DOROTHY CANFIELD

(1879–1958) was born Dorothea Frances Canfield, in Lawrence, Kansas, the daughter of James Hulme Canfield, a professor, and Flavia Camp, an artist. At the age of ten she spent a year in Paris with her mother, and the family then moved to Nebraska where she met Willa Cather who became her lifelong friend. After studying at Ohio State and Columbia Universities and at the Sorbonne, she was offered an assistant professorship at Western Reserve University in 1903. However, to avoid distressing her parents she took an administrative post at the nearer Horace Mann School and began writing short stories in her spare time. In 1905 she left to nurse her ailing mother.

Dorothy Canfield's first novel, *Gunhild*, was published in 1907 and in the same year she married James Redwood Fisher, with whom she had a son and daughter. They settled in Arlington, Vermont, the home of Dorothy Canfield's pioneering ancestors, but travelled widely. In 1911 she visited the innovative Italian school of Dr Maria Montessori, and on her return pioneered this educational method in America in: *A Montessori Mother* (1912), *A Montessori Manual* (1913), *Mothers and Children* (1914) and *Self-Reliance* (1916). Between 1916–19 she and her family moved to France to become part of the war effort. Dorothy Canfield founded a braille press and established a convalescent home for refugee French children, supporting these activities by writing, and her husband joined the ambulance service. She was later the first woman appointed to the Vermont Board of Education and was the first and only woman on the editorial board of the Book-of-the-Month Club for twenty-five years. During the Second World War Dorothy Canfield organised and led the Children's Crusade, encouraging American children to help young war victims. The death of her own son in combat in the Philippines in 1945 was devastating and she stopped writing fiction. She died of a stroke in Vermont in 1958.

A prolific and popular writer, Dorothy Canfield published poetry, translations, articles, patriotic reflections and children's books in addition to fiction and educational texts. Her other novels are: *The Squirrel Cage* (1912), *The Bent Twig* (1915), *The Brimming Cup* (1921), *Rough Hewn* (1922), *The Home-Maker* (1924), *Her Son's Wife* (1926), *The Deepening Stream* (1930), *Bonfire* (1933) and *Seasoned Timber* (1939).

THE BRIMMING CUP

DOROTHY CANFIELD

WITH A NEW INTRODUCTION BY
DOROTHY GOLDMAN

PENGUIN BOOKS – VIRAGO PRESS

PENGUIN BOOKS
Viking Penguin Inc., 40 West 23rd Street,
New York, New York 10010, U.S.A.
Penguin Books Ltd, 27 Wrights Lane, London W8 5TZ
(Publishing & Editorial) and Harmondsworth,
Middlesex, England (Distribution & Warehouse)
Penguin Books Australia Ltd, Ringwood,
Victoria, Australia
Penguin Books Canada Limited, 2801 John Street,
Markham, Ontario, Canada L3R 1B4
Penguin Books (N.Z.) Ltd, 182–190 Wairau Road,
Auckland 10, New Zealand

First published in the United States of America by
The McCall Company 1919
First published in Great Britain by Jonathan Cape, 1935
This edition first published in Great Britain by
Virago Press Limited 1987
Published in Penguin Books 1987

(CIP data available)

Printed in the United States of America by
R. R. Donnelley & Sons Company, Harrisonburg, Virginia
Set in Bulmer

Contents

PART ONE

PART TWO

PART THREE

PART FOUR

Introduction

'No one of our novelists has had the charge of writing autobiography laid at her door more frequently than has Dorothy Canfield',[1] and *The Brimming Cup* was no exception. Indeed, the parallels between her own life and that of her heroine, Marise Crittenden, are numerous. Both were talented musicians – though Dorothy Canfield gave up her hopes of a musical career because of growing deafness rather than domestic ties. Both had rather difficult relationships with their mothers; both had wide experience of European culture – Dorothy Canfield not only travelled extensively in Europe and spoke several languages but wrote her PhD thesis on Corneille and Racine. Both married for love.

Indeed, it is in their married lives that the most significant similarity between the author and her heroine lies. After their marriage in 1907, James and Dorothy Canfield Fisher did not set up home among the literary set in New York, but moved to a cottage on one of the Canfield farms in the small town of Arlington, Vermont. ('I have lived in Vermont ever since 1763' she once wrote, referring to her family's uninterrupted connection with the town.[2]) After *their* marriage in 1909, Neale and Marise Crittenden equally amazed their friends by moving to a small family property in the village of Ashley in Vermont. Both real and fictional couples devoted their lives to family and community. If Marise Crittenden organised a local choir, Dorothy Canfield had a similar commitment to provincial culture: 'Last autumn, wanting to make some money for improvements to our district school, the people of our neighbourhood (under my leadership) got together and presented a historical play ... which I wrote ... All the people in it were plain farmer-folk, who had never had any experience before in that sort of thing.'[3] Dorothy Canfield even used members of her own family as the models for the family and friends who surround her heroine. Her own daughter Sally (born in 1909) and her son James (born in 1913) were eleven and seven respectively when she was writing *The Brimming Cup*, which compares with

Marise's children, who are six, eight and ten at the beginning of the year which encompasses the major portion of the novel.

As a child Dorothy Canfield had frequently visited her father's only sister in Arlington and throughout her life she wrote to her Aunt Mattie whenever they were apart. 'Useful, busy, untroubled, zestful, cheerful [Aunt Mattie] trotted indefatigably with that quick short step of hers, familiar to generations of Arlingtonians, from library to home, from home to Church, from Church to library, till death came for her', with a kind, merciful suddenness and total unexpectedness.'[4] She died in December 1919 when *The Brimming Cup* was taking shape in its author's mind. 'Aunt Mattie lay there, august and remote, in that inexpressible peace of the newly dead, her sweet face that had never worn anything but a smile, grave and composed and infinitely in repose ... so that I almost envied her that endless quiet.' – 'I was constantly employed ... in making the most immediate decisions about a life cut short unexpectedly ... what was to be done with her old maid who had lived with her for thirty years?'[5] Readers of *The Brimming Cup* may well feel that in Aunt Mattie and her elderly maid they recognize the prototypes of Cousin Hetty whom Marise had visited so often as a child and her lifelong maid Agnes, for whose future Marise has to take responsibility after Cousin Hetty's death.

Such similarities cannot be ignored – indeed Dorothy Canfield confessed, 'I can write nothing at all about places, people or phases of life which I do not intimately know, down to the last detail'[6] – but we should consider rather carefully what we mean if we categorize any novel as autobiography. Are we assuming that Dorothy Canfield was capable of nothing more than merely recounting her own history in fictionalized form? Might it not rather be that what was essential to her as a person was essential to her as a writer? We might find it more fruitful to enquire about the nature of the experiences and ideas which were so important to her that she chose to embody them in her fiction, than to believe we have understood the sources of her creativity when we note the connections between her life and her work. What did she think about childhood and education, about Freudian psychology, about democracy? How did she incorporate these themes into her fiction? We might gain more insight into *The Brimming Cup* by asking, for example, what Vermont meant to Dorothy Canfield, rather than assuming that Marise Crittenden's experience of rural life is nothing but a public and perhaps therapeutic analysis of the author's personal decision to live there.

That Vermont was important to her is indisputable: as well as *The Brimming Cup*, two later novels, *Bonfire* (1932) and *Seasoned Timber* (1939), have significant Vermont settings. From almost the beginning of Dorothy Canfield's career until its end, she continued to write about the inhabitants of this beautiful New England state. Her first book of short stories, *Hillsboro' People*, was published in 1915 when she was thirty six, eight years after her first novel. In a manner typical of the tradition of American regional fiction from which her work sprang, *Hillsboro' People* establishes a composite, many-faceted picture of an entire community through the individual stories of the Vermonters who live in Hillsboro', a town not unlike her own Arlington. When in 1931 she published a collection of French stories entitled *Basque People*, Robert Frost commented shrewdly that 'the Basques she lived with and wrote about read to me like Vermonters'.[7] Her best loved children's book, *Understood Betsy* (1917), describes a girl's growth to maturity and independence only possible because of the freer and more challenging life she is able to lead in Vermont.

The last book Dorothy Canfield completed before her death in 1958, nearly forty years after *Hillsboro' People*, was her most considered account of Vermont, a book of non-fiction entitled *Vermont Tradition: the Biography of an Outlook on Life* (1953). '*Vermont Tradition* is an important adjunct to Dorothy's novelistic work because it proves an important point'[8], namely that the Vermont life she describes in *The Brimming Cup* as an alternative to contemporary acquisitive, materialistic, urban society actually does exist. In *Vermont Tradition* she states clearly the place that her chosen home state has in her philosophy:

> The basic, primary concern of Vermont tradition is with the conduct of human life . . . Throughout Vermont the general philosophy is that Equality must extend to the protection of everybody's personal dignity, within the community, for the backroad farmer and his wife bringing butter and eggs to the kitchen door, no less and no more than for the owner of the plywood factory . . . By unquestioned right.[9]

When we remember that old Mrs Powers does sell eggs at the kitchen door (daring to charge Mr Welles two cents more than the going rate) and that Neale Crittenden owns a lumber factory, we can see that in the thirty two years between *The Brimming Cup* and *Vermont Tradition* Dorothy Canfield's view of the relative importance of Vermonters did not change. We are not surprised to discover respect for the individual's right to order his or her own life a theme of the novel, indeed the very structure of *The Brimming Cup* embodies the insistent and integral democracy that Dorothy Canfield found in Vermont.

Standing alone at the book's centre is Marise Crittenden, cultured, talented and perhaps wasted in the small town in which she and her husband have chosen to make their lives. On 15 March 1920, the day that her youngest child goes to school for the first time, when she is alone and fearful that one of the guiding duties in her life has been removed, the outside world which she had abandoned on her marriage reappears in the contrasting forms of new neighbours, old Mr Welles and young Mr Marsh. Family duties have kept the former in the urban environment he hates all his working life, and he is now looking forward to a quiet and rural retirement in which he can cultivate his garden; the latter is his millionaire employer, eager to settle his pensioner comfortably and return to what he sees as the ease, comfort and culture of the city. The novel recounts the events of exactly one year from that day, central to which is the changing relationship of Marise and Vincent Marsh, their recognition of a mutual sexual attraction and the outcome of their passion. Since Dorothy Canfield is interested in the processes, both mental and moral, which lead up to her heroine's decision about her future, much of the action is inevitably internalized. 'You know', she wrote, 'I never have thought that my stories were suitable for the movies or for the stage, because the action takes place nearly always inside people's hearts and minds, rather than outside with gestures and actions.'[10] Indeed when a movie producer offered a large sum for the rights to *The Brimming Cup*, its author asked how he would deal with the fact that much of the action was below the surface. When it was explained to her that suitable action would be inserted to make it all clear, the offer was refused.

The internal, spiritual dilemma which Marise Crittenden faces is illuminated and given physical form by two symmetrically placed sub-plots. On either side of Marise there are the poor farmer's wife Nelly Powers and Marise's wealthy friend Eugenia Mills: women whose lives develop Marise's inner conflict into visible extremes. It is as if she is the central still consciousness of the novel with two surrogate actors performing alternative versions of her future. Nelly Powers, though she is town- not country-bred, would be entirely satisfied with her rural lot if it were not for the unwelcome attentions of Frank Warner; her horizons are limited to her family and farm. Eugenia, in contrast, is a cosmopolitan creature who finds nothing to recommend country life but the unspoken love she bears for Marise's husband, Neale. These stories reach their climaxes at the same time as Marise's, not through thought and mental anguish, but through action and even melodrama. Eugenia, who is seldom seen to stir and never to exert herself unduly, decides that she must fight for her future; if she can further the relationship between Marise and Vincent Marsh she may advance her own chances with Neale. What she does is quite simple, but causes Marise terrible mental torment. Yet even this seems insignificant when we learn that the unjustified jealousy of 'Gene Powers results in three deaths.

It would be wrong, however, to think that Nelly and Eugenia are only physical illustrations of the possible resolutions of Marise's situation. Like her they are dignified with their own chapters of interior monologue when they consider where they have arrived in their lives, their possible futures and what actions they must take to achieve them. Although fictionally the interest centres more around one woman than the others, politically the three are of equal importance. If we look carefully at three succeeding chapters 'Home Life', 'Massage Cream; Theme and Variations' and 'The Soul of Nelly Powers', it becomes apparent that Dorothy Canfield is working in the less usual, more complex form of triple comparisons. These chapters are directly comparable: Marise wants to be recognized for herself, 'not the useful house-mother, but that living core of her own self, buried, hidden, put off, choked and starved as she felt it to be'. Eugenia is equally concerned with her own identity. ' "Suppose I give up the New-Thought way, always distracting your attention to something else, always suppressing your desire, resisting the pull you want to yield to.

Suppose I try the Freud way, bringing the desire up boldly, letting yourself go, unresisting." It was worth trying.' Nelly's self-absorption is of a simpler sort:

> She would like to dance with anybody who danced good ... How she just loved to dance! Something seemed to get into her when the music struck up. She hardly knew what she was doing, felt as though she was floating around on that thick, soft moss you walked on when you went blue-berrying ... above the Eagle-Rocks ... all springy ... If you could only dance by yourself, without having to bother with partners, that was what would be nice.

Not only does the triple pattern of chapters stress the comparative structure of the novel, but the different styles and concerns bring each woman before the reader in her own person, her individuality and integrity complete. The thoughts of each woman illuminate the experience of the others – there is no sense of incongruity that Eugenia's refined sensibility sharpens our understanding of the humble farmer's wife and vice versa.

The women's triangle is only one example of the structural comparisons which are used throughout the novel. There is a variant in the repetitions which facilitate our understanding of the changes that have taken place between the repeated events. The clearest example lies in the two scenes when children come into adults' beds, seeking reassurance after nightmares. The first occurs when Marise is staying in the house of Cousin Hetty who has just died, at that crisis in her life when she must decide with whom to spend her future and whether her previous life with Neale has been the moral crusade which she had previously believed. She remembers her visits there as a child:

> the same room and the same bed ... Nothing had been changed there since those days ... [a] wave of recollection ... engulfed her ... she was again eight years old, with nothing in the world but bad dreams to fear, and Cousin Hetty there at hand as a refuge even against bad dreams. How many times had she wakened, terrified, her heart beating hammer-strokes against her ribs, and trotted shivering, in her night-gown, into Cousin Hetty's room ... The fumbling approach to the bed, the sheets held open, the kind old hand outstretched, and then the haven ... her head on the same pillow with that of the brave old woman who was afraid of nothing, who drew her up close and safe.

At the end of the book her own daughter Elly comes to her bed with the identical words that she remembers using herself: ' "it was an awful dream this time. Can't I get into bed with you?" ' Just as Marise had remembered 'the brave old woman who was afraid of nothing', Elly in her turn asks ' "Mother, aren't you and father afraid of *any*thing?" ' In Marise's reply we hear the echoes of hard-won experience and can gauge her spiritual growth.

At that moment Marise Crittenden takes her rightful place in another pattern which forms part of the novel's structure – the developing pattern of the generations. Elly has already prepared us to recognize it with her own realization:

> 'Why she herself would stop being a little girl, and would grow up and be a Mother!' ... Perhaps some day another little girl would sit there, and be just as surprised to know that *her* mother had been really and truly a little girl too, and would feel queer and shy at the idea, and all the time her mother had been only *Elly* ... It was like a procession, all half in the dark, marching forward, one after another, little girls, mothers, mothers and little girls.

It is significant that important clues to the book's meaning occur in scenes where a child takes a major role. Children were important to Dorothy Canfield, both as a mother and as a citizen – both she and her husband served several times on the local town and state school boards. (This was not an unexpected development for someone brought up in an academic atmosphere. She was born in Kansas where her father was a University Professor; he later became Chancellor of the State University of Nebraska, President of Ohio State University and finally librarian of Columbia University.) But her interest in children also extended into several different spheres of her professional life. Throughout her prolific writing career she wrote fiction and non-fiction for children and in 1912 introduced the work of Maria Montessori to America with *A Montessori Mother*, followed by *The Montessori Manual* in 1913, *Mothers and Children* in 1914 and *Self-Reliance* in 1916. The Emersonian title of the last reveals a great deal of Dorothy Canfield's beliefs about education and childrearing. For her, the Montessori method of education, with its emphasis on the child's inherent desire for learning and the importance of self-instruction, was proof of humanity's inherent goodness and its ability to respond positively to the challenges of experience. Parents and teachers have a duty to allow the children in their care to develop; while children must be protected from undue danger they must always be allowed as much freedom as they are capable of benefitting from – must be allowed to grow.

Like their mother, Marise's three children grow and mature during the novel. Most important is what happens to Paul, a rather mundane little boy, with a prosaic and matter-of-fact approach to life and a developing sense of duty. Paul's friendship with Mr Welles deepens throughout the year and he is quite unprepared for Mr Welles' growing realization that his longed-for retirement must be abandoned:

> 'I keep hearing from somebody who lives down South that the coloured folks aren't getting a real square deal. I keep wondering if maybe I oughtn't to go and live there and help her look out for them.'
> ... 'Aw, Mr Welles, I *wish't* you wouldn't! I *like* your being here. There's lots of things I've got planned we could do together.'

Before the book ends, however, Paul too has learnt that it is impossible to ignore human responsibilities. Meeting Ralph Powers he is deeply disturbed by the other boy's despair and cynicism:

> 'Mother, Ralph says ... God let his father and mother both get killed, and he don't know what the devil could do any worse than that ... He said he hated God ... Say, Mother, its *awful* hard on those Powers' kids, isn't it, not having anybody but their grandmother. Say, Mother, don't you think maybe we could ... we could ...' He turned his freckled, tanned, serious little face up to hers.

Like Mr Welles, he has accepted responsibility; he must 'look out for' Ralph. As his mother has said previously, ' "If you live in the country you're really married to humanity, for better or for worse, not just on speaking terms with it, as you are in the city." '

An understanding of the need to 'look out for' people is an important theme of *The Brimming Cup*; but equally, perhaps more, important is the individual's responsibility for his or her own spiritual and moral growth. In 'Prelude', the opening chapter, set in 1909 when Marise and Neale become engaged, Marise says ' "I never knew before that I was weak. But then I never met strength before." "You're not weak," [Neale] told her'. Much later, when she should know better, Marise is still thinking,

> What was Neale there *for*, if not for her to lean against, to protect her, to be a defending wall about her? He was so strong and so clear-headed, he could be such a wall if he chose . . . Why wouldn't Neale do it for her? Why wouldn't he put out that strength of his and crush out this strange agitation of hers, *forbid* it to her?

What in fact Neale does use his strength for is to restrain himself from usurping Marise's own responsibility for herself, from weakening her by destroying opportunities for growth, even though it could mean that he will lose her: 'he wanted her to be herself, to be all that Marise could ever grow to be, he wanted her to attain her full stature so far as any human being could do this in this life. And to do that she must be free.' Eventually she comes to recognize what he has done, to know that Neale

> had held to the certainty that his effort would not make her strong, and that she would only be free if she were strong . . . [She] had only wished to make the use of his strength which would have weakened her. Had there ever before been any man who refused to let the woman he loved weaken herself by the use of his strength? Had a man ever before held out his strong hand to a woman to help her forward, not to hold her fast? Her life was her own.

Dorothy Canfield wrote to her life-long friend Cèline Sibut in June 1920 that *The Brimming Cup* was specifically designed as 'an extremely complicated and difficult' attempt to challenge the current trend of stressing 'weakness of will power and [describing] the human being [as] prey to a sordid fate which is too strong for him to overcome'.[11] She was especially disturbed by what she considered to be the contemporary overemphasis on sex. Her friend Bradford Smith recounts that Dorothy Canfield 'was one of the early students of Freud'. By the 1920s, she told him, 'I'd been reading [Freud] a good deal – his own works, not those about him. I began reading them as soon as they appeared.'[12] She viewed Freud's emphasis on sexual appetite as one of the most serious threats to human growth. As a writer, however, she was too good a craftswoman to allow her beliefs to unbalance her fiction. In *The*

Brimming Cup, subservience to sexual passion does not exist as an isolated target, called into being by the requirements of a personal crusade and imposed on the plot; rather it is part of a wider interest with the workings of the human mind and psyche. There are, for example, more interior monologues in this novel than in any of her others, and her characters have an interest similar to her own in actually tracking down the origin of their thoughts. 'Something else slid into her mind, something watchful. She sat perfectly still so that no chance movement should disturb that mood till it could be examined and challenged.' Or, 'Oh, what did that bring to mind? What was that fleeting cobweb of thought that seemed a recurrence of a sensation only recently passed?'

It is important to understand that Dorothy Canfield was not minimizing sexual passion; indeed the book contains a deep understanding of its demands and joys. What she did not believe, however, was that it was irresistible, not when compared with the 'strong, full-grown, thought-freighted interests and richly varied sympathies and half-impersonal joys and sorrows' which are available to adults. In an interesting short story titled 'Sex Education' she allows Aunt Minnie, one of her rich gallery of older women characters, to look back after a lifetime in which her opinion of the relative importance of sex and of men and women's respective responsibility for its proper conduct, has changed radically. She criticizes her younger companions: '"And anyhow, you don't tell [your children] the truth about sex ... if they get the idea from you that it's all there is to living. It's not. If you don't get to where you want to go in it, well, there's a lot of landscape all around it a person can have a good time in."'[13]

The imagery of *The Brimming Cup* is used to support Dorothy Canfield's argument. Throughout, the two men in Marise's life are connected with different strands of imagery. Neale is almost always thought of in terms of refreshing and/or powerful forces of water. Together Marise and Neale experience 'the flood-tide of emotion'; he is 'the sustaining ocean' for her. This passion, however, is love, deeper than mere sexuality, and Neale knows it:

'if it's the mating instinct ... that may be fooling both of us, because of our youth and bodily health ... good heavens! Isn't our love deep enough to absorb that a million times over, like the water of a little brook flowing into the sea? Do you think *that*, which is only a little trickle and a harmless and natural and healthy little trickle, could unsalt the great ocean of its savour?'

This line of imagery extends in two further directions which help to clarify its significance. The first concerns the book's title. The phrase first occurs in 'Prelude', where so many of the book's themes are established, when Marise tries to explain her feelings to her new fiancé. Using the phrase *'une urne trop pleine'* from Victor Hugo's poem 'Waterloo' she says,

> 'I could see it, so vividly, an urn boiling over with the great gush of water springing up in it . . . I wanted . . . sometime to be so filled with some emotion, something great and fine, that I would be an urn too full, gushing up in a great flooding rush . . . And another phrase came into my mind, an English one . . . "The fullness of life." '

Almost at the end of the story this explanation is endorsed when Marise's children are described as 'living cups filled to the brim with life.'

Parallel to this image is Marise's dream. In 'Prelude' she says, ' "I have had dreams sometimes, that I'm in something awfully big and irresistible like a great river, flowing somewhere" '; but later in the story she changes the description in a significant manner. ' "I don't dream I'm the leaf on the current. I dream I *am* the current myself, part of it . . . the wave itself." ' She is coming to understand that she is part of life itself, learning to live for herself, not through other people, taking charge of herself and her future. If allowed their proper growth, her children will carry brimming cups in their turn too. The water imagery supports Canfield's contention that freedom and love are the essential ingredients of a fulfilled life.

If the image for love and a life fulfilled through love is water, we find the contrasting image for sexual passion is heat. Although there are general references to the 'first flare-up of passion' and the 'savage old flame', it is inevitable that most relate to Vincent Marsh and Marise. He has an 'authority which fell on her like a hot wind . . . burning lips . . . flaming eyes . . . smoky, flaming brilliance . . . [He is] fiery . . . on fire . . . the heat of his body [burned] through to her arm'. As she too becomes aroused, Marise is described as 'burning with excitement . . . [She felt] the flare-up of . . . excitement, and burned in it . . . [felt a] fierce burning response . . . burning sensations'. The imagery is not just of heat, but particularly of burning – burning, whose destructive and painful overtones connect it to the aggression which Canfield sees as part of sexual passion.

> It was as though she had physically felt the steel of his blade . . . she had an instant's absurd fear of letting him walk behind her, as though she might feel a thrust in the back . . . [Vincent is] her opponent . . . [She is] stabbed through and through by the look they had interchanged . . . [by] the dagger-like possibilities of their talk . . . [With] a thrust of sheer power . . . he wanted to hurt her once, deeply, to pierce her.

Just as Canfield makes her interest in Freudian thought part of a wider consideration of the mind, so the imagery of heat and water are part of a wider pattern of natural imagery. It is significant that the saintly Mr Welles wants to become a gardener, and that Marise offers to help him: ' "I'm a gardener," Marise was saying, "and I know a thing or two about natural processes." ' We should not be surprised that it is 'In Aunt Hetty's Garden' that a compromise to Marise's dilemma seems, momentarily, possible; nor that the villagers reveal their untutored love of beauty by coming to see 'The Night-Blooming Cereus'; nor that the Power's tragedy is preceded by 'The Fall of the Big Pine': 'So many winters, so many summers, so many suns and moons and rains and snows had gone to make it what it was. Like the men who had planted it and lived beneath its shade, it had drawn silently from the depths of the earth and the airy treasures of the sky food to grow strong and live its life'; nor that Mr Welles explains his decision to go and bear witness in the South through the parable of a falling tree whose roots cannot hold if the earth around them is washed away: ' "I guess what I ought to try to be is one more drop of water" '. Marise sees her possible future with Marsh in horticultural terms:

> it took on the shape of a glorious, uprooted plant, cut off from the very source of life, its glossy surfaces already beginning to wither and dull . . . But what beauties were there to pluck . . . would she, if she could, give up what she was now, with her myriads of roots, deep-set in the soil of human life, in order to bear the one red rose, splendid though it might be?

The vast array of natural imagery and references to nature and the natural life provide our strongest evidence for the unified nature of this novel. They create for the novel a smooth, seamless texture which can not only connect an analysis of sexuality with beliefs on personal growth, child-rearing, the treatment of blacks and the role of rural industry, but by that connection support Dorothy Canfield's belief in the importance of a rural life and underpin her commitment to Vermont.

She knew, however, that Vermont is a state of mind as much as a State of the Union and wrote:

> I'm glad you like *The Brimming Cup*'s Vermontness. It certainly is very Vermont, so much so that I wonder if real Westerners can 'get' it. I notice that most of the letters I get about it from enthusiastic readers come from Maine or Massachusetts or somewhere else in New England. But I don't *want* to be limited to being a New England writer! Me, born in Kansas![14]

The values she found there, which she incorporated into her fiction and which were as central to her life as to her art, are available everywhere. She had to know them 'intimately, down to the last detail' for that is how an artist creates, but the created fiction is available for us all. 'Every artist learns early, or he is no artist, that he must drink out of his own cup, must cultivate his own half-acre, because he never can have any other'[15]; but the half-acre of Vermont ground, the brimming cup, becomes everyone's birthright when it is translated into art.

Dorothy Goldman, Canterbury, 1986

1 Dorothea Lawrance Mann, 'Dorothy Canfield: The Little Vermonter', *The Bookman*, vol. 65, July 1927, p. 696.

2 Dorothy Canfield Fisher, *Vermont Tradition: the Biography of an Outlook on Life*, Boston, 1953, p. 3.

3 Dorothy Canfield Fisher to Paul Reynolds, 27 March 1916, Paul R. Reynolds Papers, Rare Book and Manuscript Library, Columbia University.

4 Dorothy Canfield Fisher, 'Notes on Martha Hulme Canfield for a History of St. James Church, Arlington, Dorothy Canfield Fisher Collection, University of Vermont Library.

5 Dorothy Canfield Fisher, letter to Herbert Congdon, 10 January 1920 and letter to Miss Raulett, 24 January 1920, Dorothy Canfield Fisher Collection, Russell Vermontiana Collection, Martha Canfield Memorial Library, Arlington, Vermont.

6 Bradford Smith, 'Dorothy Canfield Fisher: The Deepening Stream', *Vermont History*, Vermont Historical Society vol. 27, July 1959, p. 235.

7 Robert Frost, *Dorothy Canfield Fisher, In Memoriam*, New York, 1958.

8 Ida H. Washington, *Dorothy Canfield Fisher, A Biography*, Shelburne, Vermont, The New England Press, 1982, p. 229.

9 Dorothy Canfield Fisher, *Vermont Tradition*, pp. 8–11.

10 Dorothy Canfield Fisher to Donald Brace, 2 November 1945, Dorothy Canfield Fisher Collection, University of Vermont Library.

11 Dorothy Canfield Fisher to Cèline Sibut, 10 June 1920, Dorothy Canfield Fisher Collection, University of Vermont Library.

12 Bradford Smith, op. cit., p. 234.

13 Dorothy Canfield Fisher, 'Sex Education', *A Harvest of Stories*, New York, 1956.

14 Dorothy Canfield Fisher to Arthur Canfield, 15 June, year not known, Dorothy Canfield Fisher Collection, University of Vermont Library.

15 Arthur L. Guptil, *Norman Rockwell, Illustrator*, Preface by Dorothy Canfield Fisher, New York, 1946, pp. viii–ix.

Chapter 1: *Prelude*

An Hour in the Life of Two Modern Young People

April, 1909.

LOUNGING idly in the deserted little waiting-room was the usual shabby, bored, lonely ticket-seller, prodigiously indifferent to the grave beauty of the scene before him and to the throng of ancient memories jostling him where he stood. Without troubling to look at his watch, he informed the two young foreigners that they had a long hour to wait before the cable-railway would send a car down to the Campagna. His lazy nonchalance was faintly coloured with the satisfaction, common to his profession, in the discomfiture of travellers.

Their look upon him was of amazed gratitude. Evidently they did not understand Italian, he thought, and repeated his information more slowly, with an unrecognizable word or two of badly pronounced English thrown in. He felt slightly vexed that he could not make them feel the proper annoyance, and added, 'It may even be so late that the signori would miss the connection for the last tramway car back to Rome. It is a long walk back to the city across the Campagna.'

They continued to gaze at him with delight. 'I've got to tip him for that!' said the young man, reaching vigorously into a pocket.

The girl's answering laugh, like the inward look of her eyes, showed only a preoccupied attention. She had the concentrated absent aspect of a person who has just heard vital tidings and can attend to nothing else. She said, 'Oh, Neale, how ridiculous of you! He couldn't possibly have the least idea what he's done to deserve getting paid for.'

At the sound of her voice, the tone in which these words were pronounced, the ticket-seller looked at her hard, with a bold, intrusive, diagnosing stare: 'Lovers!' he told himself conclusively. He accepted with a vast incuriosity as to reason the coin which the young foreigner put into his hand, and, ringing it suspiciously on his table, divided his appraising attention between its clear answer to his challenge, and the sound of the young man's voice as he answered his sweetheart, 'Of course he hasn't any idea what he's done to deserve it. Who ever has? You don't suppose for a moment I've any idea what I've done to deserve mine?'

The ticket-seller smiled secretly into his dark moustache. 'I wonder if *my* voice quivered and deepened like that, when I was courting Annunziata?' he asked himself. He glanced up from pocketing the coin, and caught the look which passed between the two. He felt as though someone had laid hands on him and shaken him. '*Dio mio!*' he thought. 'They are in the hottest of it.'

The young foreigners went across the tracks and established themselves on the rocks, partly out of sight, just at the brink of the great drop to the Campagna. The setting sun was full in their faces. But they did not see it, seeing only each other.

Below them spread the divinely coloured plain, crossed by the ancient yellow river, rolling its age-old memories out to the sea, a blue reminder of the restfulness of eternity, at the rim of the weary old land. Like a little cluster of tiny, tarnished pearls, Rome gleamed palely, remote and legendary.

The two young people looked at each other earnestly, with a passionate, single-hearted attention to their own meaning, thrusting away impatiently the clinging brambles of speech which laid hold on their every effort to move closer to each other. They did not look down, or away from each other's eyes as they strove to free themselves, to step forward, to clasp the other's outstretched hands. They reached down blindly, tearing at those thorny, clutching entanglements, pulling and tugging at those tenuous, tough words which would not let them say what they meant: sure, hopefully sure that in a moment . . . now . . . with the next breath, they would break free as no others had ever done before them, and crying out the truth and glory that was in them, fall into each other's arms.

The girl was physically breathless with this effort, her lips parted, her eyebrows drawn together. 'Neale, Neale dear, if I could only tell you how I want it to be, how utterly utterly *true* I want us to be. Nothing's of any account except that.'

She moved with a shrugging, despairing gesture. 'No, no, not the way that sounds. I don't mean, you know I don't mean any old-fashioned impossible vows never to change, or be any different! I know too much for that. I've seen too awfully much unhappiness, with people trying to do that. You know what I told you about my father and mother. Oh, Neale, it's horribly dangerous, loving anybody. I never wanted to. I never thought I should. But now I'm in it, I see that it's not at all unhappiness I'm afraid of, your getting tired of me or I of you . . . everybody's so weak and horrid in this world, who knows what may be before us? That's not what would be unendurable, sickening. That would make us unhappy. But what would poison us to death . . . what I'm afraid of, between two people who try to be what we want to be to each other . . . how can I say it?' She looked at him in an anguish of endeavour, '. . . not to be true to what is deepest and most living in us . . . that would be the betrayal I'm afraid of. That's what I mean. No matter what it costs us personally, or what it brings, we must be true to that. We *must*!'

He took her hand in his silently, and held it close. She drew a long troubled breath and said, 'You *do* think we can always have between us that loyalty to what is deep and living? It does not seem too much to ask, when we are willing to give up everything else for it, even happiness?'

He gave her a long, profound look. 'I'm trying to give that loyalty to you this minute, Marise darling,' he said slowly, 'when I tell you now that I think it a very great deal to ask of life, a very great deal for any human beings to try for. I should say it was much harder to get than happiness.'

She was in despair. 'Do you think that?' She searched his face anxiously as though she found there more than in his speech. 'Yes, yes, I see what you mean.' She drew a long breath. 'I can even see how fine it is of you to say that to me now. It's like a promise of how you will try. But oh, Neale, I won't *want* life on any other terms!'

She stopped, looking down at her hand in his. He tightened his clasp. His gaze on her darkened and deepened. 'It's like sending me to get the apples of Hesperides,' he said, looking older than she, curiously and suddenly older. 'I want to say yes! It would be easy to say yes. Darling, darling Marise, you can't want it more than I! But the very intelligence that makes you want it, that makes me want it, shows me how mortally hard it would be! Think! To be loyal to what is deepest and most living in yourself . . . that's an undertaking for a lifetime's effort, with all the ups and downs and growths of life. And then to try to know what is deepest and most living in

11

another . . . and to try . . . Marise! I will try. I will try with all my might. Can anybody do more than try with all his might?'

Their gaze into each other's eyes went far beyond the faltering words they spoke. She asked him in a low voice, 'Couldn't you do more for me than for yourself? One never knows, but . . . what else is love for, but to give greater strength than we have?'

There was a moment's silence, in which their very spirits met flame-like in the void, challenging, hoping, fearing. The man's face set. His burning look of power enveloped her like the reflection of the sun. 'I swear you shall have it!' he said desperately, his voice shaking.

She looked up at him with a passionate gratitude. 'I'll never forget that as long as I live!' she cried out to him.

The tears stood in his eyes as in hers.

For the fraction of an instant, they had felt each other there, as never before they had felt any other human being: they had both at once caught a moment of flood-tide, and both together had been carried up side by side; the long, inevitable isolation of human lives from birth onward had been broken by the first real contact with another human soul. They felt the awed impulse to cover their eyes as before too great a glory.

The tide ebbed back, and untroubled they made no effort to stop its ebbing. They had touched their goal, it was really there. Now they knew it within their reach. Appeased, assuaged, fatigued, they felt the need for quiet, they knew the sweetness of sobriety. They even looked away from each other, aware of their own bodies which for that instant had been left behind. They entered again into the flesh that clad their spirits, taking possession of their hands and feet and members, and taken possession of by them again. The fullness of their momentary satisfaction had been so complete that they felt no regret, only a simple, tender pleasure as of being again at home. They smiled happily at each other and sat silent, hand in hand.

Now they saw the beauty before them, the vast plain, the mountains, the sea: harmonious, serene, ripe with maturity, evocative of all the centuries of conscious life which had unrolled themselves there.

'It's too beautiful to be real, isn't it?' murmured the girl, 'and now, the peaceful way I feel this minute, I don't mind it's being so old that it makes you feel a midge in the sunshine with only an hour or two of life before you. What if you are, when it's life as we feel it now, such a flood of it, every instant brimming with it? Neale,' she turned to him with a sudden idea, 'do you remember how Victor Hugo's "Waterloo" begins?'

'I should say not!' he returned promptly. 'You forget I got all the French I know in an American university.'

'Well, I went to college in America, myself!'

'I bet it wasn't there you learned anything about Victor Hugo's poetry,' he surmised sceptically. 'Well, how does it begin, anyhow, and what's it got to do with us?'

The girl was as unamused as he at his certainty that it had something to do with them, or she would not have mentioned it. She explained, 'It's not a famous line at all, nothing I ever heard anybody else admire. We had to learn the poem by heart, when I was a little girl and went to school in Bayonne. It starts out,

"Waterloo, Waterloo, morne plaine
Comme une onde qui bout dans une urne trop pleine,"

And that second line always stuck in my head for the picture it made. I could see it, so vividly, an urn boiling over with the great gush of water springing up in it. It gave me a feeling, inside, a real physical feeling, I mean. I wanted, oh so awfully, sometime to be so filled with some emotion, something great and fine, that I would be an urn too full, gushing up in a great flooding rush. I could see the smooth, thick curl of the water surging up and out!'

She stopped to look at him and exclaim, 'Why, you're listening! You're interested. Neale, I believe you are the only person in the world who can really pay attention to what somebody else says. Everybody else just goes on thinking his own thoughts.'

He smiled at this fancy, and said, 'Go on.'

'Well, I don't know whether that feeling was already in me, waiting for something to express it, or whether that phrase in the poem started it. But it was, for ever so long, the most important thing in the world to me. I was about fourteen years old then, and of course, being a good deal with Catholics, I thought probably it was religious ecstasy that was going to be the great flood that would brim my cup full. I used to go up the hill in Bayonne to the Cathedral every day and stay there for hours, trying to work up an ecstasy. I managed nearly to faint away once or twice, which was *something* of

13

course. But I couldn't feel that great tide I'd dreamed of. And then, little by little . . . oh, lots of things came between the idea and my thinking about it. Mother was . . . I've told you how Mother was at that time. And what an unhappy time it was at home. I was pretty busy at the house because she was away so much. And Father and I hung together because there wasn't anybody else to hang to: and all sorts of ugly things happened, and I didn't have the time or the heart to think about being "an urn too full." '

She stopped, smiling happily, as though those had not been tragic words which she had just spoken, thinking not of them but of something else, which now came out, 'And then, oh, Neale, that day, on the piazza in front of St. Peter's, when we stood together, and felt the spray of the fountains blown on us, and you looked at me and spoke out. . . . Oh, Neale, *Neale*, what a moment to have lived through! Well, when we went on into the church, and I knelt there for a while, so struck down with joy that I couldn't stand on my feet, all those wild bursts of excitement, and incredulity and happiness, that kept surging up and drenching me . . . I had a queer feeling, that awfully threadbare feeling of having been there before, or felt that before; that it was familiar, although it was so new. Then it came to me, "Why, I have it, what I used to pray for. Now at last I am the urn too full!" And it was true, I could feel, just as I dreamed, the upsurging of the feeling, brimming over, boiling up, brimming over. . . . And another phrase came into my mind, an English one. I said to myself, "The fullness of life." Now I know what it is.'

She turned to him, and caught at his hand. 'Oh, Neale, now I *do* know what it is, how utterly hideous it would be to have to live without it, to feel only the mean little trickle that seems mostly all that people have.'

'Well, I'll never have to get along without it, as long as I have you,' he said confidently.

'And I refuse to live a *minute*, if it goes back on me!' she cried.

'I imagine that old folks would think we are talking very young,' suggested the man casually.

'Don't speak of them!' She cast them away into non-existence with a gesture.

They sank into a reverie, smiling to themselves.

'How the fountains shone in the sun, that day,' she murmured; 'the spray they cast on us was all tiny opals and diamonds.'

'You're sure you aren't going to be sorry to go back to America to live, to leave all that?' asked the man. 'I get anxious about that sometimes. It seems an awful jump to go away from such beautiful historic things, back to a narrow little mountain town.'

'I'd like to know what right you have to call it narrow, when you've never even seen it,' she returned.

'Well, anybody could make a pretty fair guess that a small Vermont town isn't going to be so very *wide*,' he advanced reasonably.

'It may not be wide, but it's deep,' she replied.

He laughed at her certainty. 'You were about eleven years old when you saw it last, weren't you?'

'No, you've got it wrong. It was when we came to France to live that I was eleven, and of course I stopped going to Ashley regularly for vacations then. But I went back for several summers in the old house with Cousin Hetty, when I was in America for college, after Mother died.'

'Oh well, I don't care what it's like,' he said, 'except that it's the place where I'm going to live with you. Any place on earth would seem wide enough and deep enough, if I had you there.'

'Isn't it funny,' she mused, 'that I should know so much more about it than you? To think how I played all around your uncle's mill and house, lots of times when I was a little girl, and never dreamed . . .'

'No funnier than all the rest of it,' he demurred. 'Once you grant our existing and happening to meet out of all the millions of people in the world, you can't think up anything funnier. Just the little two-for-a-cent queerness of our happening to meet in Rome instead of in Brooklyn, and your happening to know the town where my uncle lived and owned the mill he left me . . . that can't hold a candle for queerness, for wonderfulness, compared to my having ever laid eyes on you. Suppose I'd never come to Rome at all? When I got the news of Uncle Burton's death and the bequest, I was almost planning to sail from Genoa and not come to southern Italy at all.'

She shook her head confidently. 'You can't scare me with any such hideous possibilities. It's not possible that we shouldn't ever have met, both of us being in the world. Didn't you ever study chemistry? Didn't they teach you there are certain elements that just *will* come together, no matter how you mix them up with other things?'

He made no answer, gazing out across the plain far below them, mellowing richly in the ever-softening light of the sunset.

She looked doubtfully at his profile, rather lean, with the beginning already drawn of the deep American line from the corner of the nose to the mouth, that is partly humorous and partly grim. 'Don't you believe that, Neale, that we would have come together somehow, anyhow?' she asked, 'even if you had gone straight back from Genoa to Ashley? Maybe it might have been up there after you'd begun to run the mill. Maybe I'd have gone back to America and gone up to visit Cousin Hetty again.'

He was still silent.

She said urgently, as if in alarm, 'Neale, you don't believe that we could have passed all our lives and never have *seen* each other?'

He turned on her his deep-set eyes, full of tenderness and humour and uncertainty, and shook his head. 'Yes, dear, I do believe that,' he said regretfully. 'I don't see how I can help believing it. Why, I hadn't the faintest idea of going back to settle in Ashley before I met you. I had taken Uncle Burton's mill and his bequest of four thousand dollars as a sort of joke. What could I do with them, without anything else? And what on earth did I want to do with them? Nothing! As far as I had any plans at all, it was to go home, see Father and Mother for a while, get through the legal complications of inheritance, sell the mill and house . . . I wouldn't have thought of such a thing as bothering even to go to Ashley to look at them . . . and then take the money and go off somewhere, somewhere different, and far away: to China maybe. I was pretty restless in my mind, pretty sure that nothing in our civilization was worth the candle, you know, before you arrived on the scene to put everything in focus. And if I had done all that, while you were still here in Rome, running up and down your scales, honestly . . . I know I sound awfully literal . . . but I don't see how we ever could have met, do you, dear?'

He offered her this, with a look half of apology, half of simple courage.

She considered it and him seriously, studying his face and eyes, listening retrospectively to the accent of his words, and immensely astonished him by suddenly flashing a kiss on his cheek. 'You're miraculous!' she said. 'You don't know how it feels; as though I'd been floundering in a marsh, deeper and deeper, and then all at once, when I thought I'd come to know there wasn't anything in the world *but* marsh, to come out on beautiful, fine, clean earth, where I feel the very strength of ages under my feet. You don't *know* how good it seems to have a silly, romantic remark like what I said, answered the way you did, telling the truth; how *good* it feels to be pulled down to what's what, and to know you can do it and really love me too.'

He had been so startled and moved by her kiss that he had heard her words but vaguely. 'I don't seem to catch hold of all that. What's it all about?'

'It's all about the fact that I really begin to believe that you will be loyal and tell me the truth,' she told him.

He saw cause for gravity in this, remembering the great moment so shortly back of them, and said with a surprised and hurt accent, 'Didn't you believe me, when I said I would?'

She took up his hand in hers and said rapidly, 'Dear Neale, I did believe it, for just a moment, and I can't believe anything good of anybody for longer than that, not *really* in my heart of hearts. And it's my turn to tell you some truth when I tell you about that unbelief, what I've hardly even ever told myself, right out in words.'

He was listening now, fixing on her a look of profound, intelligent attention, as she went on, stumbling, reaching out for words, discarding those she found, only her steady gaze giving coherence to her statement. 'You know, living the way I have . . . I've told you . . . I've seen a great deal more than most girls have. And then, half brought up in France with people who are clever and have their eyes wide open, people who really count, I've seen how they don't believe in humans, or goodness, or anything that's not base. They know life is mostly bad and cruel and dull and low, and above all that it's bound to fool you if you trust to it, or get off your guard a single minute. They don't *teach* you that, you know; but you see it's what they believe and what they spend all their energies trying to dodge a little, all they think they can. Then everything you read, except the silly little Bibliothèque-Rose sort of thing, makes you know that it's true . . . Anatole France, and Maupassant, and Schnitzler. Of course back in America you find lots of nice people who don't believe that. But they're so sweet you know they'd swallow anything that made things look pleasant. So you don't dare take their word for anything. They won't even look at what's bad in everybody's life, they just pretend it's not there, not in *their* husbands, or wives or children, and so you know they're fooled.' She lowered her voice, which faltered a little, but she still continued to look straight into his eyes, 'And as for love, why, I've just hated the sound of the name and . . . I'm horribly afraid of it, even now.'

He asked her gravely, 'Don't you love me? Don't you think that I love you?'

She looked at him piteously, wincing, bracing herself with an effort to be brave. 'I must try to be as honest as I want you to be. Yes, I love you, Neale, with all my heart, a thousand times more than I ever dreamed I could love anybody. But how do I know that I'm not somehow fooling myself: but that maybe all that huge unconscious inheritance from all my miserable ancestors hasn't *got* me, somehow, and you too? How do I know that I'm not being fooled by Nature and fooling you with fine words?'

She hesitated, probing deep into her heart, and brought out now, like a great and unexpected treasure, 'But, Neale, listen! I *don't* think that about you! I don't believe you're being fooled. Why, I believe in you more than in myself!' She was amazed at this and radiant.

Then she asked him, 'Neale, how do *you* manage about all this? What do you feel about all the capacity for being low and bad, that everybody has? Aren't you afraid that they'll get the best of us, inevitably, unless we let ourselves get so dull, and second-rate and passive, that we can't even be bad? Are you afraid of being fooled? Do you believe in yourself at all?'

He was silent for some time, his eyes steadily fixed on some invisible realm. When he spoke it was with a firm, natural, un-shaken accent. 'Why, yes, I think it very likely that I am being fooled all the time. But I don't think it matters the least bit in the world beside the fact that I love you. That's big enough to overtop everything else.'

He raised his voice and spoke out boldly to the undefined spectre in her mind. 'And if it's the mating instinct you mean, that may be fooling both of us, because of our youth and bodily health . . . good heavens! Isn't our love deep enough to ab-sorb that a million times over, like the water of a little brook flowing into the sea? Do you think *that*, which is only a little trickle and a harmless and natural and healthy little trickle, could unsalt the great ocean of its savour? Why, Marise, all that you're so afraid of, all that they've made you so afraid of . . . it's like the little surface waves . . . well, call it the big storm waves if you want to . . . but nothing at all, the biggest of them, compared to the stillness in the depths of the sea. Why, I love you! Do I believe in myself? Of course I believe in myself, because I have you.'

She drew a long sigh and, closing her eyes, murmured, 'I feel as though I were lifted up on a great rock.' After a moment, opening her eyes, she said, 'You are better than I, you know. I'm not at all sure that I could say that. I never knew before that I was weak. But then I never met strength before.'

'You're not weak,' he told her; adding quaintly, 'maybe a little overballasted with brains and sensitiveness and underballasted with experience, that's all. But you haven't had much chance to take on any other cargo, as yet.'

She was nettled at this, and leaving her slow, wide-winged poise in the upper airs, she veered and with swallow-like swiftness darted down on him. 'That sounds patronizing and elder-brotherish,' she told him. 'I've taken on all sorts of cargo that you don't know anything about. In ever so many ways you seem positively . . . naïve! You needn't go thinking that I'm always highstrung and fanciful. I never showed that side to anybody before, never! Always kept it shut up and locked down and danced and whooped it up before the door. You know how everybody always thinks of me as laughing all the time. I do wish everything hadn't been said already so many times. If it weren't that it's been said so often, I'd like to say that I have always been laughing to keep from crying.'

'Why don't you say it, if that is what you mean?' he proposed.

She looked at him, marvelling. 'I'm so fatuous about you!' she exclaimed; 'the least little thing you say, I see the most wonderful possibilities in it. I know *you'd* say what you meant, no matter how many thousands had said it before. And since I know it's not stupidness in you, why, it seems to me just splendidly and simply courageous, a kind of courage I'd never thought of before. I see now, how, after all, those stupid people had me beaten, because I'd always thought that a person either had to be stupid so that he didn't *know* he was saying something everybody else had said, or else not say it, even if he wanted to, ever so much, and it was just what he meant.'

'Don't you think maybe you're too much bothered about other people, anyhow?' he suggested, mildly; 'whether they're stupid or have said things or not? What difference does it make, if it's a question of what you yourself feel? I'd be just as satisfied if you gave *all* your time to discovering the wonderful possibilities in what I say. It would give me a chance to conceal the fact that I get all out of breath trying to follow what you mean.'

This surprised her into a sudden laugh, outright and ringing. He looked down at her sparkling face, brilliant in its mirth as a child's, and said seriously, 'You must instantly think of something perfectly prosaic and commonplace to say, or I shall be forced to take you in my arms and kiss you a great many times, which might have Lord knows what effect on that gloomy-minded ticket-seller back of us who already has his suspicions.'

She rose instantly to the possibilities and said smoothly, swiftly, whimsically, with the accent of drollery, 'I'm very particular about what sort of frying-pan I use. I insist on having a separate one for the *fritures* of fish, and another for the omelets, used only for that: I'm a very fine and conscientious housekeeper, I'd have you know, and all the while we lived in Bayonne I ran the house because Mother never got used to French housekeeping ways. I was the one who went to market . . . oh, the gorgeous things you get in the Bayonne market, near enough Spain, you know, for real Malaga grapes with the aroma still on them, and for Spanish quince-paste. I bossed the old Basque woman we had for cook and learned how to cook from her, using a great many onions for everything. And I learned how to keep house by the light of nature, since it had to be done. And I'm awfully excited about having a house of my own, just as though I weren't the extremely clever, cynical, disillusioned, fascinating musical genius everybody knows me to be: only let me warn you that the old house we are going to live in will need lots done to it. Your uncle never opened the dreadful room he called the parlour, and never used the south wing at all, where all the sunshine comes in. And the pantry arrangements are simply humorous, they're so inadequate. I don't know how much of that four thousand dollars you are going to want to spare for remodelling the mill, but I will tell you now, that I will go on strike if you don't give me a better cook-stove than your Uncle's Touclé had to work with.'

He had been listening with an appreciative grin to her nimble-witted chatter, but at this he brought her up short by an astonished, 'Who had? What had? What's that . . . Touclé?'

She laughed aloud again, delighted at having startled him into curiosity. 'Touclé. Touclé. Don't you think it a pretty name? Will you believe me when I say I know all about Ashley?'

'Oh, go on, tell me!' he begged. 'You don't mean to say that my Uncle Burton had pep enough to have a scandal in his life?'

'What do *you* know about your uncle?'

'Oh, I'd seen him a few times, though I'd never been up to Ashley. As long as Grandfather was alive and the mill at Adams Centre was running, Uncle Burton used to go there to see his father, and I always used to be hanging around Grandfather and the mill, and the woods. I was crazy about it all, as a boy, used to work right along with the mill-hands, and out chopping with the lumbermen. Maybe Uncle Burton noticed that.' He was struck with a sudden idea, 'By George, maybe *that* was why he left me the mill!' He cast his eye retrospectively on this idea and was silent for a moment, emerging from his meditation to say, wonderingly, 'Well, it certainly is *queer*, how things come out, how one thing hangs on another. It's enough to addle your brains, to try to start to follow back all the ways things happen . . . ways you'd never thought of as the least importance.'

'Your Uncle Burton was of some importance to *us*,' she told him. 'Miss Oldham at the *pension* said that she had just met a new American, down from Genoa, and when I heard your name I said, "Oh, I used to know an old Mr. Crittenden who ran a wood-working factory up in Vermont, where I used to visit an old cousin of mine," and that was why Miss Oldham introduced us, that silly way, as cousins.'

He said, pouncingly, 'You're running on, inconsequently, just to divert my mind from asking you again who or what Touclé is.'

'You can ask and ask all you like,' she defied him, laughing. 'I'm not going to tell you. I've got to have *some* secrets from you, to keep up the traditions of self-respecting womanhood. And anyhow I couldn't tell you, because she is different from everything else. You'll see for yourself, when we get there. If she's still alive.' She offered a compromise, 'I'll tell you what. If she's dead, I'll sit down and tell you about her. If she's still alive, you'll find out. She's an Ashley institution, Touclé is. As symbolic as the Cumean Sybil. I don't believe she'll be dead. I don't believe she'll *ever* be dead.'

'You've let the cat out of the bag enough so I've lost my interest in her,' he professed. 'I can make a guess that she's some old woman, and I bet you I won't see anything remarkable in her. Except that wild name. Is it Miss Touclé, or Mrs. Touclé?'

The girl burst into laughter at this, foolish, light-hearted mirth which drenched the air all about her with the perfume of young gaiety. 'Is it Miss Druid, or Mrs. Druid?' was all she would say.

She looked up at him, her eyes shining, and cried between her gusts of laughter, as if astonished, 'Why, I do believe we are going to be happy together. I do believe it's going to be fun to live with you.'

His appalled surprise that she had again fallen into the pit of incredulity was, this time, only half-humorous. 'For God's sake, what *did* you think!'

She answered, reasonably, 'Well, nobody ever is happy together, either in books or out of them. Of all the million, million love-affairs that have happened, does anybody ever claim any one to have been happy?'

His breath was taken away. He asked helplessly, 'Well, why *are* you marrying me?'

She replied very seriously, 'Because I can't help myself, dear Neale. Isn't that the only reason you're marrying me?'

He looked at her long, his nostrils quivering a little, gave a short exclamation which seemed to carry away all his impatience, and finally said, quietly enough, 'Why, yes, of course, if that's the way you want to put it. You can say it in a thousand thousand different ways.'

He added with a sudden fury, 'And never one of them will come anywhere near expressing it. Look here, Marise, I don't believe you have the faintest, faintest idea how big this thing is. All these fool clever ways of talking about it . . . they're just a screen set up in front of it, to my mind. It's enough sight bigger than just you or me, or happiness or unhappiness. It's the meaning of everything!'

She considered this thoughtfully. 'I don't believe I really know what you mean,' she said, 'or anyhow that I *feel* what you mean. I have had dreams sometimes, that I'm in something awfully big and irresistible like a great river, flowing somewhere; but I've never felt it in waking hours. I wish I could. It's lovely in dreams. You evidently do, even awake.'

He said, confidently, 'You will, later on.'

She ventured, 'You mean, maybe, that I'm so shaken up by

the little surface waves, chopping back and forth, that I don't feel the big current.'

'It's there. Whether you feel it or not,' he made final answer to her doubt.

She murmured, 'I wonder if there *is* anything in that silly, old-fashioned notion that men are stronger than women, and that women must lean on men's strength to live?'

'Everybody's got to lean on his own strength, sooner or later,' he told her with a touch of grimness.

'You just won't be romantic!' she cried admiringly.

'I really love you, Marise,' he answered profoundly; and on this rock-like assurance she sank down with a long breath of trust.

The sun was dipping into the sea now, emblazoning the sky with a last flaming half-circle of pure colour, but the light had left the dusky edges of the world. Already the far mountains were dimmed, and the plain, passing from one deep twilight colour to another more sombre, was quietly sinking into darkness as into the strong loving arms of ultimate dissolution.

The girl spoke in a dreamy twilight tone, 'Neale dear, this is not a romantic idea . . . honestly, I do wish we could both die right here and never go down to the plain any more. Don't you feel that? Not at all?'

His voice rang out, resonant and harsh as a bugle-note, 'No, I do not, not at all, not for a single moment. I've too much ahead of me to feel that. And so have you!'

'There comes the cable-car, climbing up to get us,' she said faintly. 'And we will go down from this high place of safety into that dark plain, and we will have to cross it, painfully, step by step. *Dare* you promise me we will not lose our way?' she challenged him.

'I don't promise you anything about it,' he answered, taking her hand in his. 'Only I'm not a bit afraid of the plain, nor the way that's before us. Come along with me, and let's see what's there.'

'Do you think you know where we are going, across that plain?' she asked him painfully; 'even where we are to *try* to go?'

'No, I don't know, now,' he answered undismayed. 'But I think we will know it as we go along because we will be to-gether.'

The darkness, folding itself like a velvet mantle about the

far mountains, deepened, and her voice deepened with it. 'Can you even promise that we won't lose each other there?' she asked sombrely.

At this he suddenly took her into his arms, silently, bending his face to hers, his insistent eyes bringing hers up to meet his gaze. She could feel the strong throbbing of his heart all through her own body.

She clung to him as though she were drowning. And indeed she felt that she was. Life burst over them with a roar, a superb flooding tide on whose strong swelling bosom they felt themselves rising, rising illimitably.

The sun had now wholly set, leaving to darkness the old, old plain, soaked with humanity.

Chapter 2: *Interlude*

March 15, 1920.
8.30 a.m.

MARISE fitted little Mark's cap down over his ears and buttoned his blue reefer coat close to his throat.

'Now, you big children,' she said, with an anxious accent, to Paul and Elly standing with their school-books done up in straps, 'be sure to keep an eye on Mark at recess-time. Don't let him run and get all hot and then sit down in the wind without his coat. Remember, it's his first day at school, and he's only six.'

She kissed his round, smooth, rosy cheek once more, and let him go. Elly stooped and took her little brother's mittened hand in hers. She said nothing, but her look on the little boy's face was loving and maternal.

Paul assured his mother seriously, 'Oh, I'll look out for Mark, all right.'

Mark wriggled and said, '*I* can looken out for myself wivout Paul!'

Their mother looked for a moment deep into the eyes of her older son, so clear, so quiet, so unchanging and true. 'You're a good boy, Paul, a real comfort,' she told him.

To herself she thought, 'Yes, all his life he'll look out for people and get no thanks for it.'

She followed the children to the door, wondering at her heavy heart. What could it come from? There was nothing in

24

life for her to fear of course, except for the children, and it was absurd to fear for them. They were all safe; safe and strong and rooted deep in health, and little Mark was stepping off gallantly into his own life as the others had done. But she felt afraid. What could she be afraid of? As she opened the door, their advance was halted by the rush upon them of Paul's dog, frantic with delight to see the children ready to be off, springing up on Paul, bounding down the path, racing back to the door, all quivering eager exultation. 'Ah, he's going *with* the children!' thought Marise wistfully.

She could not bear to let them leave her and stood with them in the open door-way for a moment. Elly rubbed her soft cheek against her mother's hand. Paul, seeing his mother shiver in the keen March air, said, 'Mother, if Father were here he'd make you go in. That's a thin dress. And your teeth are just chattering.'

'Yes, you're right, Paul,' she agreed; 'it's foolish of me!'

The children gave her a hearty round of good-bye hugs and kisses, briskly and energetically performed, and went down the stone-flagged path to the road. They were chattering to each other as they went. Their voices sounded at first loud and gay in their mother's ears. Then they sank to a murmur, as the children ran along the road. The dog bounded about them in circles, barking joyfully, but this sound too grew fainter and fainter.

When the murmur died away to silence, there seemed no sound left in the stark grey valley, empty and motionless between the steep dark walls of pine-covered mountains.

Marise stood for a long time looking after the children. They were climbing up the long hilly road now, growing smaller and smaller. How far away they were, already! And that very strength and vigour of which she was so proud, which she had so cherished and fostered, how rapidly it carried them along the road that led away from her!

They were almost at the top of the hill now. Perhaps they would turn there and wave to her.

No, of course not, she was foolish to think of such a thing. Children never remembered the people they left behind. And she was now only somebody whom they were leaving behind. She felt the cold penetrate deeper and deeper into her heart, and knew she ought to go back into the house. But she could not take her eyes from the children. She thought to herself bitterly, 'This is the beginning of the end. I've been feeling how, in their hearts, they want to escape from me when I try to hold them, or when I try to make them let me into their lives. I've given everything to them, but they never think of that. *I* think of it! Every time I look at them I see all those endless hours of sacred sacrifice. But when they look at me, do they see any of that? No! Never! They only see the Obstacle in the way of their getting what they want. And so they want to run away from it. Just as they're doing now.'

She looked after them, yearning. Although they were so far, she could see them plainly in the thin mountain air. They were running mostly, once in a while stopping to throw a stone or look up into a tree. Then they scampered on like squirrels, the fox-terrier bounding ahead.

Now they were at the top where the road turned. Perhaps, after all, they *would* remember and glance back and wave their hands to her.

Now they had disappeared, without a backward look.

She continued gazing at the vacant road. It seemed to her that the children had taken everything with them.

A gust of icy wind blew down sharply from the mountain, still snow-covered, and struck at her like a sword. She turned and went back, shivering, into the empty house.

PART I

Chapter 3: *Old Mr. Welles and Young Mr. Marsh*

An Hour in the Life of Mr. Ormsby Welles, aet. 67

March 15, 1920.
3.00 *p.m.*

HAVING lifted the knocker and let it fall, the two men stood gazing with varying degrees of attention at the closed white-painted old door. The younger, the one with the round dark head and quick dark eyes, seemed extremely interested in the door, and examined it competently, its harmoniously disposed wide panels, the shapely fan-light over it, the small panes of greenish old glass on each side. 'Beautiful old bits you get occasionally in these out-of-the-way holes,' he remarked. But the older man was aware of nothing so concrete and material. He saw the door as he saw everything else that day, through a haze. Chiefly he was concerned as to what lay behind the door. . . . 'My neighbours,' he thought; 'the first I ever had.'

The sun shone down through the bare, beautiful twigs of the leafless elms, in a still air, transparent and colourless.

The handle of the door turned, the door opened. The older man was too astonished by what he saw to speak, but after an instant's pause the younger one asked if Mr. and Mrs. Crittenden were at home and could see callers. The lean, aged, leather-coloured woman, with shiny opaque black eyes, opened the door wider and silently ushered them into the house.

As long as she was in sight they preserved a prudent silence as profound as hers, but when she had left them seated, and disappeared, they turned to each other with lifted eyebrows. 'Well, what was *that*, do you suppose?' exclaimed the younger. He seemed extremely interested and amused. 'I'm not so sure, Mr. Welles, about your being safe in never locking your doors at night, as they all tell you, up here. With that for a neighbour!' The older man had a friendly smile for the facetious intention of this. 'I guess I won't have anything that'd be worth locking doors on,' he said. He looked about him still smiling, his pleasant old eyes full of a fresh satisfaction in what he saw. The room was charming to his gaze, cheerful and homey. 'I don't believe I'm going to have anything to complain of, with the folks that live in this house,' he said, 'any more than with any of the rest of it.'

The other nodded. 'Yes, it's a very good room,' he agreed. After a longer inspection, he added with a slight accent of surprise, 'An oddly good room; stunning! Look at the colour in those curtains and the walls, and the arrangement of those prints over that Chippendale sewing-table. I wonder if it's accidental. You wouldn't think you'd find anybody up here who could achieve it consciously.'

He got to his feet with a vigorous precision of movement which the other admired. 'Well, he's grown to be considerable of a man,' he thought to himself. 'A pity his father couldn't have lived to see it, all that aliveness that had bothered them so much, down at last where he's got his grip on it. And enough of it, plenty of it, oceans of it, left so that he is still about forty times more alive than anybody else.' He looked tolerantly with his tired elderly amusement at the other, stepping about, surveying the room and every object in it.

The younger brought himself up short in front of a framed photograph. 'Why, here's a château-fort I don't know!' he said with an abrupt accent. He added, with some vehemence, 'I never even heard of it, I'm sure. And it's authentic, evidently.'

The older man sat perfectly still. He did not know what a shatto four was, nor had he the slightest desire to ask and bring the information down on him, given as the other would give it, pressingly, vividly, so that you had to listen whether you wanted to or not. Heaven knew he did not want to know about whatever it was, this time. Not about that, nor anything else. He only wanted to rest and have a little life before it was too late. It was already too late for any but the quietest sort. But that was no matter. He wouldn't have liked the other kind very well probably. He certainly had detested the sort of 'life' he'd experienced in business. The quietest sort was what he had always wanted and never got. And now it really seemed as though he was going to have it. For all his fatigued pose in the old arm-chair, his heart beat faster at the idea. He hadn't got used to being free yet. He'd heard people say that when

28

you were first married it was like that, you couldn't realize it. He'd heard one of the men at the office say that for a long time, every time he heard his bride's skirts rustle, he had to turn his head to make sure she was really there. Well, he would like now to get up and look out of that window and see if his garden was really there. *His garden!* He thought with a secret feeling, half pity and half shame, of those yellowed old seed catalogues which had come, varnished and brilliant and new, year after year, so long ago, which he'd looked at so hard and so long in the evenings, and put away to get yellow and sallow like his face . . . and his hopes. It must be almost time to 'make garden,' he thought. He had heard them saying at the store that the sap was beginning to run in the maple-trees. He would have just time to get himself settled in his house . . . he felt an absurd young flush come up under his grizzled beard at this phrase . . . 'his house,' his own house, with bookshelves, and a garden. How he loved it all already! He sat very still, feeling those savagely lopped-off tendrils put out their curling fingers once more, this time unafraid. He sat there in the comfortable old arm-chair at rest as never before. He thought, 'This is the way I'm going to feel right along, every day, all the time,' and closed his eyes.

He opened them again in a moment, moved subconsciously by the lifetime habit of making sure what Vincent was up to. He smiled at the keen look of alert, prick-eared attention which the other was still giving to that room! Lord, how Vincent did love to get things all figured out! He probably had, by this time, an exact diagram of the owners of the house all drawn up in his mind and would probably spend the hour of their call, seeing if it fitted. Not that *they* would have any notion he was doing anything but talk a blue streak, or was thinking of anything but introducing an old friend.

One thing he wanted in his garden was plenty of gladioli. Those poor, spindling, watery ones he had tried to grow in the window-box, he'd forget that failure in a whole big row all along the terrace, tall and strong, standing up straight in the country sunshine. What was the address of that man who made a specialty of gladioli? He ought to have noted it down. 'Vincent,' he asked, 'do you remember the address of that Mr. Schwatzkummerer who grew nothing but gladioli?' Vincent was looking with an expression of extreme astonishment at the sheet of music on the piano. He started at the question, stared, recollected himself, laughed, and said, 'Heavens, no, Mr.

Welles!' and went back into his own world. There were lots of things, Mr. Welles reflected, that Vincent did *not* care about just as hard as he cared about others.

In a moment the younger man came and sat down on the short, high-armed sofa. Mr. Welles thought he looked puzzled, a very unusual expression on that face. Maybe, after all, he hadn't got the owners of the house so well-plotted out as he thought he ought to. He himself, going on with his own concerns, remarked, 'Well, the name must be in the Long Island telephone directory. When you go back you could look it up and send me word.'

'Whose name?' asked Vincent blankly.

'Schwatzkummerer,' said the other.

'*What!*' cried Vincent incredulously, and then, 'Oh yes,' and then, 'Sure, yes, I'll look it up. I'm going back Thursday on the night train. I won't leave the Grand Central without going to a telephone booth, looking it up, and sending it to you on a postcard, mailed there. It ought to be here on the morning mail Saturday.'

The older man knew perfectly well that he was being a little laughed at, for his absorption in gladioli, and not minding it at all, laughed himself, peaceably. 'It would take a great deal more than a little of Vincent's fun,' he thought, 'to make me feel anything but peaceable here.' He was quite used to having people set him down as a harmless, worn-out old duffer, and he did not object to this conception of his character. It made a convenient screen behind which he could carry on his own observation and meditation uninterrupted.

'Here comes somebody,' said Vincent and turned his quick eyes towards the door, with an eager expression of attention. He really *must* have been stumped by something in the room, thought Mr. Welles, and meant to figure it out from the owners of the house themselves.

The tall, quiet-looking lady with the long dark eyes, who now came in alone, excusing herself for keeping them waiting, must of course be Mrs. Crittenden, Mr. Welles knew. He wished he could get to his feet as Vincent did, looking as though he had got there by a bound or a spring and were ready for another. He lifted himself out of his arm-chair with a heaviness he knew seemed all the heavier by contrast, took the slim hand Mrs. Crittenden offered him, looked at her as hard as he dared, and sank again into the arm-chair, as she motioned him to do. He had had a long experience in judging people quickly by

the expression of their faces, and in that short length of time he
had decided thankfully that he was really, just as he had hoped,
going to like his new neighbour as much as all the rest of it.
He gave her a propitiatory smile, hoping she might like him a
little, too, and hoping also that she would not mind Vincent.
Sometimes people did, especially nice ladies such as evidently
Mrs. Crittenden was. He observed that as usual Vincent had
cut in ahead of everybody else, had mentioned their names,
both of them, and was talking with that . . . well, the way he
did, which people either liked very much or couldn't abide.
He looked at Vincent as he talked. He was not a great talker
himself, which gave him a great deal of practice in watching
people who did. He often felt that he *saw* more than he heard,
so much more did people's faces express than their words.

He noticed that the younger man was smiling a good deal,
showing those fine teeth of his, and he had one of those instan-
taneously gone, flash-light reminiscences of elderly people . . .
the day when Mr. Marsh had been called away from the office
and had asked him to go with little Vincent to keep an appoint-
ment with the dentist. Heavens! How the kid had roared and
kicked! And now he sat there, smiling, 'making a call,' probably with that very filling in his tooth, grown-up, not even so
very young any more, with a little grey in his thick hair, what
people often called a good-looking man. How life did run
between your fingers! Well, he would close his hand tight
upon what was left to him. He noticed further that as Vincent
talked, his eyes fixed on his interlocutor, his vigorous hands
caressed with a slow circular motion the rounded arms of his
chair. 'What a three-ringed circus that fellow is,' he thought.
'I bet that the lady thinks he hasn't another idea in his head
but introducing an old friend, and all the time he's taking her
in, every inch of her, and three to one, what he'll talk about
most afterwards is the smooth hard feeling of those polished
arm-chairs.' Vincent was saying, '. . . and so, we heard in a
roundabout way too long to bother you with, about the small
old house next door being for sale, and how very quiet and
peaceful a spot this is, and the Company bought it for Mr.
Welles for a permanent home, now he has retired.'

'Pretty fine of them!' murmured the older man dutifully, to
the lady.

Vincent went on, 'Oh, it's only the smallest way for them to
show their sense of his lifetime devotion to their interests.
There's no estimating what we all owe him, for his steadiness

and loyalty and good judgment, especially during that hard period, near the beginning. *You* know, when all electrical businesses were so entirely on trial still. Nobody knew whether they were going to succeed or not. My father was one of the Directors from the first and I've been brought up in the tradition of how much the small beginning Company is indebted to Mr. Welles, during the years when they went down so near the edge of ruin that they could see the receiver looking in through the open door.'

Welles moved protestingly. He never had liked the business and he didn't like reminders that he owed his present comfort to it. Besides this was reading his own epitaph. He thought he must be looking very foolish to Mrs. Crittenden. Vincent continued, 'But of course that's of no great importance up here. What's more to the purpose is that Mr. Welles is a great lover of country life and growing things, and he's been forced to keep his nose on a city grindstone all his life until just now. I think I can guarantee that you'll find him a very appreciative neighbour, especially if you have plenty of gladioli in your garden.'

This last was one of what Welles called 'Vincent's side-wipes,' which he could inlay so deftly that they seemed an integral part of the conversation. He wondered what Mrs. Crittenden would say, if Vincent ever got through his gabble and gave her a chance. She was turning to him now, smiling, and beginning to speak. What a nice voice she had! How nice that she should have such a voice!

'I'm more than glad to have you both come in to see me, and I'm delighted that Mr. Welles is going to settle here. But Mr. . . .' she hesitated an instant, recalled the name, and went on, 'Mr. Marsh doesn't need to explain you any more. It's evident that you don't know Ashley, or you'd realize that I've already heard a great deal more about you than Mr. Marsh would be likely to tell me, very likely a good deal more than is true. I know for instance . . .' she laughed and corrected herself, '. . . at least I've been told, what the purchase price of the house was. I know how Harry Wood's sister-in-law's friend told you about Ashley and the house in the first place. I know how many years you were in the service of the Company, and how your pension was voted unanimously by the Directors, and about the silver loving-cup your fellow employees in the office gave you when you retired; and indeed every single thing about you, except the exact relation of the elderly invalid to whose care you gave up so generously so much of your life;

32

I'm not sure whether she was an aunt or a second-cousin.' She paused an instant to give them a chance to comment on this, but finding them still quite speechless, she went on. 'And now I know another thing, that you like gladioli, and that is a real bond.'

She was interrupted here by a great explosive laugh from Vincent. It was his comment on her speech to them, and for a time he made no other, eyeing her appreciatively as she and Mr. Welles talked garden together, and from time to time chuckling to himself. She gave him once a sidelong amused glance, evidently liking his capacity to laugh at seeing the ground cut away from under his feet, evidently quite aware that he was still thinking about that, and not at all about Mr. Welles and tulip-beds. Welles was relieved at this. Apparently she was going to 'take' Vincent the right way. Some ladies were frightfully rubbed the wrong way by that strange great laugh of Vincent's. And what she knew about gardening! And not only about gardening in general, but about his own garden. He was astounded at her knowledge apparently of every inch of the quadrangle of soil back of his house, and at the revelations she made to him of what could lie sleeping under a mysterious blank surface of earth. Why, a piece of old ground was like a person. You had to know it, to have any idea of all that was hidden in its bosom, good and bad. 'There never was such a place for pig-weed as the lower end of your vegetable lot,' she told him; 'you'll have to get up nights to fight it if there is plenty of rain this summer.' And again, 'Be careful about not digging too close to the east wall of your terrace. There is a border of peonies there, splendid pink ones, and you're likely to break off the shoots. They don't show so early as the red ones near the walk, that get more sun.'

'Did you ever use to *live* in that house?' he asked her, respectful of her mastery of its secrets.

She laughed. 'No, oh no. We've lived right here all the eleven years of our life in Vermont. But there's another side to the local wireless information-bureau that let me know all about you before you ever got here. We all know all about everybody and everything, you know. If you live in the country you're really married to humanity, for better or for worse, not just on speaking terms with it, as you are in the city. Why, I know about your garden because I have stood a thousand, thousand times leaning on my hoe in my own garden, discussing those peonies with old Mrs. Belham who lived there before

33

you.' This seemed to bring up some picture into her mind at which she looked for a moment, turning from it to the man beside her, with a warmth in her voice which went to his heart. 'It's been forlorn having that dear little old house empty and cold. I can't *tell* you how glad I am you have come to warm it, and live in it.'

The wonder of it overcame Mr. Welles like a wave. 'I can't believe I'm really going to!' he cried desperately. 'It doesn't seem *possible*!' He felt shamed, knowing that he had burst out too violently. What could she know of what lay back of him, that he was escaped from! What could she think of him, but that he was a foolish, bitter old man?

She did not seem to think that, looking at him attentively as though she wanted to make out just what he meant. Perhaps she did make out, for she now said gently, 'I believe you are going to like it, Mr. Welles. I believe you are going to find here what . . . what you deserve to find.' She said quietly, 'I hope we shall be good neighbours to you.'

She spoke so kindly, her look on him was so humane that he felt the water coming to his eyes. He was in a foolishly emotional state, these first days. The least little thing threw him off the track. It really *did* seem hardly possible that it was all true. That the long grind at the office was over, the business he had always hated and detested, and the long, hateful slavery at the flat finished at last, and that he had come to live out what was left to him in this lovely, peaceful valley, in that quiet welcoming little house, with this sweet woman next door! He swallowed. The corners of his mouth twitched. What an old lunatic he was. But he did not dare trust himself to speak again.

Now Vincent's voice rose. What a length of time Vincent had been silent, – he who never took a back seat for anybody! What had he been doing all this time, sitting there and staring at them with those awfully brilliant eyes of his? Very likely he had seen the silly weak tears so near the surface, had caught the sentimental twitch of the mouth. Yes, quite certainly, for now he was showing his tact by changing the subject, changing it with a vengeance. 'Mrs. Crittenden,' he was saying, 'my curiosity has been touched by that very fine photograph over there. I don't recognize the castle it shows.'

'That's in Bayonne,' she said, and paused, her eyes speculatively on him.

'No, Heavens no! You don't need to tell me that it's not

34

Bayonne, New Jersey!' he answered her unspoken question violently. This made her laugh, opening her long eyes a little. He went on, 'I've been as far as Pau, but never went into the Basque country.'

'Oh, Pau.' She said no more than this, but Welles had the impression that these words somehow had made a comment on Vincent's information. Vincent seemed to think so too, and curiously enough not to think it a very favourable comment. He looked, what he almost never looked, a little nettled, and spoke a little stiffly. 'It's a very fine specimen,' he said briefly, looking again at the photograph.

'Oh, it looks very much finer and bigger in the photograph than it really is,' she told them. 'It's only a bandbox of a thing compared with Coucy or Pierrefonds or any of the northern ones. It was built, you know, like the Cathedral at Bayonne, when the Plantagenets still held that country, but after they were practically pretty near English, and both the château and the Gothic cathedral seem queer aliens among the southern natives. I have the photograph up there on the wall only because of early associations. I lived opposite it long ago when I was a little girl.'

This, to Mr. Welles, was indistinguishable from the usual talk of people who have been 'abroad.' To tell the truth they always sounded to him more or less 'showing-off,' though he humbly tried to think it was only because he could never take any part in such talk. He certainly did not see anything in the speech to make Vincent look at her, almost with his jaw dropped. He himself paid little attention to what she was now saying, because he could not keep his mind from the lingering sweet intonations of her voice. What difference did it make where she had lived as a little girl? She was going to live next door to him now; what an awfully nice woman she was, and quite a good-looking woman too, with a very nice figure, although not in her very first youth, of course. How old could she be? Between thirty and forty of course, but you couldn't tell where. His personal taste was not for such a long face as hers. But you didn't notice that when she smiled. He liked the way she did her black hair, too, so smooth and shining and close to her head. It looked as though she'd really combed and brushed it, and most women's hair didn't.

She turned to him now, again, and said, 'Is this your very first call in Ashley? Because if it is, I mustn't miss the opportunity to cut in ahead of all the other gossips, and give you a great deal of information. You might just as well have it all in one piece now, and get it straight, as take it in little snippets from old Mrs. Powers, when she comes to bring your milk, this evening. You see I know that you are to get your milk of the Powers, and that they have plucked up courage to ask you eight cents a quart although the price around here has been, till now, six cents. You'll be obliged to listen to a great many more details from Mrs. Powers than from me, even those she knows nothing about. But of course you must be introduced to the Powers, *in toto* too. Old Mrs. Powers, a very lively old widow, lives on her farm nearly at the foot of Deer Hollow. Her married son and his family live with her. In this house, there is first of all my husband. I'm so sorry he is away in Canada just now, on lumbering business. He is Neale Crittenden, a Williams man, who in his youth had thoughts of exploring the world but who has turned out head of the "Crittenden Manufacturing Company," which is the high-sounding name of a smallish wood-working business on the other side of the field next our house. You can see the buildings and probably hear the saws from your garden. Properly speaking, you know, you don't live in Ashley but in "Crittenden's" and your house constitutes one quarter of all the residences in that settlement. There are yours, and ours, the mill-buildings, the house where an old cousin of mine lives, and the Powers' house, although that is so far away, nearly half a mile, that it is really only a farm-house in the country. *We*, you see, are the suburb of Ashley.'

Marsh laughed out again at this, and she laughed with him, their eyes, shining with amusement, meeting in a friendly glance.

'The mill is the most important member of Crittenden's, of course. Part of the mill-building is pre-Revolutionary, and very picturesque. In the lifetime of my husband's uncle, it still ran by water-power with a beautiful, enormous old mossy water-wheel. But since we took it over, we've had to put in modern machinery very prosaically and run it on its waste of slabs, mostly. All sorts of small, unimportant objects are manufactured there, things you never heard of probably. Backs of hair-brushes, wooden casters to put under beds and chairs, rollers for cotton mills. As soon as my husband returns, I'll ask him to take you through it. That and the old church are the only historic monuments in town.'

She stopped and asked him meditatively, 'What else do you

suppose I need to forestall old Mrs. Powers on? My old Cousin Hetty perhaps. She has a last name, Allen – yes, some connection with Ethan Allen. I am, myself. But everybody has always called her Miss Hetty till few people remember that she has another name. She was born there in the old house below "the Burning," and she has lived there for eighty years, and that is all her saga. You can't see her house from here, but it is part of Crittenden's all the same, although it is a mile away by the main road as you go towards the Dug-Way. But you can reach it in six or seven minutes from here by a back lane, through the Eagle Rock woods.'

'What nice names!' Mr. Welles luxuriated in them. 'The Eagle Rock woods. The Dug-Way. The Burning. Deer Hollow.'

'I bet you don't know what they mean,' Vincent challenged him. Vincent was always throwing challenges, at everything. But by this time he had learned how to dodge them. 'No, I don't know, and I don't care if I don't,' he answered happily.

It pleased him that Mrs. Crittenden found this amusing, so that she looked at him laughing. How her eyes glistened when she laughed. It made you laugh back. He risked another small attempt at facetiousness. 'Go on with the census of Crittenden's,' he told her. 'I want to know all about my future fellow-citizens. You haven't even finished up this house, anybody but your husband.'

'There is myself. You see me. There is nothing more to that. And there are the three children, Paul, Elly, and Mark . . .' She paused here rather abruptly, and the whimsical accent of good-humoured mockery disappeared. For an instant her face changed into something quite different from what they had seen. Mr. Welles could not at all make out the expression which very passingly had flickered across her eyes with a smoke-like vagueness and rapidity. He had the queerest fancy that she looked somehow scared, – but of course that was preposterous.

'Your call,' she told them both, 'happens to fall on a day which marks a turning-point in our family life. This is the very first day in ten years, since Paul's birth, that I have not had at least one of the children beside me. To-day is the opening of spring term in our country school, and my little Mark went off this morning, for the first time, with his brother and sister. I have been alone until you came.' She stopped for a moment.

37

Mr. Welles wished that Vincent could get over his habit of staring at people so. She went on, 'I have felt very queer indeed, all day. It's as though . . . you know, when you have been walking up and up a long flight of stairs, and you go automatically putting one foot up and then the other, and then suddenly . . . your upraised foot falls back with a jar. You've come to the top, and, for an instant, you have a gone feeling without your stairs to climb.'

It occurred to Mr. Welles that really perhaps the reason why some nice ladies did not like Vincent was just because of his habit of looking at them so hard. He could have no idea how piercingly bright his eyes looked when he fixed them on a speaker like that. And now Mrs. Crittenden was looking back at him, and would notice it. *He* could understand how a re-fined lady would feel as though somebody were almost trying to find a key-hole to look in at her, – to have anybody pounce on her so, with his eyes, as Vincent did. She couldn't know, of course, that Vincent went pouncing on ladies and baggage-men and office boys, and old friends, just the same way. He bestirred himself to think of something to say. 'I wish I could get up my nerve to ask you, Mrs. Crittenden, about one other person in this house,' he ventured, 'the old woman . . . the old lady . . . who let us in the door.'

At the sound of his voice Mrs. Crittenden looked away from Vincent quickly and looked at him for a perceptible moment before she heard what he had said. Then she explained, smil-ing, 'Oh, she would object very much to being labelled with the finicky title of "lady." That was Touclé, our queer old Indian woman, – all that is left of old America here. She belongs to our house, or perhaps I should say it belongs to her. She was born here, a million years ago, more or less, when there were still a few basket-making Indians left in the valley. Her father and mother both died, and she was brought up by the old Great-uncle Crittenden's family. Then my husband's Uncle Burton inherited the house and brought his bride here, and Touclé just stayed on. She always makes herself useful enough to pay for her food and lodging. And when his wife died an elderly woman, Touclé still just stayed on, till he died, and then she went right on staying here in the empty house, till my husband and I got here. We were married in Rome, and made the long trip here without stopping at all. It was dawn, a June morning, when we arrived. We walked all the way from the station at Ashley out to the old house, here at

Crittenden's. And . . . I'll never forget the astounded expression on my husband's face when Touclé rose up out of the long grass in the front yard and bade me welcome. She'd known me as a little girl when I used to visit here. She will outlive all of us, Touclé will, and be watching from her room in the woodshed chamber on the dawn of Judgment Day when the stars begin to fall.'

Mr. Welles felt a trifle bewildered by this, and showed it. She explained further, 'But seriously, I must tell you that she is a perfectly harmless and quite uninteresting old herb-gatherer, although the children in the village are a little afraid of her, because she is an Indian, the only one they have ever seen. She really *is* an Indian too. She knows every inch of our valley and the mountains better than any lumberman or hunter or fisherman in Ashley. She often goes off and doesn't come back for days. I haven't the least idea where she stays. But she's very good to our children when she's here, and I like her capacity for monumental silence. It gives her very occasional remarks an oracular air, even though you know it's only because she doesn't often open her lips. She helps a little with the housework, too, although she always looks so absent-minded, as though she were thinking of something very far away. She's quite capable of preparing a good meal for all she never seems to notice what she's up to. And she's the last member of our family except the very coming-and-going little maids I get once in a while. Ashley is unlike the rest of the world in that it is hard to get domestic servants here.

'Now let me see, whom next to introduce to you. You know all your immediate neighbours now. I shall have to begin on Ashley itself. Perhaps our minister and his wife. They live in the high-porticoed, tall-pillared white old house next door to the church in the village, on the opposite side from the churchyard. They are Ashleyans of the oldest rock. Both of them were born here, and have always lived here. Mr. Bayweather is seventy-five years old and has never had any other parish. I do believe the very best thing I can do for you is to send you straight to them, this minute. There's nothing Mr. Bayweather doesn't know about the place or the people. He has a collection of Ashleyana of all sorts, records, deeds, titles, old letters, family trees. And for the last forty years he has been very busy writing a history of Ashley.'

'A history of *Ashley*?' exclaimed Vincent.

'A history of Ashley,' she answered, level-browed.

39

Mr. Welles had the impression that a 'side-wipe' had been exchanged in which he had not shared.

Vincent now asked irrelevantly, 'Do you go to church yourself?'

'Oh yes,' she answered, 'I go, I like to go. And I take the children.' She turned her head so that she looked down at her long hands in her lap, as she added, 'I think going to church is a *refining* influence in children's lives, don't you?'

To Mr. Welles' horror this provoked from Vincent one of his great laughs. And this time he was sure that Mrs. Crittenden would take offence, for she looked up, distinctly startled, really quite as though he *had* looked in through the key-hole. But Vincent went on laughing. He even said, impudently, 'Ah, now I've caught you, Mrs. Crittenden; you're too used to keeping your jokes to yourself. And they're much too good for that.'

She looked at him hard, with a certain wonder in her eyes.

'Oh, there's no necromancy about it,' he told her. 'I've been reading the titles of your books and glancing over your music before you came in. And I can put two and two together. Who are you making fun of to yourself? Who first got off that lovely speech about the refining influence of church?'

She laughed a little, half-uneasily, a brighter colour mounting to her smooth oval cheeks. 'That's one of Mrs. Bayweather's favourite maxims,' she admitted. She added, 'But I really *do* like to go to church.'

Mr. Welles felt an apprehension about the turn things were taking. Vincent, he felt sure, was on the verge of being up to something. And he did not want to risk offending Mrs. Crittenden. He stood up. 'Thank you very much for telling us about the minister and his wife, Mrs. Crittenden. I think we'll go right along down to the village now, and pay a call on them. There'll be time enough before dinner.' Vincent of course got up too, at this, saying, 'He's the most perfect old housekeeper, you know. He's kept the neatest flat for himself and that aged aunt of his for seventy years.'

'*Seventy!*' cried Mr. Welles, scandalized at the exaggeration.

'Oh, more or less,' said Vincent, laughing. Mr. Welles noticed with no enthusiasm that his eyes were extremely bright, that he smiled almost incessantly, that he stepped with an excess of his usual bounce. Evidently something had set him off into one of his fits of wild high spirits. You could almost feel the electricity sparkle from him, as it does from a cat on a cold day. Personally, Mr. Welles preferred not to touch cats when they were like that.

'When are you going back to the city, Mr. Marsh?' asked Mrs. Crittenden, as they said good-bye at the door.

Vincent was standing below her on the marble step. He looked up at her now, and something about his expression made Mr. Welles think again of glossy fur emitting sparks. He said, 'I'll lay you a wager, Mrs. Crittenden, that there is one thing your Ashley underground news-service has not told you about us, and that is, that I've come up not only to help Mr. Welles install himself in his new home, but to take a somewhat prolonged rest-cure myself. I've always meant to see more of this picturesque part of Vermont. I've a notion that the air of this lovely spot will do me a world of good.'

As Mr. Welles opened his mouth, perhaps rather wide, in the beginning of a remark, he cut in briskly with, 'You're worrying about Schwatzkummerer, I know. Never you fear. I'll get hold of his address, all right.' He explained briefly to Mrs. Crittenden, startled by the portentous name. 'Just a specialist in gladiolus seeds.'

'*Bulbs!*' cried Mr. Welles, in involuntary correction, and knew as he spoke that he had been switched off to a side-track.

'Oh well, bulbs be it,' Vincent conceded the point indulgently. He took off his hat in a final salutation to Mrs. Crittenden, and grasping his elderly friend by the arm, moved with him down the flag-paved path.

Chapter 4: *Table Talk*

An Hour in the Home Life of Mrs. Neale Crittenden, aet. 34

March 20.

As she and Paul carried the table out to the windless, sunny side-porch, Marise was struck by a hospitable inspiration. 'You and Elly go on setting the table,' she told the children, and ran across the side-yard to the hedge. She leaned over this, calling, 'Mr. Welles! Mr. Welles!' and when he came to the door, 'The children and I are just celebrating this first really warm day by having lunch out of doors. Won't you and Mr. Marsh come and join us?'

By the time the explanations and protestations and renewals

41

of the invitation were over and she brought them back to the
porch, Paul and Elly had almost finished setting the table.
Elly nodded a country-child's silent greeting to the newcomers.
Paul said, 'Oh goody! Mr. Welles, you sit by me.'

Marise was pleased at the friendship growing up between the
gentle old man and her little boy.

'Elly, don't you want me to sit by you?' asked Marsh with a
playful accent.

Elly looked down at the plate she was setting on the table.
'If you want to,' she said neutrally.

Her mother smiled inwardly. How amusingly Elly had acquired as only a child could acquire an accent, the exact
astringent, controlled brevity of the mountain idiom.

'I think Elly means that she would like it very much, Mr.
Marsh,' she said laughingly. 'You'll soon learn to translate
Vermontese into ordinary talk, if you stay on here.'

She herself went through the house into the kitchen and
began placing on the wheel-tray all the components of the
lunch, telling them over to herself to be sure she missed none.
'Meat, macaroni, spinach, hot plates, bread, butter, water . . .
a pretty plain meal to invite city people to share. Here, I'll
open a bottle of olives. Paul, help me get this through the
door.'

As he pulled at the other end of the wheeled tray, Paul said
that Mark had gone upstairs to wash his hands, ages ago, and
was probably still fooling around in the soap-suds, and like as
not leaving the soap in the water.

'Paul the responsible!' thought his mother. As they passed
the foot of the stairs she called up, 'Mark! Come along, dear.
Lunch is served. All ready,' she announced as they pushed the
tray out on the porch.

The two men turned around from where they had been
gazing up at the mountain. 'What is that great cliff of bare
rock called?' asked Mr. Marsh.

'Those are the Eagle Rocks,' explained Marise, sitting down
and motioning them to their places. 'Elly dear, don't spread it
on your bread so *thick*. If Mr. Bayweather were here he could
probably tell you why they are called that. I have known but
I've forgotten. There's some sort of tradition, I believe . . . no,
I see you are getting ready to hear it called the Maiden's Leap
where the Indian girl leaped off to escape an unwelcome lover.
But it's not that this time: something or other about Tories and
an American spy . . . ask Mr. Bayweather.'

'Heaven forfend!' exclaimed Mr. Marsh.

Marise was amused. 'Oh, you've been lectured to on local history, I see,' she surmised.

'*I* found it very interesting,' said Mr. Welles, loyally. 'Though perhaps he does try to give you a little too much at one sitting.'

'Mr. Welles,' said Paul, with his mouth full, 'fishing season begins in ten days.'

Marise decided that she would really have to have a rest from telling Paul not to talk with food in his mouth, and said nothing.

Mr. Welles confessed that he had never gone fishing in his life, and asked if Paul would take him.

'Sure!' said Paul. 'Mother and I go, lots.'

Mr. Marsh looked at Marise inquiringly. 'Yes,' she said, 'I'm a confirmed fisherman. Some of the earliest and happiest recollections I have, are of fishing these brooks when I was a little girl.'

'Here?' asked Mr. Welles. 'I thought you lived in France.'

'There's time in a child's life to live in various places,' she explained. 'I spent part of my childhood and youth here with my dear old cousin. The place is full of associations for me. Will you have your spinach now, or later? It'll keep hot all right if you'd rather wait.'

'What is this delicious dish?' asked Mr. Marsh. 'It tastes like a man's version of creamed chicken, which is always a little too lady-like for me.'

'It's a *blanquette de veau*, and you may be sure I learned to make it in one of the French incarnations, not a Vermont one.'

Paul stirred and asked, 'Mother, where *is* Mark? He'll be late for school, if he doesn't hurry.'

'That's so,' she said, and reflected how often one used that phrase in response to one of Paul's solid and unanswerable statements.

Mark appeared just then and she began to laugh helplessly. His hands were wetly, pinkly, unnaturally clean, but his round, rosy, sunny little face was appallingly streaked and black.

Paul did not laugh. He said in horrified reproach, 'Oh, Mark! You never *touched* your face! It's piggy dirty.'

Mark was staggered for a moment, but nothing staggered him long. 'I don't get microbes off my face into my food,' he said calmly. 'And you bet there aren't any microbes left on my hands.' He went on, looking at the table disapprovingly,

43

'Mother, there isn't a many on the table *this* day, and I wanted a many.'

'The stew's awful good,' said Paul, putting away a large quantity.

' "Very," not "awful," and don't hold your fork like that,' corrected Marise, half-heartedly, thinking that she herself did not like the insipid phrase 'very good' nor did she consider the way a fork was held so very essential to salvation. 'How much of life is convention, any way you arrange it,' she thought, 'even in such an entirely unconventional one as ours.'

'It *is* good,' said Mark, taking his first mouthful. Evidently he had not taken the remarks about his face at all seriously.

'See here, Mark,' his mother put it to him as man to man, 'do you think you ought to sit down to the table looking like that?'

Mark wriggled, took another mouthful, and got up mournfully.

Paul was touched. 'Here, I'll go up with you and get it over quick,' he said. Marise gave him a quick approving glance. That was the best side of Paul. You could say what you pleased about the faults of American and French family life, but at any rate the children didn't hate each other, as English children seemed to, in novels at least. It was only last week that Paul had fought the big French-Canadian boy in his room at school, because he had made fun of Elly's rubber boots.

As the little boys clattered out she said to the two guests, 'I don't know whether you're used to children. If you're not, you must be feeling as though you were taking lunch in a boiler factory.'

Mr. Welles answered, 'I never knew what I was missing before. Especially Paul. That first evening when you sent him over with the cake, as he stood in the door, I thought, "I wish *I* could have had a little son like that!" '

'We'll share him with you, Mr. Welles.' Marise was touched by the wistfulness of his tone. She noticed that Mr. Marsh had made no comment on the children. He was perhaps one of the people who never looked at them, unless they ran into him. Eugenia Mills was like that, quite sincerely.

'May I have a little more of the *blanquette*, if I won't be considered a glutton?' asked Mr. Marsh now. 'I've sent to the city for an invaluable factotum of mine to come and look out for us here, and when he comes, I hope you'll give him the recipe.'

The little boys clattered back and began to eat again, in

44

haste with frequent demands for their mother to tell them what time it was. In spite of this precaution, the clock advanced so relentlessly that they were obliged to set off, the three of them, before dessert was eaten, with an apple in one hand and a cookie in the other.

The two men leaned back in their chairs with long breaths, which Marise interpreted as relief. 'Strenuous, three of them at once, aren't they?' she said. 'A New York friend of mine always says she can take the vibration-cure, only by listening to family talk at our table.'

'What's the vibration-cure?' asked Mr. Welles seriously.

'Oh, *I* don't know!' confessed Marise. 'I'm too busy to keep up with the latest fads in cures as Eugenia does. You may meet her here this summer, by the way. She usually spends a part of the summer with us. She is a very old school-friend of mine.'

'French or Vermont incarnation?' inquired Marsh casually. 'May I smoke? Won't you have a cigarette yourself?'

'Oh, *French*!' Marise was immensely amused, and then, remembering that the joke was not apparent, 'If you'd ever seen her, even for a moment, you'd know why I laugh. She is the embodiment of sophisticated cosmopolitanism, an expert on all sorts of esoteric, æsthetic and philosophic matters, bookbinding, historic lace, the Vedanta creed, Chinese porcelains, Provençal poetry, Persian shawls . . .'

'What nationality is she, herself?' inquired Mr. Welles with some curiosity.

Marise laughed. 'She was born in Arkansas, and brought up in Minnesota, what did you suppose? No European could ever take culture so seriously. You know how any convert always has a thousand times more fervour than the fatigued members of the faith who were born to it.'

'Like Henry James, perhaps?' suggested Marsh.

'Yes, I always envied Henry James the conviction he seems to have had, all his life, that Europeans are a good deal more unlike other people than I ever found them. It may be obtuseness on my part, but I never could see that people who lived in the Basses-Pyrénées are any more cultivated or had any broader horizons than people who live in the Green Mountains. My own experience is that when you actually live with people, day after day, year after year, you find about the same range of possibilities in any group of them. But I never advance this theory to Eugenia, who would be horrified to know that I find a strong family likeness between her New York circle and my neighbours here.'

She had been aware that Marsh was looking at her as she spoke. What a singular, piercing eye he had! It made her a little restive, as at a too-intimate contact, to be looked at so intently, although she was quite aware that there was a good deal of admiration in the look. She wondered what he was thinking about her, for it was evident that he was thinking about her, as he sent out that penetrating gaze.

But perhaps not, after all; for he now said as if in answer to her last remark, 'I have my own way of believing that, too, that all people are made of the same stuff. Mostly I find them perfectly negligible, too utterly without savour even to glance at. Once in a thousand years, it seems to me, you come across a human being who's alive as you are, who speaks your language, is your own kind, belongs to you. When you do, good Lord! What a moment!'

He pronounced this in a perfectly impersonal tone, but something about the quality of his voice made Marise flash a quick glance at him. His eyes met hers with a sudden, bold deepening of their gaze. Marise's first impulse was to be startled and displeased, but in an instant a quick fear of being ridiculous had voiced itself and was saying to her, 'Don't be countrified. It's only that I've had no contact with people-of-the-world for a year now. That's the sort of thing they get their amusement from. It would make him laugh to have it resented.' Aloud she said, rather at random, 'I usually go down once a season to the city for a visit to this old friend of mine, and other friends there. But this last winter I didn't get up the energy to do that.'

'I should think,' said Mr. Welles, 'that last winter you'd have used up all your energy on other things, from what Mrs. Powers tells me about the big chorus you always lead here in winters.'

'That does take up a lot of time,' she admitted. 'But it's a generator of energy, leading a chorus is, not a spender of it.'

'Oh, come!' protested Marsh. 'You can't put that over on me. To do it as I gather you do . . . heavens! You must pour out your energy and personality as though you'd cut your arteries and let the red flood come.'

'You pour it out all right,' she agreed, 'but you get it back a thousand times over.' She spoke seriously, the topic was vital to her, her eyes turned inward on a recollection. 'It's amazing. It's enough to make a mystic out of a granite boulder. I don't know how many times I've dragged myself to a practice-evening dog-tired physically with work and care of the children, stale morally, sure that I had nothing in me that was profitable for any purpose, feeling that I'd do anything to be allowed to stay at home, to doze on the couch and read a poor novel.' She paused, forgetting to whom she was speaking, forgetting she was not alone, touched and stirred with a breath from those evenings.

'Well . . . ?' prompted Mr. Marsh. She wondered if she were mistaken in thinking he sounded a little irritable.

'Well,' she answered, 'it has not failed a single time. I have never come back otherwise than stronger, and rested, the fatigue and staleness all gone, buried deep in something living.'

She had a moment of self-consciousness here, was afraid that she had been carried away to seem high-flown or pretentious, and added hastily and humorously, 'You mustn't think that it's because I'm making anything wonderful out of my chorus of country boys and girls and their fathers and mothers. It's no notable success that puts wings to my feet as I come home from that work. It's only the music, the hearty satisfying singing-out, by ordinary people, of what too often lies withering in their hearts.'

She was aware that she was speaking not to sympathizers. Mr. Welles looked vague, evidently had no idea what she meant. Mr. Marsh's face looked closed tight, as though he would not open to let in a word of what she was saying. He almost looked hostile. Why should he? When she stopped, a little abashed at having been carried along by her feelings, Mr. Marsh put in lightly, with no attempt at transition, 'All that's very well. But you can't make me believe that by choice you live up here all the year around. You must nearly perish away with homesickness for the big world, you who so evidently belong in it.'

'Where is the big world?' she challenged him, laughing. 'When you're young you want to go all round the globe to look for it. And when you've gone, don't you find that your world everywhere is about as big as you are?'

Mr. Marsh eyed her hard, and shook his head, with a little scornful downward thrust of the corners of his mouth, as though he were an augur who refused to lend himself to the traditional necessity to keep up the appearance of believing in an exploded religion. '*You* know where the big world is,' he said firmly. 'It's where there are only people who don't have to work, who have plenty of money and brains and beautiful possessions and

47

gracious ways of living, and few moral scruples.' He defined it with a sovereign disregard for softening phrases.

She opposed to this a meditative, 'Oh, I suppose the real reason why I go less and less to New York, is that it doesn't interest me as it used to. Human significance is what makes interest for me, and when you're used to looking deep into human lives out of a complete knowledge of them as we do up here, it's very tantalizing and tormenting and after a while gets boring, the superficial, incoherent glimpses you get in such a smooth, glib-tongued circle as the people I happen to know in New York. It's like trying to read something in a language of which you know only a few words, and having the book shown to you by jerks at that!'

Mr. Marsh remarked speculatively, as though they were speaking of some quite abstract topic, 'It may also be possible that you are succumbing to habit and inertia and routine.'

She was startled again, and nettled . . . and alarmed. What a rude thing to say! But the words were no sooner out of his mouth than she had felt a scared wonder if perhaps they were not true. She had not thought of that possibility.

'I should think you would like the concerts, anyhow,' suggested Mr. Welles.

'Yes,' said Marise, with the intonation that made the affirmation almost a negative. 'Yes, of course. But there too . . . music means so much to me, so very much. It makes me sick to see it pawed over as it is among people who make their livings out of it; used as it so often is as a background for the personal vanity or greed of the performer. Take an ordinary afternoon solo concert given by a pianist or singer . . . it always seems to me that the music they make is almost an unconsidered by-product with them. What they're really after is something else.'

Marsh agreed with her, with a hearty relish, 'Yes, musicians are an unspeakable bunch!'

'I suppose,' Marise went on, 'that I ought not to let that part of it spoil concert music for me. And it doesn't, of course. I've had some wonderful times . . . people who play in orchestra and make chamber-music are the real thing. But the music you make yourself . . . the music we make up here . . . well, perhaps my taste for it is like one's liking (some people call it perverse) for French Primitive painting, for the something so awfully touching and heart-felt that was lost when the Renaissance came up over the Alps with all its knowingness.'

'You're not pretending that you get Vermonters to make music?' protested Marsh, highly amused at the notion.

'I don't know,' she admitted, 'whether it is music or not. But it is something alive.' She fell into a muse, 'Queer, what a spider-web of tenuous complication human relationships are. I never would have thought, probably, of trying anything of the sort if it hadn't been for a childhood recollection. . . . French incarnation this time,' she said lightly to Marsh. 'When I was a little girl, a young priest, just a young parish priest, in one of the poor hill-parishes of the Basque country, began to teach the people of his parish really to sing some of the church chants. I never knew much about the details of what he did, and never spoke to him in my life, but from across half the world he has reached out to touch this corner of America. By the time I was a young lady, he had two or three big country choruses under his direction. We used to drive up first to one and then to another of those hill-towns, all white-washed houses and plane-tree atriums, and sober-eyed Basques, to hear them sing. It was beautiful. I never have had a more complete expression of beauty in all my life. It seemed to me the very soul of music; those simple people singing, not for pay, not for notoriety, out of the fullness of their hearts. It has been one of the things I never forgot, a standard, and a standard that most music produced on platforms before costly audiences doesn't come up to.'

'I've never been able to make anything out of music, myself,' confessed Mr. Welles. 'Perhaps you can convert me. I almost believe so.'

'"Gene Powers sings!" cried Marise spiritedly. 'And if he does . . .'

'Any relation to the lively old lady who brings our milk?'

'Her son. Haven't you see him yet? A powerfully built granite rock of a man. Silent as a granite rock too, as far as small talk goes. But he turns out to have a bass voice that is my joy. It's done something for him, too, I think, really and truly, without sentimental exaggeration at all. He suffered a great injustice some six or seven years ago, that turned him black and bitter, and it's only since he has been singing in our winter choir that he has been willing to mix again with anyone.'

She paused for a moment, and eyed them calculatingly. It occurred to her that she had been talking about music and herself quite enough. She would change the subject to some-

49

thing matter-of-fact. 'See here, you'll be sure to have to hear all that story from Mr. Bayweather in relentless detail. It might be your salvation to be able to say that I had told you, without mentioning that it was in a severely abridged form. He'd want to start back in the eighteenth century, and tell you all about that discreditable and unreconstructed Tory ancestor of mine who, when he was exiled from Ashley, is said to have carried off part of the town documents with him to Canada. Whether he did or not (Mr. Bayweather has a theory, I believe, that he buried them in a copper kettle on Peg-Top Hill), the fact remains that an important part of the records of Ashley are missing and that has made a lot of trouble with titles to land around here. Several times, unscrupulous land-grabbers have taken advantage of the vagueness of the titles to cheat farmers out of their inheritance. The Powers case is typical. There always have been Powerses living right there, where they do now; that big pine that towers up so over their house was planted by 'Gene's great-grandfather. And they always owned an immense tract of wild mountain land, up beyond the Eagle Rock range, along the side of the Red-Brook marsh. But after paying taxes on it for generations all during the time when it was too far away to make it profitable to lumber, it was snatched away from them, seven years ago, just as modern methods and higher prices for spruce would have made it very valuable. A lawyer from New Hampshire named Lowder turned the trick. I won't bother you going into the legal details – a question of a fake warranty deed, against 'Gene's quit-claim deed, which was all he had in absence of those missing pages from the town records. As a matter of fact, the lawyer hasn't dared to cut the lumber off it yet, because his claim is pretty flimsy; but flimsy or not, the law regards it as slightly better than 'Gene's. The result is that 'Gene can't sell it and daren't cut it for fear of being involved in a law-suit that he couldn't possibly pay for. So the Powers are poor farmers, scratching a difficult living out of sterile soil, instead of being well-to-do proprietors of a profitable estate of wood-land. And when we see how very hard they all have to work, and how soured and gloomy it has made 'Gene, and how many pleasures the Powers' children are denied, we all join in when Mrs. Powers delivers herself of her white-hot opinion of New Hampshire lawyers! I remember perfectly that Mr. Lowder – one of the smooth-shaven, thin-lipped, fish-mouthed variety, with a pugnacious jaw and an intimidating habit of talking his New Hampshire dialect out of the corner of his mouth. The poor Powers were as helpless as rabbits before him.'

It all came up before her as she talked, that horrid encounter with commercial ruthlessness: she saw again poor 'Gene's outraged face of helpless anger, felt again the heat of sympathetic indignation she and Neale had felt, recognized again the poison which triumphant unrighteousness leaves behind. She shook her head impatiently, to shake off the memory, and said aloud, 'Oh, it makes me sick to remember it! We couldn't believe, any of us, that such bare-faced iniquity could succeed.'

'There's a good deal of bare-faced iniquity riding around prosperously in high-powered cars,' said Mr. Welles, with a lively accent of bitterness. 'You have to get used to it in business life. It's very likely that your wicked Mr. Lowder in private life in New Hampshire is a good husband and father, and contributes to all the charitable organizations.'

'I won't change *my* conception of him as a pasty-faced demon,' insisted Marise.

It appeared that Mr. Marsh's appetite for local history was so slight as to be cloyed even by the very much abbreviated account she had given them, for he now said, hiding a small yawn, with no effort to conceal the fact that he had been bored, 'Mrs. Crittenden, I've heard from Mr. Welles' house the most tantalizing snatches from your piano. Won't you, now we're close to it, put the final touch to our delightful lunch-party by letting us hear it?'

Marise was annoyed by his *grand seigneur* air of certainty of his own importance, and piqued that she had failed to hold his interest. Both impressions were of a quicker vivacity than was at all the habit of her maturity. She told herself, surprised, that she had not felt this little sharp sting of wounded personal vanity since she was a girl. What did she care whether she had bored him or not? But it was with all her faculties awakened and keen that she sat down before the piano and called out to them, 'What would you like?'

They returned the usual protestations that they would like anything she would play, and after a moment's hesitation . . . it was always a leap in the dark to play to people about whose musical capacities you hadn't the faintest idea . . . she took out the Beethoven Sonata album and turned to the Sonata Pathétique. Beethoven of the early middle period was the safest guess with such entirely unknown listeners. For all that she really knew, they might want her to play Chaminade and

51

Moskowsky. Mr. Welles, the nice old man, might find even them above his comprehension. And as for Marsh, she thought with a resentful toss of her head that he was capable of saying off-hand, that he was really bored by all music -- and conveying by his manner that it was entirely the fault of the music. Well, she would show him how she could play, at least.

She laid her hands on the keys; and across those little smarting, trivial personalities there struck the clear, assured dignity and worth of her old friend . . . was there ever such a friend as that rough old German who had died so long before she was born? No one could say the human race was ignoble or had never deserved to live, who knew his voice. In a moment she was herself again.

Those well-remembered opening chords, they were by this time not merely musical sounds. They had become something within her, of her own being, rich with a thousand clustered nameless associations, something that thrilled and sang and lived a full harmonious life of its own. That first pearling down-dropping arabesque of treble notes, not only her fingers played those, but every fibre in her, answering like the vibrating wood of a violin, its very cells rearranged in the pattern which the notes had so many times called into existence . . . by the time she had finished she had almost forgotten that she had listeners.

And when, sitting for a moment, coming back slowly from Beethoven's existence to her own, she heard no sound or stir from the porch, she had only a quiet smile of tolerant amusement. Apparently she had not guessed right as to their tastes. Or perhaps she had played them to sleep.

As for herself, she was hungry for more; she reached out her hand towards that world of high, purified beauty which miraculously was always there, with open doors of gold and ivory.

. . . What now? What did she know by heart? The Largo in the Chopin Sonata. That would do to come after Beethoven.

The first plunge into this did not so intimately startle and stir her as the Beethoven movement had done. It was always like that, she thought as she played, the sound of the first note, the first chord struck when one had not played for a day or so; it was having one's closed eyes unsealed to the daylight anew, an incredulous rapture. But after that, though you didn't go on quaking and bowing your head, though you were no longer surprised to find music still there, better than you could possibly remember it, though you took it for granted, how deeply and solidly and steadfastly you lived in it and on it! It made you like the child in the Wordsworth sonnet, 'A beauteous evening, calm and free'; it took you in to worship quite simply and naturally at the Temple's inner shrine; and you adored none the less although you were not 'breathless with adoration,' like the nun; because it was a whole world given to you, not a mere pang of joy; because you could live and move and be blessedly and securely at home in it.

She finished the last note of the Largo and sat quiet for a moment. Then she knew that someone had come into the room behind her. She turned about, facing with serene, wide brows whatever might be there.

The first meeting with the eyes of the man who stood there moved her. So he too deeply and greatly loved music! His face was quite other from the hawk-like, intent, boldly imperious countenance which she had seen before. Those piercing eyes were softened and quietly shining. The arrogant lines about the mouth that could look so bitter and sceptical, were as sweet and candid as a child's.

He smiled at her, a good, grateful, peaceful smile, and nodded, as though now they understood each other with no more need for words. 'Go on . . . go on!' was all he said, very gently and softly. He sank down in an arm-chair and leaned his head back in the relaxed pose of listening.

He looked quite and exactly what Marise was feeling.

It was with a stir of all her pulses, a pride, a glory, a new sympathy in her heart, that she turned back to the piano.

Chapter 5: *A Little Girl and her Mother*

An Afternoon in the Life of Elly Crittenden, aet. 8 Years

April 6.

ELLY CRITTENDEN had meant to go straight home from school as usual with the other children, Paul and Mark, and Addie and Ralph Powers. And as usual somehow she was ever so far behind them, so far that there wasn't any use trying to catch up. Paul was hurrying to go over and see that new old man next door, as usual. She might as well *not* try, and just give up, and get home ever so late, the way she always did. Oh well,

Father wasn't at home, and Mother wouldn't scold, and it was nice to walk along just as slow as you wanted to, and feel your rubber boots squizzle into the mud. How *good* it did seem to have real mud, after the long winter of snow! And it was nice to hear the brooks everywhere, making that dear little noise and to see them flashing every-which-way in the sun, as they tumbled along downhill. And it was nice to smell that smell . . . what *was* that sort of smell that made you know the sugaring-off had begun? You couldn't smell that hot boiling sap all the way from the mountain-sides, but what you did smell made you think of the little bark-covered sap-houses up in the far woods, with smoke and white steam coming out from all their cracks, as though there was somebody inside magicking charms and making a great cloud to cover it, like Klingsor or the witch-ladies in the *Arabian Nights*. There was a piece of music Mother played, that was like that. You could almost see the white clouds begin to come streeling out between the piano-keys, and drift all around her. All but her face that always looked through.

The sun shone down so warm on her head, she thought she might take off her woollen cap. Why, yes, it was plenty warm enough. Oh, how good it felt! How *good* it did feel! Like somebody actually touching your hair with a warm, soft hand. And the air, that cool, cool air, all damp with the thousand little brooks, it felt just as good to be cool, when you tossed your hair and the wind could get into it. How *good* it did feel to be bareheaded, after all that long winter! Cool inside your hair at the roots, and warm outside where the sun pressed on it. Cool wind and warm sun, two different things that added up to make one lovely feel for a little girl. The way your hair tugged at its roots, all streaming away; every single little hair tied tight to your head at one end, and yet so wildly loose at the other; tight, strong, firm, and yet light and limber and flag-flapping . . . it was like being warm and cool at the same time, so different and yet the same.

And there, underneath all this fluttering and tossing and differences, there were your legs going on just as dumb and steady as ever, stodge, stodge, stodge! She looked down at them with interest and appreciation of their faithful, dutiful service, and with affection at the rubber boots. She owed those to Mother. Paul had scared her so, when he said, so stone-wally, the way Paul always spoke as if that settled everything, that *none* of the little girls at school wore rubber boots, and he thought Elly oughtn't to be allowed to look so queer. It made him almost ashamed of his sister, he said. But Mother had somehow . . . what *had* she said to fix it? . . . oh, well, something or other that left her her rubber boots and yet Paul wasn't mad any more.

And what could she *do* without rubber boots, when she wanted to wade through a brook, like this one, and the brooks were as they were now, all running spang full to the very edge with snow-water, the way this one did? Oo . . . Ooh . . . Ooh! how queer it did feel, to be standing most up to your knees this way, with the current curling by, all cold and snaky, feeling the fast-going water making your boot-legs shake like Aunt Hetty's old cheeks when she laughed, and yet your feet as *dry* inside! How could they feel as cold as that, without being wet, as though they were magicked? That was a *real* difference, even more than the wind cool inside your hair and the sun warm on the outside; or your hair tied tight at one end and all wobbly loose at the other. But this wasn't a nice difference. It didn't add up to make a nice feeling, but a sort of queer one, and if she stood there another minute, staring down into that swirly, snatchy water, she'd fall right over into it . . . it seemed to be snatching at *her*! Oh gracious! This wasn't much better! on the squelchy dead grass of the meadow that looked like real ground and yet you sank right into it. Oh, it was *horridly* soft, like touching the hand of that new man that had come to live with the old gentleman next door. She must hurry as fast as she could . . . it felt as though it was sucking at her feet, trying to pull her down altogether like the girl with the red shoes, and she didn't have any loaves of bread to throw down to step on. . . .

Well, there! this was better, as the ground started uphill. There was firm ground under her feet. Yes, not mud, nor soaked, flabby meadow-land, but solid earth, *solid, solid*! She stamped on it with delight. It was just as nice to have solid things *very* solid, as it was to have floaty things like clouds *very* floaty. What was horrid was to have a thing that *looked* solid, and yet was all soft, like gelatine pudding when you touched it.

Well, for goodness' sake, where *was* she? Where had she come to, without thinking a single thing about it? Right on the ridge overlooking Aunt Hetty's house to be sure, on those rocks that hang over it, so you could almost throw a stone down any one of the chimneys. She might just as well go down and make Aunt Hetty a visit now she was so near, and walk home

55

by the side-road. Of course Paul would say, nothing could keep him from saying, that she had planned to do that very thing, right along, and when she left the school-house headed straight for Aunt Hetty's cookie-jar. Well, *let* him! She could just tell him, she'd never *dreamed* of such a thing, till she found herself on those rocks.

She walked more and more slowly, letting herself down cautiously from one ledge to another, and presently stopped altogether, facing a beech-tree, its trunk slowly twisted into a spiral because it was so hard to keep alive on those rocks. She was straight in front of it, staring into its grey white-blotched bark. Now if *Mother* asked her, of course she'd have to say, yes, she had planned to, *sort of* but not quite. Mother would understand. There wasn't any use trying to tell things how they really were to Paul, because to him things weren't ever sort-of-but-not-quite. They either were or they weren't. But Mother always knew, both ways, hers and Paul's.

She stepped forward and downward now, lightened. Her legs stretched out to carry her from one mossed rock to another. 'Striding,' that was what she was doing. Now she knew just what 'striding' meant. What fun it was to *feel* what a word meant! Then when you used it, you could feel it lie down flat in the sentence, and fit into the other words, like a piece in a jig-saw puzzle when you got it into the right place. Gracious! How fast you could 'stride' down those rocks into Aunt Hetty's back yard!

Hello! Here at the bottom was some snow, a great big drift of it still left, all grey and shrunk and honey-combed with rain and wind, with a little trickle of water running away softly and quietly from underneath it, like a secret. Well, think of there being still *snow* left anywhere except on top of the mountains! She had just been thinking all the afternoon how *good* it seemed to have the snow all gone, and here she ran right into some, as if you'd been talking about a person, saying how sick and tired you were of everlastingly seeing him around, and there he was, right outside the window and hearing it all, and knowing it wasn't *his* fault he was still hanging on. You'd feel bad to know he'd heard. She felt bad now! After all, the fun the snow had given them, all that winter, sleighing and snow-shoeing and ski-running and sliding downhill. And when she remembered how *glad* she'd been to see the first snow, how she and little Mark had run to the window to see the first flakes, and had hollered, Oh goody, *goody*! And here was all there was

56

left, just one poor old forgotten dirty drift, melting away as fast as it *could*, so's to get itself out of the way. She stood looking down on it compassionately, and presently, stooping over, gave it a friendly, comforting pat with one mittened hand.

Then she was pierced with an arrow of hunger, terrible, devouring starvation! Why was it she was always so *much* hungrier just as she got out of school, than ever at mealtimes? She did hope this wouldn't be one of those awful days when Aunt Hetty's old Agnes had let the cookie-jar get empty!

She walked on fast, now, across the back yard where the hens, just as happy as she was to be on solid ground, pottered around dreamily, their eyes half-shut up. . . . Elly could just think how good the sun must feel on their feathers! She could imagine perfectly how it would be to have feathers instead of skin and hair. She went into the kitchen door. Nobody was there. She went through into the pantry. Nobody there! Nobody, that is, except the cookie-jar, larger than any other object in the room, looming up like a wash-tub. She lifted the old cracked plate kept on it for cover. *Oh*, it was *full* – a fresh baking! And raisins in them! The water ran into her mouth in a little gush. Oh *my*, how good and cracklesome they looked! And how beautifully the sugar sprinkled on them would grit against your teeth as you ate it! Oh *gracious*!

She put her hand in and touched one. There was nothing that felt like a freshly baked cookie; even through your mitten you could *know*, with your eyes shut, it was a cookie. She took hold of one, and stood perfectly still. She could take that, just as easy! Nobody would miss it, with the jar so full. Aunt Hetty and Agnes were probably house-cleaning, like everybody else, upstairs. Nobody would ever know. The water of desire was at the very corners of her mouth now. She felt her insides surging up and down in longing. *Nobody* would know!

She opened her hand, put the cookie back, laid the plate on the top of the jar, and walked out of the pantry. Of course she couldn't do that. What had she been thinking of – such a stealy, common thing, and she *Mother's* daughter!

But, oh! It was awful, having to be up to Mother! She sniffed forlornly and drew her mitten across her nose. She *had* wanted it so! And she was just *dying*, she was so hungry. And Mother wouldn't even let her *ask* people for things to eat. Suppose Aunt Hetty didn't think to ask her!

She went through the dining-room, into the hall, and called

upstairs, 'Aunt Hetty! Aunt Hetty!' She was almost crying she felt so sorry for herself.

'Yis,' came back a faint voice, very thin and high, the way old people's voices sounded when they tried to call loud. 'Up in the east-wing garret.'

She mounted the stairs heavily, pulling herself along by those spindling old red balustrades, just like so many old laths, noticing that her rubber boots left big hunks of mud on the white-painted stairs, but too miserable to care.

The door to the east-wing garret was open. Aunt Hetty was there, bossing Agnes, and they were both 'dudsing,' as Elly called it to herself, leaning over trunks, disappearing in and out of closets, turning inside out old bags of truck, sorting over, and, for all Elly could see, putting the old duds back again, just where they had been before. Grown-ups did seem to run round in circles, so much of their time!

She sat down wearily on an ugly little old trunk near the door. Aunt Hetty shut up a drawer in a dresser, turned to Elly, and said, 'Mercy, child, what's the matter? Has the teacher been scolding you?'

'No, Aunt Hetty,' said Elly faintly, looking out of the window.

'Anybody sick at your house?' asked Aunt Hetty, coming towards the little girl.

'No,' said Elly, shaking her head.

'Don't you feel well?' asked Aunt Hetty, laying one wrinkled, shaky old hand on her shoulder.

'No, Aunt Hetty,' said Elly, her eyes large and sad.

'Maybe she's hungry,' suggested Agnes, in a muffled voice from the depths of a closet.

'Are you?' asked Aunt Hetty.

'YES,' cried Elly.

Aunt Hetty laughed. 'Well, I don't know if there are any cookies in the house or not,' she said, 'we've been so busy house-cleaning. Agnes, did you bake any cookies this morning?'

Elly was struck into stupor at this. Think of not *knowing* if there were any cookies in the house!

Agnes appeared, tiny and old and stooped and wrinkled, like her mistress. She had a big, rolled-up woollen-covered comforter in her arms, over which she nodded. 'Yes, I made some. You told me to make some every Wednesday,' she said. She went on, looking anxiously at Aunt Hetty, 'There ain't any moth-holes in this. Was this the comfortable you meant? I

58

thought this was the one you told me to leave out of the camphor chest. I thought you told me . . .'

'You know where to find the cookies, don't you, Elly?' asked Aunt Hetty, over her shoulder, trotting rapidly like a little dry, wind-blown leaf towards Agnes and the comforter.

'Oh *yes*, Aunt Hetty!' shouted Elly, half-way down the stairs.

Aunt Hetty called after her, 'Take all you want . . . three or four. They won't hurt you. There's no egg in our recipe.'

Elly was there again, in the empty pantry, before the cookie-jar. She lifted the cracked plate again. . . . But, oh! how differently she did feel now! . . . and she had a shock of pure, almost solemn, happiness at the sight of the cookies. She had not only been good and done as Mother would want her to, but she was going to have *four* of those cookies. Three *or* four, Aunt Hetty had said! As if anybody would take three if he was let to have four! Which ones had the most raisins? She knew of course it wasn't *so very* nice to pick and choose that way, but she knew Mother would let her, only just laugh a little and say it was a pity to be eight years old if you couldn't be a little greedy!

Oh, how happy she was! How light she felt! How she floated back up the stairs! What a perfectly sweet old thing Aunt Hetty was! And what a nice old house she had, though not so nice as home, of course. What pretty mahogany balusters, and nice white stairs! Too bad she had brought in that mud. But they were house-cleaning anyhow. A little bit more to clean up, that was all. And what *luck* that they were in the east-room garret, the one that had all the old things in it, the hoop-skirts and the shells and the old scoop-bonnets, and the four-poster bed and those fascinating old cretonne bags full of treasures.

She sat down near the door on the darling little old hair-covered trunk that had been Great-grandfather's, and watched the two old women at work. The first cookie had disappeared now, and the second was well on the way. She felt a great appeasement in her insides. She leaned back against the old dresses hung on the wall and drew a long breath.

'Well,' said Aunt Hetty, 'you've got neighbours up your way, so they tell me. Funny thing, a city man coming up here to live. He'll never stick it out. The summer may be. But that's all. You just see, come autumn, if he don't light out for New York again.'

Elly made no comment on this. She often heard her elders

say that she was not a talkative child, and that it was hard to get anything out of her. That was because mostly they wanted to know about things she hadn't once thought of noticing, and weren't a bit interested when she tried to talk about what she *had* noticed. Just imagine trying to tell Aunt Hetty about that poor old grey snow-bank out in her woods, all lonely and scrumpled up! She went on eating her cookie.

'How does he like it, anyhow?' asked Aunt Hetty, bending the upper part of her out of the window to shake something. 'And what kind of a critter is he?'

'Well, he's rather an old man,' said Elly. She added conscientiously, trying to be chatty, 'Paul's crazy about him. He goes over there all the time to visit. I like him all right. The old man seems to like it here all right. They both of them do.'

'Both?' said Aunt Hetty, curving herself back into the room again.

'Oh, the other one isn't going to *live* here, like Mr. Welles. He's just come to get Mr. Welles settled, and to make him a visit. His name is Mr. Marsh.'

'Well, what's *he* like?' asked Aunt Hetty, folding together the old wadded petticoat she had been shaking.

'Oh, he's all right too,' said Elly. She wasn't going to say anything about that funny softness of his hands, she didn't like, because that would be like speaking about the snow-drift; something Aunt Hetty would just laugh at, and call one of her notions.

'Well, what do they *do* with themselves, two great hulking men set off by themselves?'

Elly tried seriously to remember what they did do. 'I don't see them, of course, much in the morning before I go to school. I guess they get up and have their breakfast, the way anybody does.'

Aunt Hetty snorted a little, 'Gracious, child, a person needs a corkscrew to get anything out of you. I mean all day, with no chores, or farmin', or *any*thing.'

'I don't *know*,' Elly confessed. 'Mr. Clark, of course, he's busy cooking and washing dishes and keeping house, but . . .'

'Are there *three* of them?' Aunt Hetty stopped her dudsing in her astonishment. 'I thought you said two.'

'Oh well, Mr. Marsh sent down to the city and had this Mr. Clark come up to work for them. He doesn't call him "Mr. Clark" – just "Clark," short like that. I guess he's Mr. Marsh's hired man in the city. Only he can do everything in the house, too. But I don't feel like calling him "Clark" because he's grown-up, and so I call him "*Mr*. Clark."' She did not tell Aunt Hetty that she sort of wanted to make up to him for being somebody's servant and being called like one. It made her mad and she wanted to show he could be a mister as well as anybody. She began on the third cookie. What else could she say to Aunt Hetty, who always wanted to know the news so? She brought out, 'Well, *I* tell you, in the afternoon, when I get home, mostly old Mr. Welles is out in his garden.'

'*Gardin!*' cried Aunt Hetty. 'Mercy on us, making garden the fore-part of April. Where does he think he's living? Florida?'

'I don't believe he's exactly making garden,' said Elly. 'He just sort of pokes around there, and looks at things. And sometimes he sits down on the bench and just *sits* there. He's pretty old, I guess, and he walks kind of tired, always.'

'Does the other one?' asked Aunt Hetty.

This made Elly sit up, and say very loud, 'No, *indeedy*!' She really hadn't thought before how very *un*tired Mr. Marsh always seemed. She added, 'No, the other one doesn't walk tired, nor he doesn't poke around in the garden. He takes long tramps way back of the mountains, over Burnham way.'

'For goodness' sakes, what's he find up there?'

'He likes it. He comes over and borrows our maps and things to study, and he gets Mother to tell him all about everything. He gets Touclé to tell him about the back trails, too.'

'Well, he's a smart one if he can get a word out of Touclé.'

'Yes, he does. Everybody talks to him. You *have* to if he starts in. He's very lively.'

'Does he get *you* to talk?' asked Aunt Hetty, laughing at the idea.

'Well, some,' stated Elly soberly. She did not say that Mr. Marsh always seemed to her to be trying to get some secret out of her. She didn't *have* any secret that she knew of, but that was the way he made her feel. She dodged him mostly, when she could.

'What's the news from your father?'

'Oh, he's all right,' said Elly. She fell to thinking of Father and wishing he would come back.

'When's he going to get through his business up there?'

'Before long, I guess. Mother said maybe he'd be back here next month.' Elly was aware that she was again not being talkative. She tried to think of something to add. 'I'm very

61

much obliged for these cookies,' she said. 'They are awfully good.'

'They're the kind your mother always liked, when she was your age,' said Aunt Hetty casually. 'I remember how she used to sit right there on Father's hair-trunk and eat them and watch me just like you now.'

At this statement Elly could feel her thoughts getting bigger and longer and higher, like something being opened out. 'And the heaven was removed as a scroll when it is rolled up.' That sentence she'd heard in church and never understood, and always wondered what was behind, what they had seen when the scroll was rolled up. . . . Something inside her now seemed to roll up as though she were going to see what was behind it. How much longer time was than you thought! Mother had sat there as a little girl . . . a little girl like her. Mother who was now grown-up and *finished*, knowing everything, never changing, never making any mistakes. Why, how *could* she have been a little girl! And such a short time ago that Aunt Hetty remembered her sitting there, right there, maybe come in from walking across that very meadow, and down those very rocks. *What had she been thinking about, that other little girl who had been Mother?* 'Why' . . . Elly stopped eating, stopped breathing for a moment. 'Why, she herself would stop being a little girl, and would grow up and be a Mother!' She had always known that, of course, but she had never *felt* it till that moment. It made her feel very sober; more than sober, rather holy. Yes, that was the word – holy – like the hymn. Perhaps some day another little girl would sit there, and be just as surprised to know that *her* mother had been really and truly a little girl too, and would feel queer and shy at the idea, and all the time her mother had been only *Elly*. But would she *be* Elly any more, when she was grown up? What would have happened to Elly? And after that little girl, another; and one before Mother; and back as far as you could see, and forwards as far as you could see. It was like a procession, all half in the dark, marching forward, one after another, little girls, mothers, mothers and little girls, and then more . . . what for . . . oh *what for*?

She was a little scared. She wished she could get right up and go *home* to Mother. But the procession wouldn't stop . . . wouldn't stop. . . .

Aunt Hetty hung up the last bag. 'There,' she said, 'that's all we can do here to-day. Elly, you'd better run along home.

The sun'll be down behind the mountain *now* before you get there.'

Elly snatched at the voice, at the words, at Aunt Hetty's wrinkled, shaking old hand. She jumped up from the trunk. Something in her face made Aunt Hetty say, 'Well, you look as though you'd most dropped to sleep there in the sun. It does make a person feel lazy this first warm March sun. I declare this morning I didn't want to go to work house-cleaning. I wanted to go and spend the day with the hens, singing over that little dozy ca-a-a-a they do, in the sun, and stretch one leg and one wing till they most broke off, and ruffle up all my feathers and let 'em settle back very slow, and then just *set*.'

They had started downstairs before Aunt Hetty had finished this, the little girl holding tightly to the wrinkled old hand. How peaceful Aunt Hetty was! Even the smell of her black woollen dresses always had a *quiet* smell. And she must see all those hunks of mud on the white stairs, but she never said a word. Elly squeezed her hand a little tighter.

What was it she had been thinking about on the hair-trunk that made her so glad to feel Aunt Hetty peaceful? Oh yes, that Mother had been there, where she was, when she was a little girl. Well, gracious! What of that? She'd always known that Mother had visited Aunt Hetty a lot and that Aunt Hetty had been awfully good to her, and that Mother loved Aunt Hetty like everything. What had made it seem so queer, all of a sudden?

'Well,' said Aunt Hetty at the front door, 'step along now. I don't want you should be late for supper.' She tipped her head to look around the edge of the top of the door and said, 'Well, I declare, just see that moon showing itself before ever the sun gets down.'

She walked down the path a little way with Elly, who still held her hand. They stood together looking up at the mountain, very high and blue against the sky that was green . . . yes, it really was a pale, clear green, at the top of the mountain-line. People always said the sky was blue, except at sunset-time, like now, when it was filling the Notch right to the top with every colour that could be.

'The lilacs will begin to swell soon,' said Aunt Hetty.

'I saw some pussy-willows out, to-day,' answered Elly.

The old woman and the little girl lifted their heads, threw them back, and looked up long into the sky, purely, palely high above them.

'It's quite a sightly place to live, Crittenden's is,' said Aunt Hetty.

Elly said nothing, it being inconceivable to her that she could live anywhere else.

'Well, good-bye,' said Aunt Hetty. It did not occur to her to kiss the little girl. It did not occur to Elly to want a kiss. They squeezed their hands together a little bit more, and then Elly went down the road, walking very carefully.

Why did she walk so carefully, she wondered? She felt as though she were carrying a cup, full up to the brim of something. And she mustn't let it spill. What was it so full of? Aunt Hetty's peacefulness, maybe.

Or maybe just because it was beginning to get twilight. That always made you feel as though something was being poured softly into you, that you mustn't spill. She was glad the side-road was so grass-grown. You could walk on it, so still, like this, and never make a sound.

She thought again of Father and wished he would come home. She *liked* Father. He was solid. He was solid like that solid earth she liked so much to walk on. It was just such a comfort to feel him. Father was like the solid ground and Mother was like the floaty clouds. Why, yes, they were *every* way like what she had been thinking about. . . . Father was the warm sun on the outside, and Mother was the cool wind on the inside. Father was the end that was tied tight and firm so you *knew* you couldn't lose it, and Mother was the end that streamed out like flags in the wind. But they weren't either of them like that slinky, swirly water, licking at you, in such a hurry to get on past you and get what it was scrambling to get, whatever that was.

Well, of all things! There was old Mr. Welles, coming towards her. *He* must be out taking a walk too. How slowly he went! And kept looking up the way she and Aunt Hetty had, at the sky and the mountains. He was quite close now. Why . . . why, he didn't know she was there. He had gone right by her and never even saw her and yet had been so close she could see his face plainly. He must have been looking very hard at the mountains. But it wasn't hard the way he was looking, it was soft. How soft his face had looked, almost quivery, almost . . . But that was silly to think of . . . almost as though he felt like crying. And yet all shining and quiet, too, as if he'd been in church.

Well, it *was* a little bit like being in church, when you could

64

see the twilight come down very slow like this, and settle on the tree-tops and then down through them towards you. You always felt as though it was going to do something to you when it got to you; something peaceful, like old Aunt Hetty.

She was at her own front path now, it was really almost dark. Mother was playing the piano. But not for either of the boys. It was grown-up music she was playing. Elly hesitated on the flagged stones. Maybe she was playing for Mr. Marsh again. She advanced slowly. Yes, there he was, sitting on the door-step, across the open door, leaning back his head, smoking, sometimes looking out at the sunset, and sometimes looking in towards the piano.

Elly made a wide circuit under the apple-trees, and went in the side-door. Touclé was only just setting the table. Elly would have plenty of time to get off her rubber boots, look up her old felt slippers, and put them on before supper time. Gracious! Her stockings were wet. She'd have to change them, too. She'd just stay upstairs till Mr. Marsh went away. She didn't feel to talk to him.

When out of her window she saw him step back across the grass to Mr. Welles' house, Elly came downstairs at once. The light in the living-room made her blink, after all that outdoor twilight and the indoor darkness of her room upstairs.

Mother was still at the piano, her hands on the keys, but not playing. At the sight of her, Elly's heart filled and brightened. Her busy, busy thoughts stopped for the first time that day. She felt as you do when you've been rowing a boat a long time and finally, almost where you want to go, you stop and let her slide in on her own movement, quiet and soft and smooth, and reach out your hand to take hold of the landing-place. Elly reached out her arm and put it around Mother's neck. She stood perfectly quiet. There wasn't any need to be anything *but* quiet now you'd got to where you were going.

She had been out on the rim of the wheel, all around and around it, and up and down the spokes. But now she was at the centre where all the spokes ended.

She closed her eyes and laid her head on Mother's soft shoulder.

'Did you have a good walk, all by yourself, dear?' asked Mother.

'Oh yes, it was all right,' said Elly.

65

'Your feet aren't wet, are they?'

'No,' said Elly, 'I took off my boots just as soon as I came in, and changed my stockings.'

Chapter 6: *Things Take Their Course*

A Couple of Hours from Mr. Welles' New Life

§ 1

April 10.

ONE of the many things which surprised Mr. Welles was that he seemed to need less sleep than in the city. Long hours in bed had been one of the longed-for elements of the haven of rest which his retiring from the office was to be. Especially as he had dragged himself from bed to stop the relentless snarl of his alarm-clock, had he hoped for late-morning sleeps in his new home, when he could wake up at seven, feel himself still heavy, unrefreshed, unready for the day, and turn on the pillow to take another dose of oblivion.

But here, after the first ten days of almost prostrate relaxation, he found himself waking even before the dawn, and lying awake in his bed, waiting almost impatiently for the light to come so that he could rise to another day. He learned all the sounds of the late night and early morning, and how they had different voices in the dark; the faint whisper of the maple-branches, the occasional stir and muffled chirp of a bird, the hushed, secret murmur of the little brook which ran between his garden and the Crittenden yard, and the distant, deeper note of the Necronsett River as it rolled down the Ashley valley to the Notch. He could almost tell, without opening his eyes, when the sky grew light over the Eagle Rocks, by the way the night voices lifted, and carried their sweet, muted notes up to a clearer, brighter singing.

When that change in the night voices came, he sat up in bed, turning his face from the window, for he did not want any mere partial glimpse for his first contact with the day, and got into his clothes, moving cautiously not to waken Vincent, who always sat up till all hours and slept till ten. Down the stairs in his stocking-feet, his shoes in his hand; a pause in the living-room to thread and fasten shoe-laces; and then, his silly old

66

heart beating fast, his hand on the door-knob. The door slowly opened, and the garden, his own shining garden, offered itself to him anew, so fresh in the dew and the pale gold of the slanting morning sun-rays, that he was apt to swallow hard as he first stepped out into it and stood still, with bare head lifted, drawing one long breath after another.

He was seldom alone in those early hours, although the house slept profoundly behind him; a robin, the only bird whose name he was sure of, hopped heavily and vigorously about on the sparkling grass; a little brown bird of whose name he had not the slighest notion, but whose voice he knew very well by this time, poured out a continuous cascade of quick, high, eager notes from the top of the elm; a large toad squatted peaceably in the sun, the loose skin over its forehead throbbing rhythmically with the life in it; and over on the steps of the Crittendens' kitchen, the old Indian woman, as motionless as the toad, fixed her opaque black eyes on the rising sun, while something about her, he could never decide what, throbbed rhythmically with the life in her. Mr. Welles had never in all his life been so aware of the rising sun, had never so felt it like something in himself as on those mornings when he walked in his garden and glanced over at the old Indian.

Presently, the Crittenden house woke, so to speak, with one eye, and took on the aspect of a house in which someone is astir. First came the fox-terrier, inevitable precursor of his little master, and then, stepping around Touclé as though she were a tree or a rock, came his little partner Paul, his freckled face shining with soap and the earliness of the hour. Mr. Welles was apt to swallow hard again, when he felt the child's rough, strong fingers slip into his.

'Hello, Mr. Welles,' said Paul.

'Hello, Paul,' said Mr. Welles.

'I thought sure I'd beat you to it for once, this morning,' was what Paul invariably said first. 'I can't seem to wake up as early as you and Touclé.'

Then he would bring out his plan for that particular morning walk.

'Maybe we might have time to have me show you the back-road by Cousin Hetty's, and get back by the men's short-cut before breakfast, maybe? Perhaps?'

'We could try it,' admitted Mr. Welles cautiously. It tickled him to answer Paul in his own prudent idiom. Then they set off, surrounded and encompassed by the circles of mad delight which Médor wove about them, rushing at them once in a while, in a spasm of adoration, to leap up and lick Paul's face.

Thus on one of these mornings in April, they were on the back-road to Cousin Hetty's, the right-hand side solemn and dark with tall pines, where the ground sloped up towards the Eagle Rocks; jungle-like with blackberry brambles and young pines on the left side where it had been lumbered some years ago. Paul pointed out proudly the thrifty growth of the new pines and explained it by showing the several large trees left standing at intervals down the slope towards the Ashley valley. 'Father always has them do that, so the seeds from the old trees will seed up the bare ground again. Gosh! You'd ought to hear him light into the choppers when they forget to leave the seed-pines or when they cut under six inches butt diameter.'

Mr. Welles had no more notion what cutting under six inches butt diameter meant than he had of the name of the little brown bird who sang so sweetly in his elm; but Paul's voice and that of the nameless bird gave him the same pleasure. He tightened his hold of the tough, sinewy little fingers, and looked up through the glorious brown columns of the great pines towards where the sky-line showed, luminous, far up the slope.

'That's the top of the Eagle Rocks, where you see the sky,' explained his small cicerone, seeing the direction of his eyes. 'The Powerses lost a lot of sheep off over them last year. A dog must ha' started running them down in the pasture. And you know what fools sheep are. Once they get scared they can't think of anything to do except just to keep a-running till something gets in their way. About half of the Powers flock just ran themselves off the top of the Rocks, although the dog had stopped chasing them, way down in the valley. There wasn't enough of them left even to sell to the butcher in Ashley for mutton. Ralph Powers, he's about as old as I am, maybe a little bit older, well, his father had given him a ewe and two twin lambs for his own, and didn't they all three get killed that day! Ralph felt awful bad about it. He don't ever seem to have any luck, Ralph don't.'

. . . How sweet it was, Mr. Welles thought to himself, how awfully sweet to be walking in such pine-woods, on the early morning, preceded by such a wildly happy little dog, with a little boy whose treble voice ran on and on, whose strong little hand clasped yours so tightly, and who turned up to you eyes of such clear trust! Was he the same man who for such endless years had been a part of the flotsam cast out every morning

68

into the muddy, brawling flood of the city street and swept along to work which had always made him uneasy and suspicious of it?

'There's the whistle,' said Paul, holding up a finger. 'Father has the first one blown at half-past six, so's the men can have time to get their things ready and start; and not have to hurry.'

At this a faint stirring of interest in what the child was saying broke through the golden haze of the day-dream in which Mr. Welles was walking. 'Where do they come from, anyhow, the men who work in your father's mill?' he asked. 'Where do they live? There are so few homes at Crittenden's.'

'Oh, they live mostly over the hill in the village, in Ashley. There are lots of old houses there, and once in a while now they even have to build a new one, since the old ones are all filled up. Mr. Bayweather says that before Father and Mother came here to live and really run the mill, that Ashley Street was all full of empty houses, without a light in them, that the old folks had died out of. But now the men have bought them up and live in them. It's just as bright, nights! With windows lighted up all over. Father's had the electric current run over there from the mill, now, and that doesn't cost anything except . . .'

Mr. Welles' curiosity satisfied, he fell back into his old shimmer of content and walked along, hearing Paul's voice only as one of the morning sounds of the newly awakened world.

Presently he was summoned out of this day-dream by a tug at his hand. Paul gave out the word of command, 'We turn here, so's to get into the men's short-cut.'

This proved to be a hard-trodden path, lying like a loosely thrown-down string, over the hill pasture-land which cut Ashley village off from Crittenden's mill. It was to get around this rough tract that the road had to make so long a detour.

'Oh, I see,' said Mr. Welles. 'I'd been thinking that it must bother them a lot to come the two miles along the road from the village.'

'Sure,' said Paul. 'Only the ones that have got Fords come that way. This is ever so much shorter. Those that step along fast make it easy in twelve or fifteen minutes. There they come now, the first of them.' He nodded backward along the path where a distant dark line of men came treading swiftly and steadily forward, tin pails glistening in their hands.

'Some of those in that first bunch are really choppers by rights,' Paul diagnosed them with a practised eye, 'but of course nobody does much chopping come warmer weather. But Father never lays off any men unless they want to be. He fixes some jobs for them in the lumber-yard or in the mill, so they live here all the year around, same's the regular hands.'

The two stood still now, watching the men as their long, powerful strides brought them rapidly nearer. Back of them the sun rose up splendid in the sparkling, dustless mountain air. The pasture grass on either side of the sinuous path lay shining in the dew. Before them the path led through a grove of slim, white birches, tremulous in a pale cloud of light green.

'Well, they've got a pretty good way to get to their work, all right,' commented Mr. Welles.

'Yep, pretty good,' agreed Paul. 'It's got tramped down so it's quite smooth.'

A detachment of the file of tall, strongly built, roughly dressed men had now reached them, and with friendly, careless nods and greetings to Paul, they swung by, smoking, whistling, calling out random remarks and jokes back and forth along the line.

'Hello, Frank. Hello, Mike. Hello, Harry. Hello, Jombastiste. Hello, Jim.' Paul made answer to their repeated, familiar, 'Hello, Paul.'

Mr. Welles drew back humbly from out their path. These were men, useful to the world, strong for labour. He must needs stand back with the child.

With entire unexpectedness, he felt a wistful envy of those men, still valid, still fit for something. For a moment it did not seem as sweet as he had thought it would always be to feel himself old, old and useless.

§ 2

April 12.

He was impatient to be at the real work of gardening and one morning applied seriously to Mrs. Crittenden to be set at work. Surely this must be late enough, even in this 'suburb of the North Pole,' as Vincent called Vermont. Well, yes, Mrs. Crittenden conceded to him, stopping her rapid manipulation of an oiled mop on the floor of her living-room, if he was in such a hurry, he could start getting the ground ready for the sweet-peas. It wouldn't do any harm to plant them now, though it might not do any good either; and he mustn't be surprised to find occasional chunks of earth still frozen. She would be over in a little while to show him about it. Let him get his pick-mattock, spade, and rake ready, up by the corner of his stone wall.

He was waiting there, ten minutes later, the new implements (bought at Mrs. Crittenden's direction days and days ago) leaning against the wall. The sun was strong and sweet on his bared white head, the cool earth alive under his feet, freed from the tension of frost which had held it like stone when he had first trod his garden. He leaned against the stone wall, laid a century ago by who knew what other gardener, and looked down respectfully at the strip of ground along the stones. There it lay, blank and brown, shabby with the litter of broken, sodden stems of last year's weeds, and unsightly with half-rotten lumps of manure. And that would feed and nourish . . .

For an instant there stood there before his flower-loving eyes the joyful tangle of fresh green vines, the pearly many-coloured flesh of the petals, their cunning, involved symmetry of form – all sprung from a handful of wrinkled yellow seeds and that ugly mixture of powdered stone and rotten decay.

It was a wonderful business, he thought.

Mrs. Crittenden emerged from her house now, in a short skirt, rough heavy shoes, and old flannel shirt. She looked, he thought, ever so trig and energetic and nice; but suddenly aware that Vincent was gazing idly out of an upper window at them, he guessed that the other man would not admire the costume. Vincent was so terribly particular about how ladies dressed, he thought to himself, as he moved forward, mattock in hand.

'I'm ashamed to show you how dumb I am about the use of these tools,' he told her, laughing shamefacedly. 'I don't suppose you'll believe me, but honestly I never had a pick-mattock in my hand till I went down to the store to buy one. I might as well go the whole hog and confess I'd never even heard of one till you told me to get it. Is this the way you use it?' He jabbed ineffectually at the earth with the mattock, using a short tight blow with a half-arm movement. The tool jarred itself half an inch into the ground and was almost twisted out of his hand.

'No, not quite,' she said, taking the heavy tool out of his hand. If she were aware of the idle figure at the upper window, she gave no sign of it. She laid her strong, long, flexible hands on the handle, saying, 'So, you hold it this way. Then you swing it up, back of your head. There's a sort of knack to that. You'll soon catch it. And then, if the ground isn't very hard, you don't need to use any strength at all on the downward stroke. Let Old Mother Gravity do the work. If you aim it right, its own weight is enough for ordinary garden soil, that's not in sod. Now watch.'

She swung the heavy tool up, shining in the bright air, all her tall, supple body drawn up by the swing of her arms, cried out, 'See, now I relax and just let it fall,' and bending with the downward rush of the blade, drove it deep into the brown earth. A forward thrust of the long handle ('See, you use it like a lever,' she explained), a small earthquake in the soil, and the tool was free for another stroke.

At her feet was a pool of freshly stirred fragments of earth, loose, friable, and moist, from which there rose in a gust of the spring breeze an odour unknown to the old man and thrilling.

He stooped down, thrust his hand into the open breast of earth, and took up a handful of the soil which had lain locked in frost for half a year and was now free for life again. Over it his eyes met those of the beautiful woman beside him.

She nodded. 'Yes, there's nothing like it, the smell of the first earth stirred every spring.'

He told her, wistfully, 'It's the very first stirred in all my life.'

They had both lowered their voices instinctively, seeing Vincent emerge from the house-door and saunter towards them immaculate in a grey suit. Mr. Welles was not at all glad to see him at this moment. 'Here, let me have the mattock,' he said, taking it out of Mrs. Crittenden's hands, 'I want to try it myself.'

He felt an anticipatory impatience of Vincent's everlasting talk, to which Mrs. Crittenden always had, of course, to give a polite attention; and imitating as well as he could the free, upward swing of his neighbour, he began working off his impatience on the unresisting earth. But he could not help hearing that, just as he expected, Vincent plunged at once into his queer, abrupt talk. He always seemed to think he was going right on with something that had been said before, but really, for the most part, as far as Mr. Welles could see, what he said had nothing to do with anything. Mrs. Crittenden must really be a very smart woman, he reflected, to seem to know what he meant, and always to have an answer ready.

Vincent, shaking his head, and looking hard at Mrs. Crittenden's rough clothes and the handful of earth in her fingers, said with an air of enforced patience with obvious unreasonableness, 'You're on the wrong track, you know. You're just all off. Of course with you it can't be pose as it looks when other people do it. It must be simply muddle-headed thinking.'

He added, very seriously, 'You infuriate me.'

Mr. Welles, pecking feebly at the ground, the heavy mattock apparently invested with a malicious life of its own, twisting perversely, heavily lop-sided in his hands, thought that this did not sound like a polite thing to say to a lady. And yet the way Vincent said it made it sound like a compliment, somehow. No, not that; but as though it were awfully important to him what Mrs. Crittenden did. Perhaps that counted as a compliment.

He caught only a part of Mrs. Crittenden's answer, which she gave, lightly laughing, as though she did not wish to admit that Vincent could be so serious as he sounded. The only part he really heard was when she ended, '. . . oh, if we are ever going to succeed in forcing order on the natural disorder of the world, it's going to take everybody's shoulder to the wheel. Women can't stay ornamental and leisurely, and elegant, nor even always nice to look at.'

Mr. Welles, amazed at the straining effort he needed to put forth to manage that swing which Mrs. Crittenden did so easily, took less than his usual small interest in the line of talk which Vincent was so fond of springing on their neighbour. He heard him say, with his air of always stating a foregone conclusion, something so admitted that it needed no emphasis, 'It's Haroldbellwrightism, pure and simple, to imagine that anything you can ever do, that anybody can ever do, will help bring about the kind of order *you're* talking about, order for everybody. The only kind of order there ever will be, is what you get when you grab a little of what you want out of the chaos, for your own self, while there's still time, and hold on to it. That's the only way to get anywhere for yourself. And as for doing something for other people, the only satisfaction you can give anybody is in beauty.'

Mr. Welles swam out of the breakers into clear water. Suddenly he caught the knack of the upward swing, and had the immense satisfaction of bringing the mattock down squarely, buried to the head in the earth.

'There!' he said proudly to Mrs. Crittenden, 'how's that for fine?'

He looked up at her, wiping the sweat from his forehead. He wondered for an instant if she really looked troubled, or if he only imagined it. There was no doubt about how Vincent looked, as though he thought Mr. Welles, exulting over a blow with a mattock, an old imbecile in his dotage.

Mr. Welles never cared very much whether he seemed to Vincent like an old imbecile or not, and certainly less than nothing about it to-day, intoxicated as he was with the air, the sun, and his new mastery over the soil. He set his hands lovingly to the tool and again and again swung it high over his head, while Vincent and Mrs. Crittenden strolled away, still talking. . . . 'Doesn't it depend on what you mean by "beauty"?' Mrs. Crittenden was saying.

Chapter 7: *The Night-Blooming Cereus*

An Evening in the Life of Mrs. Neale Crittenden

April 20.

NOWADAYS she so seldom spoke or acted without knowing perfectly well what she was about, that Marise startled herself almost as much as her callers by turning over that leaf in the photograph album quickly and saying with abruptness, 'No, never mind about that one. It's nothing interesting.'

Of course this brought out from Paul and little Mark, hanging over her shoulder and knee, the to-be-expected shouts of, 'Oh, let's see it! What is it?'

Marise perceived that they scented something fine and exciting such as Mother was always trying to keep from them, like one man choking another over the edge of a cliff, or a woman lying on her back with the blood all running from her throat. Whenever pictures like that were in any of the magazines that came into the house, Marise took them away from the little boys, although she knew helplessly that this naturally made them extremely keen not to miss any chance to catch a glimpse of such a one. She could see that they thought it queer, there being anything so exciting in this old album of dull snapshots and geographical picture-postcards of places and churches and ruins and things that Father and Mother had seen, so long ago.

74

But you never could tell. The way Mother had spoken, the sound of her voice, the way she had flapped down the page quick, the little boys' practised ears and eyes had identified all that to a certainty with the actions that accompanied pictures she didn't want them to see. So, of course, they clamoured, 'Oh *yes*, Mother, just one look!'

Elly as usual said nothing, looking up into Mother's face. Marise was extremely annoyed. She was glad that Elly was the only one who was looking at her, because, of course, dear old Mr. Welles' unobservant eyes didn't count. She was glad that Mr. Marsh kept his gaze downward on the photograph marked 'Rome from the Pincian Gardens,' although through the top of his dark, close-cropped head she could fairly feel the racing, inquiring speculations whirling about. Nor had she any right to resent that. She supposed people had a right to what went on in their own heads, so long as they kept it to themselves. And it had been unexpectedly delicate and fine, the way he had come to understand, without a syllable spoken on either side, that that piercing look of his made her uneasy; and how he had promised her, wordlessly always, to bend it on her no more.

Why in the world had it made her uneasy, and why, a thousand times why, had she felt this sudden unwillingness to look at the perfectly commonplace photograph, in this company? Something had burst up from the subconscious and flashed its way into action, moving her tongue to speak and her hand to action before she had the faintest idea it was there . . . like an action of youth! And see what a silly position it had put her in!

The little boys had succeeded with the inspired tactlessness of children in emphasizing and exaggerating what she had wished could be passed over unnoticed, a gesture of hers as inexplicable to her as to them. Oh well, the best thing, of course, was to carry it off matter-of-factly, turn the leaf back, and *let* them see it. And then refute them by insisting on the literal truth of what she had said.

'There!' she said carelessly; 'look at it then.'

The little boys bent their eager faces over it. Paul read out the title as he had been doing for the other photographs, ' "View of the Campagna from the top of the cable-railway at Rocca di Papa. Rome in the distance." '

She had to sustain, for an instant, an astonished and disconcerted look from all those eyes. It made her quite genuinely break into a laugh. It was really a joke on them. She said to

75

the little boys mischievously, 'What did Mother say? Do you find it very interesting?'

Paul and Mark stared hard at the very dull photograph of a cliff and a plain and not even a single person or donkey in it, and gave up the riddle. Mother certainly *had* spoken to them in that hide-it-away-from-the-children voice, and yet there was nothing there.

Marise knew that they felt somehow that Mother had unfairly slipped out between their fingers, as grown-ups are always doing. Well, it wasn't fair. She hated taking advantage of them like that. It was a sort of sin against their awakening capacity to put two and two together and make a human total, and understand what went on about them.

But it hadn't been against *their* capacity to put two and two together that she had instinctively thrown up that warding-off arm, which hadn't at all warded off attention, but rather drawn it hard and scrutinizing, in spite of those down-dropped sharp eyes. Well, there was no sum he could do with only two, and slight probability he would ever get the other two to put with it . . . whatever the other two might be.

Mr. Welles' pleasant old voice said, 'It's a very pretty picture, I'm sure. They certainly have very fine views about the Eternal City. I envy you your acquaintance with all those historic spots. What is the next one?'

Dear old Mr. Welles! What a restful presence! How unutterably sweet and uncomplicated life could be with a good big dose of simplicity holding everything in a clear solution, so that it never occurred to you that what things seemed was very different from what they were.

'Ready to turn over, dears?' she asked the little boys. This time she was in her usual control of the machine, regulated what she did from the first motion to the last, made her voice casual but not elaborately so, and put one arm around Mark's slim little shoulder with just the right degree of uninterest in those old and faded photographs.

Very deep down, at the edge of consciousness, something asked her, 'Why did you try to hide that photograph?'

She could not answer this question. She didn't know why, any more than the little boys did. And it wouldn't do now, with the need to be mistress-of-the-house till a call ended, to stop to try to think it out. Later on, to-night, after the children were in bed, when she was brushing her hair . . . oh, probably she'd find as you so often did, when you went after the cause of some unexpected little feeling, that it came from a meaningless fortuitous association of ideas, like Elly's hatred of grape-jelly because she had once taken some bitter medicine in it.

' "View of the Roman Aqueduct, taken from the tramway line to Tivoli," ' read out Paul.

'Very pretty view,' said Mr. Welles.

Mr. Marsh's silences were as abysmal as his speech was Niagara-like on occasion. He said nothing.

Elly stirred and looked towards the doorway. Touclé stood there, her shoe-button eyes not blinking in the lamplight although she probably had been sitting on the steps of the kitchen, looking out into the darkness, in the long, motionless vigil which made up Touclé's evenings. As they all turned their faces towards her, she said, 'The cereus is going to bloom to-night,' and disappeared.

Marise welcomed this diversion. Ever since that absurd little gesture about the photograph, she had felt thickening about her . . . what? What you call 'depression' (whatever that meant), the dull hooded apparition that came blackly and laid its leaden hand on your heart. This news was just the thing. It would change what was threatening to stand stagnant and charge it with fresh running currents. She got up briskly to her feet.

'Come on, children,' she said. 'I'll let you sit up beyond bed-time to-night. Scatter quick, and put on your things. We'll all go down the road to the Powers' house and see the cereus in bloom.'

The children ducked quickly out of the room, thudding along softly in their felt slippers. Scramblings, chatterings, and stamping sounded back from the front hall, as they put on their boots and wraps.

'Wouldn't you like to come, too?' she asked the men, rescuing them from the rather high-and-dry position in which this unexpected incident had left them. It was plainly, from their faces, as inexplicable as unexpected. She explained, drawing a long, plain, black silk scarf closely about her head and shoulders, 'Why, yes, do come. It's an occasion as uniquely Ashleyian as pelota is Basque. You, Mr. Marsh, with your exhaustive inquiries into the habits and manners of Vermont mountaineers, your data won't be complete unless you've seen Nelly Powers' night-blooming cereus in its one hour of glory. Seriously, I assure you, you won't encounter anything like it anywhere else.'

77

As Marsh looked at her, she noted with an inward amusement that her words had lighted a smouldering glow of carefully repressed exasperation in her eyes. It made her feel quite gay and young to be teasing somebody again. She was only paying him back in his own coin. He himself was always telling everybody about his deep interest in the curious quaint ways of these mountaineers. And if he didn't have a deep interest in their curious quaint ways, what else could he give as a reason for staying on in the valley?

The men turned away to get their hats. She settled the folds of her heavy black silk mantilla more closely about her head, glancing at herself in the mirror. She smiled back with sympathy at the smiling face she saw there. It was not so often since the war that she saw her own face lighted with mirth.

Gravely, something deep on the edge of the unconscious called up to her, 'You are talking and feeling like a coquette.'

She was indignant at this, up in arms to defend human freedom. 'Oh, what a hateful, little-villagey, prudish, nastyminded idea!' she cried to herself. 'Who would have thought that narrowness and priggishness could rub off on a person's mind like that! Mrs. Bayweather could have thought that! Mercy! As if one civilized being can't indulge in a light touch or two in human intercourse with another!'

The two men were ready now, and all the party of six jostled each other cheerfully as they went out of the front door. Paul had secured the hand of old Mr. Welles and led him along with an air of proprietary affection.

'Don't you turn out the lamp, or lock the door, or *any*thing?' asked the old man, now.

'Oh no, we won't be gone long. It's not more than half a mile to the Powers'. There's not a soul in the valley who would think of going in and rummaging . . . let alone taking anything. And we never have tramps. We are too far from the railroad,' said Marise.

'*Well!*' exclaimed the other, looking back as they went down the path, 'it certainly looks queer to me, the door standing open into this black night, and the light shining in that empty room.'

Elly looked back too. She slipped her hand out of her mother's and ran towards the house. She darted up to the door and stood there, poised like a swallow, looking in.

'What does she want?' asked Mr. Welles with the naïve conviction of the elderly bachelor that the mother must know everything in the child's mind.

78

'I don't know,' admitted Marise. 'Nobody ever knows exactly what is in Elly's mind when she does things. Maybe she is looking to see that her kitten is safe.'

The little girl ran back to them.

'What did you want, dear?' asked her mother.

'I just wanted to look at it again,' said Elly. 'I *like* it, like that, all quiet, with nobody in it. The furniture looks as though it were having a good rest from us.'

'Oh, listen to the frogs!' screamed Mark, out of the darkness where he had run to join Touclé.

Elly and Paul sprang forward to join their little brother.

'What in the world are we going to see?' asked Marsh. 'You forget you haven't given us the least idea.'

'You are going to see,' Marise set herself to amuse them, 'you're going to see a rite of the worship of beauty which Ashley, Vermont, has created out of its own inner consciousness.'

She had succeeded in amusing at least one of them, for at this Mr. Marsh gave her the not disagreeable shock of that singular, loud laugh of his. It was in conversation like something-or-other in the orchestra . . . the cymbals, that must be it . . . made you jump, and tingle with answering vibrations.

'Ashleyians in the rôle of worshippers of beauty!' he cried, out of the soft, moist, dense darkness about them.

'None so blind as those who won't see,' she persisted. 'Just because they go to it in overalls and gigham aprons, instead of peplums and sandals.'

'What *is* a night-blooming cereal?' asked Mr. Welles, patient of the verbose by-play of his companions that never got anybody anywhere.

What an old dear Mr. Welles was! thought Marise. It was like having the sweetest old uncle bestowed on you as a pendant to dear Cousin Hetty.

'. . . -eus, not -eal,' murmured Marsh; 'not that I know any more than you what it is.'

Marise felt suddenly wrought upon by the mildness of the spring air, the high, tuneful shrillness of the frogs' voices, the darkness, sweet and thick. She would not amuse them; no, she would really tell them, move them. She chose the deeper intonations of her voice, she selected her words with care, she played upon her own feeling, quickening it into genuine emotion as she spoke. She would make them feel it too.

'It is a plant of the cactus family, as native to America as

79

is Ashley's peculiar sense of beauty which you won't acknowledge. It is as ugly to look at, the plant is, all spines and thick,
graceless, fleshy pads; as ugly as Ashley life looks to you. And
this crabbed, ungainly plant-creature is faithfully, religiously
tended all the year around by the wife of a farmer, because
once a year, just once, it puts forth a wonderful exotic flower of
extreme beauty. When the bud begins to show its colour she
sends out word to all her neighbours to be ready. And we are
all ready. For days, in the back of our minds as we go about
our dull, routine life, there is the thought that the cereus is near
to bloom. Nelly and her grim husband hang over it day by
day, watching it slowly prepare for its hour of glory. Sometimes when they cannot decide just the time it will open, they
sit up all through a long night, hour after hour of darkness and
silence, to make sure that it does not bloom unseen. When they
see that it is about to open, they fling open their doors, wishing
above everything else to share that beauty with their fellows.
Their children are sent to announce, as you heard Touclé say
to-night, "The cereus is going to bloom." And all up and down
this end of the valley, in those ugly little wooden houses that
look so mean and dreary to you, everywhere people, tired from
their day's struggle with the earth, rise up and go their
pilgrimage through the night . . . for what? To see something
rare and beautiful.'

She stopped speaking. On one side of her she heard the
voice of the older man say with a quiver, 'Well, I can understand why your neighbours love you.'

With entire unexpectedness Marsh answered fiercely from
the other side, '*They* don't love her! They're not capable of it!'

Marise started, as though a charged electric wire had fallen
across her arm. Why was there so often a note of anger in his
voice?

For a moment they advanced silently, pacing forward, side
by side, unseen but not unfelt by each of the others.

The road turned now and they were before the little house,
every window alight, the great pine sombre and high before it.
The children and Touclé were waiting at the door. They all
went in together, shaking hands with the mistress of the house,
neatly dressed, with a clean, white flounced apron. 'Nelly's
garment of ceremony!' thought Marise.

Nelly acknowledged, with a graceful, silent inclination of her
shining blonde head, the presence of the two strangers whom
Marise presented to her. What an inscrutable fascination

Nelly's silence gave to her! You never knew what strange thoughts were going on behind that proud taciturnity. She showed the guests to chairs, of which a great many, mostly already filled, stood about the centre table, on which sprawled the great, spiny, unlovely plant. Marise sat down, taking little Mark on her knees. Elly leaned against her. Paul sat close beside old Mr. Welles. Their eyes were on the big pink bud enthroned in the uncomeliness of the shapeless leaf-pads.

'Oh!' said Elly, under her breath, 'it's not open yet! We're going to *see* it open, this time!' She stared at it, her lips parted. Her mother looked at her, tenderly aware that the child was storing away an impression to last her life long. Dear, strangely compounded little Elly, with her mysticism, and her greediness and her love of beauty all jumbled together! A neighbour leaned from her chair to say to Mrs. Crittenden, 'Warm for this time of year, ain't it?' And another remarked, looking at Mark's little trousers, 'That material come out real good, didn't it? I made up what I got of it into a dress for Pearl.' They both spoke in low tones, but not constrained or sepulchral, for they smiled and nodded as though they had meant something else and deeper than what they had said. They looked with a kindly expression for a moment at the Crittenden children and then turned back to their gaze on the flower-bud.

Nelly Powers, walking with a singular lightness for so tall a woman, ushered in another group of visitors – a tall, unshaven farmer, his wife, three little children clumping in on shapeless cow-hide boots, and a baby, fast asleep, its round bonneted head tucked in the hollow of its mother's gingham-clad shoulder. They sat down, nodding silent greetings to the other neighbours. In turning to salute them, Marise caught a glimpse of Mr. Marsh, fixing his brilliant scrutiny first on one and then on another of the company. At that moment he was gazing at Nelly Powers, 'taking her in,' thought Marise, from her beautiful hair to those preposterously high-heeled shoes she always would wear on her shapely feet. His face was impassive. When he looked neutral like that, the curious irregularity of his features came out strongly. He looked like that bust of Julius Cæsar, the bumpy, big-nosed, strong-chinned one, all but that thick, closely cut, low-growing head of dark hair.

She glanced at Mr. Welles, and was surprised to find that he was looking neither at the people nor the plant. His arm was around his favourite Paul, but his gaze seemed turned inward, as though he were thinking of something very far away. He

81

looked tired and old, it seemed to her, and without that quietly shining aspect of peace which she found so touching. Perhaps he was tired. Perhaps she ought not to have brought him out, this evening, for that long walk over rough country roads. How much older he was than his real age in years! His life had used him up. There must have been some inner maladjustment in it!

There was a little stir in the company, a small inarticulate sound from Elly. Marise saw everyone's eyes turn to the centre of the room and look back to the plant. The big pink bud was beginning visibly to swell.

A silence came into the room. No one coughed, or stirred, or scraped a chair-leg. It was as though a sound would have wounded the flower. All those human souls bowed themselves. Almost a light shone upon them . . . a phrase from Dante came to Marise's mind . . . 'la mia menta fu percossa da un fulgore . . .'

With a quick involuntary turn she looked at Marsh, fearing his mockery of her, 'quoting the *Paradiso*, about Vermont farmers!' as though he could know, for all those sharp eyes of his, what was going on hidden in her mind!

All this came and went in an instant, for she now saw that one big, shining petal was slowly, slowly, but quite visibly uncurling at the tip. From that moment on, she saw nothing, felt nothing but the opening flower, lived only in the incredibly leisurely, masterful motion with which the grotesquely shaped protecting petals curled themselves back from the centre. Their motion was so slow that the mind was lost in dreaminess in following it. Had that last one moved? No, it stood still, poised breathlessly . . . and yet, there before them, revealed, exultant, the starry heart of the great flower shimmered in the lamplight.

Then she realized that she had not breathed. She drew in a great marvelling aspiration, and heard everyone about her do the same. They turned to each other with inarticulate exclamations, shaking their heads wonderingly, their lips a little apart as they drew long breaths.

Two very old women, rubbing their age-dimmed eyes, stood up, tiptoed to the table, and bent above the miraculously fine texture of the flower their worn and wrinkled faces. The petals cast a clear, rosy reflection upon their sallow cheeks. Some of the younger mothers took their little children over to the table and lifting them up till their round shining eyes were on a level with the flower, let them gaze their fill at the mysterious splendour of stamen and pistil.

'Would you like to go quite close and look at it, children?' Marise asked her own brood.

The little boys stepped forward at once, curiously, but Elly said, 'No, oh *no*!' and backed off till she stood leaning against Touclé's knee. The old woman put her dark hand down gently on the child's soft hair and smiled at her. How curious it was to see that grim, battered old visage smile! Elly was the only creature in the world at whom the old Indian ever smiled, indeed almost the only thing in the house which those absent old eyes ever seemed to see. Marise remembered that Touclé had smiled when she first took the baby Elly in her arms.

A little murmur of talk arose now from the assembled neighbours. They stood up, moved about, exchanged a few laconic greetings, and began putting their wraps on. Marise remembered that Mr. Welles had seemed tired and as soon as possible set her party in motion.

'Thank you so much, Nelly, for letting us know,' she said to the farmer's wife, as they came away. 'It wouldn't seem like a year in our valley if we didn't see your cereus in bloom.'

She took Elly's hand in one of hers, and with Mark on the other side walked down the path to the road. The darkness was intense there, because of the gigantic pine-tree which towered above the little house. 'Are you there, Paul?' she called through the blackness. The little boy's voice came back, 'Yes, with Touclé, we're ahead.' The two men walked behind.

Elly's hand was hot and clasped her mother's very tightly. Marise bent over the little girl and divined in the darkness that she was crying. 'Why, Elly darling, what's the matter?' she asked.

The child cried out passionately, on a mounting note, 'Nothing, nothing! *Nothing!*' She flung her arms around her mother's neck, straining her close in a wild embrace. Little Mark, on the other side, yawned and staggered sleepily on his feet. Elly gave her mother a last kiss, and ran on ahead, calling over her shoulder, 'I'm going to walk by myself!'

'*Well!*' commented the old gentleman.

Mr. Marsh had not been interested in this episode and had

83

stood gazing admiringly up at the huge pine-tree, divining its bulk and mass against the black sky.

'Like Milton's Satan, isn't it?' was his comment as they walked on, 'with apologies for the triteness of the quotation.'

For a time nothing was said, and then Marsh began, 'Now I've seen it, your rite of the worship of beauty. And do you know what was really there? A handful of dull, insensitive, primitive beings, hardened and calloused by manual toil and atrophied imaginations, so starved for any variety in their stupefyingly monotonous life that they welcome anything, anything at all as a break . . . only if they could choose, they would infinitely prefer a two-headed calf or a bearded woman to your flower. The only reason they go to see that is because it is a curiosity, not because of its beauty, because it blooms once a year only, at night, and because there is only one of them in town. Also because everybody else goes to see it. They go to look at it only because there aren't any movies in Ashley, nor anything else. And you know all this just as well as I do.'

'Oh, Mr. Welles,' Marise appealed to him, 'do you think that is the truth of the facts?'

The old man pronounced judgment gently. 'Well, I don't know that *any*thing is the truth. I should say that both of you told the truth about it. The truth's pretty big for any one person to tell. Isn't it all in the way you look at it?' He added, 'Only personally I think Mrs. Crittenden's the nicest way.'

Marsh was delighted with this. 'There! I hope you're satisfied. You've been called "nice." That ought to please any good American.'

'I wonder, Mr. Welles,' Marise said in an ostentatiously casual tone, 'I wonder if Mr. Marsh had been an ancient Greek, and had stood watching the procession going up the Acropolis hill, bearing the thank-offerings from field and loom and vineyard, what do you suppose he would have seen? Dullness and insensitiveness in the eyes of those Grecian farmer-lads, no doubt, occupied entirely with keeping the oxen in line; a low vulgar stare of bucolic curiosity as the country girls, bearing their woven linen, looked up at the temple. Don't you suppose he would have thought they managed those things a great deal more artistically in Persia?'

'Well, I don't know much about the ancient Greeks,' said Mr. Welles mildly, 'but I guess Vincent would have been about the same wherever he lived.'

'Who is satisfied with the verdict now?' triumphed Marise.

But she noticed that Marsh's attack, although she considered that she had refuted it rather neatly, had been entirely efficacious in destroying the aura of the evening. Of the genuine warmth of feeling which the flower and the people around it had roused in her heart, not the faintest trace was left. She had only a cool interested certainty that her side had a perfectly valid foundation for arguing purposes. Mr. Marsh had accomplished that, and more than that, a return from those other centres of feeling to her preoccupation with his own personality.

He now went on, 'But I'm glad to have gone. I saw a great deal else there than your eccentric plant and the vacancy of mind of those sons of toil, cursed, soul-destroying toil. For one thing, I saw a woman of very great beauty. And that is always so much gained.'

'Oh yes,' cried Marise, 'that's so. I forgot that you could see that. I've grown so used to the fact that people here don't understand how splendidly handsome Nelly Powers is. Their taste doesn't run to the statuesque, you know. They call that grand silent calm of her stupidness! Ever since 'Gene brought her here as a bride, a year after we came to live in Crittenden's, I have gone out of my way to look at her. You should see her hanging out the clothes on a windy day. One sculptured massive pose after another. But even to see her walk across the room and bend that shining head is thrilling.'

'I saw something else, too,' went on Marsh, a cool voice speaking out of the darkness. 'I saw that her black, dour husband is furiously in love with her and furiously jealous of that tall, ruddy fellow with an expressive face, who stood by the door in shirt-sleeves and never took his eyes from her.'

Marise was silent, startled by this shouting out of something she had preferred not to formulate.

'Vincent, you see too much,' said Mr. Welles resignedly. The phrase ran from his tongue as though it were a familiar one.

Marise said slowly, 'I've sometimes thought that Frank Warner did go to the Powers' a good deal, but I haven't wanted to think anything more.'

'What possible reason in the world have you for not wanting to?' asked Marsh with the most authentic accent of vivid and astonished curiosity.

'What reason . . .?' she repeated blankly.

He said dispassionately, 'I don't like to hear *you* make such a flat, conventional, rubber-stamp comment. Why in the world shouldn't she love a fine, ardent, *living* man better than that knotty, dead branch of a husband? A beautiful woman and a living, strong, vital man, they belong together. Whom God hath joined . . . Don't try to tell me that your judgment is maimed by the Chinese shoes of outworn ideas, such as the binding nature of a mediæval ceremony. That doesn't marry anybody, and you know it. If she's really married to her husband, all right. But if she loves another man, and knows in her heart that she would live a thousand times more fully, more deeply with him . . . why, she's *not* married to her husband, and nothing can make her. You know that!'

Marise sprang at the chance to turn his own weapons of mockery against him. 'Upon my word, who's idealizing the Yankee mountaineer now?' she cried, laughing out as she spoke at the idea of her literal-minded neighbours dressed up in those trailing rhetorical robes. 'I thought you said they were so dull and insensitive they could feel nothing but an interest in two-headed calves, and here they are, characters in an Italian opera. I only wish Nelly Powers were capable of understanding those grand languages of yours and then know what she thought of your idea of what's in her mind. And as for 'Gene's jealousy, I'll swear that it amounts to no more than a vague dislike for Frank Warner's "all the time hanging around and gassin' instead of stickin' to work." And you forget, in your fine modern clean-sweep, a few old-fashioned facts like the existence of three Powers children, dependent on their mother.'

'You're just fencing, not really talking,' he answered imperturbably. 'You can't pretend to be sincere in trying to pull that antimacassar home-and-mother stuff on me. Ask Bernard Shaw, ask Freud, ask Mrs. Gilman, how good it is for children's stronger, better selves to live in the enervating, hot-house concentration on them of an unbalanced, undeveloped woman, who has let everything else in her personality atrophy except her morbid preoccupation with her own offspring. That's really the meaning of what's sentimentally called "mothering." Probably it would be the best thing in the world for the Powers children if their mother ran away with that fine broth of a lad.'

'But Nelly loves her children and they love her!' Marise brought this out abruptly, impulsively, and felt, as she heard the words, that they had a flat, naïve sound, out of key with the general colour of this talk, like a C Major chord introduced into Debussy nuances.

'Not much she doesn't, nor they her. Any honest observer of

86

life knows that the only sincere relation possible between the young and the old (after the babies are weaned) is hostility. We hated our elders, because they got in our way. And they'll hate us as soon as they get the strength to, because we'll be in their way. And we will hate them because they will want to push us off the scene. It's impossible to ignore the gulf. Most human tragedies come from trying to pretend it's not there.'

'Why, Mr. Welles,' cried Marise again, 'what do you say to such talk? Don't you find him perfectly preposterous?'

Mr. Welles answered a little absently. 'Oh, I'm pretty well used to him, by now. And all his friends in the city are talking like that now. It's the fashion. I'm so old that I've seen a good many fashions in talk come and go. I never could see that people *acted* any differently, no matter which way they talk.' As he finished, he drew a long sigh, which had obviously no connection with what he had been saying. With the sigh, came an emanation from him of dispirited fatigue. Marise wished she dared draw his hand upon her arm and ask him to lean on her as they walked.

Nothing more was said for a time. Marise lost herself in the outdoor wideness of impression that always came to her under a night sky, where she felt infinity hovering near. She was aware of nothing but the faint voice of the pines, the distant diminuendo of the frog's song, the firm elastic quality of the ground under her feet, so different from the iron rigidity of the winter earth, and the cool soft pressure of the night air on her cheeks, when, like something thrust into her mind from the outside, there rose into her consciousness, articulate and complete, the reason why she had shrunk from looking at the photograph of Rocca di Papa. It was because it was painful to her, intimately painful and humiliating to remember how she and Neale had felt there, the wild, high things they had said to each other, that astounding flood of feeling which had swept them away at the last. What had become of all that? Where now was that high tide?

Of course she loved Neale, and he loved her; there was nobody like Neale, yes, all that; but oh! the living flood had been ebbing, ebbing out of their hearts. They were not *alive* as they had been alive when they had clung to each other, there on that age-old rock, and felt the tide of all the ages lift them high.

It must have been ebbing for a long time before she realized it because, hurried, absorbed, surrounded incessantly by small

87

cares as she was, hustled and jostled in her rôle of mother and mistress-of-the-house in servantless America, with the primitive American need to do so much with her own hands, she had not even had the time to know the stupid, tragic thing that was happening to her . . . that she was turning into a slow, vegetating plant instead of a human being. And now she understood the meaning of the strange dejection she had felt the day when little Mark went off to school with the others. How curiously jaded and apprehensive she had felt that morning, and when she had gone downstairs to see the callers who arrived that day. That was the first time she had *felt* that the tide was ebbing.

All this went through her mind with the cruel swiftness of a sword-flash. And the first reaction to it, involuntary and reflex, was to crush it instantly down, lest the man walking at her side should be aware of it. It had come to her with such loud precision that it seemed it must have been audible.

As she found herself still on the dark country road, cloaked and protected by the blackness of the starless night, she was struck with wonder, as though she had never thought of it before, at the human body, its opaque, inscrutable mystery, the locked, sealed strong-box of unimaginable secrets which it is. There they were, the three of them, stepping side by side, brushing each other as they moved; and as remote from each other as though they were on different stars. What were the thoughts, powerful, complex, under perfect control, which were being marshalled in that round, dark head? She felt a little afraid to think; and turned from the idea to the other man with relief. She knew (she told herself), as though she saw inside, the tired, gentle, simple, wistful thoughts that filled the white head on her other side.

With this, they were again at the house, where the children and Touclé had preceded them. Paul was laughing and saying, 'Elly's the looniest kid! She's just been saying that Father is like . . .' Elly, in a panic, sprang up at him, clapping her hand over his mouth, crying out, 'No, Paul, you shan't tell! *Don't!*'

The older, stronger child pulled himself away and, holding her at arm's length, continued, 'She said Father was like the end of her hair that's fastened into her head, and Mother was the end that flaps in the wind, and Mr. Marsh was like the Eagle Rock brook, swirly and hurrying the way it is in the spring."

Elly, half crying, came to her mother. 'Mother, it's nasty-horrid in Paul to tell when I didn't want him to.'

Marise began taking off the little girl's coat. 'It wasn't very kind in Paul, but there was nothing in those funny little fancies to hide, dear.'

'I don't care about you and Father!' explained the child. 'Only . . .' She looked at Mr. Marsh from under down-bent brows.

'Why, Elly, I am very much complimented, I'm sure,' Marsh hastened to tell her, 'to be compared with such a remarkably nice thing as a brook in spring-time. I didn't suppose any young lady would ever have such a poetic idea about me.'

'Oh . . .' breathed Elly, relieved, 'well . . .'

'Do you suppose you little folks can get yourselves to bed without me?' asked Marise. 'If one of you big children will un-button Mark in the back, he can manage the rest. I must set a bread-sponge before I go upstairs.'

They clung to her imploringly. 'But you'll be upstairs in time to kiss us good night in our beds,' begged Elly and Mark together. Paul also visibly hung on his mother's answer.

Marise looked down into their clear eyes and eager faces, reaching out to her ardently, and she felt her heart melt. What darlings they were! What inestimable treasures! How sweet to be loved like that!

She stooped over them and gathered them all into a great armful, kissing them indiscriminately. 'Yes, of course, I will . . . and give you an extra kiss now!' she cried.

She felt Marsh's eyes on her, sardonically.

She straightened herself, saying with affectionate roughness, 'There, that's enough. Scamper along with you. And don't run around with bare feet!'

She thought to herself that she supposed this was the sort of thing Marsh meant when he spoke about hot-house enervating concentration. She had been more stung by that remark of his than she had been willing to acknowledge to Marsh or to her-self.

But for the moment, any further reflection on it was cut short by the aspect of Mr. Welles' face. He had sunk into a chair near the lamp, with an attitude and an expression of such weariness, that Marise moved quickly to him. 'See here, Mr. Welles,' she said impulsively, 'you have something on your mind, and I've got the mother-habit so fastened on me that I can't be discreet and pretend not to notice it. I want to make you say what the trouble is, and then fix it right, just as I would for one of mine.'

The old man looked up at her gratefully and reaching out one of his wrinkled hands took hers in it. 'It does me good to have you so nice to me,' he said, 'but I'm afraid even you can't fix it right. I've had a rather distressing letter to-day, and I can't seem to get it out of my mind.'

'Schwatzkummerer can't send the gladioli,' conjectured Marsh.

For the first time since he had entered the house, Marise felt a passing dislike for him. She had often felt him to be hard and ruthless, but she had never seen anything cheap in him, before, she thought.

'What was your letter?' she asked the older man.

'Oh, nothing in the least remarkable, nothing new,' he said heavily. 'I've got a cousin whom I haven't seen since she was a little, little girl, though she must be somewhere near my age, now. She has been a teacher in a school for Negroes, down in Georgia, for years, most of her life. But I had sort of lost track of her, till I had to send her some little family trinkets that were left after my old aunt died. Her letter, that I received to-day, is in answer to that. And while she was writing, she gave me her news, and told me a good deal about conditions down there. Pretty bad, I should think it, pretty bad.'

A little spasm crossed his face. He shook his head, as though to shake off a clinging filament of importunate thought.

'What's the trouble? Do they need money, the school?' asked Marise with a vague idea of getting up a contribution.

'No, my cousin didn't say anything about that. It's not so simple. It's the way the Negroes are treated. No, not lynchings, I knew about them. But I knew they don't happen every day. What I hadn't any idea of, till her letter came, was how every day, every minute of every day, they're subject to indignity that they can't avoid, how they're made to feel themselves outsiders and unwelcome in their own country. She says the Southern white people are willing to give them anything that will make good day-labourers of them, almost anything in fact except the thing they can't rise without, ordinary human respect. It made a very painful impression on my mind, her letter, very. She gave such instances. I haven't been able to get it out of my mind. For instance, one of the small things she told me . . . it seems incredible . . . is that Southern white people won't give the ordinary title of respect of Mr. or Mrs.

or Dr. even to a highly educated Negro. They call them by their first names, like servants. Think what an hourly pin-prick of insult that must be. Ever since her letter came, I've been thinking about it, the things she told me, about what happens when they try to raise themselves and refine themselves, how they're made to suffer intimately for trying to be what I thought we all wanted all Americans to be.' He looked at Marise with troubled eyes. 'I've been thinking how it would feel to be a Negro myself. What a different life would be in front of your little Elly if she had Negro blood!'

Marise had listened to him in profound silence. Sheer, unmixed astonishment filled her mind, up to the brim. Of all the totally unexpected things for Mr. Welles to get wrought up about!

She drew a long breath. How eternally disconcerting human beings are! There she had been so fatuously sure, out there on the walk home, that she knew exactly what was in that old white head. And all the time it had been this. Who could have made the faintest guess at that? It occurred to her for the first time that possibly more went on under Mr. Welles' gently fatigued exterior than she thought.

She found not a word to say, so violent and abrupt was the transition of subject. It was as though she had been gazing down through a powerful magnifying-glass, trying to untangle with her eyes a complicated twist of moral fibres, inextricably bound up with each other, the moral fibres that made up her life . . . and in the midst of this, someone had roughly shouted in her ear, 'Look up there, at that distant cliff. There's a rock on it, all ready to fall off!'

She could not be expected all of a sudden, that way, to refocus her eyes. And the rock was so far away. And she had such a dim sense of the people who might be endangered by it. And the confusion here, under the microscope of her attention, was so vital and immediate, needing to be understood and straightened before she could go on with her life.

She looked at the old man in an astonishment which she knew must seem fairly stupid to him, but she could not bring out anything else. What was it to her, whether a Negro physician was called Dr. or 'Jo'?

Mr. Welles patted her hand, released it, smiled at her kindly, and stood up. 'I'm pretty tired. I guess we'd better be getting along home, Vincent and I.'

'Well, I should say we *would* better be getting along home to

bed!' agreed the other man, coming forward and slipping his
arm under the older man's. 'I'll tuck you up, my old friend,
with a good hot toddy inside you, and let you sleep off this
outrageously crazy daylight nightmare you've cooked up for
yourself. And don't wake up with the fate of the Japanese
factory-hand sitting on your chest, or you'll get hard to live
with.'

Mr. Welles answered this with literal good faith. 'Oh, the
Japanese factory-hands, they're not on the conscience of Americans.'

'But, when I see an aged and harmless inhabitant of Ashley,
Vermont, stretching his poor old protesting conscience till it
cracks, to make it reach clear down to the Georgia Negroes,
how do I know where he's going to stop?'

The old man turned to their hostess. 'Well, good night, Mrs.
Crittenden. I enjoyed seeing that wonderful flower very much.
I wonder if I could grow one like it? It would be something to
look forward to, to have the flower open in your own house.'

To Marise he looked so sweet and good, and like a tired old
child, that she longed to kiss him good night, as she had her
own. But even as she felt the impulse, she had again a startled
sense of how much more goes on under the human surface than
ever appears. Evidently Mr. Welles, too, was a locked and
sealed strong-box of secrets.

In the doorway Marsh stopped abruptly and said, looking at
the dense, lustreless black silk wrap about Marise's head and
shoulders, 'What's that thing? I meant to ask you when you
put it on.'

She felt as she often did when he spoke to her, as startled as
though he had touched her. What an extraordinarily living
presence he was, so that a word from him was almost like an
actual personal contact. But she took care not to show this.
She looked down casually at the soft, opaque folds of her wrap.
'Oh, this is a thousand years old. It dates from the Bayonne
days. It's Basque. It's their variation, I imagine, on the
Spanish mantilla. They never wear hats, the Basque women.
The little girls, when they have made their first communion,
wear a scarf of light net, or open transparent lace. And when
they marry they wear this. It's made of a special sort of silk,
woven just for this purpose. As far away as you can see a
woman in the Basque country, if she wears this, you know she's
married.'

'Oh, you do, do you?' said Marsh, going out after his companion.

They were very far from the Negroes in Georgia.

Chapter 8: *What Goes On Inside*

Half an Hour in the Life of a Modern Woman

May 8.

MARISE looked at the clock. They all three looked at the clock. On school mornings the clock dominated their every instant. Marise often thought that the swinging of its great pendulum was as threatening as the Pendulum that swung in the Pit. Back and forth, back and forth, bringing nearer and nearer the knife-edge of its dire threat that nine o'clock would come and the children not be in school. Somehow they must all manage to break the bonds that held them there and escape from the death-trap before the fatal swinging menace reached them. The stroke of nine, booming out in that house, would be like the Crack o' Doom to the children.

Marise told Paul not to eat so fast, and said to Elly, who was finishing her lessons and her breakfast together, 'I let you do this, this one time, Elly, but I don't want you to let it happen again. You had plenty of time yesterday to get that done.'

She stirred her coffee and thought wistfully, 'What a policeman I must seem to the children. I wish I could manage it some other way.'

Elly, her eyes on the book, murmured in a low chanting rhythm, her mouth full of oatmeal, 'Delaware River, Newcastle, Brandywine, East Branch, West Branch, Crum Creek, Schuylkill.'

Paul looked round at the clock again. His mother noted the gesture, the tension of his attitude, his preoccupied expression, and had a quick inner vision of a dirty, ragged, ignorant, gloriously free little boy on a raft on the Mississippi river, for whom life was not measured out by the clock, in thimbleful doses, but who floated in a golden liberty on the very ocean of eternity. 'Why can't we bring them up like Huckleberry Finns!' she thought, protestingly, pressing her lips together.

Then she laughed inwardly at the thought of certain sophisticated friends and their opinion of her life. 'I daresay we do seem to be bringing them up like Huckleberry Finns, in the minds of any of the New York friends, Eugenia Mills for instance!' She remembered with a passing gust of amusement the expression of slightly scared distaste which Eugenia had for the children. 'Too crudely quivering lumps of life-matter for Eugenia's taste,' she thought, and then, 'I wonder what Marsh's feeling towards children really is, children in general. He seems to have the greatest capacity to ignore their existence at all. Or does he only seem to do that, because I have grown so morbidly conscious of their existence as the only thing vital in life? That's what he thinks, evidently. Well, I'd like to have him live a mother's life and see how he'd escape it!'

'Mother,' said Paul seriously, 'Mother, Mark isn't even awake yet, and he'll never be ready for school.'

'Oh, his teacher had to go to a wedding to-day. Don't you remember? He doesn't have any school till the afternoon session.'

She thought to herself, 'What a sense of responsibility Paul has! He is going to be one of the pillars of the earth, one of those miraculous human beings who are mixed in just the right proportions, so that they aren't pulled two ways at once. *Two* ways! Most of us are pulled a thousand ways! It is one of the injustices of the earth that such people aren't loved as much as impulsive, selfish, brilliant natures like dear little Mark's. Paul has had such a restful personality! Even when he was a baby, he was so straight-backed and robust. There's no yellow streak in Paul, such as too much imagination lets in. I know all about that yellow streak, alas!'

The little boy reached down lovingly, and patted the dog, sitting in a rigid attitude of expectancy by his side. As the child turned the light of his countenance on those adoring dog-eyes, the animal broke from his tenseness into a wriggling fever of joy.

' "Oh, my God, my dear little God!" ' quoted Marise to herself, watching uneasily the animal's ecstasy of worship. 'I wish dogs wouldn't take us so seriously. We don't know so much more than they, about anything.' She thought, further, noticing the sweetness of the protecting look which Paul gave to Médor, 'All animals love Paul, anyhow. Animals know more than humans about lots of things. They haven't that horrid perverse streak in them that makes humans dislike people who

94

are too often in the right. Paul is like my poor father. Only I'm here to see that Paul is loved as Father wasn't. Médor is not the only one to love Paul. *I* love Paul. I love him all the more because he doesn't get his fair share of love. And old Mr. Welles loves him, too, bless him!'

'Roanoke River, Staunton River, Dan River,' murmured Elly, swallowing down her chocolate. She stroked a kitten curled up on her lap.

'What shall I have for lunch to-day?' thought Marise. 'There are enough potatoes left to have them creamed.'

Like a stab came the thought, 'Creamed potatoes to please our palates and thousands of babies in Vienna without milk enough to *live*!' She shook the thought off, saying to herself, 'Well, would it make any difference to those Viennese babies if I deprived my children of palatable food?' and was aware of a deep murmur within her, saying only half-articulately, 'No, it wouldn't make any literal difference to those babies, but it might make a difference to you. You are taking another step along the road of hardening of heart.'

All this had been the merest muted arpeggio accompaniment to the steady practical advance of her housekeeper's mind. 'And beefsteak . . . Mark likes that. At fifty cents a pound! What awful prices. Well, Neale writes that the Canadian lumber is coming through. That'll mean a fair profit. What better use can we put profit to, than in buying the best food for our children's growth. Beefsteak is not a sinful luxury!'

The arpeggio accompaniment began murmuring, 'But the Powers children. Nelly and 'Gene can't afford fifty cents a pound for beefsteak. Perhaps part of their little Ralph's queerness and abnormality comes from lack of proper food. And those white-cheeked little Putnam children in the valley. They probably don't taste meat, except pork, more than once a week.' She protested sharply, 'But if their father won't work steadily, when there is always work to be had?' And heard the murmuring answer, 'Why should the children suffer because of something they can't change?'

She drew a long breath, brushed all this away with an effort, asking herself defiantly, 'Oh, what has all this to do with *us*?' And was aware of the answer, 'It has everything to do with us, only I can't figure it out.'

Impatiently she proposed to herself, 'But while I'm trying to figure it out, wouldn't I better just go ahead and have beefsteak to-day?' and wearily, 'Yes, of course, we'll have beef-steak as usual. That's the way I always decide things.'

She buttered a piece of toast and began to eat it, thinking, 'I'm a lovely specimen, anyhow, of a clear-headed, thoughtful modern woman, muddling along as I do.'

The clock struck the half-hour. Paul rose as though the sound had lifted him bodily from his seat. Elly did not hear, her eyes fixed dreamily on her kitten, stroking its rounded head, lost in the sensation of the softness of the fur.

Her mother put out a reluctant hand and touched her quietly. 'Come, dear Elly, about time to start to school.'

As she leaned across the table, stretching her neck towards the child, she caught a glimpse of herself in the mirror on the other side of the room, and thought, 'Oh, how awful! I begin to look as Cousin Hetty does, with a scrawny neck . . .'

She repulsed the thought vigorously. 'Well, what does it matter if I do? There's nothing in my life, any more, that depends on my looking young.'

At this thought, something perfectly inchoate, which she did not recognize, began clawing at her. She pushed it off, scornfully, and turned to Elly, who got up from the table and began collecting her books into her school-bag. Her face was rosy and calm with the sweet ineffable confidence of a good child who has only good intentions. As she packed her books together, she said, 'Well, I'm ready. I've done my grammar, indefinite pronouns, and I can say all those river-tributaries backwards. So now I can start. Good-bye, Mother dear.' Marise bent to kiss the shining little face. 'Good-bye, Elly.'

To herself she thought, as her face was close to the child's, 'I wonder if I look to my little girl as Cousin Hetty used to look to me?' and startled and shocked that the idea kept recurring to her, assuming an importance she was not willing to give it, she cried out to herself, 'Oh, stop being so paltry about that!'

Aloud she said, 'Don't forget to put your rubbers on. Have you a clean handkerchief? Oh, *Elly*, look at your nails! Here, hand me the nail-file over there, Paul. I'll clean them more quickly than you, dear.'

As she cleaned the nails, one eye on the grimly relentless clock, the ideas flicked through her mind like quick, darting flames. 'What mediæval nonsense we do stuff into the school-children's head. What an infamous advantage we take of the darlings' trust in us and their docility to our purposes! My dear little daughter with her bright face of desire-to-do-her-best! What wretched chaff she is getting for that quick, imaginative brain of hers! It's not so bad for Paul, but . . . oh, even for him what nonsense! Rules of grammar, names of figures of speech . . . stuff left over from scholastic hair-splitting! And the tributaries of rivers . . .!' She glanced up for an instant and was struck into remorse by the tranquil expression of peace in the little girl's clear eyes, bent affectionately on her mother. 'Oh, my poor, darling little daughter,' she thought, 'how *can* you trust anything in this weak and wicked world as you trust your broken reed of a mother? I don't know, dear child, any more than you do, where we are going, nor how we are going to get there. We are just stumbling along, your father and I, as best we can, dragging you and your brothers along with us. And all we can do for you, or for each other, is to love you and . . .'

Elly withdrew her hand. 'There, Mother, I know they're clean enough now. I'm afraid I'll be late if I don't go. And you know she scolds like everything if anybody's late.' She repeated in a rapid murmur, 'The tributaries of the Delaware on the left bank are . . .'

Her mother's mind went back with a jerk to the question of river-tributaries. 'And what's the use of cramming her memory with facts she could find in three minutes in any Atlas if by any strange chance she should ever, ever need to know about the tributaries of the Delaware? As well set her to learning the first page of the Telephone Directory! Why don't I do the honest thing by her and say to her that all that is poppy-cock?'

An inner dialogue flashed out, lunge, parry, riposte, like rapier blades at play. 'Because if I told her it is nonsense, that would undermine her faith in her teacher and her respect for her.'

'But why *should* she respect her teacher if her teacher does not deserve that sort of respect? Ought even a little child to respect anything or anybody merely because of a position of authority and not because of intrinsic worth? No, of course not.'

'Oh, you know that's only wild talk. Of course you couldn't send the child to school, and keep her under her teacher, unless you preserve the form of upholding the teacher's authority.'

'Yes, but in Heaven's name, why *do* we send her to school? She could learn twenty times more, anywhere else.'

'Because sending her to school keeps her in touch with other children, with her fellow-beings, keeps her from being "queer" or different. She might suffer from it as she grew up, might desire more than anything in the world to be like others.'

Elly had been staring at her mother's face for a moment, and now said, 'Mother, what *makes* you look so awfully serious?'

Marise said ruefully, 'It's pretty hard to explain to a little girl. I was wondering whether I was as good a mother to you as I ought to be.'

Elly was astonished to the limit of astonishment at this idea. 'Why, Mother, how *could* you be any better than you are?' She threw herself on her mother's neck, crying, 'Mother, I wish you never looked serious. I wish you were always laughing and cutting up, the way you used to. Seems to me since the war is over, you're more soberer than you were before, even, when you were so worried about Father in France. I'd rather you'd scold me than look serious.'

Paul came around the table, and shouldered his way against Elly up to a place where he touched his mother. 'Is that masculine jealousy, or real affection?' she asked herself, and then, 'Oh, what a *beast*! To be analysing my own children!' And then, 'But how am I ever going to know what they're like if I don't analyse them?'

The dog, seeing the children standing up, half ready to go out, began barking and frisking, and, wriggling his way to where they stood all intertwined, stood up with his fore-paws against Paul. The kitten had been startled by his approach and ran rapidly up Marise as though she had been a tree, pausing on her shoulder to paw at a loosened hair-pin.

Marise let herself go on this wave of eager young life, and thrust down into the dark all the razor-edged questions. 'Oh, children! children! take the kitten off my back!' she said, laughing and squirming. 'She's tickling me with her whiskers. Oh, *ow*!' She was reduced to helpless mirth, stooping her head, reaching up futilely for the kitten, who had retreated to the nape of her neck and was pricking sharp little pin-pointed claws through to the skin. The children danced about chiming out peals of laughter. The dog barked excitedly, standing on his hind-legs, and pawing first at one and then at another. Then Paul looked at the clock, and they all looked at the clock. The children, flushed with fun, crammed on their caps, thrust their arms into coats, bestowed indiscriminate kisses on their mother and the kitten, and vanished for the morning, followed

98

by the dog, pleading with little whines to be taken along too. The kitten got down and began soberly to wash her face.

There was an instant of appalling silence in the house, the silence that is like no other, the silence that comes when the children have just gone. Through it, heavy-footed and ruthless, Marise felt something advancing on her, something which she dreaded and would not look at.

From above came a sweet, high, little call, 'Mo-oo-ther!' Oh, a respite – Mark was awake!

His mother sprang upstairs to snatch at him as he lay, rosy and smiling and sleepy. She bent over him intoxicated by his beauty, by the flower-perfection of his skin, by the softness of his sleep-washed eyes.

She heard almost as distinctly as though the voice were in her ear, 'Oh, you mothers use your children as other people use drugs. The child-habit, the drug-habit, the baby-habit, the morphine habit . . . two different ways of getting away from reality.' That was what Marsh had said one day. What terribly tarnishing things he did say. How they did make you question everything. She wondered what Neale would say to them.

She hoped to have a letter from Neale to-day. She hoped so, suddenly, again, with such intensity, such longing, such passion that she said to herself, 'What nonsense that was, that came into my head, out on the road in the dark, the other night, that Neale and I had let the flood-tide of emotion ebb out of our hearts! What could have put such a notion into my head?' What crazy, fanciful creatures women are! Always reaching out for the moon. Yes, that must have been the matter with her lately, that Neale was away. She missed him so, his strength and courage and affection.

'I'm awfully hungry,' remarked Mark in her ear. 'I feel the hole right *here*.' He laid a small shapely hand on the centre of his pyjama-clad body, but he kept the other hand and arm around his mother's neck, and held her close where he had pulled her to him in his little bed. As he spoke he rubbed his peach-like cheek softly against hers.

A warm odour of sleep and youth and clean, soaped skin came up from him. His mother buried her face in it as in a flower.

'Ooh!' he cried, laughing richly, 'you're tickling me.'

'I *mean* to tickle you!' she told him savagely, worrying him as a mother-cat does her kitten. He laughed delightedly, and wriggled to escape her, kicking his legs, pushing at her softly with his hands, reaching for the spot back of her ear. 'I'll tickle *you*,' he crowed, tussling with her, disarranging her hair, thudding his little body against her breast, as he thrashed about. The silent house rang with their laughter and cries.

They were both flushed, with lustrous eyes, when the little boy finally squirmed himself with a bump off the bed and slid to the floor.

At this point the kitten came walking in, innocent-eyed and grave. Mark scrambled towards her on his hands and knees. She retreated with a comic series of stiff-legged, sideways jumps, that made him roll on the floor, chuckling and giggling, and grabbing futilely for the kitten's paws.

Marise had stood up and was putting the loosened strands of her hair back in place. The spell was broken. Looking down on the laughing child, she said dutifully, 'Mark, the floor's cold. You mustn't lie down on it. And, anyhow, you're ever so late this morning. Hop up, dear, and get into your clothes.'

'Oh, Mother, *you* dress me!' he begged, rolling over to look up at her pleadingly.

She shook her head. 'Now, Mark, that's silly. A great big boy like you, who goes to school. Get up quick and start right in before you take cold.'

He scrambled to his feet and padded to her side on rosy bare feet. 'Mother, you'll have to 'tay here, anyhow. You know I can't do those back buttons. And I always get my drawer-legs twisted up with my both legs inside my one leg.'

Marise compromised. 'Well, yes, if you'll hurry. But not if you dawdle. Mother has a lot to do this morning. Remember, I won't help you with a single thing you can do yourself.'

The child obediently unbuttoned his pyjamas and stepping out of them reached for his undershirt. His mother, looking at him, fell mentally on her knees before the beautiful, living body. 'Oh, my son, the straight, strong darling! My precious little son!' She shook with that foolish aching anguish of mothers, intolerable. . . . 'Why must he stop being so pure, so *safe*? How can I live when I am no longer strong enough to protect him?'

Mark remarked plaintively, shrugging himself into the sleeves of his shirt, 'I've roden on a horse, and I've roden on a dog, and I've even roden on a cow, but I've never roden on a camel, and I *want* to.'

The characteristic Mark-like unexpectedness of this made her smile.

'You probably will, some day,' she said, sitting down.

'But I've never even *sawn* a camel,' complained Mark. 'And Elly and Paul have, and a elephant too.'

'Well, you're big enough to be taken to the circus this year,' his mother promised him. 'This very summer we'll take you.'

'But I want to go *now*!' clamoured Mark, with his usual disregard of possibilities, done in the grand style.

'Don't dawdle,' said his mother, looking around for something to read, so that she would seem less accessible to conversation. She found the newspaper under her hand, on the table, and picked it up. She had only glanced at the head-lines yesterday. It took a lot of moral courage to read the newspapers in these days. As she read, her face changed, darkened, set.

The little boy, struggling with his underwear, looked at her and decided not to ask for help.

She was thinking as she read, 'The Treaty muddle worse than ever. Great Britain sending around to all her colonies asking for the biggest navy in the world. Our own navy constantly enlarged at enormous cost. Constantinople to be left Turkish because nobody wants anybody else to have it. Armenian babies dying like flies and evening cloaks advertised to sell for six hundred dollars. Italy land-grabbing. France frankly for anything except the plain acceptance of the principles we thought the war was to foster. The same reaction from those principles starting on a grand scale in America. Men in prison for having an opinion . . . what a hideous bad joke on all the world that fought for the Allies and for the holy principles they claimed! To think how we were straining every nerve in a sacred cause two years ago. Neale's enlistment. Those endless months of loneliness. That constant terror about him. And homes like that all over the world . . . with *this* as the result. Could it have been worse if we had all just grabbed what we could get for ourselves, and had what satisfaction we could out of the baser pleasures?'

She felt a mounting wave of horror and nausea, and knowing well from experience what was on its way fought desperately to ward it off, reading hurriedly a real-estate item in the newspaper, an account of a flood in the West, trying in vain to fix her mind on what she read. But she could not stop the advance of what was coming. She let the newspaper fall with a shudder as the thought arrived, hissing, gliding with venomous swiftness along the familiar path it had so often taken to her heart . . . 'suppose this reactionary outburst of hate and greed and intolerance and imperialistic ambitions all around means that the "peace" is an armed truce only, and that in fifteen years the whole nightmare will start over.'

She looked down at the little boy, applying himself seriously to his buttons. 'In fifteen years' time my baby will be a man of twenty-one.'

Wild cries broke out in her heart. 'No, oh no! I couldn't live through another. To see them all go, husband and sons! Not another war! Let me live quickly, anyhow, somehow, to get it over with . . . and die before it comes.'

The little boy had been twisting himself despairingly, and now said in a small voice, 'Mother, I've tried and I've tried, and I can't do that back button.'

His mother heard his voice and looked down at him uncomprehendingly for a moment. He said, less resigned, impatience pricking through his tone, 'Mother, I *told* you I never could reach that button behind.'

She bent from her chair, mechanically secured the little garment, and then, leaning back, looked down moodily at her feet. The little boy began silently to put on and lace up his shoes.

Marise was aware of a dimming of the light in the inner room of her consciousness, as though one window after another were being darkened. A hushed, mournful twilight fell in her heart. Melancholy came and sat down with her, black-robed. What could one feel except Melancholy at the sight of the world of humanity, poor world, war-ridden, broken in health, ruined in hope, the very nerves of action cut by the betrayal of its desperate efforts to be something more than base.

.   .   .   .

Was that really Melancholy? Something else slid into her mind, something watchful. She sat perfectly still so that no chance movement should disturb that mood till it could be examined and challenged. There was certainly something else in her heart beside sorrow over the miseries of the after-war world.

She persisted in her probing search, felt a cold ray of daylight strike into that gloom and recognized with amazement and chagrin what else it was! Disgusting! There in the very bottom of her mind lay still that discomfort at beginning to look like Cousin Hetty! And so that wound to her vanity had slowly risen again into her consciousness and clothed itself in the ampler, nobler garments of impersonal Melancholy. . . . '*Oh*,' she cried aloud, impatiently, contemptuous of herself, 'what picayune creatures human beings are! I'm ashamed to be one!'

She started up and went to the window, looking out blankly at the mountain wall, as she had at the newspaper, not seeing what was there, her eyes turned inward. 'Wait now, wait. Don't go off, half-cocked. Go clear through with this thing,' she exhorted herself. 'There *must* be more in it than mere childish, silly vanity.' She probed deep and brought up, 'Yes, there is more to it. In the first place I was priggish and hypocritical when I tried to pretend that it was nothing to me when I looked in the glass and saw for the first time that my youth has begun to leave me. That was Anglo-Saxon pretence, trying to seem to myself made of finer stuff than I really am. It's really not cheerful for any woman, no matter on what plane, to know that the days of her physical flowering are numbered. I'd have done better to look straight at that, and have it out with myself.'

She moved her head very slightly, from side to side. 'But there was more than that. There was more than that. What was it?' She leaned her ear as if to listen, her eyes very large and fixed. 'Yes, there *was* the war, and the awfulness of our disappointment in it, too, after all. There was the counsel of despair about everything, the pressure on us all to think that all efforts to be more than base are delusions. We were so terribly fooled with our idealistic hopes about the war . . . who knows but that we are being fooled again when we try for the higher planes of life? Perhaps those people are right who say that to grab for the pleasures of the senses is the best . . . those are *real* pleasures, at least. Who knows if there is anything else?'

Something like a little, far-away tolling said to her, 'There was something else. There was something else.'

This time she knew what it was. 'Yes, there was that other aspect of the loss of physical youth, when you think that the pleasures of the senses are perhaps all there are. There was the inevitable despairing wonder if I had begun to have out of my youth all it could have given, whether . . .'

There tolled in her ear, 'Something else, something else there.' But now she would not look, put her hands over her eyes, and stood in the dark, fighting hard lest a ray of light should show her what might be there.

A voice sounded beside her. Touclé was saying, 'Have you got one of your headaches? The mail-carrier just went by. Here are the letters.'

She took down her hands, and opened her eyes. She felt that something important hung on there being a letter from Neale. She snatched at the handful of envelopes and sorted them over, her fingers trembling. Yes, there it was, the plain stamped envelope with Neale's firm regular handwriting.

She felt as though she were a diver whose lungs had almost collapsed, who was being drawn with heavenly swiftness up to the surface of the water. She tore open the envelope and read, 'Dearest Marise.' It was as though she had heard his voice.

She drew in a great audible breath and began to read. What a relief it was to feel herself all one person, not two or three, probing hatefully into each other!

But there was something she had not done, some teasing, unimportant thing she ought to finish before going on with the letter. She looked up vacantly, half-absently, wondering what it was. Her .eyes fell on Touclé. Touclé was looking at her, Touclé who so seldom looked at anything. She felt a momentary confusion as though surprised by another person in a room she had thought empty. And after that, uneasiness. She did not want Touclé to go on looking at her.

'Mark hasn't had his breakfast yet,' she said to the old Indian woman. 'Won't you take him downstairs, please, and give him a dish of porridge for me?'

Chapter 9

'The Gent Around the Lady
and
The Lady Round the Gent'

An Evening in the Life of Mr. Vincent Marsh

May 25.

'COME in, come in!' cried an old black-clad woman, with a white apron, who opened the door wider into the flaring brilliance of the lamp-lit kitchen. 'I'm *real* glad you felt to come to one of our dances. They're old-fashioned, but *we* like 'em.' She closed the door behind them and added cordially, 'Now Mr. Welles is going to live here, he'll have to learn to shake his feet along with the rest of us.'

Mr. Welles was frankly terrified at the idea. 'Why, I never dreamed of dancing in all my life!' he cried. 'I only came to look on.' He hesitated to divest himself of his overcoat, panic-struck and meditating flight. Vincent fell upon him from one side and the lively old woman from the other. Together they stripped the older man of his wraps. 'Never too late to learn,' old Mrs. Powers assured him briskly. 'You dance with *me* and I'll shove ye around, all right. There ain't a quadrille ever danced that I couldn't do backwards with my eyes shut, as soon as the music strikes up.' She motioned them towards the door. 'Step right this way. The folks that have come are all in the settin'-room.'

As they followed her, Vincent said, 'Mrs. Powers, aren't you going to dance with me, too?'

'Oh, of course I be,' she answered smartly, 'if you ask me.'

'Then I ask you now,' he urged, 'for the first dance. Only I don't know any more than Mr. Welles how to dance a quadrille. But I'm not afraid.'

'I guess there ain't much ye *be* afraid of,' she said admiringly. They came now into the dining-room and caught beyond that a glimpse of the living-room. Both wore such an unusual aspect of elegance and grace that Vincent stared, stopping to look about him. 'Looks queer, don't it,' said Mrs. Powers, 'with the furniture all gone. We always move out everything we *can*, up garret, so's to leave room for dancing.'

Oh yes, that was it, Vincent thought; the shinily varnished cheap furniture had almost disappeared, and the excellent proportions of the old rooms could be seen. Lamps glowed from every shelf, their golden light softened by great sprays of green branches with tender young leaves, which were fastened everywhere over the doors, the windows, banked in the corner. The house smelled like a forest, indescribably fresh and spicy.

'There ain't many flowers yet; too early,' explained Mrs. Powers apologetically, 'so we had to git green stuff out'n the woods to kind of dress us up. 'Gene he *would* have some pine boughs too. He's crazy about pine-trees. I always thought that was one reason why he took it so hard when we was done out of our wood-land. He thinks as much of that big pine in front of the house as he does of a person. And to-night he's got the far room all done up with pine boughs.'

They arrived in the living-room now, where the women and children clustered on one side, and the men on the other, their lean boldly marked faces startlingly clear-cut in the splendour of fresh shaves. The women were mostly in light-coloured waists and dark skirts, their hair carefully dressed. Vincent noticed, as he nodded to them before taking his place with the men, that not a single one had put powder on her face. Their eyes looked shining with anticipation. They leaned their heads together and chatted in low tones, laughing and glancing sideways at the group of men on the other side of the room. Vincent wondered at the presence of the children. When she arrived, he would ask Marise about that. At the inward mention of the name he felt a little shock, which was not altogether pleasurable. He narrowed his eyes and shook his head slightly, as though to toss a lock of hair from his forehead, a gesture which was habitual with him when he felt, with displeasure, an unexpected emotion not summoned by his will. It passed at once.

On joining the dark-suited group of men he found himself next to young Frank Warner, leaning, loose-jointed and powerful, against the wall, and not joining in the talk of weather, pigs, roads, and spring ploughing which rose from the others. Vincent looked at him with approval. He felt strongly drawn to this splendid, primitive creature, and knew perfectly well why. He liked anybody who had pep enough to have an original feeling, not one prescribed by the ritual and taboo of his particular tribe.

'Hello, Frank,' he said. 'Have a cigarette?'

'We'll have to go out if we smoke,' said Frank.

'Well, why shouldn't we?' suggested Vincent, looking around him. 'There's nothing to do here, yet.'

Frank tore himself loose from the supporting wall with a jerk, and nodded. Together they stepped out of the front door, unused by the guests, who all entered by the kitchen. At first it was as though they had plunged into black velvet curtains, so great was the contrast with the yellow radiance of the room they had left. They looked back through the unshaded windows and saw the room as though it were an illustration in a book, or a scene in a moving-picture play, the men grouped in a dark mass on one side, the women, smiling, bending their heads towards each other, the lamps glowing on the green branches and on the shining eyes of all those pleasure-expectant human beings.

As they looked, Nelly Powers came in from another room, doubtless the 'far room' of which her mother-in-law had spoken. She was carrying a large tray full of cups. She braced herself against the weight of the earthenware and balancing herself with a free swinging motion on her high-heeled shoes walked with an accentuation of her usual vigorous poise.

'By George, she's a beauty!' cried Vincent, not sorry to have an opportunity to talk of her with his companion.

Frank made no comment. Vincent laughed to himself at the enormous capacity for silence of these savages, routing to the imagination of a civilized being. He went on, determined to get some expression from the other, 'She's one of the very handsomest women I ever saw anywhere.'

Frank stirred in the darkness as though he were about to speak. Vincent cocked his ear and prepared to listen with all the prodigious sharpness of which he knew himself capable. If he could only once make this yokel speak her name, he'd know . . . all he wanted to know.

Frank said, 'Yes, she's good-looking all right.'

Vincent kept silence, pondering every tone and overtone of the remark. He was astonished to find that he had no more direct light than ever on what he wanted to know. He laughed again at his own discomfiture. There were the two extremes, the super-sophisticated person who could control his voice so that it did not give him away, and the utter rustic whose voice had such a brute inexpressiveness that his meaning was as effectively hidden. He would try again. He said casually, 'She's an enough-sight better-looking specimen than her husband. However does it happen that the best-looking women are always caught by that sort of chimpanzees? How did she ever happen to marry 'Gene, anyhow?'

The other man answered, literally, 'I don't know how she did happen to marry him. She don't come from around here. 'Gene was off working in a mill, down in Massachusetts, Adams way, and they got married there. They only come back here to live after they'd had all that trouble with lawyers and lost their wood-land. 'Gene's father died about that time. It cut him pretty hard. And 'Gene and his wife they come back to run the farm.'

At this point they saw, looking in at the lighted dumb-show in the house, that new arrivals had come. Vincent felt a premonitory clap of his heart and set his teeth in his cigarette. Yes, Marise had come, now appeared in the doorway, tall, framed in green-leafed branches, the smooth pale oval of her face lighted by the subtle smile, those dark long eyes! By God! What would he not give to know what went on behind that smile, those eyes!

She was unwinding from her head the close, black nun-like wrap that those narrow primitive country-women far away on the other side of the globe had chosen to express their being united to another human being. And a proper lugubrious symbol it made for their lugubrious, prison-like, primitive view of the matter.

Now she had it off. Her sleek, gleaming dark head stood poised on her long, thick, white throat. What a woman! What she could be in any civilized setting!

She was talking to Nelly Powers now, who had come back and stood facing her in one of those superb poses of hers, her yellow braids heavy as gold. It was Brunhilda talking to Leonardo da Vinci's Ste. Anne. No, heavens no! Not a saint, a musty, penitential negation like a saint! Only, of course, the Ste. Anne wasn't a saint either, but da Vinci's glorious Renaissance stunt at showing what an endlessly desirable woman he could make if he put his mind on it.

'What say, we go in,' suggested Frank, casting away the butt of his cigarette. 'I think I hear old Nate beginning to tune up.'

They opened the door and stepped back, the laughing confusion of their blinking entrance, blinded by the lights, carrying off the first moments of greeting. In the midst of this, Vincent heard the front door open and, startled to think that anyone else had used that exit, turned his head, and saw with some dismay that 'Gene had followed them in. How near had he been to them in the black night while they talked of his wife's mismated beauty? He walked past them giving no sign, his strong long arms hanging a little in front of his body as he moved, his shoulders stooped apparently with their own weight. From the dining-room came a sound which Vincent did not recognize as the voice of any instrument he had ever heard: a series of extraordinarily rapid staccato scrapes, playing over and over a primitively simple sequence of notes. He stepped to the door to see what instrument was being used and saw an old man with a white beard and long white hair, tipped back in a chair, his eyes half shut, his long legs stretched out in front of him, patting with one thick boot. Under his chin was a violin, on the strings of which he jiggled his bow back and forth spasmodically, an infinitesimal length of the horse-hair being used for each stroke, so that there was no sonority in the tones. Vincent gazed at him with astonishment. He had not known that you could make a violin, a real violin, sound like that.

Old Mrs. Powers said at his elbow, 'The first sets are forming, Mr. Marsh.' She called across to Frank Warner, standing very straight with Nelly Powers' hand on his arm, 'Frank, you call off, wun't ye?'

Instantly the young man, evidently waiting for the signal, sent out a long clear shout, 'First sets *fo-orming*!'

Vincent was startled by the electrifying quality of the human voice when not hushed to its usual smothered conversational dullness.

'Two sets formed in the living-room! Two in the dining-room! One in the far room!' chanted Frank. He drew a deep breath which visibly swelled his great chest and sang out, resonantly, 'Promenade *to* your places!'

He set the example, marching off through the throng with Nelly by his side.

'Frank, he generally calls off,' explained old Mrs. Powers. 'It's in his family to. His father always did before him.' She looked around her, discerned something intelligible in what looked like crowding confusion to Vincent and told him hurriedly, 'Look-y-here, we'll have to git a move on, if we git into a set. They're all full here.' Frank appeared in the doorway, alone, and lifted a long high arm. '*One* couple needed in the far room!' he proclaimed with stentorian dignity and seriousness.

'Here we are!' shouted old Mrs. Powers, scrambling her way through the crowd, and pulling Vincent after her. He could see now that the couples about him were indeed in their places, hand in hand, facing each other, gravely elate and confident. The younger ones were swinging their bodies slightly, in time to the sharply marked beat of the fiddle, and in the older ones, the pulse throbbed almost visibly as they waited.

He felt the breath of pines on him, resinous, penetrating, stimulating. He was in a small, square room with a low ceiling, dense and green with pine boughs, fastened to the walls. The odour was as strange an accompaniment to dancing as was that furiously whirling primitive iteration of the fiddle.

'Over here!' cried Mrs. Powers, dragging masterfully at her

partner. She gave a sigh of satisfaction, caught at his hand and held it high. 'All ready, Frank,' she said.

Facing them, near the doorway stood Frank and Nelly, their heads up, Nelly's small high-heeled shoe thrust forward, their clasped hands held high. Vincent felt his blood move more quickly at the spectacle they made. On one side stood Marise Crittenden, her fingers clasped by the huge knotted hand of 'Gene Powers, and on the other was rounded, rosy old Mr. Bayweather holding by the hand the oldest Powers child, a pretty blonde girl of twelve.

Frank's voice pealed out above the jig-jig-jigging of the fiddle. '*Salute* your partners!'

Vincent had a qualm of a feeling he thought he had left behind him with his boyhood, real embarrassment, fear of appearing at a disadvantage. What in the world did their antiquated lingo *mean*? Was he to *kiss* that old woman?

Mrs. Powers said reassuringly, 'Don't you worry. Just do what the others do.'

As she spoke she was holding out her skirts and dipping to a curtsy. A little later, he caught at the idea and sketched a bow such as to his astonishment he saw the other men executing. Was he in old Versailles or Vermont?

He felt his hand seized by the old woman's. Such a hearty zest was in her every action that he looked at her amazed.

'Balance to the corners, right!' chanted Frank, sending his voice out like a bugle so that it might be heard in all the rooms.

With perfect precision and poise, the men and women of the couples separated, stepped swayingly, each towards the nearest of the couple to their right, and retreated.

'Balance to corners, left!'

The same movement was executed to the other side.

'First couple forward and back!' shouted Frank.

Marise and 'Gene advanced, hand in hand, to meet the old clergyman and the little girl. They met in the middle, poised an instant on the top wave of rhythm and stepped back, every footfall, every movement, their very breathing, in time to the beat-beat-beat of the fiddle's air which filled the room as insistently as the odour of the pines.

Mrs. Powers nodded her white head to it and tapped her foot. Marsh had not ventured to remove his eyes from the weaving interplay of the dancers in his own set. Now, for an instant, he glanced beyond them into the next room. He received an impression of rapid, incessant, intricate shifting to and fro, the whole throng of dancers in movement as swift and disconcerting to the eyes as the bits of glass in a kaleidoscope. It made him literally dizzy to see it, and he turned his eyes back to his own set.

The air changed, but not the rhythm, and all the men broke out in a hoarse chant, singing to a whirring, rapid tune,

'*Oh*, pass right through and never mind who
    And leave the girl behind you.
Now come right back on the same old track
    And *swing* the girl behind you!'

In obedience to these chanted commands, the four who were executing the figure went through labyrinthine manœuvres, forward and back, dividing and reuniting. The old clergyman held out his hand to Mrs. Crittenden, laughing as he swung her briskly about. 'Gene bent his great bulk solemnly to swing his own little daughter. Then with neat exactitude, on the stroke of the beat, they were all back in their places.

'*Second* couple forward and back!' sang out Frank, prolonging the syllables in an intoned chant like a muezzin calling from a tower. Vincent felt himself being pushed and shoved by Mrs. Powers through the intricate figure.

'Now come right back on the same old track
    And *swing* the girl behind you!'

The men shouted loudly, stamping in time, with such a relish for the beat of the rhythm that it sang itself through to the motor-centres and set them throbbing. Vincent found himself holding Nelly Powers at arm's length and swinging her till his head whirled. She was as light as sea-foam, dreamy, her blue eyes shining.

'*Grand* right and left!' shouted Frank.

Vincent's hand was seized by the little Powers girl. She swung him competently and passed him on to her mother, who swam past him like a goddess, a golden aroma of health and vivid sensual seduction trailing from her as she moved.

Then it was Marise's hand in his . . . how strange, how strange . . . that hand which knew the secrets of Debussy's heart. . . . She grasped his fingers firmly and looked at him full, laughingly, her face as open as a child's . . . the many-sided tantalizing creature! She pulled him about and was gone.

And there was old Mrs. Powers in her place, absurdly light and elastic, treading the floor in her flat, old-woman's shoes with brilliant precision.

'*All* promenade!' cried Frank, this time his voice exultant that the end was successfully reached.

He seized Nelly by the waist and danced with her the length of the room, followed by the other couples. The music stopped. He released her instantly, made a strange, stiff little bow, and turned away. The set was over.

'There!' said Mrs. Powers, breathing quickly. ''Twan't so hard as you thought 'twas goin' to be, was it?'

'Good evening,' said Mr. Bayweather on the other side, wiping the pink roll at the back of his neck. 'What do you think of our aboriginal folk-dancing? I'll warrant you did not think there was a place in the United States where the eighteenth-century dances had had an uninterrupted existence, did you?'

'I assure you I had never thought about the subject at all,' said Vincent, edging away rapidly towards escape.

'Fascinating historical phenomenon, I call it,' said the clergyman. 'Analogous to the persistence of certain parts of old English speech which is to be observed in the talk of our people. For instance in the eighteenth-century English vocabulary, the phrase . . .'

His voice died away in the voices of the people Vincent had put resolutely between them, shoving his way through the crowd recklessly. He was struck by the aspect of the people, their blood warmed, their lips moist, their eyes gleaming. The rooms were growing hot, and the odour of pines was heavy in the air.

He found himself next to Nelly Powers, and asked her to dance with him, 'Although I don't know at all how to do it,' he explained. She smiled, silently, indifferently, confidently, and laid her hand on his arm in token of accepting his invitation. Vincent had a passing fancy that she did not care at all with whom she danced, that the motion itself was enough for her. But he reflected that it was probably that she did not care at all whether she danced with *him*.

From the other end of the room came Frank's deep-mouthed shout, 'The set is forming! Promenade *to* your places!'

Nelly moved swiftly in that direction and again Vincent found himself opposite Frank, dancing this time with Marise Crittenden.

The music broke out into its shaking, quavering iteration of the pulse of the dance.

'Salute your partners!'

This time Vincent knew what to do, and turning, bowed low to Nelly, who made him a deep curtsy, her toe pointed, instep high, her eyes shining, looking straight at him but evidently not seeing him. The music seemed to float her off on a cloud.

'Chassay *to* the corners, right!'

Vincent untangled the difference between 'chassay' and 'balance' and acquitted himself. Now that his first panic of astonishment was over, he observed that the figures of the dance were of great simplicity, all but the central part, the climax.

When the preliminary part was over, the music changed and again the men broke out into their accompanying chant. This time it ran,

> 'The gent around the lady
> *and*
> The lady around the gent.
> *Then*
> The lady around the lady
> *and*
> The gent around the gent.'

Somewhere in the hypnotic to-and-fro of those swaying, poised, alert human figures, he encountered Marise, coming on her suddenly, and finding her standing stock-still.

'*Around* me!' she commanded, imperatively, nodding and laughing. 'Just as the song says.'

> 'The gent around the lady,'

sang the men.

Frank was circling about Nelly, his eyes on hers, treading lightly, his tall body apparently weighing no more than thistledown. It was as though he were weaving a charm.

Vincent ended his circle.

The men sang, '*And* the lady around the gent.'

Marise and Nelly stepped off, overlaying the men's invisible circle with one of their own.

The room beyond boiled with the dervish-like whirling of the dancers. The fiddle rose louder and shriller, faster and faster. The men sang at the tops of their voices, and beat time heavily. Under cover of this rolling clamour, Vincent called out boldly to Marise, 'A symbol of life! A symbol of our life!' and did not know if she heard him.

> *'Then*
> The lady around the lady.'

Nelly and Marise circled each other.

> *'And*
> The gent around the gent.'

He and Frank followed them.

His head was turning, the room staggered around him. Nelly's warm, vibrant hand was again in his. They were in their places. Frank's voice rose, resounding, '*Pro*menade all!'

Nelly abandoned herself to his arms, in the one brief moment of close physical contact of the dance. They raced to the end of the room.

The music stopped abruptly, but it went on in his head.

The odour of pines rose pungent in the momentary silence. Everyone was breathing rapidly. Nelly put up a hand to touch her hair. Vincent, reflecting that he would never acquire the native-born capacity for abstaining from chatter, said, because he felt he must say something, 'What a pleasant smell those pine branches give.'

She turned her white neck to glance into the small room lined with the fragrant branches, and remarked, clearly and dispassionately, 'I don't like the smell.'

Vincent was interested. He continued, 'Well, you must have a great deal of it, whether you like it or not, from that great specimen by your front door.'

She looked at him calmly, her eyes as blue as precious stones. 'The old pine-tree,' she said, 'I wish it were cut down, darkening the house the way it does.' She spoke with a sovereign impassivity, no trace of feeling in her tone. She turned away.

Vincent found himself saying almost audibly, 'Oh *ho!*' He had the sensation, very agreeable to him, of combining two clues to make a certainty. He wished he could lay his hands on a clue to put with Marise Crittenden's shrinking from the photograph of the Rocca di Papa.

He had not spoken to Marise that evening, save the first greetings, and his impudent shout to her in the dance, and now turned to find her. On the other side of the room she was installed, looking extraordinarily young and girl-like, between Mr. Welles and Mr. Bayweather, fanning first one and then the other elderly gentleman and talking to them with animation. They were both in need of fanning, puffing and panting hard. Mr. Welles indeed was hardly recognizable, the usual pale quiet of his face broken into red and glistening laughter.

'I see you've been dancing,' said Vincent, coming to a halt in front of the group and wishing the two old gentlemen in the middle of next week.

'Old Mrs. Powers got me,' explained Mr. Welles. 'You never saw anything so absurd in your life.' He went on to the others, 'You simply can't imagine how remarkable this is for me. I never, *never* danced and I no more thought I ever *would* . . .'

Mr. Bayweather ran his handkerchief around and around his neck in an endeavour to save his clerical collar from complete ruin, and said, panting still, 'Best thing in the world for you, Mr. Welles.'

'Yes indeed,' echoed Marise. 'We'll have to prescribe a dance for you every week. You look like a boy, and you've been looking rather tired lately.' She had an idea and added, accusingly, 'I do believe you've gone on tormenting yourself about the Negro problem!'

'Yes, he has!' Mr. Bayweather unexpectedly put in. 'And he's not the only person he torments about it. Only yesterday when he came down to the rectory to see some old deeds, didn't he expatiate on that subject and succeed in spoiling the afternoon. I had never been forced to think so much about it in all my life. He made me very uncomfortable, very! What's the use of going miles out of your way, I say, out of the station to which it has pleased God to place us? I believe in leaving such insoluble problems to a Divine Providence.'

Marise was evidently highly amused by this exposition of one variety of ministerial principle, and looked up at Vincent over her fan, her eyes sparkling with mockery. He savoured with an intimate pleasure her certainty that he would follow the train of her thought; and he decided to try to get another rise out of the round-eyed little clergyman. 'Oh, if it weren't the Negro problem, Mr. Bayweather, it would be free-will or predestination, or capital and labour. Mr. Welles suffers from a duty-complex, inflamed to a morbid degree by a life-long compliance to a mediæval conception of family responsibility.'

Mr. Bayweather's eyes became rounder than ever at this,

and Vincent went on, much amused, 'Mr. Welles has done his duty with discomfort to himself so long that he has the habit. His life at Ashley seems too unnaturally peaceful to him. I'd just as soon he took it out with worrying about the Negroes. They are so safely far away. I had been on the point of communicating to him my doubts as to the civic virtues of the Martians, as a safety valve for him.'

Marise laughed out, as round a peal as little Mark's, but she evidently thought they had gone far enough with their fooling, for she now brought the talk back to a safe, literal level by crying, 'Well, there's one thing sure, Mr. Welles can't worry his head about *any* of the always-with-us-difficulties of life, as long as he is dancing an Ashley quadrille.'

Mr. Welles concurred in this with feeling. 'I'd no idea I would ever experience anything so . . . so . . . well, I tell you, I thought I'd left *fun* behind me, years and years ago.'

'Oh, what you've had is nothing compared to what you're going to have,' Marise told him. 'Just wait till old Nate strikes up the opening bars of "The Whirlwind" and see the roof of the house fly off. See here,' she laid her hand on his arm. 'This is leap-year. I solemnly engage you to dance "The Whirlwind" with me.' She made the gesture of the little-boy athlete, feeling the biceps of one arm, moving her forearm up and down. 'I'm in good health, and good muscle, because I've been out stirring up the asparagus bed with a spading-fork. I can shove you around as well as old Mrs. Powers, if I do say it who shouldn't.'

Vincent looked down at her, bubbling with light-hearted merriment, and thought, 'There is no end to the variety of her moods!'

She glanced up at him, caught his eyes on her and misinterpreted their wondering expression. 'You think I'm just silly and childish, don't you?' she told him challengingly. 'Oh, don't be such an everlasting adult. Life's not so serious as all that!'

He stirred to try to protest, but she went on, 'It's dancing that sets me off. Nelly Powers and I are crazy about it. And so far as my observation of life extends, our dances here are the only social functions left in the world that people really *enjoy* and don't go to merely because it's the thing to. It always goes to my head to see people enjoy themselves. It's so sweet.'

Mr. Welles gave her one of his affectionate pats on her hand.

116

Vincent asked her casually, 'What's the idea of making a family party of it and bringing the children too?'

She answered dashingly, 'If I answer you in your own language, I'd say that it's because their households are in such a low and lamentably primitive condition that they haven't any slave-labour to leave the children with, and so bring them along out of mere brute necessity. If I answer you in another vocabulary, I'd say that there is a close feeling of family unity, and they *like* to have their children with them when they are having a good time, and find it pleasant to see mothers dancing with their little boys and fathers with their little girls.'

Without the slightest premonition of what his next question was to bring out, and only putting it to keep the talk going, Vincent challenged her, 'Why don't you bring your own, then?' He kept down with difficulty the exclamation which he inwardly added, 'If you only knew what a relief it is to see you for once, without that intrusive, tiresome bunch of children!'

'Why, sometimes I do,' she answered in a matter-of-fact tone. 'But I just had a telegram from my husband saying that he is able to get home a little sooner than he thought, and will be here early to-morrow morning. And the children voted to go to bed early so they could be up bright and early to see him.'

Vincent continued looking down on her blankly for an instant, after she had finished this reasonable explanation. He was startled by the wave of anger which spurted up over him like flame.

He heard Mr. Welles make some suitable comment, 'How nice.' He himself said, 'Oh really,' in a neutral tone, and turned away.

For a moment he saw nothing of what was before him, and then realized that he had moved next to Frank Warner, who was standing by Nelly Powers, and asking her to dance with him again. She was shaking her head, and looking about the room uneasily. Vincent felt a gust of anger again. 'Oh, go *to* it, Frank!' he said, in a low fierce tone. 'Take her out again, as often as you like. Why shouldn't you?'

Nelly gave him one of her enigmatic looks, deep and inscrutable, shrugged her shoulders, put her hand on Frank's arm, and walked off with him.

'They're the handsomest couple in the room,' said Vincent, at random to a farmer near him, who looked at him astonished by the heat of his accent. And then, seeing that Nelly's husband was in possible earshot, Vincent raised his voice recklessly. 'They're the handsomest couple in the room,' he repeated resentfully. 'They ought always to dance together.'

If 'Gene heard, he did not show it, the granite impassivity of his harsh face unmoved.

Vincent went on towards the door, his nerves a little relieved by this outburst. He would go out and have another cigarette, he thought, and then take his old man-child home to bed. What were they doing in this absurd place?

The music began to skirl again as he stepped out and closed the door behind him.

He drew in deeply the fresh night-air, and looking upward saw that the clouds had broken away and that the stars were out, innumerable, thick-sown, studding with gold the narrow roof of sky which, rising from the mountains on either side, arched itself over the valley. He stood staring before him, frowning, forgetting what he had come out to do. He told himself that coming from that yelling confusion inside, and the glare of those garish lamps, he was stupefied by the great silence of the night. There was nothing clear in his mind, only a turmoil of eddying sensations which he could not name. He walked down to the huge dark pine, the pine which 'Gene Powers loved like a person, and which his wife wished were cut down. What a ghastly prison marriage was, he thought, a thing as hostile to the free human spirit as an iron ball-and-chain.

He looked back at the little house, tiny as an insect before the great bulk of the mountains, dwarfed by the gigantic tree, ridiculous, despicable in the face of Nature, like the human life it sheltered. From its every window poured a flood of yellow light that was drunk up in a twinkling by the vastness of the night's obscurity.

He leaned against the straight, sternly unyielding bole of the tree, folding his arms and staring at the house. What a beastly joke the whole business of living!

A thousand ugly recollections poured their venom upon him from his past life. Life, this little moment of blind, sensual groping and grabbing for something worth while that did not exist, save in the stultification of the intelligence. All that you reached for, so frantically, it was only another handful of mud, when you held it.

Past the yellow squares of the windows, he saw the shapes of the dancers, insect-tiny, footing it to and fro. And in one of those silhouettes he recognized Marise Crittenden.

He turned away from the sight and struck his fist against the rough bark of the tree. What an insane waste and confusion ruled everywhere in human life! A woman like that to be squandered . . . an intelligence fine and supple, a talent penetrating and rare like hers for music, a strange personal beauty like that of no other woman, a depth one felt like mid-ocean, a capacity for fun like a child's and a vitality of personality, a power for passion that pulsed from her so that to touch her hand casually set one thrilling . . .! And good God! What was destiny doing with her? Spending that gold like water on three brats incapable of distinguishing between her and any good-natured woman who would put on their shoes and wash their faces for them. Any paid Irish nurse could do for them what their mother bent the priceless treasure of her temperament to accomplish. The Irish nurse would do it better, for she would not be aware of anything else better, which she might do, and their mother knew well enough what she sacrificed . . . or if she did not know it yet, she would, soon. She had betrayed that to him, the very first time he had seen her, that astonishing first day, when, breathing out her vivid charm like an aureole of gold mist, she had sat there before him, quite simply the woman most to his taste he had even seen . . . *here*! That day when she had spoken about the queerness of her feeling 'lost' when little Mark went off to school, because for the first time in years she had had an hour or so free from those ruthless little leeches who spent their lives in draining her vitality. He had known, if she had not, the significance of that feeling of hers, the first time she had had a moment to raise her eyes from her trivial task and see that she had been tricked into a prison. That very day he had wanted to cry out to her, as impersonally as one feels towards a beautiful bird caught in a net, 'Now, *now*, burst through, and spread your wings where you belong.'

It was like wiping up the floor with cloth of gold. In order that those three perfectly commonplace, valueless human lives might be added to the world's wretched population, a nature as rare as a jewel was being slowly ground away. What were the treasures to whom she was being sacrificed? Paul, the greasy, well-intentioned, priggish burgher he would make; Elly, almost half-witted, a child who stared at you like an imbecile when asked a question, and who evidently scarcely knew that her mother existed, save as cook and caretaker. And Mark, the passionate, gross, greedy baby. There were the three walls of the prison where she was shut away from any life worthy of her.

And the fourth wall . . .

The blackness dropped deeper about him, and within him. There they were dancing, those idiots, dancing on a volcano if ever human beings did, in the little sultry respite from the tornado which was called the world-peace. Well, that was less idiotic than working, at least. How soon before it would break again, the final destructive hurricane, born of nothing but the malignant folly of human hearts, and sweep away all that they now agonized and sweated to keep? What silly weakness to spend the respite in anything but getting as much of what you wanted as you could, before it was all gone in the big final smash-up, and the yellow or black man were on top.

With a bitter relish he felt sunk deep in one of his rank re-actions against life and human beings. Now at least he was on bed-rock. There was a certain hard, quiet restfulness in scorn-ing it all so whole-heartedly as either stupid or base.

At this a woman's face hung suddenly there in the blackness. Her long eyes seemed to look directly into his, a full revealing look such as they had never given him in reality. His hard quiet was broken by an agitation he could not control. No, no, there was something there that was not mud. He had thought he would live and die without meeting it. And there it was, giving to paltry life a meaning, after all, a troubling and im-mortal meaning.

A frosty breath blew down upon him from the mountains. A long shudder ran through him.

The sensation moved him to a sweeping change of mood, to a furious resentment as at an indignity. God! What was he doing? Who was this moping in the dark like a boy?

The great night stood huge and breathless above him as before, but now he saw only the lamp-lit house, tiny as an insect, but vibrant with eager and joyous life. With a strong, resolute step he went rapidly back to the door, opened it wide, stepped in, and walked across the floor to Marise Crittenden. 'You're going to dance the next dance with *me*, you know,' he told her.

Chapter 10: *At the Mill*

§ 1

An Afternoon in the Life of Mr. Neale Crittenden, aet. 38

May 27.

THE stenographer, a pale, thin boy, with a scarred face and very white hands, limped over to the manager's desk with a pile of letters to be signed. 'There, Captain Crittenden,' he said, pride in his accent.

Neale was surprised and pleased. 'All done, Arthur?' He looked over the work hastily. 'Good work, good work.' He leaned back, looking up at the other. 'How about it, anyhow, Arthur? Is it going to work out all right?'

The stenographer looked at him hard and swallowed visibly. 'I never dreamed I'd be fit to do anything I like half so well. I thought when I was in the hospital that I was done for, for sure. Captain Crittenden, if you only knew what my mother and I think about what you've done for . . .'

Neale dodged hastily. 'That's all right. That's all right. If you like it, that's all that's necessary. And I'm not Captain any more.'

'I forget, sir,' said the other apologetically.

'Can you sit down and take a second batch right now? I want to get through early. Mrs. Crittenden's going to bring some visitors to see the place this afternoon, and I'll have to be with them more or less.'

He looked at the clock. It was half-past three. Marise had said she would be there about four. He gave a calculating glance at the stack of letters. He would never be able to get through those. 'We'll have to get a move on,' he remarked. 'Things got pretty well piled up while I was away.'

He began to dictate rapidly, steadily, the end of a sentence clearly in his mind before he pronounced the first word. He liked to dictate and enjoyed doing it well. The pale young stenographer bent over his note-book, his disfigured face intent and serious.

'Turned out all right, Arthur has,' thought Neale to himself. 'I wasn't so far off, when I thought of the business college for him.' Then he applied himself single-mindedly to his dictation, taking up one letter after another, with hardly a pause in his voice. But for all his diligence, he had not come to the bottom of the pile when four o'clock struck; nor ten minutes later when, glancing out of the window, he saw Marise and the children with Mr. Bayweather and the two other men coming across the mill-yard. Evidently Mr. Bayweather had dropped in just as they were going to start and had come along. He stopped dictating and looked at the group with a certain interest. Marise and the children had had a good deal to say yesterday about the new-comers to Crittenden's.

It seemed to him that the impression he had received of them had been as inaccurate as such second-hand impressions were apt to be. The older man was just like any elderly business man, for all he could see, nothing so especially attractive about him, although Marise had said in her ardent way that he was 'the sort of old American you love on sight, the kind that makes you home-sick when you meet him in Europe.' And as for Mr. Marsh, he couldn't see any signs of his being such a record-breaking live-wire as they had all said. He walked along quietly enough, and was evidently as resigned as any of them to letting Mr. Bayweather do all the talking. On the other hand, none of them had told him what a striking-looking fellow he was, so tall, and with such a bold carriage of that round dark head.

'Here they come, Arthur,' he remarked. 'No more time. But I'll try to squeeze in a minute or two, while they are here, to finish up these last ones.'

The young man followed the direction of his eyes and nodded. He continued looking at the advancing group for a moment, and as he stood up, 'You could tell that Mr. Marsh is a millionaire by the way his clothes fit, couldn't you?' he remarked, turning to go back to his desk in the outer office.

They were coming down the hall now. Neale went forward to open the door, met and breasted the wave of children who after hugging casually at his knees and arms swept by; and stepped forward to be presented to the new-comers. They had not crossed the threshold, before his first impression was reversed in one case. Marsh was a live-wire all right. Now that

122

he had seen his eyes, he knew what Elly had meant when she said that when he looked at you it was like lightning.

Mr. Bayweather barely waited for the first greetings to be pronounced before he burst out, 'Do they say, "backwards and forwards" or "back and forth"?'

Neale laughed. Old Bayweather was perennial. 'Backwards and forwards, of course,' he said. 'English people always say everything the longest possible way.' He explained to the others, 'Mr. Bayweather is an impassioned philologist . . .'

'So I have gathered,' commented Marsh.

'. . . and whenever any friends of his go on travels, they are always asked to bring back some philological information about the region where they go.'

He turned to Marise (how sweet she looked in that thin yellow dress). 'Where do you want your personally conducted to begin, dear?' he asked her. (Lord! How good it seemed to get back to Marise!)

Mr. Bayweather cut in hastily, 'If I may be permitted to suggest, I think a history of the mill would be advisable as a beginning. I will be glad to tell the new-comers about this. I've just been working the subject up for a chapter in my history of Ashley.'

Neale caught an anguished side-glance from Marise and sent back to her a shrugged message of helplessness in the face of Destiny. The man didn't live who could head old Bayweather off when he got started on local history. And besides, this would give him time to get those last three letters finished. Aloud he said, 'I wouldn't dare say a word about history in Mr. Bayweather's presence. I have a few letters to finish. I'll just step into the outer office and be ready to start when you've heard the history lecture.' He turned to the children, who were tapping on the typewriter. 'Look here, kids, you'd be better off where you won't break anything. Get along with you out into the mill-yard and play on the lumber-piles, why don't you? Paul, you see if you can tell yellow birch from oak this time!'

He and the children beat a retreat together into the outer office, where he bent over Arthur's desk and began to dictate in a low voice, catching, as he did so, an occasional rotund phrase from the disquisition in the other room. '. . . the glorious spirit of manly independence of the Green Mountain Boys . . .'

To himself Neale thought, 'He'd call it bolshevism if he met it to-day. . . .'

'. . . second building erected in the new settlement, 1766, as a fort. . . . No, *no*, Mr. Marsh, *not* against the Indians! Our early settlers *here* never had any trouble with the Indians.'

Neale laughed to himself at the clergyman's resentment of any ignorance of any detail of Ashley's unimportant history.

'. . . as a fort against the York State men in the land-grant quarrels with New Hampshire and New York, before the Revolution.' Neale, smiling inwardly, bet himself a nickel that neither of the two strangers had ever heard of the Vermont land-grant quarrels, and found himself vastly tickled by the profound silence they kept on the subject. They were evidently scared to death of starting old Bayweather off on another line. They were safe enough, if they only knew it. It was inconceivable to Mr. Bayweather that any grown person should not know all about early Vermont history.

At this point Marise came out of the office, her face between laughter and exasperation. She clasped her hands together and said, 'Can't you do *any*thing?'

'In a minute,' he told her. 'I'll just finish these two letters and then I'll go and break him off short.'

Marise went on to the accountant's desk, to ask about his wife, who sang in her winter chorus.

He dictated rapidly: 'No more contracts will go out to you if this stripping of the mountain-land continues. Our original contract has in it the clause which I always insist on, that trees smaller than six inches through the butt shall not be cut. You will please give your choppers definite orders on this point, and understand that logs under the specified size will not be accepted at the mill.' He held out to the stenographer the letter he was answering. 'Here, Arthur, copy the name and address off this. It's one of those French-Canadian names, hard to spell if you don't see it.'

He paused an instant to hear how far Mr. Bayweather had progressed, and heard him saying, 'In the decade from 1850 on, there was a terrible and scandalous devastation of the mountain-land . . .' and said to himself, 'Half-way through the century. I'll have time to go on a while. All ready, Arthur.' He dictated: 'On birch brush-backs of the model specified, we can furnish you any number up to . . .' He wound his way swiftly and surely through a maze of figures and specifications without consulting a paper or record, and drawing breath at the end, heard Mr. Bayweather pronouncing his own name. '. . . Mr. Crittenden has taught us all a great deal about the economic aspects of a situation with which we had had years of more familiarity than he. His idea is that this mountainous part of New England is really not fit for agriculture. Farming in the usual sense has been a losing venture ever since the Civil War high prices for wool ceased. Only the bottoms of the valleys are fit for crops. Most of our county is essentially forest-land. And his idea of the proper use to make of it, is to have a smallish industrial population engaged in wood-working, who would use the bits of arable land in the valleys as gardens to raise their own food. He has almost entirely reorganized the life of our valley, along these lines, and I dare say he cannot at all realize himself the prodigious change from hopelessness and slow death to energy and forward-looking activity which his intelligent grasp of the situation has brought to this corner of the earth.'

The young stenographer had heard this too, and had caught the frown of annoyance which the personal reference brought to Neale's forehead. He leaned forward and said earnestly, 'It's so, Captain . . . Mr. Crittenden. It's so!'

Mr. Bayweather went on, 'There is enough wood in the forests within reach of the mill to keep a moderate-sized wood-working factory going indefinitely, cutting by rotation and taking care to leave enough trees for natural reforestation. But of course that has not been the American way of going at things. Instead of that steady, continuous use of the woods, which Mr. Crittenden has shown to be possible, furnishing good, well-paid work at home for the men who would be otherwise forced off into cities, our poor mountains have been lumbered every generation or so, on an immense, murderous, slashing scale, to make a big sum of money for somebody in one operation. When old Mr. Burton Crittenden's nephew came to town it was a different story. Mr. Neale Crittenden's ideal of the lumber business is, as I conceive it, as much a service to mankind as a doctor's is.'

Neale winced, and shook his head impatiently. How ministers did put the Sunday-school rubber-stamp on everything they talked about – even legitimate business.

'And as Mrs. Crittenden's free-handed generosity with her musical talent has transformed the life of the region as much as Mr. Crittenden's high and disinterested . . .'

'Oh *gosh*, Arthur, never mind about the rest!' murmured
125

Neale, moving back quickly into the inner office to create a diversion. 'All ready?' he asked in a loud, hearty voice, as he came up to them. 'Up to 1920 by this time, Mr. Bayweather?' He turned to Marsh, 'I'm afraid there is very little to interest you, with your experience of production on a giant scale, in a business so small that the owner and manager knows every man by name and everything about him.'

'You couldn't show me anything more *out* of my own experience,' answered Marsh, 'than just that. And as for what I know about production on a giant scale, I can tell you it's not much. I did try to hook on, once or twice, years ago – to find out something about the business that my father spent his life in helping to build up, but it always ended in my being shooed out of the office by a rather irritable manager who knew I knew nothing about any of it, and who evidently hated above everything else having amateur directors come horning in on what was no party of theirs. "If they get their dividends all right, what more do they want?" was his motto. I never was able to make any sense out of it. It's all on such a preposterously big scale now. Once in a while, touring, I have come across one of our branch establishments and have stopped my car to see the men come out of the buildings at quitting-time. That's as close as I have ever come. Do you really know their *names*?'

'I can't pronounce all the French-Canadian names to suit them, but I know them all, yes. Most of them are just the overflow of the rural population around here.'

He said to himself in congratulation, 'Between us, we pried old Bayweather loose from his soft soap, pretty neatly,' and gave the man before him a look of friendly understanding. He was a little startled, for an instant, by the expression in the other's bright eyes, which he found fixed on him with an intentness almost disconcerting. 'Does he think I'm trying to put something over on him?' he asked himself with a passing astonishment, 'or is he trying to put something over on me?' Then he remembered that everyone had spoken of Marsh's eyes as peculiar; it was probably just his habit. 'He can look right through me and out at the other side, for all *I* care!' he thought indifferently, meeting the other's gaze with a faintly humorous sense of something absurd.

Marise had come back now, and was saying, 'You really must get started, Neale, the men will be quitting work soon.'

'Yes, yes, this minute,' he told her, and led the way with Mr.

Welles, leaving Marise and Mr. Bayweather to be showman for Mr. Marsh. He now remembered that he had not heard the older man say a single word as yet, and surmised that he probably never said much when the fluent Mr. Marsh was with him. He wondered a little, as they made their way to the saw-mill, what Marise saw in either of them to interest her so much. Oh well, they were a change, of course, from Ashley and Crittenden's people, and different from the Eugenia Mills bunch, in New York, too.

He stood now, beside Mr. Welles, in the saw-mill, the ringing high crescendo scream of the saws filling the air. Marise stood at the other end talking animatedly to the two she had with her. Marise was a wonder on conversation anyhow. What could she find to say, now, for instance? What in the world was there to say to an ex-office manager of a big electrical company about a wood-working business?

His eyes were caught by what one of the men was doing and he yelled at him sharply, 'Look out there, Harry! Stop that! What do I have a guard-rail there for, anyhow?'

'What was the matter?' asked Mr. Welles, startled.

'Oh, nothing much. One of the men dodging under a safety-device to save him a couple of steps. They get so reckless about those saws. You have to look out for them like a bunch of bad children.'

Mr. Welles looked at him earnestly. 'Are you . . . have you . . . . Mr. Bayweather has told us so much about all you do for the men . . . how they are all devoted to you.'

Neale looked and felt annoyed. Bayweather and his palaver! 'I don't do anything for them, except give them as good wages as the business will stand, and as much responsibility for running things as they'll take. Beyond that, I let them alone. I don't believe in what's known as "welfare work." I wouldn't want them messing around in my private life, and I don't believe they'd like me in theirs.'

The necessity to raise his voice to a shout in order to make himself heard above the tearing scream of the saws made him sound very abrupt and peremptory, more so than he had meant. As he finished speaking his eyes met those of the older man, and were held by the clarity and candour of the other's gaze. They were like a child's eyes in that old face. It was as though he had been abrupt and impatient to Elly or Mark.

As he looked he saw more than candour and clarity. He saw a deep weariness.

127

Neale smoothed his forehead, a little ashamed of his petulance, and drew his companion further from the saws where the noise was less. He meant to say something apologetic, but the right phrase did not come to him. And as Mr. Welles said nothing further, they walked on in silence. They passed through the first and second floors of the mill, where the handling of the smaller pieces was done, and neither of them spoke a word. Neale looked about him at the familiar, familiar scene, and found it too dull to make any comment on. What was there to say? This was the way you manufactured brush-backs and wooden boxes and such-like things, and that was all. The older men bent over their lathes quietly, the occasional woman-worker smartly hammering small nails into the holes already bored for her, the big husky boys shoved the trucks around, the elevator droned up and down, the belts flicked as they sped around and around. Blest if he could think of any explanation to make to a grown man on so simple and everyday a scene. And yet he did not enjoy this silence because it seemed like a continuation of his grumpiness of a few minutes ago. Well, the next time the old fellow said anything, he'd fall over himself to be nice in his answer.

Presently as they came to the outside door, Mr. Welles remarked with a gentle dignity, in evident allusion to Neale's cutting him short, 'I only meant that I was very much interested in what I see here, and that I would like very much to know more about it.'

Neale felt he fairly owed him an apology. He began to understand what Marise meant when she had said the old fellow was one you loved on sight. It was her way, emotionally heightened as usual, of saying that he was really a very nice old codger. 'I'll be glad to tell you anything you want to know, Mr. Welles,' he said. 'But I haven't any idea what it is that interests you. You fire ahead and ask questions and I'll agree to answer them.'

'That's what I'd like, all right. And remember, if I ask anything you don't want to talk about . . .' He referred evidently to Neale's impatience of a few minutes ago.

'There aren't any trade secrets in the wood-working business,' said Neale, laughing. 'Better come along and see our drying-room as we talk. We've had to make some concession to modern haste and use kiln-drying, although I season first in the old way as long as possible.' They stepped out of the door and started across the mill-yard.

Mr. Welles said with a very faint smile in the corner of his pale old lips, 'I don't believe you want to show me any of this, Mr. Crittenden. And honestly, that isn't what interests me about it. I wouldn't know a drying-room from a steam-laundry.'

Neale stopped short, and surveyed his companion with amusement and admiration. 'Good for you!' he cried. 'Tell the truth and shame the devil and set an example to all honest men. Mr. Welles, you have my esteem.'

The old man had a shy smile at this. 'I don't tell the truth that way to everybody,' he said demurely.

Neale liked him more and more. 'Sir, I am yours to command,' he said, sitting down on the steps, 'ask ahead!'

Mr. Welles turned serious, and hesitated. 'Mr. Bayweather said . . .' he began and looked anxiously at Neale.

'I won't bite even if he did,' Neale reassured him.

Mr. Welles looked at him with the pleasantest expression in his eyes. 'It's a great relief to find that we can get on with one another,' he said, 'for I must admit to you that I have fallen a complete victim to Mrs. Crittenden. I . . . I love your wife.' He brought it out with a quaint, humorous roundness.

'You can't get up any discussion with me about that,' said Neale. 'I do myself.'

They both laughed, and Mr. Welles said, 'But you see, caring such a lot about her, it was a matter of great importance to me what kind of husband she had. I find actually seeing you very exciting.'

'You're the first who ever found it so, I'm sure,' said Neale, amused at the idea.

'But it wasn't this I wanted to say,' said Mr. Welles. He went back and said again, 'Mr. Bayweather said your idea of business is service, like a doctor's?'

Neale winced at the Bayweather priggishness of this way of putting it, but remembering his remorse for his earlier brusqueness, he restrained himself to good humour and the admission, 'Making allowance for ministerial jargon, that's something like a fair statement.'

He was astonished at the seriousness with which Mr. Welles took this. What was it to him? The old man looked at him, deeply, unaccountably, evidently entirely at a loss. 'Mr. Crittenden,' he said abruptly, 'to speak right out, that sounded to me like the notion of a nice idealistic woman, who has never been in business. You see, I've *been* in a business office all my life!'

Neale found his liking for the gentle, troubled old man enough for him to say truthfully, 'Mr. Welles, I don't mind talking to you about it. Sure, yes I can understand how having a minister put it that way . . . Lord! How the old boy does spill over! And yet, why should I care? I'm ashamed of letting harmless Mr. Bayweather get on my nerves so.'

Mr. Welles started to speak, found no words, and waved an arm as if to imply that *he* understood perfectly. This made Neale laugh a little, and gave him a picture of the helplessness of a newcomer to Ashley, before the flood-tide of Mr. Bayweather's local learning.

He went on, 'He sort of taints an honest idea, doesn't he, by his high-falutin' way of going on about it?'

He hesitated, trying to think of simple words to sum up what he had, after all, never exactly formulated because it had been so much an attitude he and Marise had silently grown into. It was hard, he found, to hit on any expression that said what he wanted to; but after all, it wasn't so very important whether he did or not. He was only trying to make a nice tired old man think himself enough respected to be seriously talked to. He'd just ramble on, till Marise brought the other visitors up to them.

And yet as he talked, he got rather interested in his statement of it. A comparison of baseball and tennis ethics came into his mind as apposite, and quite tickled him by its aptness. Mr. Welles threw in an occasional remark. He was no man's fool, it soon appeared, for all his mildness. And for a time he seemed to be interested.

But presently Neale noticed that the other was looking absent and no longer made any comments. That was what happened, Neale reflected with an inward smile, as he slowed down and prepared to stop, when anybody succeeded in getting you started on your hobby. They were bored. They didn't really want to know after all. It was like trying to tell folks about your travels.

But he was astonished to the limit of astonishment by what Mr. Welles brought out in the silence which finally dropped between them. The old man looked at him very hard and asked, 'Mr. Crittenden, do you know anything about the treatment of the Negroes in the South?'

Neale sat up blinking. 'Why no, nothing special, except that it's a fearful knot we don't seem to get untied,' he said. 'I contribute to the support of an agricultural school in Georgia, but I'm afraid I never take much time to read the reports they send me. Why do you ask?'

'Oh, no particular reason. I have a relative down there, that's all.'

Marise and the others came out of a door at the far end of the building now, and advanced towards them slowly. Neale and Mr. Welles watched them.

Neale was struck again by Marsh's appearance. As far away as you could see him, he held the eye. 'An unusual man, your friend Mr. Marsh,' he remarked. 'Mrs. Crittenden tells me that he is one of the people who have been everywhere and done everything and seen everybody. He looks the part.'

Mr. Welles made no comment on this for a moment, his eyes on the advancing group. Marise had raised her parasol of yellow silk. It made a shimmering halo for her dark, gleaming hair, as she turned her head towards Marsh, her eyes narrowed and shining as she laughed at something he said.

Then the old man remarked, 'Yes, he's unusual, all right, Vincent is. He has his father's energy and push.' He added in a final characterization, 'I've known him ever since he was a little boy, and I never knew him not to get what he went after.'

§ 2

How the Same Thing Looked to Mr. Welles

As they walked along towards the mill, Mr. Welles had a distinct impression that he was going to dislike the mill-owner, and as distinct a certainty as to where that impression came from. He had received too many by the same route not to recognize the shipping label. Not that Vincent had ever said a single slighting word about Mr. Crittenden. He couldn't have, very well, since they neither of them had ever laid eyes on him. But Vincent never needed words to convey impressions into other people's minds. He had a thousand other ways better than words. Vincent could be silent, knock off the ashes from his cigarette, recross his legs, and lean back in his chair in a manner that slammed an impression into your head as though he had yelled it at you.

But to be fair to Vincent, Mr. Welles thought probably he had been more than ready to soak up an impression like the one he felt. They'd had such an awfully good time with Mrs. Crittenden and the children, it stood to reason the head of the house would seem to them like a butter-in and an outsider in a happy family group.

More than this, too. As they came within hearing of the industrial activity of the mill, and he felt his heart sink and turn sore and bitter, Mr. Welles realized that Vincent had very little to do with his dread of meeting the mill-owner. It was not Mr. Crittenden he shrank from, it was the mill-owner, the business man . . . business itself.

Mr. Welles hated and feared the sound of the word and knew that it had him cowed, because in his long life he had known it to be the only reality in the world of men. And in that world he had known the only reality to be that if you didn't cut the other fellow's throat first he would cut yours. There wasn't any other reality. He had heard impractical, womanish men say there was, and try to prove it, only to have their economic throats cut considerably more promptly than any others. He had done his little indirect share of the throat-cutting always. He was not denying the need to do it. Only he had never found it a very cheerful atmosphere in which to pass one's life. And now he had escaped, to the only other reality, the pleasant, gentle, slightly unreal world of women, nice women, and children and gardens. He was so old now that there was no shame in his sinking into that for what time he had left, as other old fellows sank into an easy chair. Only he wished that he could have got along without being reminded so vividly, as he would be by this trip to the business-world, of what paid for the arm-chair, supported the nice women and children. He wished he hadn't had to come here, to be forced to remember again that the inevitable foundation for all that was pleasant and liveable in private life was the grim determination on the part of a strong man to give his strength to 'taking it out of the hide' of his competitors, his workmen, and the public. He'd had a vacation from that, and it made him appallingly depressed to take another dose of it now. He sincerely wished that sweet Mrs. Crittenden were a widow with a small income from some impersonal source with no uncomfortable human associations with it. He recalled with a sad cynicism the story Mrs. Crittenden had told them about the clever and forceful lawyer who had played the dirty trick on the farmer here in Ashley, and done him out of his wood-land. She had been very much wrought up about that, the poor lady, without having the least idea that probably her husband's business life was full of such knifings-in-the-back, all with the purpose of making a quiet life for her and the children.

Well, there was nothing for it but to go on. It wouldn't last long, and Mr. Welles' back was practised in bowing to weather he didn't like but which passed if you waited a while.

They were going up the hall now, towards a door marked 'Office,' the children scampering ahead. The door was opening. The tall man who stood there, nodding a welcome to them, must be Mr. Crittenden.

So that was the kind of man he was. Nothing special about him. Just a nice-looking American business man, with a quiet, calm manner and a friendly face.

To the conversation which followed and which, like all such conversations, amounted to nothing at all, Mr. Welles made no contribution. What was the use? Mr. Bayweather and Vincent were there. The conversation would not flag. So he had the usual good chance of the silent person to use his eyes. He looked mostly at Mr. Crittenden. Well, he wasn't so bad. They were usually nice enough men in personal relations, business men. This one had good eyes, very nice when he looked at the children or his wife. They were often good family men, too. There was something about him, however, that wasn't just like all others. What was it? Not clothes. His suit was cut off the same piece with forty million other American business-suits. Not looks, although there was an outdoor ruddiness of skin and clearness of eye that made him look a little like a sailor. Oh yes, Mr. Welles had it. It was his voice. Whenever he spoke, there was something . . . something *natural* about his voice, as though it didn't ever say things he didn't mean.

Well, for Heaven's sake here was the old minister started off again on one of his historical spiels. Mr. Welles glanced cautiously at Vincent to see if he were in danger of blowing up, and found him looking unexpectedly thoughtful. He was evidently not paying the least attention to Mr. Bayweather's account of the eighteenth-century quarrel between New Hampshire and Vermont. He was apparently thinking of something else, very hard.

He himself leaned back in his chair, but half of one absent

ear given to Mr. Bayweather's lecture, and enjoyed himself looking at Mrs. Crittenden. She was pretty, Mrs. Crittenden was. He hadn't been sure the first day, but now he had had a chance to get used to her face being so long and sort of pointed, and her eyes long too, and her black eyebrows running back almost into her hair: he liked every bit of her face. It looked so different from anybody else's. He noticed with an inward smile that she was fidgety under Mr. Bayweather's historical talk. *He* was the only person with any patience in that whole bunch. But at what a price had he acquired it!

By and by Mrs. Crittenden got up quietly and went out into the other office as if on an errand.

Mr. Bayweather took advantage of her absence to tell them a lot about how much the Crittendens had done for the whole region and what a golden thing Mrs. Crittenden's music had been for everybody, and about an original conception of business which Mr. Crittenden seemed to have. Mr. Welles was not interested in music, but he was in business and he would have liked to hear a great deal more about this, but just at this point, as if to cut the clergyman off, in came Mr. Crittenden, very brisk and prompt, ready to take them around the mill.

Vincent stood up. They all stood up. Mr. Welles noted that Vincent had quite come out of his brown study and was now all there. He was as he usually was, a wire charged with a very high-voltage current.

They went out now, all of them together, but soon broke up into two groups. He stayed behind with Mr. Crittenden and pretended to look at the machinery of the saw-mill, which he found very boring indeed, as he hadn't the slightest comprehension of a single cog in it. But there was something there at which he really looked. It was the expression of Mr. Crittenden's face as he walked about, and it was the expression on the faces of the men as they looked at the boss.

Mr. Welles, not being a talker, had had a great deal of opportunity to study the faces of others, and he had become rather a specialist in expressions. Part of his usefulness in the office had come from that. He had catalogued in his mind the different looks on human faces, and most of them connected with any form of business organization were infinitely familiar to him, from the way the casual itinerant temporary labourer looked at the boss of his gang, to the way the star salesman looked at the head of the house.

But here was a new variety to him, these frank and familiar glances thrown in answer to the nodded greeting or short sentence of the boss as he walked about. They were not so much friendly (although they were that too), as they were familiar and open, as though nothing lay hidden behind the apparent expression. It was not often that Mr. Welles had encountered that, a look that seemed to hide nothing.

He wondered if he could find out anything about this from Mr. Crittenden and put a question to him about his relations with his men. He tried to make it tactful and sensible-sounding, but as he said the words, he knew just how flat and parlour-reformerish they sounded; and it didn't surprise him a bit to have the business man bristle up and snap his head off. It had sounded as though he didn't know a thing about business – he, the very marrow of whose bones was soaked in a bitter knowledge that the only thing that could keep it going was the fear of death in every man's heart, lest the others get ahead of him and trample him down.

He decided that he wouldn't say another thing, just endure the temporary boredom of being trotted about to have things explained to him, which he hadn't any intention of trying to understand.

But Mr. Crittenden did not try to explain. Perhaps he was bored himself, perhaps he guessed the visitor's ignorance. He just walked around from one part of the big, sunshiny shops to another, taking advantage of this opportunity to look things over for his own purposes. And everywhere he went, he gave and received back that curious, new look of openness.

It was not noisy here as in the saw-mill, but very quiet and peaceful, the bee-like whirring of the belts on the pulleys the loudest continuous sound. It was clean, too. The hardwood floor was being swept clean of sawdust and shavings all the time, by a lame old man, who pottered tranquilly about, sweeping and cleaning and putting the trash in a big box on a truck. When he had it full, he beckoned to a burly lad, shoving a truck across the room, and called in a clear, natural, friendly voice, 'Hey, Nat, come on over.' The big lad came, whistling, pushed the box off full, and brought it back empty, still whistling airily.

There were a good many work-people in sight. Mr. Welles made a guessing estimate that the business must keep about two hundred busy. And there was not one who looked harried by his work. The big, cluttered place heaped high with piles of curiously shaped pieces of wood, filled with oddly contrived saws and lathes and knives and buffers for sawing and turning and polishing and fitting those bits of wood, was brooded over as by something palpable by an emanation of order. Mr. Welles did not understand a detail of what he was looking at, but from the whole, his mind, experienced in business, took in a singularly fresh impression that everybody there knew what he was up to, in every sense of the word.

He and Mr. Crittenden stood for a time looking at and chatting to a grey-haired man who was polishing smoothly planed oval bits of board. He stopped as they talked, ran his fingers over the satin-smooth surface with evident pleasure, and remarked to his employer, 'Mighty fine maple we're getting from the Warner lot. See the grain in that!'

He held it up admiringly, turning it so that the light would show it at its best, and looked at it respectfully. 'There's no wood like maple,' he said. Mr. Crittenden answered, 'Yep. The Warner land is just right for slow-growing trees.' He took it out of the workman's hand, looked it over more closely with an evident intelligent certainty of what to look for, and handed it back with a nod that signified his appreciation of the wood and of the workmanship which had brought it to that state.

There had been about that tiny, casual human contact a quality which Mr. Welles did not recognize. His curiosity rose again. He wondered if he might not succeed in getting some explanation out of the manufacturer, if he went about it very tactfully. He would wait for his chance. He began to perceive with some surprise that he was on the point of quite liking Mrs. Crittenden's husband.

So he tried another question, after a while, very cautiously, and was surprised to find Mr. Crittenden no longer snappish, but quite friendly. It occurred to him as the pleasantest possibility that he might find his liking for the other man returned. That *would* be a new present hung on the Christmas tree of his life in Vermont.

On the strength of this possibility, and banking on the friendliness in the other man's eyes, he drove straight at it, the phrase which the minister had used when he said that Mr. Crittenden thought of business as an ideal service to humanity as much as doctoring. That had sounded so ignorant and ministerial he hadn't even thought of it seriously, till after this contact with

the man of whom it had been said. The best way with Crittenden was evidently the direct one. He had seen that in the first
five minutes of observation of him. So he would simply tell
him how bookish and impossible it had sounded, and see what
he had to say. He'd probably laugh and say the minister had
it all wrong, of course, regular minister's idea.

And so presently they were off, on a real talk, beyond what
he had hoped for, and Crittenden was telling him really what
he had meant. He was saying in his firm, natural, easy voice,
as though he saw nothing specially to be self-conscious about
in it, 'Why, of course I don't rank lumbering and wood-working with medicine. Wood isn't as vital to human life as quinine,
or a knowledge of what to do in typhoid fever. But after all,
wood is something that people have to have, isn't it? Somebody has to get it out and work it up into usable shape. If he
can do this, get it out of the woods without spoiling the future
of the forests, drying up the rivers and all that, and have it
transformed into some finished product that people need in
their lives, it's a sort of plain, everyday service, isn't it? And to
do this work as economically as it can be managed, taking as
low a price as you can get along with instead of screwing as
high a price as possible out of the people who have to have it,
what's the matter with that, as an interesting problem in in-
genuity? I tell you, Mr. Welles, you ought to talk to my wife
about this. It's as much her idea as mine. We worked it out
together, little by little. It was when Elly was a baby. She was
the second child, you know, and we began to feel grown-up.
By that time I was pretty sure I could make a go of the business. And we first began to figure out what we were up to.
Tried to see what sort of a go we wanted the business to have.
We first began to make some sense out of what we were doing
in life.'

Mr. Welles found himself overwhelmed by a reminiscent ache
at this phrase and burst out, his words tinged with the bitterness he tried to keep out of his mind, 'Isn't that an awful moment when you first try to make some sense out of what you are
doing in life! But suppose you had gone on doing it, always,
always, till you were an old man, and *never* succeeded! Suppose all you seemed to be accomplishing was to be able to hand
over to the sons of the directors more money than was good for
them? I tell you, Mr. Crittenden, I've often wished that once,
just once, before I died I could be *sure* that I had done anything that was of any use to anybody.' He went on, nodding

his head, 'What struck me so about what Mr. Bayweather said is that I've often thought about doctors myself, and envied them. They take money for what they do, of course, but they miss lots of chances to make more, just so's to be of some use. I've often thought when they were running the prices up and up in our office just because they could, that a doctor would be put out of his profession in no time by public opinion, if he ever tried to screw the last cent out of everybody, the way business men do as a matter of course.'

Mr. Crittenden protested meditatively against this. 'Oh, don't you think maybe there's a drift the other way among decent business people now? Why, when Marise and I were first trying to get it clear in our own heads, we kept it pretty dark, I tell you, that we weren't in it only for what money we could make, because we knew how loony we'd seem to anybody else. But don't you see any signs that lately maybe the same idea is striking lots of people in America?'

'No, I do *not*!' said Mr. Welles emphatically. 'With a profiteer on every corner!'

'But look-y-here, the howl about profiteers, isn't that something new? Isn't that a dumb sort of application to business of the doctor's standard of service? Twenty years ago, would anybody have thought of doing anything but uneasily admiring a grocer who made all the money he could out of his business? "Why shouldn't he?" people would have thought then. Everybody else did. Twenty years ago, would anybody have dreamed of legally preventing a rich man from buying all the coal he wanted, whether there was enough for everybody, or not?'

Mr. Welles considered this in unconvinced silence. Mr. Crittenden went on, 'Why, sometimes it looks to me like the difference between what's legitimate in baseball and in tennis. Every ball-player will try to bluff the umpire that he's safe when he knows the baseman tagged him three feet from the bag; and public opinion upholds him in his bluff if he can get away with it. But like as not, the very same man who lies like a trooper on the diamond, if he went off that very afternoon to play tennis would never dream of announcing "out" if his opponent's ball really had landed in the court – not if it cost him the set and match – whether anybody was looking at him or not. It's "the thing" to try to get anything you can put over in baseball, anything the umpire can't catch you at. And it's not "the thing" in tennis. Most of the time you don't even have any umpire. That's it: that's not such a bad way to put it. My wife and I wanted to run our business on the tennis standard and not on the baseball one. Because I believe, ultimately you know, in fixing things – everything – national life as well, so that we'll need as few umpires as possible. Once get the tennis standard adopted . . .'

Mr. Welles said mournfully, 'Don't get started on politics. I'm too old to have any hopes of that!'

'Right you are there,' said Mr. Crittenden. 'Economic organization is the word. That's one thing that keeps me so interested in my little economic laboratory here. Political parties are as prehistoric as the mastodon, if they only knew it.'

Mr. Welles said, 'But the queer thing is that you make it work.'

'Oh, anybody with a head for business could make it work. You've got to know how to manage your machine before you can make it go, of course. But that's not saying you have to drive it somewhere you don't want to get to. I don't say that that workman back there who was making such a beautiful job of polishing that maple could make it go. He couldn't.'

Mr. Welles persisted. 'But I've always thought, I've always *seen* it, or thought I had . . . that life-and-death competition is the only stimulus that's strong enough to stir men up to the prodigious effort they have to put out to *make* a go of their business, start the machine running. That, and the certainty of all they could get out of the consumer as a reward. You know it's held that there's a sort of mystic identity between all you can get out of the consumer and the exact amount of profit that'll just make the business go.'

Mr. Crittenden said comfortably, as though he were talking of something that did not alarm him, 'Oh, well, the best of the feudal seigneurs mournfully believed that a sharp sword and a long lance in their own hands were the strongholds of society. The wolf-pack idea of business will go the same way.' He explained in answer to Mr. Welles' vagueness as to this term, 'You know, the conception that if you're going to get hair-brushes or rubber coats or mattresses or what-not enough for humanity manufactured, the only way is to have the group engaged in it form a wolf-pack, hunting down the public to extract from it as much money as possible. The salesmen and advertisers take care of this extracting. Then this money's to be fought for, by the people engaged in the process, as wolves fight over the carcass of the deer they have brought down together. This is the fight between the directors of labour and the working men. It's ridiculous to hold that such a wasteful and incoherent system is the only one that will arouse men's energies enough to get them into action. It's absurd to think that business men . . . they're the flower of the nation, they're America's specialty, you know . . . can only find their opportunity for service to their fellow-men by such haphazard contracts with public service as helping raise money for a library or heading a movement for better housing of the poor, when they don't know anything about the housing of the poor, nor what it ought to be. Their opportunity for public service is right in their own legitimate businesses, and don't you forget it. Everybody's business is his best way to public service, and doing it that way, you'd put out of operation the professional uplifters who uplift as a business, and can't help being priggish and self-conscious about it. It makes me tired the way professional idealists don't see their big chance. They'll take all the money they can get from business for hospitals, and laboratories, and to investigate the sleeping sickness or the boll-weevil, but that business itself could rank with public libraries and hospitals as an ideal element in the life on the globe . . . they can't open their minds wide enough to take in that.'

Mr. Welles had been following this with an almost painful interest and surprise. He found it very agitating, very upsetting. Suppose there had been something there, all the time. He must try to think it out more. Perhaps it was not true. But here sat a man who had made it work. Why hadn't he thought of it in time? Now it was too late. Too late for him to do anything. Anything? The voice of the man beside him grew dim to him, as, uneasy and uncertain, his spirits sank lower and lower. Suppose all the time there had been a way out besides beating the retreat to the women, the children, and the gardens? Only now it was too late! What was the use of thinking of it all?

For a moment he forgot where he was. It seemed to him that there was something waiting for him to think of it . . .

But oddly enough, all that presented itself to him, when he tried to look, was the story that had nothing to do with anything, which his cousin had told him in a recent letter, of the fiery sensitive young Negro doctor, who had worked his way through medical school, and hospital-training, gone South to practise, and how he had been treated by the white people in the town where he had settled. He wondered if she hadn't exaggerated all that. But she gave such definite details. Perhaps Mr. Crittenden knew something about that problem. Perhaps he had an idea about that, too, that might be of help. He would ask him.

PART II

Chapter 11: *In Aunt Hetty's Garden*

§ 1

June 10.

MARISE bent to kiss the soft withered cheek. 'Elly is a *real* Vermonter, but I'm not. She can get along with just "Hello, Aunt
Hetty," but that's not enough for me,' she said tenderly to the
old woman; 'I have to kiss you.'

'Oh, you can do as you like, for all of me,' answered the other
with an unsparing indifference.

Marise laughed at the quality of this, taking the shaky old
hand in hers with a certainty of affection returned. She went
on, 'This is a regular descent on you, Cousin Hetty. I've come
to show you off, you and the house and the garden. This is Mr.
Welles who has settled next door to us, you know, and this is
Mr. Marsh who is visiting him for a time. And here are the
children, and Eugenia Mills came up from the city last night
and will be here perhaps, if she gets up energy after her afternoon nap, and Neale is coming over from the mill after closing-
hours, and we've brought along a basket supper and, if you'll
let us, we're going to eat it out in your garden, under Great-
great-grandmother's willow-tree.'

Cousin Hetty nodded dry, though not uncordial greetings to
the strangers and said crisply, 'You're welcome enough to sit
around anywhere you can find, and eat your lunch here, but
where you're going to find anything to show off, beats me.'

'Mr. Welles is interested in gardens and wants to look at
yours.'

'Not much to look at,' said the old lady uncompromisingly.

'I don't want to look at a *garden*!' clamoured little Mark,
outraged at the idea. 'I want to be let go up to Aunt Hetty's
yattic where the sword and 'pinning-wheel are.'

'Would all you children like that best?' asked Marise.

Their old kinswoman answered for them, 'You'd better believe they would. You always did yourself. Run along, now,

children, and don't fall on the attic stairs and hurt yourselves on the wool-hetchels.'

The fox-terrier, who had hung in an anguish of uncertainty and hope and fear on the incomprehensible words passing between little Mark and the grown-ups, perceiving now that the children ran clattering towards the stairs, took a few agitated steps after them, and ran back to Marise, shivering, begging with his eyes, in a wriggling terror lest he be forbidden to follow them into the fun. Marise motioned him along up the stairs, saying with a laughing, indulgent, amused accent, 'Yes, yes, poor Médor, you can go along with the children if you want to.'

The steel sinews of the dog's legs stretched taut on the instant, in a great bound of relief. He whirled with a ludicrous and undignified haste, slipping, his toe-nails clicking on the bare floor, tore across the room and dashed up the stairs, drunk with joy.

'If strong emotions are what one wants out of life,' commented Marise lightly, to Marsh, 'one ought to be born a nervous little dog, given over to the whimsical tyranny of humans.'

'There are other ways of coming by strong emotions,' answered Marsh, not lightly at all.

'What in the world are wool-hetchels?' asked Mr. Welles as the grown-ups went along the hall towards the side-door.

'Why, when I was a girl, and we spun our own wool yarn . . .' began Cousin Hetty, trotting beside him and turning her old face up to his.

Marsh stopped short in the hall-way with a challenging abruptness that brought Marise to a standstill also. The older people went on down the long dusky hall to the door and out into the garden, not noticing that the other two had stopped. The door swung shut behind them.

Marise felt the man's dark eyes on her, searching, determined. They were far from those first days, she thought, when he had tacitly agreed not to look at her like that, very far from those first days of delicacy and lightness of touch.

With a determination as firm as his own, she made her face and eyes opaque, and said on a resolutely gay note, 'What's the matter? Can't you stand any more information about early times in Vermont? You must have been having too heavy a dose of Mr. Bayweather. But *I* like it, you know. I find it awfully interesting to know so in detail about any past period of human life; as much so . . . why not? . . . as researches into which provinces of France used half-timber houses, and how late?'

'You like a great many things!' he said impatiently.

'We must get out into the garden with the others, or Cousin Hetty will be telling her old-time stories before we arrive,' she answered, moving towards the door.

She felt her pulse knocking loud and swift. Strange how a casual interchange of words with him would excite and agitate her. But it had been more than that. Everything *was*, with him.

He gave the sidewise toss of his head, which had come to be so familiar to her, as though he were tossing a lock of hair from his forehead, but he said nothing more, following her down the long hall in silence.

It was as though she had physically felt the steel of his blade slide gratingly once more down from her parry. Her mental attitude had been so entirely that of a fencer, on the alert, watchfully defensive against the quick-flashing attack of the opponent, that she had an instant's absurd fear of letting him walk behind her, as though she might feel a thrust in the back. 'How ridiculous of me!' she told herself with an inward laugh of genuine amusement. 'Women are as bad as fox-terriers for inventing exciting occasions out of nothing at all.'

Then in a gust of deep anger, instantly come, instantly gone, 'Why do I tolerate this for a moment? I was perfectly all right before. Why don't I simply send him about his business, as I would any other bold meddler?'

But after this, with an abrupt shift to another plane, 'That would be acting preposterously, like a silly, self-consciously virtuous matron. What earthly difference does it make to me what a casual visitor to our town says or does to amuse himself in his casual stay, that may end at any moment? And how scarifyingly he would laugh at me, if he knew what comic relics of old prudish reflexes are stirred up by the contact with his mere human lovingness. Heavens! How he would laugh to know me capable of being so "guindée," so personal, fearing like any school-girl a flirtation in any man's conversation. He must never see a trace of that. No matter how startled I ever am, he mustn't see anything but a smooth, amused surface. It would be intolerable to have him laugh at me.'

Her hand was on the latch, when a deep, muffled murmur

144

from the depths admonished her, 'Personal vanity . . . that's what's at the bottom of all that you are telling yourself. It is a vain woman speaking, and fearing a wound to her vanity.'

She resented this, pushed it back, and clicked the latch up firmly, stepping out into the transparent gold of the late-afternoon sunshine. She turned her head as her companion came up behind her on the garden path, half expecting to have his eyes meet hers with a visible shade of sardonic mockery, and prepared to meet it half-way with a similar amusement at the absurdity of human beings, herself included.

He was not looking at her at all, but straight before him, unconscious for an instant that she had turned her eyes on him, and in this instant before the customary mask of self-consciousness dropped over his face, she read there, plain and startling to see, unmistakable to her grown woman's experience of life, the marks of a deep, and painful, and present emotion.

All of her hair-splitting speculations withered to nothing. She did not even wonder what it was that moved him so strangely and dreadfully. There was no room for thought in the profound awed impersonal sympathy which with a great hush came upon her at the sight of another human being in pain.

He felt some intimate emanation from her, turned towards her, and for the faintest fraction of time they looked at each other through a rent in the veil of life.

Cousin Hetty's old voice called them cheerfully, 'Over here, this way under the willow-tree.'

They turned in that direction, to hear her saying, '. . . that was in 1763 and of course they came on horseback, using the Indian trails the men had learned during the French and Indian wars. Great-grandmother (she was a twelve-year-old girl then) had brought along a willow switch from their home in Connecticut. When the whole lot of them decided to settle here in the valley, and her folks took this land to be theirs, she stuck her willow switch into the ground, alongside the brook here, and this is the tree it grew to be. Looks pretty battered up, don't it, like other old folks.'

Mr. Welles tipped his pale, quiet face back to look up at the great tree, stretching its huge, stiff old limbs, mutilated by time and weather, across the tiny, crystal brook dimpling and smiling and murmuring among its many-coloured pebbles. 'Queer, isn't it,' he speculated, 'how old the tree has grown, and how the brook has stayed just as young as ever.'

'It's the other way around between 'Gene Powers' house and his pine-tree,' commented Aunt Hetty. 'The pine-tree gets bigger and finer and stronger all the time, seems 'sthough, and the house gets more battered and feeble-looking.'

Marise looked across at Marsh and found his eyes on her with an expression she rarely saw in them, almost a peaceful look, as of a man who has had something infinitely satisfying fall to his lot. He smiled at her gently, a good, quiet smile, and looked away into the extravagant splendour of a row of peonies.

Marise felt an inexplicable happiness, clear and sunny like the light in the old garden. She sat down on the bench and fell into a more relaxed and restful pose than she had known for some time. What a sweet and gracious thing life could be after all! Could there be a lovelier place on earth than here among Cousin Hetty's flower-children? Dear old Cousin Hetty, with her wrinkled, stiff exterior, and those bright living eyes of hers. She was the willow-tree outside and the brook inside, that's what she was. What tender childhood recollections were bound up with the sight of that quiet old face.

'And those rose-bushes,' continued the old woman, 'are all cuttings my great-great-grandmother brought up from Connecticut, and *they* came from cuttings our folks brought over from England, in 1634. If 'twas a little later in the season, and they were in bloom, you'd see how they're not nearly so double as most roses. The petals are bigger and not so curled up, more like wild roses.'

She sat down beside the others on the long wooden bench, and added, 'I never dig around one of those bushes, nor cut a rose to put in a vase, without I feel as though Great-great-grandmother and Grandmother and all the rest were in me, still alive.'

'Don't you think,' asked Marise of the two men, 'that there is something awfully sweet about feeling yourself a part of the past generations, like that? As we do here. To have such a familiarity with any corner of the earth . . . well, it seems to me like music, the more familiar it is, the dearer and closer it is . . . and when there are several generations of familiarity back of you. . . . I always feel as though my life were a part of something much bigger than just *my* life, when I feel it a continuation of their lives, as much as of my own childhood. It always seems deep and quieting to me.'

Mr. Welles assented wistfully, 'It makes me envious.'

Marsh shook his head, sending up a meditative puff of smoke. 'If you want to know how it really strikes me, I'll have to say it sounds plain sleepy to me. Deep and quieting all right, sure enough. But so's opium. And in my experience, most things just get duller and duller, the more familiar they are. I don't begin to have time in my life for the living I want to do, my own self! I can't let my grandmothers and grand-fathers come shoving in for another whirl at it. They've had their turn. And my turn isn't a minute too long for me. Your notion looks to me . . . lots of old accepted notions look like that to me . . . like a good big dose of soothing syrup to get people safely past the time in their existences when they might do some sure-enough personal living on their own hook.' He paused and added in a meditative murmur, 'That time is so damn short as it is!'

He turned hastily to the old lady with an apology. 'Why, I *beg* your pardon! I didn't realize I had gone on talking aloud. I was just thinking along to myself. You see, your soothing syrup is working on me, the garden, the sun, the stillness, all the grandmothers and grandfathers sitting around. I am al-most half asleep.'

'I'm an old maid, I know,' said Cousin Hetty piquantly. 'But I'm not a proper Massachusetts old maid. I'm Vermont, and a swear-word or two don't scare me. I was brought up on first-hand stories of Ethan Allen's talk, and . . .'

Marise broke in hastily, in mock alarm, 'Now, Cousin Hetty, don't you start in on the story of Ethan Allen and the cow-shed that was too short. I won't have our city visitors scan-dalized by our lack of . . .'

Cousin Hetty's laughter cut her short, as merry and young a sound as the voice of the brook. 'I hadn't thought of that story in years!' she said. She and Marise laughed together, looking at each other. But they said nothing else.

'Aren't you going to *tell* us?' asked Mr. Welles with a genuine aggrieved surprise which tickled Cousin Hetty into more laughter.

'I shall not rest day or night till I have found someone who knows that story,' said Marsh, adding, 'Old Mrs. Powers must know it. And *she* will love to tell it to me. It is evidently the sort of story which is her great specialty.'

They all laughed, foolishly, light-heartedly.

Marise consciously delighted in the laughter, in the silly, light tone of their talk, in the feeling of confidence and security which bathed her as warmly as the new wine of the spring sunshine. She thought passingly, swiftly, with her habitual, satiric wonder at her own fancifulness, of her earlier notions about steel blades and passes and parries, and being afraid to walk down the hall with her 'opponent' back of her.

Her opponent, this potent, significant personality, lounging on the bench beside her, resting in the interval of a life the intensity of which was out of her world altogether, the life, all power, of a modern rich man in great affairs; controlling vast forces, swaying and shaping the lives of thousands of weaker men as no potentate had ever done, living in the instants he allowed himself for personal life (she felt again the pang of her sympathy for his look of fierce, inexplicable pain) with a concentration in harmony with the great scale of his other activities. It was, just as the cheap novels called it, a sort, a bad, inhuman, colourful, fascinating sort of modern version of the superman's life, she reflected. She had been ridiculous to project her village insignificance into that large-scale landscape.

A distant whistle blew a long, full note, filling the valley with its vibrations.

'Is that a train, at this hour?' murmured Mr. Welles. His voice was sunk to a somnolent monotone, his hands folded over his waistcoat moved slowly and rhythmically with his breathing. It was evident that he did not in the least care whether it was a train or not.

'Oh *no*!' said Marise severely, disapproving the vagueness and inaccuracy of his observation. 'That's the mill-whistle, blowing the closing-hour. You're no true Ashleyan, not to have learned the difference between the voices of the different whistles of the day.'

She turned to Marsh tilting her wings for a capricious flight. 'I think it's part of the stubborn stiff-jointedness of human imagination, don't you, that we don't hear the beauty of those great steam-whistles. I wonder if it's not unconscious art that gave to our mighty machines such voices of power.'

'Isn't it perhaps ostentatious to call the family saw-mill a "mighty machine"?' inquired Marsh mildly. He sat at the end of the bench, his arm along the back behind Mr. Welles, his head turned to the side, his soft hat pulled low over his forehead, looking at the garden and at Marise out of half-shut, sleepy eyes.

Marise went on, drawing breath for a longer flight. 'When the train comes sweeping up the valley, trailing its great beautiful banner of smoke, I feel as though it were the crescendo announcing something, and at the crossing, when that noble rounded note blares out . . . why, it's the music for the setting. Nothing else could cope with the depth of the valley, the highness and blackness of its mountain walls, and the steepness of the Eagle Rocks.'

'I call that going some, "noble rounded note"!' murmured Marsh, lifting his eyebrows with a visible effort and letting his eyes fall half shut, against the brilliance of the sunshine.

Marise laughed, and persisted. 'Just because it's called a steam-whistle, we won't hear its beauty and grandeur till something else has been invented to take its place, and then we'll look back sentimentally and regret it.'

'Maybe *you* will,' conceded Marsh.

The two elder looked on, idly amused at this give-and-take.

'And I don't suppose,' continued Marise, 'to take another instance of modern lack of imagination, that you have ever noticed, as an element of picturesque power in modern life, the splendid puissance of the traffic cop's presence in a city street.'

They all had a protesting laugh at this, startled for an instant from their dreaminess.

'Yes, and if I could think of more grandiloquent words to express him, I'd use them,' said Marise defiantly, launching out into yet more outrageous flights of rhetoric. 'I could stand for hours on a street corner, admiring the completeness with which he is transfigured out of the human limitations of his mere personality, how he feels, flaming through his every vein and artery, the invincible power of THE LAW, freely set over themselves by all those turbulent, unruly human beings, surging around him in their fiery speed-genii. He raises his arm. It is not a human arm, it is the decree of the entire race. And as far as it can be seen, all those wilful fierce creatures bow themselves to it. The current boils past him in one direction. He lets it go till he thinks fit to stop it. He sounds his whistle, and raises his arm again in that inimitable gesture of omnipotence. And again they bow themselves. Now that the priest before the altar no longer sways humanity as he did, is there anywhere else, any other such visible embodiment of might, majesty, and power as . . .'

'Gracious me, Marise!' warned her old cousin. 'I know you're only running on with your foolishness, but I think you're going pretty far when you mix a policeman up with priests and altars and things. I don't believe Mr. Bayweather would like that very well.'

'He wouldn't mind,' demurred Marise. 'He'd think it an interesting historical parallel.'

'Mrs. Bayweather would have a thing or two to say.'

'Right you are. *Mrs.* Bayweather would certainly say something!' agreed Marise.

She stood up. 'I'm hypnotized into perfect good-for-nothingness like the rest of you by the loveliness of the afternoon and the niceness of everybody. Here it is almost eating-time and I haven't even opened the baskets. No, don't you move,' she commanded the others, beginning to stir from their nirvana to make dutiful offers of help. 'I'll call the children. And Neale will be here in a moment.'

She went back to the house, down the long walk, under the grape-arbour, still only faintly shaded with sprigs of pale green. She was calling, 'Children! *Children!* Come and help with the supper.'

She vanished into the house. There was a moment or two of intense quiet, in which the almost horizontal rays of the setting sun poured a flood of palpable gold on the three motionless figures in the garden.

Then she emerged again, her husband beside her, carrying the largest of the baskets, the children struggling with other baskets, a pail, an ice-cream freezer, while the dog wove circles about them, wrought to exaltation by the complicated smell of the eatables.

'Neale was just coming in the front gate,' she explained, as he nodded familiarly to the men and bent to kiss the old woman's cheek. 'Cousin Hetty, just *look* at Elly in that nightcap of Great-aunt Pauline's. Doesn't she look the image of that old daguerreotype of Grandmother? See here, Mark, who said you could trail that sword out here? That belongs in the attic.'

'Oh, let him, let him,' said Cousin Hetty peaceably. 'There's nothing much less breakable than a sword. He can't hurt it.'

'I've woren it lots of times before,' said Mark. 'Aunt Hetty always let me to. Favver, won't you 'trap it tight to me, so's I won't 'traddle it so much.'

'Mother,' said Elly, coming up close to Marise, as she stood unpacking the dishes, 'I was looking inside that old diary, the one in the red leather cover, your grandmother's, I guess, the diary she wrote when she was a young lady. And she was having a perfectly dreadful time whether she could believe the Doctrine of the Trinity. She seemed to feel so bad about it. She wrote how she couldn't sleep nights, and cried, and everything. It was the Holy Ghost she couldn't make any sense out of. Mother, what in the world *is* the Doctrine of the Trinity?'

'For mercy's sakes!' cried Cousin Hetty. 'I never saw such a family! Elly, what won't you be up to next? I can't call that a proper thing for a little girl to talk about, right out, so.'

'Mother, *you* tell me,' said Elly, looking up into her mother's face with the expression of tranquil trust which was like a visible radiance. Marise always felt scared, she told herself, when Elly looked at her like that. She made a little helpless shrugged gesture of surrender with her shoulders, setting down on the table a plate of cold sliced lamb. 'Elly, darling, I can't stop just this minute to tell you about it, and anyhow I don't understand any more about it than Grandmother did. But I don't care if I don't. The first quiet minute we have together, I'll tell you enough so you can understand why *she* cared.'

'All right, when I go to bed to-night I'll remind you to,' Elly made the engagement definite. She added, with a shout, 'Oh, Mother, *chicken* sandwiches! Oh, I didn't know we were going to have *chicken* sandwiches. Mother, can't we begin now? I'm awfully hungry.'

'Hello,' said Neale, looking back towards the house. 'Here comes Eugenia, arisen from her nap. Paul, run back into the house and bring out another chair. Marise, have you explained who Eugenia is?'

'Oh *là, là,* no!' exclaimed Marise. 'I forgot they didn't know her. Quick, you do it, Neale.'

'Old friend of my wife's, sort of half-cousin several times removed, schoolmates in France together, the kind of old family friend who comes and goes in the house at will,' said Neale rapidly. 'Cultivated, artistic, and so on.'

'Oh, *Neale*, how slightingly you put it!' cried Marise under her breath. 'She's made herself into one of the rarest and most finished creations!'

Neale went on rapidly in a low tone as the new-comer

stepped slowly down the path, 'She toils not, neither does she spin . . . doesn't have to. Highbrow, very, and yet stylish, very! Most unusual combination.' He added as final information, 'Spinster, by conviction,' as he stepped forward to greet her.

The other two men stood up to be presented to the newcomer, who, making everything to Marise's eyes seem rough and countrified, advanced towards them, self-possessed and indifferent to all those eyes turned on her. In her gleaming, supple dress of satin-like ivory jersey, she looked some tiny, finished, jewel-object, infinitely breakable, at which one ought only to look if it were safely behind glass.

'There is someone of Marsh's own world, the "great world" he speaks of,' thought Marise. She was not aware of any wistfulness in her recognition of this fact, but she was moved to stand closer to her husband, and once as she moved about, setting the table, to lay her fingers for an instant on his hand.

'We're going to have ice-cream, Eugenia,' announced Paul, leaning on the arm of her chair after she and all the others were seated again.

'That's good news,' she said equably. She laid a small, beautiful hand on the child's shoulder, and with a smooth, imperceptible movement set him a little further from her. Paul did not observe this manœuvre, but his mother did, with an inward smile. 'Paul, don't hang on Eugenia like that,' she called to him.

'But she smells so sweet!' protested the little boy.

Mr. Welles held out a sympathizing hand and drew the child to him. He too had seen that gesture.

'Come here, all you little folks,' ordered Marise, now seriously beginning to serve the meal, 'and start waiting on the table.'

'Cold lamb!' cried Cousin Hetty with enthusiasm. 'I'm so glad. Agnes won't touch mutton or lamb. She says they taste so like a sheep. And so we don't often have it.'

'Paul, can you be trusted to pour the hot chocolate?' asked his mother. 'No, Neale, don't get up. I want to see if the children can't do it all.'

From where she sat at the foot of the table, she directed the operations. The children stepped about, serious, responsible, their rosy faces translucent in the long, searching, level rays sent up by the sun, low in the Notch. Dishes clicked lightly, knives and forks jingled, cups were set back with little clinking noises on saucers. All these indoor sounds were oddly diminished and unresonant under the open sky, just as the chatting, laughing flow of the voices, even though it rose at times to bursts of mirth which the children's shouts made noisy, never drowned out the sweet, secret talk of the brook to itself.

Marise was aware of all this, richly and happily aware of the complexities of an impression whose total seemed to her, for the moment, felicity itself. It pleased her, all, every bit of it, pleased and amused her; the dear children, Paul worshipping at the shrine of Eugenia's elegancies, Mark the absurd darling with that grotesque sword between his legs, Elly devouring her favourite sandwich with impassioned satisfaction and wondering about the Holy Ghost; Cousin Hetty, ageless, pungent, and savoury as one of her herbs; Mr. Welles, the old tired darling come into his haven, loving Paul as he would his own grandson; Eugenia, orchid-like against their apple-blossom rusticity; Marsh . . . how tremendously more *simpático* he had seemed this afternoon than ever before, as though one might really like him, and not just find him exciting and interesting; Neale, dear Neale with his calm eyes into which it did everyone good to look. All of them at ease, friendly, enjoying food, the visible world, and each other. Where, after all, were those traditional, troubling, insoluble intricacies of human relationships which had been tormenting her and darkening her sky? It was all so good and simple if one could only remain good and simple oneself. There was no lightning to fear in that lucent sunset air.

Presently, as the talk turned on flowers and the dates of their blooming, Eugenia said to her casually, 'Marisette, here we are the first of June and past, and the roses here are less advanced than they were at Tivoli the last of March. Do you remember the day when a lot of us sat outdoors and ate a picnic dinner, just as we do now? It was the day we climbed Monte Cavo.'

Marise explained, 'Miss Mills is a friend who dates back even before my husband's time, back to our student days in Rome.' To Eugenia she said, 'You're giving us both away and showing how long ago it is, and how you've forgotten about details. We never could have climbed up Monte Cavo, the day we went to Tivoli. They don't go on the same excursion at all.'

'That's true,' agreed Eugenia indifferently, 'you're right. Monte Cavo goes with the Rocca di Papa expedition.'

Before she could imagine a possible reason, Marise felt her

hands go cold and moist. The sky seemed to darken and lower above her. Eugenia went on, 'And I never went to Rocca di Papa with you at all, I'm sure of that. That was a trip you took after you had dropped me for Neale. In fact, it was on that very expedition that you got formally engaged, don't you remember? You and Neale walked over from Monte Cavo and only just caught the last car down.'

Ridiculous! Preposterous! Marise told herself that it was not possible that her hands were trembling so. It was merely a physical reaction, such as one had when startled by some trivial sudden event. But she couldn't make them stop trembling. She couldn't make them stop.

What nonsense to be so agitated. Nobody could remember the name from that evening, weeks and weeks ago. And what if they did? What could they make of it?

It seemed to her that dusk had fallen in the garden. Where was that lucent sunset air?

She heard Eugenia's voice going on, and Neale chiming in with a laugh, and did not understand what they said. Surely everybody must have forgotten.

She hazarded a quick glance at Mr. Welles' face and drew a long breath of relief. He had forgotten, that was evident. She looked beyond him to Marsh. He too would certainly have forgotten.

He was waiting for her eyes. And when they met his, she felt the lightning flash. He had not forgotten.

§ 2

Marsh suddenly found it unbearable. He wasn't used to keeping the curb on himself like this, and he hadn't the least intention of learning how to do it. A fierce, physical irritability overcame him, and he stopped short in the hall, just because he could not stand the silly chatter that was always flowing from these silly people about their foolish affairs. If they only knew what he was leaving unsaid!

He had not meant to make Marise halt, too, his movement having been a mere unconsidered reflex, but of course she did stop, apparently surprised by the brusqueness of his action, and faced him there in the dusky hall-way. She was so close to him that he could see every detail of her face and person, just as he could at night when he closed his eyes; so close that for an instant he felt her breath on his face. He ground his teeth, minded, that instant, to throw down the trumpery little wall of convention. It couldn't stand, he knew with an experienced certainty of his own power that it couldn't stand for an instant against him. The day he chose to put his shoulder to it, down it would go in a heap of rubble.

But the wall was not all. Usually it was all. But with this woman it was nothing, a mere accident. Beyond it she stood, valid, and looked at him out of those long eyes of hers. *What was in her mind?* She looked at him now, quietly, just as usual, made some light casual remark, and effortlessly, as though she had some malign and invincible charm, she had passed from out his power again, and was walking with that straight, sure tread of hers, down to the door.

If he could have done it, he would have struck at her from behind.

He could get no hold on her, could not take the first step. All during those weeks and weeks, he had thrown out his net, and had caught enough facts, Lord knows. But had he any certainty that he had put them together right? He had not yet caught in her any one tone or look or phrase that would give him the unmistakable clue. He had set down words and words and words that would tell him what her life really was, if he only knew the alphabet of her language. He might be making a fool of himself with his almost certainty that she was conscious of having outgrown, like a splendid tropical tree, the wretched little kitchen-garden where fate had transplanted her. When he could stamp down his heat of feeling and let his intelligence have a moment's play, he was perfectly capable of seeing that he might be misinterpreting everything he had observed. For instance, that evening over the photograph-album with her betrayal of some strong feeling of distaste for the place near Rome. It was evident, from her tone, her look, her gesture, that the name of it brought up some acutely distasteful memory to her, but that could mean anything, or nothing. It might be merely some sordid accident, as that a drunken workman had said something brutal to her there. Women of her sort, he knew, never forgot those things. Or any one of a thousand such incidents. He would never know the significance of that gesture of shrinking of hers.

As he walked behind her, he looked hard at her back, with its undulating, vase-like beauty, so close to him; and felt her immeasurably distant. She opened the door now and went out into the sunlight, stepping a little to one side as though to make room for him to come up beside her. He found that he knew every turn of her head, every poise of her shoulders and action of her hands, the whole rhythm of her body, as though they were his own. And there she passed from him, far and remote.

A sudden certainty of foreordained defeat came over him, as he had never known before. He was amazed at the violence of his pain, intolerable, intolerable!

She turned her head quickly and caught his eyes in this instant of inexplicable suffering.

What miraculous thing happened then? It seemed to him that her face wavered in golden rays, from the radiance of her eyes. For she did not withdraw her gaze. She looked at him with an instant, profound sympathy and pity, no longer herself, transfigured, divine by the depth of her humanity.

The sore bitterness went out from his heart.

A voice called. She turned away. He felt himself following her. He looked about him, light-headed with relief from pain. The quiet, flowering world shimmered rainbow-like. What a strange power one human being could have with another that a look could be an event!

He walked more slowly, feeling with a curious pleasure the insatiable desire for possession ebbing from him. Why not let it ebb entirely? Why not enjoy the ineffable sweetness of what he could have? That was what would please her, what she would like, what she would give, freely. In this moment of hush, he quite saw how it would be possible, although he had never for a moment before in his life believed it. Yes, possible and lovely. After all, he must stop some time, and take the slower pace. Why not now, when there was a certain and great prize to be won . . .?

People talked around him. He talked and did not know his own words. Marise spun those sparkling webs of nonsense of hers, and made him laugh, but the next moment he could not have told what she had said. He must somehow have been very tired to take such intense pleasure in being at rest.

Her husband came, that rough and energetic husband. The children came, the children whose restless, selfish, noisy preying on their mother usually annoyed him so, and still the charm was not broken. Marise, as she always did when her husband and children were there, retreated into a remote plane of futile busyness with details that servants should have cared for; answering the children's silly questions, belonging to everyone, her personal existence blotted out. But this time he felt still, deep within him, the penetrating sweetness of her eyes as she had looked at him.

A tiresome, sophisticated friend of Marise's came, too, somehow intruding another personality into the circle, already too full, and yet he was but vaguely irritated by her. She only brought out by contrast the thrilling quality of Marise's golden presence. He basked in that, as in the sunshine, and thought of nothing else.

Possibilities he had never dreamed of stretched before him, possibilities of almost impersonal and yet desirable existence. Perhaps this was the turning-point of his life. He supposed there really was one, some time, for everybody.

'. . . Rocca di Papa . . .' someone had said. Or had he dreamed it? He awoke with an inward bound, like a man springing up from sleep at a sudden noise. His first look was for Marise. She was pale. He had not dreamed it.

The voice went on . . . the new-comer's, the one they called Eugenia . . . yes, she had known them in Italy. Marise had just said they had been friends before her marriage.

The voice went on. How he listened as though crouched before the keyhole of a door! Only three or four sentences, quite casual and trivial in content, pronounced in that self-consciously cosmopolitan accent. Then the voice stopped.

It had said enough for him. Now he knew. Now he had that clue.

He had the sensation of rising to his full height, exultantly, every faculty as alert as though he had never been drugged to sleep by those weak notions of renunciation. The consciousness of power was like a sweet taste in his mouth. The deep, fundamental, inalienable need for possession stretched itself, titanic and mighty, refreshed, reposed, and strengthened by the involuntary rest it had had.

He fixed his eyes on Marise, waiting for the first interchange of a look. He could see that her hands were trembling; and smiled to himself. She was looking at the old man.

Now, in a moment she would look at him.

There were her eyes. She had looked at him. Thunder rolled in his ears.

Chapter 12: *Heard from the Study*

June 20.

FROM his desk in the inner room where he finally buckled down to those estimates about the popple-wood casters, Neale could follow, more or less closely, as his attention varied, the evening activities of the household.

First there had been the clinking and laughter from the dining-room and kitchen where Marise and the children cleared off the table and washed the dishes. How sweet their voices sounded, all light and gay! Every occasion for being with their mother was fun for the kids. How happy Marise made them! And how they throve in that happiness, like little plants in the sunshine!

When you really looked at what went on about you, how funny and silly lots of traditional ideas did seem. That notion, solemnly accepted by the would-be sophisticated moderns, for instance, that a woman of beauty and intelligence was being wasted unless she was engaged in being the 'emotional inspiration' of some man's life: which meant in plain English, stimulating his sexual desire to that fever-heat which they called impassioned living. As if there were not a thousand other forms of deep fulfilment in life. People who thought that, how narrow and cramped they seemed, and blinded to the bigness and variety of life! But then, of course, everybody hadn't had under his eyes a creature genuinely rich and various, like Marise, and hadn't seen how all children feasted on her charm like bees on honey, and how old people adored her, and how, just by being herself, she enriched and civilized every life that touched her, and made every place she lived in a home for the human spirit. And Heaven knew she was, with all that, the real emotional inspiration of a man's life, a man who loved her a thousand times more than in his ignorant and passionate youth.

Come, this wasn't work. He might as well have stayed out with the family and helped with the dishes. This was being like Eugenia Mills, who always somehow had something to do upstairs when there was any work to do downstairs. Eugenia was a woman who somehow managed to stand from under life, anyhow, had been the most successful draft-dodger he knew. No call had been urgent enough to get *her* to the recruiting station to shoulder her share of what everybody had to do. But what did she get out of her successful shirking? She was in plain process of drying up and blowing away.

He turned to his desk and drew out the papers which had the figures and estimates on that popple. He would see if the Warner woodlot had as much popple and basswood on it as they thought. It would, of course, be easiest to get it off that lot, if there were enough of it to fill the order for casters. The Hemmingway lot and the Dornwood lot oughtn't to be lumbered except in winter, with snow for the sleds. But you could haul straight downhill from the Warner lot, even on wheels, using the back lane in the Eagle Rocks woods. There was a period of close attention to his papers, when he heard nothing at all of what went on in the rooms next his study. His mind was working with the rapid, trained exactitude which was a delight to him, with a sure, firm grasp on the whole problem in all its complicated parts.

Finally he nodded with satisfaction, pushed the papers away, and lighted his pipe, contentedly. He had it by the tail.

He leaned back in his chair, drawing on the newly lighted pipe and ruminating again. He thought to himself that he would like to see any other man in the valley who could make an estimate like that, and be sure of it, who would know what facts to gather and where to get them, on the cost of cutting and hauling in different seasons, on mill-work and transportation and overhead expenses, and how to market and where, and how to get money and how to get credit and how to manage these cranky independent Yankees and the hot-tempered irresponsible Canucks. It was all very well for advanced radicals to say that the common workmen in a business were as good as the head of the concern. They weren't and that was all there was to be said about it. Any one of them, any single one of his employees, put in his place as manager, would run the business into a hole as deep as hell inside six months. And if you put the whole lot of them at it, it would only be six weeks instead of six months before the bust-up.

There again, what people kept saying about life, things clever people said and that got accepted as the clever things *to* say,

how awfully beside the mark they seemed to you when you found
out actual facts by coming up against them. What a difference
some first-hand experience with what you were talking about
did make with what you said. What clever folks ought to say
was not that the workmen were as good as the head or the
same sort of flesh and blood, because they weren't; but that
the head exploited his natural capacities out of all proportion,
getting such an outrageous share of the money they all made
together, for doing what was natural to him, and what he
enjoyed doing. Take himself for instance. If by some freak,
he could make more money out of being one of the hands,
would he go down in the ranks, stand at a machine all day and
cut the same wooden shapes, hour after hour: or drive a team
day after day where somebody else told him to go? You bet
your life he wouldn't! He didn't need all the money he could
squeeze out of everybody concerned to make him do his job as
manager. His real pay was the feeling of managing, of doing
a job he was fitted for, and that was worth doing.

How fine it had always been of Marise to back him up in
that view of the business, not to want him to cheat the umpire,
even if he could get away with it, even though it would have
meant enough sight more money for them, even though the
umpire didn't exist as yet, except in his own conscience, in his
own idea of what he was up to in his business. Never once had
Marise had a moment of that backward-looking hankering for
more money that turned so many women into pillars of salt
and their husbands into legalized sneak-thieves.

He pulled out some of the letters from Canada about the
Powers case, and fingered them over a little. He had brought
them home this evening, and it wasn't the first time either, to
try to get a good hour alone with Marise to talk it over with
her. He frowned as he reflected that he seemed to have had
mighty little chance for talking anything over with Marise since
his return. There always seemed to be somebody sticking
around; one of the two men next door, who didn't have anything to do *but* stick around, or Eugenia, who appeared to have
settled down entirely on them this time. Well, perhaps it was
just as well to wait a little longer and say nothing about it, till
he had those last final verifications in his hands.

What in thunder did Eugenia come to visit them for, anyhow? Their way of life must make her sick. Why did she
bother? Oh, probably her old affection for Marise. They had
been girls together, of course, and Marise had been good to

her. Women thought more of those old-time relations than men. Well, he could stand Eugenia if she could stand them, he guessed. But she wasn't one who grew on him with the years.

He had less and less patience with those fussy little ways, found less and less amusing those frequent, small cat-like gestures of hers, picking off an invisible thread from her sleeve, rolling it up to an invisible ball between her white finger and thumb, and casting it delicately away; or settling a ring, or brushing off invisible dust with a flick of a polished finger-nail; all these manœuvres executed with such leisure and easy deliberation that they didn't make her seem restless, and you knew she calculated that effect. A man who had had years with a real, living woman like Marise didn't know whether to laugh or swear at such mannerisms and the self-consciousness that underlay them.

There she was coming down the stairs now, when she heard Marise at the piano, with the children, and knew there was no more work to be done. Pshaw! He had meant to go out and join the others, but now he would wait a while, till he had finished his pipe. A pipe beside Eugenia's perfumed cigarettes always seemed so gross. And he wanted to lounge at his ease, stretch out in his arm-chair with his feet on another. Could you do that, with Eugenia fashion-plating herself on the sofa?

He leaned back smoking peacefully, listening to Marise's voice brimming up all around the children's as they romped through 'The raggle-taggle gypsies, oh!'

What a mastery of the piano Marise had, subduing it to the slender pipe of those child-voices as long as they sang, and rolling out sumptuous harmonies in the intervals of the song. Lucky kids! Lucky kids! to have childhood memories like that.

He heard Paul say, 'Now let's sing "Massa's in the cold, cold ground," ' and Elly shriek out, 'No, Mother, *no*! It's so *terribly* sad! I can't stand it!' And Paul answer with that certainty of his always being in the right, 'Aw, Elly, it's not fair. Is it, Mother, fair to have Elly keep us from singing one of the nicest songs we have, just because she's so foolish?'

His father frowned. Queer about Paul. He'd do anything for Elly if he thought her in trouble, would stand up for her against the biggest bully of the school-yard. But he couldn't keep himself from . . . it was perhaps because Paul could not *understand* that . . . now how could Marise meet this little problem in family equity, he wondered? Her solutions of the children's knots always tickled him.

161

She was saying, 'Let's see. Elly, it doesn't look to me as though you had any right to keep Paul from singing a song he likes. And, Paul, it doesn't seem as though you had any right to make Elly listen to a song that makes her cry. Let's settle it this way. We can't move the piano, but we can move Elly. Elly dear, suppose you go 'way out through the kitchen and shut both doors and stand on the back porch. Touclé will probably be there, looking out, the way she does evenings, so you won't be alone. I'll send Mark out to get you when we're through. And because it's not very much fun to stand out in the dark, you can stop and get yourself a piece of cocoa-nut cake as you go through the pantry.'

Neale laughed silently to himself as he heard the doors open and shut and Elly's light tread die away. How perfectly Marise understood her little daughter! It wasn't only over the piano that Marise had a mastery, but over everybody's nature. She played on them as surely, as richly as on any instrument. That's what he called real art-in-life. Why wasn't it creative art, as much as anything, her Blondin-like accuracy of poise among all the conflicting elements of family-life, the warring interests of the different temperaments, ages, sexes, natures? Why wasn't it an artistic creation, the unbroken happiness and harmony she drew out of those elements, as much as the picture the painter drew out of the reds and blues and yellows on his palette? If it gave an actor a high and disinterested pleasure when he had an inspiration, or heard himself give out a true and freshly found intonation, or make exactly the right gesture, whether anybody in the audience applauded him or not, why wouldn't the mother of a family and maker of a home have the same pleasure, and by heck! just as high and disinterested, when she had once more turned the trick, had an inspiration, and found a course that all her charges, young and old, could steer together? Well, there was one, anyhow, of Marise's audience who often gave her a silent hand-clap of admiration.

The wailing, lugubrious notes of the negro lament rose now, Paul's voice loud and clear and full of relish. 'It takes a heavy stimulant to give Paul his sensations,' thought his father. 'What would take the hide right off of Elly, just gives him an agreeable tingle.' His pipe went out as he listened, and he reached for a match. The song stopped. Someone had come in. He heard Paul's voice cry joyfully, 'Oh goody, Mr. Welles, come on up to the piano.'

Neale leaned forward with a slightly unpleasant stirring of

his blood and listened to see if the old man had come alone. No, of course he hadn't. He never did.

There was Eugenia's voice saying, 'Good evening, Mr. Marsh.' She would move over for him on the sofa and annex him with a look. Well, let her have him. He was her kind more than theirs, the Lord knew. Probably he was used to having that sort of woman annex him.

Neale moved his head restlessly and shifted his position. His pipe and his arm-chair had lost their savour. The room seemed hot to him and he got up to open a window. Standing there by the open sash, looking out into the blue, misty glory of an overclouded moonlight night, he decided that he would not go in at all and join them. He felt tired and out of sorts, he found. And they were such infernal talkers, Eugenia and Marsh. It wore you out to hear them, especially as you felt all the time that their speculations on life and human nature were so *far* off, that it would be just wasting your breath to try to set them right. He'd stay here in the study and smoke and maybe doze off a little, till they went away. Marise had known he had business figuring to do, and she would have a perfectly valid excuse to give them for his non-appearance. Not that he had any illusions as to anybody there missing him at all.

He heard Mark's little voice sound shrilly from the pantry, 'Come on, Elly. It's all right. I've even putten away the book that's got that song.'

Some splendid, surging shouts from the piano and the voices began on 'The Battle Hymn of the Republic.' Neale could hear Mr. Welles' shaky old bass booming away this time. He was probably sitting down with Paul on his knees. It was really nice of the old codger to take such a fancy to Paul, and be able to see those sterling qualities of his through Paul's surface unloveliness that came mostly from his slowness of imagination.

The voices stopped; Elly said, 'That song sounds as if it were proud of itself.' Her father's heart melted in the utter prostration of tenderness he felt for his little daughter. How like Elly! What a quick intelligence animated the sensitive, touching, appealing, defenceless darling that Elly was! Marise must have been a little girl like that. Think of her growing up in such an atmosphere of disunion and flightiness as that weak mother of hers must have given her. Queer, how Marise didn't seem to have a trace of that weakness, unless it was that funny physical impressionableness of hers, that she could laugh at herself, but that still wrought on her, so that if measles were going the rounds, she could see symptoms of measles in everything the children did or didn't do; or that well-known habit of hers, that even the children laughed about with her, of feeling things crawling all over her for hours after she had seen a caterpillar. Well, that was only the other side of her extraordinary sensitiveness, that made her know how everybody was feeling, and what to do to make him feel better. She had often said that she would certainly die if she ever tried to study medicine, because, as fast as she read of a symptom she would have it herself. But she wouldn't die. She'd live and make a crackerjack of a doctor, if she'd ever tried it, enough sight better than some callous brute of a boy with no imagination.

'One more song before bed-time,' announced Marise. 'And we'll let Mark choose. It's his turn.'

A long silence, in which Neale amusedly divined Mark torn between his many favourites. Finally the high sweet little treble, 'Well, let's make it "Down Among the Dead Men."'

At which Neale laughed silently again. What a circus the kids were!

The clock struck nine as they finished this, and Neale heard the stir and shifting of chairs. Paul said, 'Mother, Mr. Welles and I have fixed it up that he's going to put us to bed to-night, if you'll let him.' Amused surprise from Marise: Mr. Welles' voice saying he really would like it, never had seen any children in their nightgowns except in the movies; Paul saying, 'Gracious! We don't wear nightgowns like women. We wear pyjamas!'; Mark's voice crying, 'We'll show you how we play foot-fight on the rug. We have to do that barefoot, so each one can tickle ourselves'; as usual, no sound from Elly probably still revelling in the proudness of 'The Battle Hymn of the Republic.'

A clatter of feet on the stairs, the chirping voices muffled by the shutting of a door overhead, and Eugenia's voice, musical and carefully modulated, saying, 'Well, Marisette, you look perfectly worn out with fatigue. You haven't looked a bit well lately, anyhow. And I'm not surprised. The way those children take it out of you!'

'Damn that woman!' thought Neale. That sterile life of hers had starved out from her even the capacity to understand a really human existence when she saw it. Not that she had *ever* seemed to have any considerable seed-bed of human possibilities to be starved, even in youth, if he could judge from his memory, now very dim, of how she had seemed to him in

Rome, when he had first met her, along with Marise. He remembered that he had said of her fantastically to a fellow in the *pension*, that she reminded him of a spool of silk thread. And now the silk thread had all been wound off, and there was only the bare wooden spool left.

'It's not surprising that Mrs. Crittenden gets tired,' commented Marsh's voice. 'She does the work of four or five persons.'

'Yes,' agreed Eugenia, 'I don't know how she does it . . . cook, nurse, teacher, housekeeper, welfare-worker, seamstress, gardener . . .'

'Oh, let up, let up!' Neale heard Marise say, with an impatience that pleased him. She must have been at the piano as she spoke, for at once there rose, smiting to the heart, the solemn, glorious, hopeless chords of the last part of the Pathetic Symphony. Heavens! How Marise could play!

When the last dull, dreary, beautiful note had vibrated into silence, Eugenia murmured, 'Doesn't that always make you want to crawl under the sod and pull the daisies over you?'

'Ashes, ashes, not daisies,' corrected Marsh dreamily.

There was, thought Neale, listening critically to their intonations, a voluptuous, perverse pleasure in despair which he found very distasteful. Despair was a real and honest and deadly emotion. Folks with appetites sated by having everything they wanted oughtn't to use despair as a sort of condiment to perk up their jaded zest in life. 'Confounded playactors!' he thought, and wondered what Marise's reaction to them was.

He foresaw that it was going to be too much for his patience to listen to them. He would get too hot under the collar and be snappish afterwards. Luckily he was in the library. There were better voices to listen to. He got up, ran his forefinger along a shelf, and took down a volume of Trevelyan, *Garibaldi and the Thousand*. The well-worn volume opened of itself at a familiar passage, the description of the battle of Calatafimi. His eye lighted in anticipation. There was a man's book, he thought. But his pipe was out. He laid the book down to light it before he began to read. In spite of himself he listened to hear what they were saying now in the next room. Eugenia was talking and he didn't like what she was saying about those recurrent dreams of Marise's, because he knew it was making poor Marise squirm. She had such a queer, Elly-like shyness about that notion of hers, Marise had. It evidently meant more to her than she had ever been able to make him understand. He couldn't see why she cared so much about it, hated to have it talked about casually. But he wasn't Eugenia. If Marise didn't want it talked about casually, by George he wasn't the one who would mention it. They'd hardly ever spoken of them, those dreams, even to each other. People had a right to moral privacy, if they wanted it, he supposed, even married women. There was nothing so ruthless anyhow as an old childhood friend, to whom you had made foolish youthful confidences and who brought them out any time he felt like it.

'You ought to have those dreams of yours psycho-analysed, Marisette,' Eugenia was saying. To Marsh she went on in explanation, 'Mrs. Crittenden has always had a queer kind of dream. I remember her telling me about them, years ago, when we were girls together, and nobody guessed there was anything in dreams. She dreams she is in some tremendous rapid motion, a leaf on a great river-current, or a bird blown by a great wind, or foam driven along by storm-waves, isn't that it, Marisonne?'

Neale did not need the sound of Marise's voice to know how she hated this. She said, rather shortly for her, as though she didn't want to say a word about it, and yet couldn't leave it uncorrected, 'Not exactly. I don't dream I'm the leaf on the current. I dream I *am* the current myself, part of it. I'm the wind, not the bird blown by it; the wave itself; it's too hard to explain.'

'Do you still have those dreams once in a while, Marisette, and do you still love them as much?'

'Oh, yes, sometimes.'

'And have you ever had the same sensation in your waking moments? I remember so well you used to say that was what you longed for, some experience in real life that would make you have that glorious sense of irresistible forward movement. We used to think,' said Eugenia, 'that perhaps falling in love would give it to you.'

'No,' said Marise. 'I've never felt it out of my dreams.'

Neale was sorry he had elected to stay in the study. If he were out there now, he could change the conversation, come to her rescue. Couldn't Eugenia see that she was bothering Marise!

'What do you suppose Freud would make out of such dreams?' asked Eugenia, evidently of Marsh.

'Why, it sounds simple enough to me,' said Marsh, and

Neale was obliged to hand it to him that the very sound of his voice had a living, real, genuine accent that was a relief after Eugenia. He didn't talk half-chewed and wholly undigested nonsense, the way Eugenia did. Neale had heard enough of his ideas to know that he didn't agree with a word the man said, but at least it was a vital and intelligent personality talking.

'Why, it sounds simple enough to me. Americans have fadded the thing into imbecility, so that the very phrase has become such a bromide one hates to pronounce it. But of course the commonplace that all dreams are expressions of suppressed desires is true. And it's very apparent that Mrs. Crittenden's desire is a very fine one for freedom and power and momentum. She's evidently not a back-water personality. Though one would hardly need psycho-analysis to guess that!' He changed the subject as masterfully as Neale could have done. 'See here, Mrs. Crittenden, that Tschaikowsky whetted my appetite for more. Don't you feel like playing again?'

The idea came over Neale, and in spite of his uneasy irritation, it tickled his fancy that possibly Marsh found Eugenia just as deadly as he did.

Marise jumped at the chance to turn the talk, for in an instant the piano began to chant again, not Tschaikowsky, Neale noted, but some of the new people whom Marise was working over lately. He couldn't understand a note of them, nor keep his mind on them, nor even try to remember their names. He had been able to get just as far as Debussy and no further, he thought whimsically, before his brain-channels hardened in incipient middle age.

He plunged into Trevelyan and the heart-quickening ups and downs of battle.

Some time after this, he was pulled back from those critical and glorious hours by the consciousness, gradually forcing itself on him on two discomforts; his pipe had gone out and Eugenia was at it again. He scratched a match and listened in spite of himself to that smooth liquid voice. She was still harping on psycho-analysis. Wasn't she just the kind of woman for whom that would have an irresistible fascination! He gathered that Marise was objecting to it just as sweepingly as Eugenia was approving. How women did hate half-tones and reasonable qualifications!

'I'm a gardener,' Marise was saying, 'and I know a thing or two about natural processes. The thing to do with a manure pile is not to paw it over and over, but to put it safely away in the dark, underground, and never bother your head about it again except to watch the beauty and vitality of the flowers and grains that spring from the earth it has fertilized.'

Neale, as he held the lighted match over his pipe, shook his head. That was all very well, put picturesquely as Marise always put things; but you couldn't knock an idea on the head just with an apt metaphor. There was a great deal more to be said about it, even if fool half-baked faddists like Eugenia did make it ridiculous. In the first place it was nothing so new. Everybody who had ever encountered a crisis in his life and conquered it, had . . . why, he himself . . .

He felt his heart beat faster, and before he knew what was coming, he felt a great, heart-quickening gust of fresh salt air blow over him, and felt himself far from the book-tainted stagnant air of that indoor room. He forgot to light his pipe and sat motionless, holding the burning match till it flared up at the end and scorched his fingers. Then he dropped it with a startled oath, and looked quickly around him.

In that instant he had lived over again the moment in Nova Scotia when he had gone down to the harbour just as the battered little tramp-steamer was pulling out, bound for China.

Good God! What an astonishing onslaught that had been! How from some great, fierce, unguessed appetite the longing for wandering, lawless freedom had burst up! Marise, the children, their safe, snug middle-class life, how they had seemed only so many drag-anchors to cut himself loose from and make out to the open sea! If the steamer had been still close enough to the dock so that he could have jumped aboard, how he would have leaped! He might have been one of those men who disappeared mysteriously from out a prosperous and happy life, and are never heard of again. But it hadn't been close enough. The green oily water widened between them; and he had gone back with a burning heart to that deadly little country hotel.

Well, had he buried it and forced himself to think no more about it? No. Not on your life he hadn't. He'd stood up to himself. He'd asked himself what the hell was the matter, and he'd gone after it, as any grown man would. It hadn't been fun. He remembered that the sweat had run down his face as though he'd been handling planks in the lumber-yard in midsummer.

And what had he found? He'd found that he'd never got

over the jolt it had given him, there on that aimless youthful trip through Italy, with China and the Eastern seas before him, to fall in love and have all those plans for wandering cut off by the need for a safe, stable life.

Then he'd gone on. He'd asked himself, if that's so, *then* what? He hadn't pulled any of the moralizing stern-duty stuff; he knew Marise would rather die than have him doing for her something he hated out of stern duty. It was an insult, anyhow, unless it was a positively helpless cripple in question, to do things for people out of duty only. And to mix what folks called 'duty' up with love, that was the devil. So he hadn't.

That was the sort of thing Marise had meant, so long ago, when they were first engaged, that was the sort of thing she had asked him never to do. He'd promised he never would, and this wasn't the first time the promise had held him straight to what was, after all, the only decent course with a woman like Marise, as strong as she was fine. Anything else would be treating her like a child, or a dependant, as he'd hate to have her treat him, or anybody treat him.

So this time he'd asked himself right out what he really wanted and needed in life, and he'd been ready, honestly ready, to take any answer he got, and dree his weird accordingly, as the best thing for everybody concerned, as the only honest thing, as the only thing that would put any bed-rock under him, as what Marise would want him to do. If it meant tramp-steamers, why it had to be tramp-steamers. Something could be managed for Marise and the children.

This was what he had asked. And what answer had he got? Why, of course, he hankered for the double-jointed, lawless freedom that the tramp-steamer stood for. He guessed everybody wanted that, more or less. But he wanted Marise and the children a damn sight more. And not only Marise and the children. He hadn't let himself lay it all on their backs, and play the martyr's rôle of the forcibly domesticated wild male. No, he wanted the life he had, outside the family, his own line of work; he wanted the sureness of it, the coherence of it, the permanence of it, the clear conscience he had about what he was doing in the world, the knowledge that he was creating something, helping men to use the natural resources of the world without exploiting either the natural resources or the men; he wanted the sense of deserved power over other human beings. That was what he really wanted most of all. You could call it smug and safe and bourgeois if you liked. But the plain fact remained that it had more of what really counted for him than any other life he could see possible. And when he looked at it, hard, with his eyes open, why the tramp-steamer to China sailed out of school-boy theatrical clouds and showed herself for the shabby, sordid little substitute for a real life she would have been to him.

He'd have liked to have that too, of course. You'd *like* to have everything! But you can't. And it is only immature boys who whimper because you can't have your cake and eat it too. That was all there was to that.

What he had dug for was to find his deepest and most permanent desires, and when he had found them, he'd come home with a happy heart.

It even seemed to him that he had been happier and quieter than before. Well, maybe Marise's metaphor had something in it, for all it was so flowery and high falutin. Maybe she would say that what he had done was exactly what she'd described, to dig it under the ground and let it fertilize and enrich his life.

Oh Lord! how a figure of speech always wound you up in knots if you tried to use it to say anything definite!

He relighted his pipe, this time with a steady hand, and a cool eye; and turned to Trevelyan and Garibaldi again. He'd take that other side of himself out in books, he guessed.

He had now arrived at the crucial moment of the battle, and lifted his head and his heart in anticipation of the way Garibaldi met that moment. He read, 'To experienced eyes the battle seemed lost. Bixio said to Garibaldi, "General, I fear we ought to retreat." Garibaldi looked up as though a serpent had stung him. *"Here we make Italy or die!"* he said.'

'That's the talk!' cried Neale, to himself. The brave words resounded in the air about him, and drowned out the voices from the next room.

Chapter 13: *Along the Eagle Rock Brook*

July 1.

PAUL was very much pleased that Mr. Welles agreed with him so perfectly about the hour and place for lunch. But then Mr. Welles was awfully nice about agreeing. He said, now, 'Yes, I believe this would be the best place. Here by the pool, on that big rock, as you say. We'll be drier there. Yesterday's rain has made everything in the woods pretty wet. That's a good idea of yours, to build our fire on the rock, with water all around. The fire couldn't possibly spread.' Paul looked proudly at the rain-soaked trees and wet soggy leaves which his forethought had saved from destruction and strode across the brook in his rubber boots, with the first instalment of dry pine branches.

'Aren't you tired?' he said protectingly to his companion. 'Whyn't you sit down over there and undo the lunch-basket? I'll make camp. Father showed me how to make a camp-fire with only one match.'

'All right,' said Mr. Welles. 'I do feel a little leg-weary. I'm not so used to these mountain scrambles as you are.'

'I'll clean the fish, too,' said Paul; 'maybe you don't like to. Elly can't abide it.' He did not say that he did not like it very well himself, having always to get over the sick feeling it gave him.

'I never did it in my life,' confessed Mr. Welles. 'You see, I always lived in towns till now.'

Paul felt very sorry for Mr. Welles, and shook his head pityingly as he went off for more firewood.

When he had collected a lot, he began to lay the sticks. He did it just as Father had showed him, but it seemed lots harder to get them right. And it took a lot more than one match to get it started. He didn't have a bit of breath left in him, by the time he finally got it going. And my, weren't his hands black! But he felt very much set up, all the same, that he had done it. In his heart Paul knew that there was nothing anybody could do which he could not.

They hung the slimpsy slices of bacon from forked sticks, Paul showing Mr. Welles how to thread his on, and began to cook them around the edges of the fire, while the two little trout frizzled in the frying-pan. 'I'm so glad we got that last one,' commented Paul. 'One wouldn't have been very much.'

'Yes, it's much better to have one apiece,' agreed Mr. Welles.

When the bacon was done (only burned a little at the edges, and still soft in the thicker places in the centre of the slice), and the fish the right brown, and 'most shrunk up to nothing, they each of them put a trout and a piece of bacon on his slice of bread and butter, and gracious! didn't it taste good.

'You must have done this before,' said Mr. Welles respectfully; 'you seem to know a good deal about camping.'

'Oh, I'm a good camper, all right,' agreed Paul. 'Mother

and I have gone off in the woods, lots of times. When I was littler, I used to get spells when I was bad. I do still, even now, once in a while.'

Mr. Welles did not smile, but continued gravely eating his bread and bacon, his eyes on the little boy.

'I don't know what's the matter. I feel all snarled up inside. And then the first thing you know I've done something awful. Mother can tell when it first gets started in me, the least little teenty bit. *How* can she tell? And then she takes me off camping. She pretends it's because she's feeling snarled up, herself. But it's not. She never is. Why not?'

He considered this in silence, chewing slowly on a vast mouthful of bread. 'Anyhow, we leave the little children with Touclé, if she's there,' (he stopped here an instant to inspect Mr. Welles to make sure he was not laughing because he had called Elly and Mark the 'little children.' But Mr. Welles was not laughing at him. He was listening, *really* listening, the way grown-ups almost never did, to hear what you had to say. He did like Mr. Welles. He went on,) 'or if Touclé's off somewhere in the woods herself, we leave them down at the Powers' to play with Addie and Ralph, and we light out for the woods, Mother and I. The snarleder up I feel, the farther we go. We don't fish or anything. Just leg it, till I feel better. Then we make a fire and eat.'

He swallowed visibly a huge lump of unchewed bread, and said, uncorking a thermos bottle, 'I asked Mother to put up some hot coffee.'

Mr. Welles seemed surprised. 'Why, do you drink coffee?'

'Oh no, none of us kids ever take it. But I thought you'd like some. Grown-up folks mostly do, when they eat out of doors.'

Mr. Welles took the cup of steaming coffee, ready sugared and creamed, without even saying thank you, but in a minute, as they began their second round of sandwiches, filled this time with cold ham from home, he said, 'You've got quite a way of looking out for folks, haven't you?'

'I like to,' said Paul.

'*I* always liked to,' said Mr. Welles.

'I guess you've done quite a lot of it,' conjectured the little boy.

'Quite a lot,' said the old man thoughtfully.

Paul never liked to be left behind and now spoke out, 'Well, I expect I'll do a good deal, too.'

'Most likely you will,' agreed the old man.

He spoke a little absently, and after a minute said, 'Paul, talking about looking out for folks makes me think of something that's bothering me like everything lately. I can't make up my mind about whether I ought to go on, looking out for folks, if I know folks that need it. I keep hearing from somebody who lives down South, that the coloured folks aren't getting a real square deal. I keep wondering if maybe I oughtn't to go and live there and help her look out for them.'

Paul was so astonished at this that he opened his mouth wide, without speaking. When he could get his breath, he shouted, 'Why, Mr. Welles, go away from Ashley to live!' He stared hard at the old man, thinking he must have got it twisted. But Mr. Welles did not set him straight, only stared down at the ground with a pale, bothered-looking face and sort of twitched his mouth to one side.

The little boy moved over closer to him, and said, looking up at him with all his might, 'Aw, Mr. Welles, I *wish*'*t* you wouldn't! I *like* your being here. There's lot of things I've got planned we could do together.'

It seemed to him that the old man looked older and more tired at this. He closed his eyes and did not answer. Paul felt better. Mr. Welles couldn't have been in earnest.

How still it was in the woods that day. Not the least little flutter from any leaf. The sunlight looked as green, as green, coming down through the trees that way, like the light in church when the sun came in through the stained-glass windows.

The only thing that budged at all was a bird . . . was it a flicker? . . . he couldn't make out. It kept hopping around in that big beech-tree across the brook. Probably it was worried about its nest and didn't like to have people so near. And yet they sat as still, he and Mr. Welles, as still as a tree, or the shiny water in the pool.

Mr. Welles opened his eyes and took the little boy's rough, calloused hand in his. 'See here, Paul, maybe you can help me make up my mind.'

Paul squared his shoulders.

'It's this way. I'm pretty nearly used up, not good for much any more. And the Electrical Company wanted to fix everything the nicest way for me to live. And they have. I hadn't any idea anything could be so nice as living next door to you folks in such a place as Crittenden's. And then making friends with you. I'd always wanted a little boy, but I thought I was so old no little boy would bother with me.'

He squeezed the child's fingers and looked down on him lovingly. For a moment Paul's heart swelled up so he couldn't speak. Then he said, in a husky voice, 'I *like* to.' He took a large bite from his sandwich and repeated roughly, his mouth full, 'I *like* to.'

Neither said anything more for a moment. The flicker . . . yes, it was a flicker . . . in the big beech kept changing her position, flying down from a top branch to a lower one, and then back again. Paul made out the hole in the old trunk of the tree where she'd probably put her nest, and wondered why she didn't go back to it.

'Have you got to the Civil War in your history yet, Paul?'

'Gee, yes, 'way past it. Up to the Philadelphia Exposition.'

Mr. Welles said nothing for a minute, and Paul could see by his expression that he was trying to think of some simple baby way to say what he wanted to. Gracious! didn't he know Paul was in the seventh grade? '*I* can understand all right,' he said roughly.

Mr. Welles said, 'Well, all right. If you can, you'll do more than I can. You know how the coloured people got their freedom then. But something very bad had been going on there in slavery, for ever so long. And bad things that go on for a long time can't be straightened out in a hurry. And so far, it's been too much for everybody to get this straightened out. The coloured people . . . they're made to suffer all the time for being born the way they are. And that's not right . . . in America . . .'

'Why don't they stand up for themselves?' asked Paul scornfully. He'd like to see anybody who would make him suffer for being born the way he was.

Mr. Welles hesitated again. 'It looks to me this way. People can fight for some things . . . their property, and their vote and their work. And I guess the coloured people have got to fight for those, themselves. But there are some other things . . . some of the nicest . . . why, if you fight for them, you tear them all to pieces, trying to get them.'

Paul did not have the least idea what this meant.

'If what you want is to have people respect what you are worth, why, if you fight them to make them, then you spoil what you're worth. Anyhow, even if you don't spoil it, fighting about it doesn't put you in any state of mind to go on being your best. That's a pretty hard job for anybody.'

Paul found this very dull. His attention wandered back to that queer flicker, so excited about something.

The old man tried to get at him again. 'Look here, Paul, Americans that happen to be coloured people ought to have every bit of the same chance to amount to their best that any Americans have, oughtn't they?'

Paul saw this. But he didn't see what Mr. Welles could do about it, and said so.

'Well, I couldn't do a great deal,' said the old man sadly, 'but more than if I stayed here. It looks as though they needed, as much as anything else, people to just have the same feeling towards them that you have for anybody who's trying to make the best of himself. And I could do that.'

Paul got the impression at last that Mr. Welles was in earnest about this. It made him feel anxious. 'Oh *dear*!' he said, kicking the toe of his rubber boot against the rock. He couldn't think of anything to say, except that he hated the idea of Mr. Welles going.

But just then he was startled by a sharp cry of distress from the bird, who flew out wildly from the beech, poised herself in the air, beating her wings and calling in a loud scream. The old man, unused to forests and their inhabitants, noticed this but vaguely, and was surprised by Paul's instant response. 'There must be a snake after her eggs,' he said excitedly. 'I'll go over and chase him off.'

He started across the pool, gave a cry, and stood still, petrified. Before their eyes, without a breath of wind, the huge beech solemnly bowed itself and with a great roar of branches, whipping and crushing the trees about, it fell, its full length thundering on the ground, a great mat of shaggy roots uptorn, leaving an open wound in the stony mountain soil. Then, in a minute, it was all as still as before.

Paul was scared almost to death. He scrambled back to the rock, his knees shaking, his stomach sick, and clung to Mr. Welles with all his might. 'What made it fall? There's no wind! What made it fall?' he cried, burying his face in the old man's coat. 'It might just as easy have fallen this way, on us, and killed us! What made it fall?'

Mr. Welles patted Paul's shoulder, and said, 'There, there,' till Paul's teeth stopped chattering and he began to be a little ashamed of showing how it had startled him. He was also a little put out that Mr. Welles had remained so unmoved. 'You don't know how dangerous a big tree *is*, when it falls!' he said, accusingly, to defend himself. 'If you'd lived here more, and heard some of the stories . . .! Nate Hewitt had his back broken with a tree falling on him. But he was cutting that one down, and it fell too soon. Nobody had touched this one! And there isn't any wind. What *made* it fall? Most every winter, some man in the lumber-camp on the mountain gets killed or smashed up, and lots of horses too.'

He felt much better now, and he did want to find out whatever had made that tree fall. He sat up, and looked back at it, just a mess of broken branches and upset leaves, where a minute before there had been a tall living tree! 'I'm going over to see what made it fall,' he said.

He splashed across the pool and poked around with a stick in the hole in the ground, and almost right away he saw what the reason was. He ran back to tell Mr. Welles. 'I see now. The brook had kept sidling over that way, and washed the earth from under the rocks. It just didn't have enough ground left to hold on to.'

He felt all right now he knew some simple reason for what had looked so crazy. He looked up confidently at the old man, and was struck into awed silence by the expression of Mr. Welles' face.

'Paul,' said Mr. Welles, and his voice wasn't steady, 'I guess what I ought to try to be is one more drop of water in the brook.'

Paul stared hard. He did not understand this either, but he understood the expression in that tired, old face. Mr. Welles went on, 'That wrong feeling about coloured people, not wanting them to be respected as much as any American, is . . . that's a tree that's got to come down. I'm too old to take an axe to it. And, anyhow, if you cut that sort of thing down with an axe, the roots generally live and start all over again. If we can just wash the ground out from under it, with enough people thinking differently, maybe it'll fall, roots and all, of its own weight. If I go and live there and just am one more person who respects them when they deserve it, it'll help *that* much, maybe, don't you think?'

Paul had understood more what Mr. Welles' face and voice said to him than the words. He kept on looking into the old man's eyes. Something deep inside Paul said 'yes' to what Mr. Welles' eyes were asking him.

'How about it, Paul?' asked the old man.

The child gave a start, climbed up beside him, and took hold of his hand. 'How about it? How about it?' asked Mr. Welles in a very low tone.

The little boy nodded. 'Maybe,' he said briefly. His lips shook. Presently he sniffed and drew his sleeve across his nose. He held the old hand tightly.

'Oh dear!' he said again, in a small, miserable voice.

The old man made no answer.

The two sat motionless, leaning against each other. A ray of sun found the newly opened spot in the roof of the woods, and it seemed to Paul it pointed a long steady finger down on the fallen beech.

At first Paul's throat ached, and his eyes smarted. He felt heavy and sore, as though he hadn't eaten the right thing for lunch.

But by and by this went away. A quiet came all over him, so that he was better than happy. He laid his head against Mr. Welles' shoulder and looked up into the worn, pale old face, which was now also very quiet and still as though he too were better than happy.

He held Paul close to him.

Paul had a great many mixed-up thoughts. But there was one that was clear. He said to himself solemnly, 'I guess I know who I want to be like when I grow up.'

By and by, he stirred and said, 'Well, I guess I better start to pack up. Don't you bother. I'll pack the things away. Mother showed me how to clean the frying-pan with sand and moss.'

Chapter 14: *Beside the Onion-Bed*

July 10.

MARISE pulled nervously and rapidly at the weeds among the onions, and wiped away with her sleeve the drops that ran down her hot, red face. She was not rebellious at the dusty, tiresome task, nor aware of the merciless heat of the early-summer sun. She was not indeed thinking at all of what she was doing, except that the physical effort of stooping and reaching and pulling was a relief to her, made slightly less oppressive the thunder-heavy moral atmosphere she breathed. She was trying to think, but the different impressions came rushing into her mind with such vehement haste that they dashed against each other brutally, to her entire confusion.

When she tried to think out an answer to this perfectly preposterous idea of old Mr. Welles, why should a thousand other horrifying ideas which she had been keeping at bay pour in through the door, once opened to probing thought? What possible connection could there be between such a fantastic crazy notion as his, and those other heaving, looming possibilities which rolled themselves higher and murkier the longer she refused to look at them? She snatched at the weeds, twitching them up, flinging them down, reaching, straining, the sun molten on her back, the sweat stinging on her face. It was a silly impression of course, but it seemed to her that if she hurried fast enough with the weeds, those thoughts and doubts could not catch up with her.

She had put them off, and put them off while Neale was away, because they scared her, and she didn't want to look at them without Neale. But he had been back for weeks now and still she put them off. All those tarnishing sayings, those careless, casual negations of what she had taken for axioms; that challenge to her whole life dropped from time to time as though it were an accepted commonplace with all intelligent beings. . . .

Was her love for the children only an inverted form of sensual egotism, an enervating slavery for them, really only a snatched-up substitute for the personal life which was ebbing away from her? Was her attitude towards her beloved music a lazy, self-indulgent one, to keep it to herself and the valley here? Was that growing indifference of hers to dress and trips to the city, and seeing Eugenia's smart crowd there, a sign of mental dry-rot? Was it a betrayal of what was alive in her own personality to go on adapting herself to the inevitable changes in her relations with Neale, compromising, rather than . . .

'Aren't you awfully hot to go on doing that?' asked Neale, coming up behind her, from the road. She was startled because she had not heard him approach on the soft, cultivated ground of the garden. And as she turned her wet, crimson face up to his, he was startled himself. 'Why, what's the matter, dear?' he asked anxiously.

She sank back to a sitting position, drawing a long breath, mopping her forehead with her sleeve, as unconscious of her looks before Neale as though she had still been alone. She motioned him down beside her. 'Oh, Neale, I'm so glad! How'd you happen to be so early? Maybe if we stay right out here, where the children won't know where we are, we can have a few minutes quite to ourselves. Touclé is going to get tea to-night. Neale, sit down a minute. I want to tell you something. I'm awfully upset. I went over to help Mr. Welles transplant his brussels sprouts, and we got to talking. Neale, what do you suppose has been in his mind all this time we've been thinking him so happy and contented here?'

'Doesn't he like Crittenden's? Find it dull?'

'No, no, not that, a bit. He *loves* it. It's heart-breaking to see how much he loves it!' She stopped, her voice shaking a little, and waited till she could get it under control. Her husband took her stained, dusty hand in his. She gave his fingers a little pressure, absently, not noting what she did, and seeing the corner of his handkerchief showing in the pocket of his shirt, she pulled it out with a nervous jerk, and wiped her face all over with it.

He waited in silence.

'Listen, Neale, I know it will sound perfectly crazy to you, at first. But you might as well believe it, for he is serious. It seems he's been getting lots more letters from that niece or cousin of his, down in Georgia. She tells him about things, how the Negroes are treated, all the Jim Crow business carried into every single detail of every single minute of every single day. It seems they're not badly treated as long as they'll stay day-labourers or servants, but . . . oh well, there's no need to go on with telling you . . . *you* know. We all know well enough what the American attitude is. Only I didn't think it could be so bad, or so everlastingly kept up every minute, as this cousin tells him. I suppose she ought to know. She's lived there for forty years. She keeps citing instances she's seen.' Marise broke out with a fierce, blaming sharpness, 'I don't see what *business* she had, writing him that way. I think it was beastly of her. Why couldn't she let him alone!'

She felt her husband waiting patiently for her to quiet down and go on more coherently, and knew that his patience came from a long acquaintance with her mental habits, a certainty that her outbursts of feeling generally did quiet down if one waited: and across her genuine absorption in the story she was telling there flitted, bat-like, a distaste for being known so well as all that! There was something indiscreet and belittling in it, she thought, with an inward fastidious recoil. But this had gone, entirely, in a moment, and she was rushing on, 'And, Neale, what *do* you think? She has worked on him, and he has worked on himself till he's got himself in a morbid state. He thinks perhaps he ought to leave Ashley that he loves so much and go down to live where this horrid cousin lives.. . .'

Her husband's astonishment at this was as great as she could have desired. None of Neale's usual, unsurprised acceptance of everything that happened as being in the nature of things, which occasionally so rubbed her the wrong way, and seemed to her so wilfully phlegmatic. He was sincerely amazed and astounded; that was plain from his exclamation, his tone, his face. Of course he wasn't as outraged as she, but that wasn't to be expected, since he hadn't seen so much of that dear old life-worn man, nor grown so protectingly fond of him. She revelled in Neale's astonishment as bearing out her own feeling. 'Isn't it crazy, Neale? Don't you think it crazy? *Is* there the slightest justification for it? You feel, just as I do, don't you, that it's a perfectly unbalanced, fanatical, *fool*ish thing to think of doing, his going down into that hopeless mess?'

But her husband had had a moment's time, while she exclaimed, to get back to his usual unhurried post in life. 'It's certainly about as unexpected as anything I ever heard of,' he admitted. 'I should have to know a lot more about it, before I could be sure what to think.'

An old impatience, at an old variance between their ways of thought, came out with an edge in Marise's tone as she said hotly, 'Oh, *Neale*, don't take that line of yours! You know all there is to know, now! What else could you find out? You know how he's given all his life to looking out for his family, ending up with years of that bed-ridden old aunt the others wished on to him, just because he was too soft-hearted to get out from under. You know how anxious the Company was to do something to make up to him for all the years of service he gave them. And you know how happy he has been here, how he's loved it all, and fathered every root and seed in his garden, and how he and Paul have struck up such a sweet affection, and how he could be happier and happier.' She struck her hands together. 'Oh, Neale, I can't have him do such a foolish, useless thing, and spoil his life! It's not as if he'd be of any use down in Georgia. You know how the Southern white people detest Northerners coming down and interfering with the Negroes. Maybe they're wrong. But they're the people who live there. What could *he* do against them? What under the sun could one tired-out old man accomplish in a situation that every American knows to be simply impossible?' She looked hard at her husband's thoughtful face and threw herself against him with a petulant gesture. 'Now, Neale, don't go and justify him! Don't say you think he's right.'

He put his arm about her shoulders, hot and wet under their gingham covering, and she leaned against him, the gesture as unconsidered and unconscious for the one as the other. 'No, I'm not going to try to justify him. I suppose I think he's very foolish. But I must say it shows a pretty fine spirit. I take off my hat to his intention.'

'Oh yes, his intention . . .' conceded Marise. 'He's an old saint, of course. Only he mustn't be allowed to ruin his life and break everybody's heart, even if he is a saint.'

'That's the way saints usually run their business, isn't it?' asked Neale. 'And I'd like to know how anybody's going to keep him from doing it, if he decides he ought to.'

'Oh yes, we can,' urged Marise, sitting up with energy. 'We can, every one of us, throw ourselves against it, argue with him, tell him that it seems to us not only foolish, and exaggerated, and morbid, but conceited as if he thought what *he* did would count so very much. We can make him feel that it would be sort of cheating the Company, after what they've done for him; we can just mass all our personalities against it, use moral suasion, get excited, work on his feelings . . . she has done that, that cousin!'

'I wouldn't want to do that,' said Neale quietly. 'You can, if you think best.'

She recognized a familiar emergence of granite in his voice and aspect and cried out on it passionately, 'Now, *Neale!*'

He knew perfectly well what this meant, without further words from her. They looked at each other, an unspoken battle going on with extreme rapidity between them, over ground intimately familiar. In the middle of this, she broke violently into words, quite sure that he would know at which point she took it up. 'You carry that idea to perfectly impossible lengths, Neale. Don't you ever admit that we ought to try to make other people act the way we think best, even when we *know* we're right and they're wrong?'

'Yes,' admitted her husband, 'I should think we were bound to. If we ever *were* sure we were right and they wrong.'

She gave the impression of vibrating with impatience and cried out, 'That's pettifogging. Of course there are times when

181

we are sure. Suppose you saw a little child about to take hold of the red-hot end of a poker?'

'A child is different,' he opposed her. 'All grown-ups are responsible for all children. I suppose I'd keep him from taking hold of it. And yet I'm not dead sure I'd be right. If I thought he was only just going to touch it, to see if it really would burn him as people had told him, I guess I'd let him.'

'You always get around things,' she said blamingly, 'but there *are* cases when you could be sure. Suppose you saw Aunt Hetty just about to take poison, or Frank Warner getting Nelly Powers to run away with him?'

He was startled by this, and asked quickly with a change of tone, 'Whatever made you think of that? Are Frank and Nelly . . .?'

'Oh, it just came into my head. No, I haven't heard anybody has said anything, noticed anything. But I had a sort of notion that 'Gene doesn't like Frank hanging around the house so much.'

'Well . . .' commented her husband, with a lively accent of surprise. 'I hadn't dreamed of such a thing. And it throws a light on something I happened to see this afternoon, on my way home. I came round the back way, the ravine road below the Eagle Rocks. I wanted to see about some popple we're thinking of buying from the Warners, on the shoulder beyond the Rocks. It didn't occur to me, of course, that anybody else would be up there, but just at the peak of the shoulder I saw 'Gene Powers, lying down beside a big beech-tree. He didn't hear me, walking on the pine-needles. And for a minute I stood there, and honestly didn't know what to do.'

'How do you mean . . . "lying down"?' asked Marise, not visualizing the scene. 'As though he were sick?'

'No, not a bit that way. Not on his back, but on his face, looking over the edge of the ridge. All strung up like a bow, his head down between his shoulders and shot forwards like a cat stalking something. *I* tell you, he made me think of a hunter when he thinks he sees a deer. I thought probably he had. I've seen a buck and some does up there lately. Then he saw me and jumped up very quickly and came down past me. I was going to say, just for the sake of saying something, "Laying your plans for next deer-week?" But as he went by and nodded, he looked at me with such an odd expression that I thought I'd better not. The idea came to me that maybe 'Gene does poach and occasionally take a deer out of season.

182

Meat is so high it wouldn't be surprising. They have a pretty hard time scraping along. I don't know as I'd blame him if he did shoot a deer once in a while.

'Well, after I'd been on beyond and made my estimate on the popple, I came back that way. And as I passed where he'd been lying, I thought, just for curiosity, I'd go up and see if I could see what he'd been looking at so hard. I got up to the big beech where he'd been, and looked over. And I got the surprise of my life. He couldn't have been looking at deer, for on the other side the cliff drops down sheer, and you look right off into air, across the valley. I was so surprised I stood there, taken aback. The afternoon train went up the valley while I stood there, staring. It looked so tiny. You're really very high on those rocks. I noticed you could see your Cousin Hetty's house from there, and the mill and the Powers house. That looked like a child's plaything, so little, under the big pine. And just as I looked at that, I saw a man come out from the house, get on a horse, and ride away.'

'Why, that must have been Frank,' said Marise. 'He rides that roan mare of his as much as he drives her.'

'Yes, that's what came into my mind when you spoke his name just now in connection with Nelly. I hadn't thought anything of it, before.'

There was a moment's silence as they looked at each other.

'Oh, *Neale!*' said Marise, on a deep note. 'How awful! You don't suppose there is anything in his jealousy. . . . Nelly is as inscrutable in her way as 'Gene.'

'Heavens! how should I know ? But my guess is that 'Gene is making a fool of himself for nothing. Nelly doesn't strike me as being the sort of woman to . . .'

'But Frank is awfully good-looking and dashing, and lots younger than 'Gene. And Nelly is young too and perfectly stunning to look at. And she's not one of our native valley girls, you know. It may seem very dull and cooped-up here, so far from town, and shops. She may envy her sisters, still living back in West Adams with city life around them.'

'Oh, it's possible enough, I suppose,' admitted Neale. 'But she seems perfectly contented, and thinks the world of the children.'

Marise's face clouded. The phrase had recalled her dark preoccupations of a moment ago. 'Lots of people nowadays would say she seems to be fond of the children because she is using them to fill up a lack in her life,' she said sombrely;

'that 'Gene no longer satisfied her, and that she fed on the children because she was starving emotionally.' Her husband making no comment on this, she went on, 'Neale, don't you think that people are saying horrid, distressing things nowadays? About marriage I mean, and all relations between men and women and between parents and children?' Her heart was beating faster as she finished this question. The subject was broached at last. Where would it lead them? Where would it lead them? She shut her eyes at the thought.

'There's a good deal to be said about all that, that's pretty horrid and perfectly true,' remarked Neale casually. He tilted his hat farther over his eyes and leaned back, propping himself on one elbow.

'*Neale!*' she protested, shocked and repelled. She had hoped for something very different from Neale. But she thought, in a momentary exasperation with him, she might have known she would not get it. He always took everything so abstractedly, so impersonally.

'I don't see any use in pretending there's not,' he advanced with a reasonable, considering air. 'I don't see that intimate human relationships are in any *more* of a mess than other human relations. International ones, for instance, just now. But they certainly are in considerable of a mess, in a great many cases. It is evident that lots of times they're managed all wrong.'

Marise was so acutely disappointed that she felt a quavering ache in her throat, and kept silence for a moment. So this was what she had looked forward to, as a help. What was Neale there *for*, if not for her to lean against, to protect her, to be a defending wall about her? He was so strong and so clear-headed, he could be such a wall if he chose. How stern and hard he was, the core of him!

'Neale,' she said after a moment, 'I wonder if you even *know* what things are being said about what we've always believed in . . . motherhood for instance, and marriage?'

She had been unable to keep the quaver out of her voice, and at the sound of it, he sat up instantly, astonished, solicitous, tender. 'Why, darling, what's the matter?' he said again, moving closer to her, bending over her.

'How *can* you think such things without their making you perfectly miserable, without making you want to go straight and cut your throat?' she cried out on his callousness.

He put his arm about her again, not absently this time, and

184

drew her close. She thought angrily, 'He thinks it's just a fit of nerves I can be soothed out of like a child,' and pulled away from him.

He looked at her, his attentive, intelligent look, and let his arm drop. And yet, although he was serious now, she was sure that he saw only that the subject agitated her, and did not see any possibility that it might touch them both, personally.

'I have to think whatever I'm convinced is true, whether it makes me miserable or not, don't I?' he said gently. 'And it does make me miserable, of course. Who can help being miserable at the spectacle of such rich possibilities as human life is full of, mismanaged and spoiled and lost?'

'But, Neale, do you realize that people are thinking, books are being written to prove that parents' love for their children is only self-love, hypocritically disguised, and sometimes even sexual love camouflaged; and that anybody is better for the children to be with than their mother; and that married people, after the first flare-up of passion is over, hate each other instead of loving?'

'I daresay there's a certain amount of truth in that, occasionally. It would certainly explain some of the inexplicable things we all see happen in family life,' he remarked.

Marise started and cried out piercingly, 'Neale, how can you say such things to *me*!'

He looked at her keenly again, keenly and penetratingly, and said, 'I'm not one of those who think it inherent in the nature of women to take abstract propositions personally always. But I do think they will have to make a big effort to get themselves out of a mighty old acquired habit of thinking every general observation is directed at them personally.'

She flashed out indignantly at him, 'How can you help taking it personally when it shakes the very foundations of our life?'

He was astonished enough at this to suit even her. His face showed the most genuine amazed incapacity to understand her. 'Shakes the . . . why, Marise dear, what are you talking about? You don't have to believe about *yourself* all the generalizing guesses that people are writing down in books, do you, if it contradicts your own experience? Just because you read that lots of American men had flat-foot and were refused at the recruiting station for that, you don't have to think your own feet flat, do you? If you do think so, all you have to do is to start out and walk on them, to know for sure they're all right.

Heavens and earth! People of our age, who have really lived, don't need somebody in a book to tell them what's happening to them. Don't you *know* whether you really love Elly and Mark and Paul? If you don't, I should think a few minutes' thought and recollection of the last ten years would tell you, all right. Don't you *know* whether we hate each other, you and I?'

Marise drew a long breath of relief. This was the sort of talk she wanted. She clutched at the strong hand which seemed at last held out to her. She did so want to be talked out of it all. 'Oh good! then, Neale, you don't believe any of that sort of talk? You were only saying so for argument.'

He withdrew the hand. 'Yes, I do believe a good deal of it, as a general proposition. What I'm saying, what I'm always saying, dear, and trying my best to live, is that everybody must decide for himself when a general proposition applies to him, what to believe about his own life and its values. Nobody else can tell him.'

She approached along another line. 'But, Neale, that's all very well for you, because you have so much withstandingess in you. But for me, there are things so sacred, so intimate, so much a part of me, that only to have some rough hand laid on them, to have them pulled out and pawed over and thought about . . . it frightens me so, sets me in such a quiver! And they don't seem the same again. *Aren't* there things in life so high and delicate that they can't stand questioning?'

He considered this a long time, visibly putting all his intelligence on it. 'I can't say, for you,' he finally brought out. 'You're so much finer and more sensitive than I. But I've never in all these years seen that your fineness and your sensitiveness makes you any less strong in the last analysis. You suffer more, respond more to all the implications of things; but I don't see that there is any reason to think there's any inherent weakness in you that need make you afraid to look at facts.'

He presented this testimony to her, seriously, gravely. It took her breath, coming from him. She could only look at him in speechless gratitude and swallow hard. Finally she said, falteringly, 'You're too good, Neale, to say that. I don't deserve it. I'm awfully weak, many times.'

'I wouldn't say it, if it weren't so,' he answered, 'and I didn't say you weren't weak sometimes. I said you were strong when all was said and done.'

Even in her emotion, she had an instant's inward smile at the

186

Neale-like quality of this. She went on, 'But don't you think there is such a thing as spoiling beautiful elements in life, with handling them, questioning them, for natures that aren't naturally belligerent and ready to fight for what they want to keep? For instance, when somebody says that children in a marriage are like drift-wood left high on the rocks of a dwindled stream, tokens of a flood-time of passion now gone by. . . .' She did not tell him who had said this. Nor did he ask. But she thought by his expression that he knew it had been Vincent Marsh.

He said heartily, 'I should just call that a nasty-minded remark from somebody who didn't know what he was talking about. And let it go at that.'

'There, you see,' she told him, 'that rouses your instinct to resist, to fight back. But it doesn't mine. It just makes me sick.'

'Marise, I'm afraid that you *have* to fight for what you want to keep in this world. I don't see any way out of it. And I don't believe that anybody else can do your fighting for you. You ask if it's not possible to have beautiful, intimate things spoiled by questioning, criticisms, doubts. Yes, I do think it is, for young people, who haven't learned anything of life at first hand. I think they ought to be protected till they have been able to accumulate some actual experience of life. That's the only weapon for self-defence anybody can have, what he has learned of life, himself. Young people are apt to believe what older people tell them about life, because they don't know anything about it, yet, themselves, and I think you ought to be careful what is questioned in their presence. But I don't see that mature people ought to be protected unless you want to keep them childish, as women used to be kept. Nothing is your own, if you haven't made it so, and kept it so.'

'But, Neale, it's so sickeningly *hard*! Why do it? Why, when everything seems all right, pry into the deep and hidden roots of things? I don't *want* to think about the possibility of some dreadful dry-rot happening to married people's feelings towards each other, as they get older and get used to each other. It's soiling to my imagination. What's the use?'

She had so hoped he would help her to sweep them all back to the cellar labelled 'morbid' and lock them down in the dark again. Any other man would be, she thought, amazed at him, *any* other husband! She focussed all her personality passionately to force him to answer as she wished.

He fell into another thoughtful silence, glanced up at her once sharply and looked down again. She always felt afraid of him when he looked like that. No, not afraid of him, but of the relentless thing he was going to say. Presently he said it. 'What's the use? Why, the very fact you seem afraid of it . . . I can't imagine why . . . shows there would be some use. To turn your back on anything you're afraid of, that's fatal, always. It springs on you from behind.'

She cried out to him in a sudden anguish that was beyond her control, 'But *suppose you face it and still it springs!*'

Her aspect, her accent, her shaken voice gave him a great start. He faced her. He looked at her as though he saw her for the first time that day. And he grew very pale as he looked. Something wordless passed between them. Now he knew at last what she was afraid of.

But he did not flinch. He said desperately, in a harsh voice, 'You have to take what comes to you in life,' and was grimly silent.

Then with a gesture as though to put away something incredible, approaching him, he went on more quietly, 'But my experience is that it doesn't dare spring if you walk right up to it. Generally you find you're less afraid of everything in the world, after that.'

She had been frightened, stabbed through and through by the look they had interchanged, by the wordless something which had passed between them. But now she wondered suddenly, passionately, amazedly, if he had really understood all the dagger-like possibilities of their talk.

'Neale,' she challenged him, 'don't you put *any* limits on this? Isn't there *any*where you'd stop out of sheer respect? Nothing too hallowed by . . .'

'Nothing. Nothing,' he answered her, his face pale, his eyes deep and enduring. 'It's lying down, not to answer the challenge when it comes. How do you know what you have to deal with if you won't look to see? You may find out that something you have been trusting is growing out of a poisonous root. That does happen. What's the use of pretending that it couldn't to you, as to anybody else? And what's the use of having lived honestly, if you haven't grown brave enough to do whatever needs to be done? If you are scared by the idea that your motherhood may be only inverted sensuality, or if you think there is any possibility that the children would be better

188

off in other hands, or if you think . . . if you think there is any other terrifying possibility in our life here, for God's sake look into your own heart and see for yourself! It all sounds like nonsense to me, but . . .'

She snatched at the straw, she who longed so for help. 'Oh, Neale, if *you* think so, I know . . .'

'I won't *have* you taking my word for it!' he told her roughly. '*I* can't tell what's back of what you do. And you oughtn't to take my word for it if I tried to. Nobody on earth can make your decision for you, but you yourself.' The drops stood out on his forehead as he spoke, and ran down his pale face.

She quivered and was silent for a moment. Then, 'Neale, where shall I get the strength to do that?' she asked.

He looked full in her face. 'I don't know anywhere to go for strength but out of one's naked human heart,' he said.

She shrank from the rigour of this with a qualm of actual fear. 'I think I must have something else,' she told him wildly.

'I don't know,' he returned. 'I don't know at all about that. I'm no mystic. I can't help you there, dear. But I know, as well as I know anything on earth, that anything that's worth having in anybody's life, his parenthood, his marriage, his love, his ambition, can stand any honest challenge it can be put to. If it can't, it's not valid and ought to be changed or discarded.' His gaze on her was immeasurably steady.

She longed unspeakably for something else from him, some warming, comforting assurance of help, some heartening, stimulating encouragement along that stark, bleak way.

Somehow they were standing up now, both pale, looking profoundly into each other's eyes. Something almost palpable, of which not a word had been spoken aloud, came and stood there between them, and through it they still looked at each other. They had left words far behind now, in the fierce velocity of their thoughts.

And yet with the almost physical unity of their years of life together, each knew the other's thoughts.

She flung herself against him as though she had cried out to him. He put his arms strongly, tenderly about her, as though he had answered.

With no words she had cried out, silently, desperately to him, 'Hold me! Hold me!'

And with no words, he had answered, silently, desperately, 'No one can hold you but yourself.'

A shouting babble of voices rose in the distance. The children crying to each other came out of the house door and raced down the flag-stone walk. 'There they are! In the garden! By the onion-bed! Father! Mother! We've been looking for you everywhere. Touclé says if you'll let her, she'll boil down some maple syrup for us to wax on ice for dessert.'

They poured into the garden, children, cat and fox-terrier, noisy, insistent, clamorous. Mark, always frankly greedy of his mother's attention, pushed in jealously between his parents, clinging to his mother's knees. He looked up in her face and laughed out his merry peal, 'Oh, Mother, what a dirty face! You've been suspiring and then you've wiped your forehead with your dirty hand, the way you say I mustn't. How funny you look! And you've got a great, long tear in your sleeve, too.'

Behind them, tiny, smooth and glistening, Eugenia Mills strolled to the edge of the garden, as far as the flag-stones went, and stood waiting, palpably incapable of taking her delicate bronze slippers into the dust.

'You've missed a kitchen call from that lively, earthy old Mrs. Powers and her handsome daughter-in-law,' she announced casually. 'Touclé says they brought some eggs. What a stunning creature that Nelly is! There's temperament for you! Can't you just feel the smouldering, primitive fire hidden under that scornful silence of hers?'

'Mother, may we tell Touclé to put the syrup on to boil?' begged Elly. Her hair was tangled and tousled, with bits of bark sticking in it, and dried mud was caked on her hands and bare legs. Marise thought of the repugnance she must have aroused in Eugenia.

'Mother,' said Paul, 'Mr. Welles is going to give me a fishing-rod, he says. A *real* one. Boughten.'

'Oh, I want one too!' cried Mark, jumping up and down. 'I want one too.'

'You're too little. Mother, *isn't* Mark too little? And anyhow, he always breaks everything. You do, Mark, you know you do. I take *care* of my things!'

Someone in the confusion stepped on the fox-terrier's toes and he set up a shrill, aggrieved yelping. The children pawed at her with dirty hands.

'Good evening, Mr. Marsh,' said Eugenia, looking over her shoulder at the dark-haired figure in flannels approaching from the other house. She turned and strolled across the grass to meet him, as white and gleaming as he.

A sick qualm of self-contempt shook Marise. For, high and clear above everything else, there had come into her mind a quick discomfort at the contrast between her appearance and that of Eugenia.

Chapter 15: *Home Life*

July 20.

THE heat was appalling even early in the morning, right after breakfast. There were always three or four such terrific days, even up here in the mountains, to remind you that you lived in America and had to take your part of the ferocious extremes of the American climate.

And of course this had to be the time when Touclé went off for one of her wandering disappearances. Marise could tell that by the aspect of the old woman as she entered the kitchen that morning, her reticule bag bulging out with whatever mysterious provisions Touclé took with her. You never missed anything from the kitchen.

Marise felt herself in such a nervously heightened state of sensitiveness to everything and everybody in those days, that it did not surprise her to find that for the first time she received something more than a quaint and amusing impression from the old aborigine. She had never noticed it before, but sometimes there was something about Touclé's strange, battered, leathery old face . . . what was it? The idea came to her a new one, that Touclé was also a person, not merely a curious and enigmatic phenomenon.

Touclé was preparing to depart in the silent, unceremonious, absent-minded way she did everything, as though she were the only person in the world. She opened the screen door, stepped out into the torrid glare of the sunshine and, a stooped, shabby, feeble old figure, trudged down the path.

'Where does she go?' thought Marise, and 'What was that expression on her face I could not name?'

Impulsively she went out quickly herself, and followed after the old woman.

'Touclé! Touclé!' she called, and wondered if her voice in these days sounded to everyone as nervous and uncertain as it did to her.

The old woman turned and waited till the younger had overtaken her. They were under the dense shade of an old maple, beside the road, as they stood looking at each other.

As she had followed, Marise regretted her impulse, and had wondered what in the world she could find to say, but now that she saw again the expression in the other's face, she cried out longingly, 'Touclé, where do you go that makes you look peaceful?'

The old woman glanced at her, a faint surprise appearing in her deeply lined face. Then she looked at her, without surprise, seriously as though to see what she might read in the younger woman's eyes. She stood for a long moment, thinking. Finally she sat down on the grass under the maple-tree, and motioned Marise to sit beside her. She meditated for a long time, and then said, hesitatingly, 'I don't know as a white person could understand. White people . . . nobody ever asked me before.'

She sat silent, her broad, dusty feet in their elastic-sided, worn, run-over shoes straight before her, the thick, horny eyelids dropped over her eyes, her scarred old face carved into innumerable deep lines. Marise wondered if she had forgotten that anyone else was there. She turned her own eyes away, finally, and looking at the mountains saw that black thunderclouds were rolling up over the Eagle Rocks. Then the old woman said, her eyes still dropped, 'I tell you how my uncle told me, seventy-five years ago. He said people are like fish in an underground brook, in a black cave. He said there is a place, away far off from where they live, where there is a crack in the rock. If they went 'way off they could get a glimpse of what daylight is. And about once in so often they need to swim there and look out at the daylight. If they don't they lose their eyesight from always being in the dark. He said that a lot of Indians don't care whether they lose their eyesight or not, so long's they can go on eating and swimming around. But good Indians do. He said that as far as he could make out, none of the white people care. He said maybe they've lost their eyes altogether.'

Without a move of her sagging, unlovely old body, she turned her deep black eyes on the flushed, quivering, beautiful woman beside her. 'That's where I go,' she answered. 'I go 'way off to be by myself, and get a glimpse of what daylight is.'

She got up to her feet, shifted her reticule from one hand to the other, and without a backward look trudged slowly down the dusty road, a stooped, shabby, feeble old figure.

Marise saw her turn into a wood-road that led up towards the mountain, and disappear. Her own heart was burning as she looked. Nobody would help her in her need. Touclé went away to find peace, and left her in the black cave. Neale stood . . .

A child's shriek of pain and loud wailing calls for 'Mother! Mother! *Mother!*' sent her back running breathlessly to the house. Mark had fallen out of the swing and the sharp corner of the board had struck him, he said, 'in the eye! in the eye!' He was shrieking and holding both hands frantically over his left eye. This time it might be serious, might have injured the eye-ball. Those swing-boards were deadly. Marise snatched up the screaming child and carried him into the kitchen, terrible perspectives of blindness hag-riding her imagination; saying to herself with one breath, 'It's probably nothing,' and in the next seeing Mark groping his way about the world with a cane all his life long.

She opened the first-aid box on the kitchen-shelf, pulled out a roll of bandage and a length of gauze, sat down with Mark in her lap near the faucet, and wet the gauze in cold water. Then she tried in vain to induce him to take down his hands so that she could see where the blow had struck.

But the terrified, hysterical child was incapable of hearing what she said, incapable of doing anything but scream louder and louder when she tried to pull down those desperately tight little hands held with frantic tenseness over the hurt eye. Marise could feel all his little body quivering and taut. His shrieks were like those of someone undergoing the most violent torture.

She herself responded nervously and automatically to his condition, felt herself begin to tighten up, and knew that she was equally ready to shake him furiously, or to burst into anguished tears of sympathy for his pain.

Wait now . . . wait . . . what was the thing to do for Mark? What would untie those knots of fright and shock? For Paul it would have been talk of the bicycle he was to have for his birthday; for Elly a fairy-story of a piece of candy! For Mark . . .

High above the tumult of Mark's shrieks and her own spasmodic reactions to them she sent her intelligence circling quietly . . . and in an instant . . . oh yes, that was the thing. 'Listen, Mark,' she said in his ear, stopping her effort to take down his hands, 'Mother's learned a new song, a *new* one, awfully funny. And ever so long too, the way you like them.' She put her arms about him and began, hearing herself with difficulty through his cries.

> 'On yonder hill there stands a damsel,
> Who she is, I do not know.'

('How preposterous we must sound, if Eugenia is listening,' she thought to herself as she sang, 'out-yelling each other this way!')

> 'I'll go and court her for her beauty.
> She must answer "yes" or "no." '

As usual Mark fell helpless before the combination of music and a story. His cries diminished in volume. She said in his ear, 'And then the Lady sings,' and she tuned her voice to a young-ladyish, high sweetness and sang,

> 'My father was a Spanish Captain,
> Went to sea a month ago,'

Mark made a great effort and choked down his cries to heaving sobs as he tried to listen,

> 'First he kissed me, then he left me;
> Bade me *always* answer "no." '

She told the little boy, now looking up at her out of the one eye not covered by his hands, 'Then the gentleman says to her,' she made her voice loud and hearty and bluff,

> 'Oh, Madam, in your face is beauty,
> On your lips red roses grow.
> Will you take me for your lover?
> Madam, answer "yes" or "no." '

She explained in an aside to Mark, 'But her father had told her she must always answer just the one thing, "no," so she had to say,' she turned up in the mincing, ladylike key again, and sang,

> 'Oh no, John, no, John, no.'

Mark drew a long quivering breath through parted lips and sat silent, his one eye fixed on his mother, who now sang in the loud, lusty voice,

> 'Oh, Madam, since you are so cruel,
> And that you do scorn me so,
> If I may not be your lover,
> Madam, will you let me *go*?'

And in the high, prim voice, she answered herself,

> 'Oh no, John, no, John, *no*!'

A faint smile hovered near Mark's flushed face. He leaned towards his mother as she sang, and took down his hands so that he could see her better. Marise noted instantly, with a silent exclamation of relief, that the red angry mark was quite outside the eye-socket, harmless on the bone at one side. Much ado about nothing as usual with the children. Why *did* she get so frightened each time? Another one of Mark's hair-breadth escapes.

She reached for the cold wet compress and went on, singing loudly and boldly, with a facetious wag of her head (how tired she was of all this manœuvring!),

> 'Then I will stay with you for ever
> If you will not be unkind.'

She applied the cold compress on the hurt spot and put out her hand for the bandage-roll, singing with an ostentatiously humorous accent and thinking with exasperation how all this was delaying her in the thousand things to do in the house,

> 'Madam, I have vowed to love you;
> Would you have me change my mind?'

She wound the bandage around and around the little boy's head, so that it held the compress in place, singing in the high, sweet voice,

> 'Oh no, John, no, John, NO.'

She went on with a heavy, mock solemnity, in the loud voice,

'Oh, hark, I hear the church-bells ringing;
Will you come and be my wife?'

She pinned the bandage in place at the back of Mark's head,

'Or, dear Madam, have you settled
To live single all your life?'

She gathered the child up to her, his head on her shoulder, his face turned to her, his bare, dusty, wiry little legs wriggling and soiling her white skirt; and sang, rollickingly,

'Oh no, John, no, John, NO!'

'There, that's all,' she said in her natural voice, looking down at Mark. She said to herself rebelliously, 'I've expended enough personality and energy on this performance to play a Beethoven sonata at a concert,' and found she was quoting something Vincent Marsh had said about her life, the day before.

There was a moment while the joke slowly penetrated to Mark's six-year-old brain. And then he laughed out, delightedly, 'Oh, Mother, that's a beaut! Sing it again. Sing it again! Now I know what's coming, I'll like it such a lots betterer.'

Marise cried out in indignant protest, 'Mark! When I've sat here for ten minutes singing to you, and all the work to do, and the sun getting like red-hot fire every minute.'

'What must you got to do?' asked Mark challengingly.

'Well, the very first thing is to get dinner ready and in the fireless cooker, so we can turn out the oil-stove and cool off this terrible kitchen.'

Mark looked up at her and smiled. He had recently lost a front tooth and this added a quaintness to the splendour of his irresistible smile. 'You could sing as you get the dinner ready,' he said insinuatingly, 'and I'll help you.'

Marise smothered an impulse to shout to the child, 'No, no, go away! Go away! I can't have you bothering around. I've got to be by myself, or I don't know what will happen!' She thought of Touclé, off in the green and silent woods, in a blessed solitude. She thought of Eugenia up in her shaded room, stretched on the chaise-longue in a thin silk room-gown, she thought of Neale and his stern eyes . . . she looked down on the dusty, tanned, tousle-headed little boy, with the bandage around his head, his one eye looking up at her pleadingly, his dirty little hand clutching at the fold of her skirt; and drearily and unwillingly she summoned herself to self-control. 'All right, Mark, that's true. I could sing while I peel the potatoes. You could wash them for me. That would help.'

They installed themselves for this work. The acrid smell of potato-parings rose in the furnace-like heat of the kitchen, along with the singing voice, asking and answering itself. Mark listened with all his might, laughing and wriggling with appreciation. When his mother had finished and was putting the potatoes into the boiling water, he said exultantly, 'He got around *her*, all right, I should say what!'

Paul burst in now, saying, 'Mother, Mother!' He stopped short and asked, 'What you got on your head, Mark?'

The little boy looked surprised, put his hand up, felt the bandage, and said with an off-hand air, 'Oh, I bunked my head on the corner of the swing-board.'

'I know,' said Paul, 'I've done it lots of times.' He went on, 'Mother, my pig has lice. You can just *see* them crawling around under his hair. And I got out the oil Father said to use, but I can't do it. It says on the can to rub it on with a stiff little brush. I don't see how ever in the world you're going to get your pig to stand still while you do it. When I try to, he just squeals and runs away.'

His mother said with decision, from where she stooped before the open ice-box door, 'Paul, if there is anything in the world I know nothing about, it is pigs. I haven't the slightest idea what to do.' She shut the heavy door with a bang more energetic than was necessary to latch it, and came back towards the stove with a raw, red piece of uncooked meat on a plate.

'Oh, how nasty meat looks, raw,' said Mark, with an accent of disgust.

'You eat it with a good appetite when I've cooked it,' remarked his mother, somewhat grimly, putting it in a hot pan over the fire. An odour of searing fibres and smoke and frying onions rose up in the hot, still air of the kitchen.

'If I could have guessed we'd have such weather, I'd never have ordered a pot-roast,' thought Marise, vexed.

'Please, Mother, *please*,' begged Paul.

'Please what?' asked his mother, who had forgotten the pig.

'Henry!' said Paul. 'If you could see how he scratches and scratches and how the behind of his ears is all scabs he's so bitten.'

'Wouldn't Eugenia and Vincent Marsh love this conversation?' thought Marise, turning the meat in the pan and starting back from the spatters of hot fat.

'Mother, don't you see, I agreed to take care of him with Father, and so I *have* to. He's just like my child. You wouldn't let one of *us* have lice all over, and scabs on our . . .'

'Oh stop, Paul, for Heaven's sake!' said his mother.

Through the smoke and smell and heat, the sensation of her underclothing sticking hotly to her limbs, the constant dogging fear and excitement that beset her, and the causeless twanging of her nerves, there travelled to her brain, along a channel worn smooth by the habit of her thought about the children, the question, 'What is it that makes Paul care so much about this?' And the answer, almost lost in the reverberation of all those other questions and answers in her head, was, 'It comes from what is best in Paul, his feeling of personal responsibility for the welfare of others. That mustn't be hindered.' Aloud, almost automatically, she said, in a neutral tone, 'Paul, I don't think I can do a single thing for you and Henry, but I'll go with you and look at him and see if I can think of anything. Just wait till I get this and the potatoes in the fireless cooker.'

Paul made a visible effort, almost as though he were swallowing something too large for his throat, and said ungraciously, 'I suppose I ought to help you in here then.'

'I suppose so,' said his mother roughly, in an exact imitation of his manner.

Paul looked at her quickly, laughing a little, sheepishly. He waited a moment, during which time Mark announced that he was going out to the sand-pile, and then said, in a pleasant tone, 'What can I do?'

His mother nodded at him with a smile, refrained from the spoken word of approbation which she knew he would hate, and took thought as to what he might do that would afflict him least. 'You can go and sweep off the front porch, and straighten out the cushions and chairs, and water the porch-box geraniums.'

He disappeared, whistling loudly, 'Massa's in the cold, cold ground.' Marise hoped automatically that Elly was not in earshot to hear this.

She felt herself tired to the point of exhaustion by the necessity always to be divining somebody's inner processes, putting herself in somebody else's skin and doing the thing that would reach him in the right way. She would like, an instant, just an instant, to be in her own skin, she thought, penetrated with a sense of the unstable equilibrium of personal relations. To keep the peace in a household of young and old highly differentiated personalities was a feat of the Blondin variety; the least inattention, the least failure in judgment, and opportunities were lost for ever. Her sense of the impermanence of the harmony between them all had grown upon her of late, like an obsession. It seemed to her that her face must wear the strained, propitiatory smile she had so despised in her youth on the faces of older women, mothers of families. Now she knew from what it came . . . balancing perpetually on a tightrope from which . . .

Oh, her very soul felt crumpled with all this pressure from the outside, never-ending!

The worst was not the always recurring physical demands, the dressing and undressing the children, preparing their food and keeping them clean. The crushing part was the moral strain; to carry their lives always with you, incalculably different from each other and from your own. And not only their present lives, but the insoluble question of how their present lives were affecting their future. Never for a moment from the time they are born to be free from the thought, 'Where are they? What are they doing? Is that the best thing for them?' till every individual thought of your own was shattered, till your intelligence was atrophied, till your sensibilities to finer things were dulled and blunted.

Paul came back. 'About ready for Henry?' he asked. 'I've finished the porch.'

She put the two tightly closed kettles inside the fireless cooker and shut down the lid. 'Yes, ready for Henry,' she said.

She washed her hot, moist face in cold water, drank a glass, put on a broad-brimmed garden hat, and set out for the field back of the barn. The kitchen had been hot, but it seemed cool compared to the heat into which they stepped from the door. It startled Marise so that she drew back for an instant. It seemed to her like walking through molten metal. 'Mercy! what heat!' she murmured.

'Yes, ain't it great?' said Paul, looking off, down the field, 'just what the corn needs.'

'You should say "isn't," not "ain't," ' corrected his mother.

'But it'll be cooler soon,' said Paul. 'There's a big thunderstorm coming up. See, around the corner of the mountain. See how black it is now over the Eagle Rocks.' He took her hand in his bramble-scarred little fingers, and led her along, talking proudly of his own virtue. 'I've moved Henry's pen to-day, fresh, so's to get him on new grass, and I put it under the shade of this butternut tree.'

They were beside the pen now, looking over the fence at the grotesque animal, twitching his gross and horribly flexible snout, as he peered up at them out of his small, intelligent eyes, sunk in fat, and almost hidden by the fleshy, hairy triangles of his ear-flaps.

'Don't you think Henry is a *very* handsome pig?' asked Paul.

'I think you take very good care of him,' she answered. 'Now what is the matter about the oil you can't put on? Doesn't he like it?'

'He hasn't felt it yet. He won't even let me try. Look!' The child climbed over the fence and made a quick grab at the animal, which gave an alarmed, startled grunt, wheeled with astonishing nimbleness, and darted away in a short-legged gallop.

'Look there, that's the way he always does!' said Paul in an aggrieved tone.

Marise considered the pig for a moment. He had turned again and was once more staring at her, his quivering, fleshy snout in the air, a singularly alert expression of attention animating his heavy-jowled countenance.

'Are there any things he specially likes?' she asked Paul.

'He likes to eat, of course, being a pig,' said Paul, 'and he loves you to scratch his back with a stick.'

'Oh, then it's easy. Come outside the pen. Now listen. You go back to the barn and get whatever it is you feed him. Then you put that in the trough, and let him begin to eat, quietly. Then take your oil and your brush, and moving very slowly so that you don't startle him, lean over the fence and begin to brush it on his back where he likes to be rubbed. If he likes the feel of it, he'll probably stand still. I'll wait here, till you see how it comes out.'

She moved away a few paces, and sank down on the grass under the tree, as though the heat had flung her there. The grass crisped dryly under her, as though it too were parched.

She closed her eyes and felt the sun beating palpably on the lids . . . or was it that hot inward pulse still throbbing . . .? Why wouldn't Neale do it for her? Why wouldn't he put out that strength of his and crush out this strange agitation of hers, *forbid* it to her? Then there was nothing in her but intense discomfort, as though that were a universe of its own. A low, distant growl of thunder shook the air with a muffled, muted roar.

After a time, a little voice back of her announced in a low, cautious tone, 'Mother, it *works*! Henry loves it!'

She turned her head and saw the little boy vigorously rubbing the ears and flanks of the pig, which stood perfectly still, its eyes half shut, rapt in a beatitude of satisfaction.

Marise turned her head away and slid down lower on the grass, so that she lay with her face on her arm. She was shaking from head to foot as though with sobs. But she was not crying. She was laughing hysterically. 'Even for the pig!' she was saying to herself. 'A symbol of my life!'

She lay there a long time after this nervous fit of laughter had stopped, till she heard Paul saying, 'There, I've put it on every inch of him.' He added with a special intonation, 'And now I guess maybe I'd better go in swimming.'

At this Marise sat up quickly, with an instant experienced divination of what she would see.

In answer to her appalled look on him, he murmured apologetically, 'I didn't know I was getting so *much* on me. It sort of spattered.'

It was, of course, as she led the deplorable object towards the house that they encountered Eugenia under a green-lined white parasol, on the way back from the garden, carrying an armful of sweet-peas.

'I thought I'd fill the vases with fresh flowers before the rain came,' she murmured, visibly sheering off from Paul.

'Eugenia ought not to carry sweet-peas,' thought Marise. 'It ought always to be orchids.'

In the bathroom as she and Paul took off his oil-soaked clothes, Mark's little voice called to her, 'Mother! Mo-o-other!'

'Yes, what is it?' she answered, suspending operations for a moment to hear.

'Mother, if I had to kill all the ants in the world,' called Mark, 'I'd a great deal rather they were all gathered up together in a heap than running around every-which-way, wouldn't you?'

'For goodness' *sakes*, what a silly baby thing to say!' commented Paul with energy.

Marise called heartily to Mark, 'Yes, indeed I would, dear.'

Paul asked curiously, 'Mother, how can you answer him like that, such a *fool* thing!'

Marise felt another wave of hysterical laughter mounting at the idea of the difficulty in perceiving the difference in degree of flatness between Mark's remarks and those of Paul.

But it suddenly occurred to her that this was the time for Elly's hour at the piano, and she heard no sound. She hastily laid out the clean clothes for Paul, saw him started on the scrub in the bath-tub, and ran downstairs to see if she could find Elly, before the storm broke, turning over in her mind Elly's favourite nooks.

The air was as heavy as noxious gas in the breathless pause before the arrival of the rain.

In the darkened, shaded hall stood a man's figure, the face turned up towards her, the look on it meant for her, her only, not the useful house-mother, but that living core of her own self, buried, hidden, put off, choked and starved as she had felt it to be all that morning. That self rose up now, passionately grateful to be recognized, and looked back at him.

Thunder rolled among the distant hills.

She felt her pulse whirling with an excitement that made her lean against the wall, as he took a great stride towards her, crying out, 'Oh, make an end . . . make an end of this . . .'

The door behind him opened, and Elly ran in, red-faced and dusty. 'Mother, Mother, Reddy has come off her nest. And there are twelve hatched out of the fourteen eggs! Mother, they are such darlings! I wish you'd come and see. Mother, if I practise *good*, won't you come afterwards and look at them?'

'You should say "practise well," not "good," ' said Marise, her accent openly ironical.

The wind, precursor of the storm falling suddenly on the valley, shook the trees till they roared.

Over the child's head she exchanged with Vincent Marsh a long reckless look, the meaning of which she made no effort to understand, the abandon of which she made no effort to restrain.

With a dry, clattering, immediate rattle, without distance or dignity, the thunder broke threateningly over the house.

Chapter 16: *Massage-Cream; Theme and Variations*

July 20.

THE hardest thing for Eugenia about these terribly hard days of suspense was to keep her self-control in her own room. Of course for her as for any civilized being, it was always possible to keep herself in hand with people looking on. But for years she had not had to struggle so when alone for poise and self-mastery. Her room at the Crittendens', which had been hers so long, and which Marise had let her furnish with her own things, was no longer the haven of refuge it had been from the bitter, raw crudity of the Vermont life. She tried to fill the empty hours of Neale's daily absences from the house with some of the fastidious, delicate occupations of which she had so many, but they seemed brittle in her hot hands, and broke when she tried to lean on them. A dozen times a day she interrupted herself to glance with apprehension at her reflection in the mirror, the Florentine mirror with the frame of brown wood carved, with the light, restrained touch of a good period, into those tasteful slender columns. And every time she looked, she was horrified and alarmed to see deep lines of thought, of hope, of impatience, of emotion, criss-crossing fatally on her face.

Then she would sit down before her curving dressing-table, gather the folds of her Persian room-dress about her, lift up her soul and go through those mental and physical relaxing exercises which the wonderful lecturer of last winter had explained. She let her head and shoulders and neck droop like a wilted flower-stem, while she took into her mind the greater beauty of a wilted flower over the crass rigidity of a growing one; she breathed deeply and slowly and rhythmically, and summoned to her mind far-off and rarely, difficultly, beautiful things; the tranquil resignation of Chinese roofs, tempered with the merry human note of their tilted corners; Arabian traceries; cunningly wrought, depraved wood-carvings in the corners of Gothic cathedrals; the gay and amusing pink rotundities of a Boucher ceiling. When she felt her face calm and unlined again, she put on a little massage-cream, to make doubly sure, and rubbed it along where the lines of emotion had been.

But half an hour afterwards, as she lay stretched in the chaise-longue by the window, reading Claudel, or Strindberg, or Rémy de Gourmont, she would suddenly find that she was not thinking of what was on the page, that she saw there only Marise's troubled eyes while she and Marsh talked about the inevitable and essential indifference of children to their parents and the healthiness of this instinct; about the foolishness of the parents' notion that they would be formative elements in the children's lives; or on the other hand, if the parents did succeed in forcing themselves into the children's lives, the danger of sexual mother-complexes. Eugenia found that instead of thrilling voluptuously, as she knew she ought, to the precious pain and bewilderment of one of the thwarted characters of James Joyce, she was, with a disconcerting and painful eagerness of her own, bringing up to mind the daunted silence Marise kept when they mentioned the fact that of course everybody nowadays knew that children are much better off in a big, numerous, robust group than in the nervous, tight isolation of family life; and that a really trained educator could look out for them much better than any mother, because he could let them alone as a mother never could.

She found that such evocations of facts poignantly vital to her personally were devastatingly more troubling to her facial calm than any most sickening picture in d'Annunzio's portrayal of small-town humanity in which she was trying to take the proper, shocked interest. Despite all her effort to remain tranquil she would guess by the stir of her pulses that probably she had lost control of herself again, and going to the mirror would catch her face all strained and tense in a breathless suspense.

But if there was one thing which life had taught her, it was persevering patience. She drew from the enamelled bonbonnière one of the curious, hard sweetmeats from Southern China; lifted to her face the spicy-sweet spikes of the swamp-orchid in her Venetian glass vase; turned her eyes on the reproduction of the Gauguin *Ja Orana Maria*, and began to draw long, rhythmic breaths, calling on all her senses to come to her rescue. She let her arms and her head and her shoulders go limp again, and fixed her attention on rare and beautiful things of beauty . . . abandoning herself to the pictures called up by a volume of translated Japanese poems she had recently read . . . temples in groves . . . bells in the mist . . . rain on willow-trees . . . snow falling without wind. . . . How delicate and suggestive those poems were! How much finer, more subtle than anything in the Aryan languages!

She came to herself cautiously, glanced at her face in the mirror, and reached for the carved ivory pot of massage-cream.

She decided then she would sew a little, instead of reading. The frill of lace in her net dress needed to be changed . . . such a bore having to leave your maid behind. She moved to the small, black-lacquered table where her work-box stood and leaned on it for a moment, watching the dim reflection of her pointed white fingers in the glistening surface of the wood. They did not look like Marise's brown, uncared-for hands. She opened the inlaid box and took from it the thimble which she had bought in Siena, the little antique masterpiece of North Italian gold-work. What a fulfilment of oneself it was to make life beautiful by beautifying all its implements. What a revelation it might be to Neale, how a woman could make everything she touched exquisite, to Neale who had only known Marise, subdued helplessly to the roughness of the rough things about her, Marise who had capitulated to America and surrendered to the ugliness of American life.

But none of that, none of that! She was near the danger-line again. She felt the flesh on her face begin to grow tense, and with her beautiful, delicate forefingers she smoothed her eyebrows into relaxed calm again.

She must keep herself occupied incessantly; that was the only thing possible. She had been about to have recourse to the old, old tranquillizer of women, the setting of fine stitches. She would fix her mind on that . . . a frill of lace for the net dress . . . which lace? She lifted the cover from the long, satin-covered box and fingered over the laces in it, forcing herself to feel the suitable reaction to their differing physiognomies, to admire the robustness of the Carrick-Macross, the boldness of design of the Argentan, the complicated fineness of the English Point. She decided, as harmonizing best with the temperament of the net dress, on Malines, a strip of this perfect, first-Napoleon Malines. What an aristocratic lace it was, with its cobwebby *fond-de-neige* background and its four-petalled flowers in the scrolls. Americans were barbarians indeed that Malines was so little known; in fact hardly recognized at all. Most Americans would probably take this priceless creation in her hand for something bought at a ten-cent store, because of its simplicity and classic reticence of design. They always wanted, as they would say themselves, something more to show for their money. Their only idea of 'real lace,' as they vulgarly called it (as if anything could be lace that wasn't real), was that showy, awful Brussels, manufactured for exportation, which was sold in those terrible tourists' shops in Belgium, with the sprawling patterns made out of coarse braid and *appliquéd* on, not an organic part of the life of the design.

She stopped her work for a moment to look more closely at the filmy lace in her hand, to note if the mesh of the *réseau* were circular or hexagonal. She fancied that she was the only American woman of her acquaintance who knew the difference, who had the least culture in the matter of lace . . . except Marise, of course, and it was positively worse for Marise to have been initiated and then turn back to commonness, than for those other well-meaning, Philistine American women who were at least innocently ignorant. Having known the exquisite lore of lace, how could Marise have let it and all the rest of the lore of civilization drop for these coarse occupations of hers, now? How could she have let life coarsen her, as it had, how could she have fallen into such common ways, with her sun-browned hair, and her roughened hands, and her inexactly adjusted dresses, and the fatal middle-aged lines beginning to show from the corner of the ear down into the neck, and not an effort made to stop them? But as to wrinkles, of course a woman as unrestrained as Marise was bound to get them early. She had never learned the ABC of woman's wisdom, the steady cult of self-care, self-beautifying, self-refining. How long would it be before Neale . . .

No! None of that! She must get back to impersonal thoughts. What was it she had selected as subject for consideration? It had been lace. What about lace? Lace . . .? Her mind balked, openly rebellious. She could not make it think of lace again. She was in a panic, and cast about her for some strong defence . . . oh! just the thing . . . the new hat.

She would try on the new hat which had just come from New York. She had been waiting for a leisurely moment, really to be able to put her attention on that.

She opened the gaily printed round pasteboard box, and took out the creation. She put it on with care, low over her eyebrows, adjusting it carefully by feel, before she looked at herself to get the first impression. Then, hand-glass in hand, she began to study it seriously from various angles. When she was convinced that from every view-point her profile had the unlovely and inharmonious silhouette fashionable that summer, she drew a long breath of relief, and took it off gently, looking at it with pleasure. Nothing gives one such self-confidence, she reflected, as the certainty of having the right sort of hat. How much better 'chic' was than beauty!

With the hat still in her hand, her very eyes on it, she saw there before her, as plainly as though in a crystal ball, Marise's attitude as she had stood with Marsh that evening before at the far end of the garden. Her body drawn towards his, the poise of her head, all of her listening intently while he talked . . . one could see how he was dominating her. A man with such a personality as his, regularly hypnotic when he chose, and practised in handling women, he would be able to do anything he liked with an impressionable creature like Marise, who as a girl was always under the influence of something or other. It was evident that he could put any idea he liked into Marise's head just by looking at her hard enough. She had seen him do it . . . helped him do it, for that matter!

And so Neale must have seen. Anybody could! And Neale was not raising a hand, nor so much as lifting an eyebrow, just letting things take their course.

What could that mean except that he would welcome . . .

Oh Heavens! her pulse was hammering again. She sprang up and ran to the mirror. Yes, the mirror showed a face that scared her; haggard and pinched with a fierce desire.

There were not only lines now, there was a hollow in the cheek . . . or was that a shadow? It made her look a thousand years old. Massage would do that no good! And she had no faith in any of those 'flesh-foods.' Perhaps she was underweight. The hideous strain and suspense of the last weeks had told on her. Perhaps she would better omit those morning exercises for a time, in this intense heat. Perhaps she would better take cream with her oatmeal again. Or perhaps cream of wheat would be better than oatmeal. How ghastly that made her look! But perhaps it was only a shadow. She could not summon courage enough to move and see. Finally she took up her hand-mirror, framed in creamy ivory, with a carved jade bead hanging from it by a green silk cord. She went to the window to get a better light on her face. She examined it, holding her breath; and drew a long, long sigh of respite and relief. It *had* been only a shadow!

But what a fright it had given her! Her heart was quivering yet. What unending vigilance it took to protect yourself from deep emotions. When it wasn't one, it was another that sprang on you unawares.

Another one *was* there, ready to spring also, the suddenly conceived possibility, like an idea thrust into her mind from the outside, that there might be some active part she could play in what was going on in this house. People did sometimes. If some chance for this offered . . . you never could tell when . . . a word might be . . . perhaps something to turn Marise from Neale long enough to . . .

She cast this idea off with shame for its crudeness. What vulgar raw things would come into your head when you let your mind roam idly . . . like cheap melodrama . . .

She would try the Vedanta deep-breathing exercises this time to quiet herself; and after them, breathing in and out through one nostril, and thinking of the Infinite, as the Yogi had told her.

She lay down flat on the bed for this, kicking off her quilted satin *mules*, and wriggling her toes loose in their lace-like silk stockings. She would lie on her back, look up at the ceiling, and fix her mind on the movement up and down of her navel in breathing, as the Vedanta priest recommended to quiet the spirit. Perhaps she could even say,

'Om . . . om . . . om . . .'

as they did.

No, no she couldn't. She still had vestiges of that stupid, gross Anglo-Saxon self-consciousness clinging to her. But she would outgrow them yet.

She lay there quiet and breathed slowly, her eyes fixed on the ceiling. And into her mind there slowly slid a cypress-shaded walk with Rome far below on one side, and a sun-ripened, golden, old wall on the other. She stood there with Marise, both so young, so young! And down the path towards them came a tall figure, with a bold clear face, a tender full-lipped mouth, and eyes that both smiled and were steady.

Helplessly she watched him come, groaning in spirit at what she knew would happen; but she could not escape till the ache in her throat swelled and broke, as she saw that his eyes were for Marise and his words, and all of his very self for which she . . .

So many years . . . so many years . . . with so much else in the world . . . not to have been able to cure that one ache . . . and she did not want to suffer . . . she wanted to be at rest, and have what she needed. The tears rose brimming to her eyes, and ran down on each side of her face to the pillow. Poor Eugenia! Poor Eugenia!

She was almost broken this time, but not entirely. There was some fight left in her. She got up from the bed, clenched her hands tightly, and stood in the middle of the floor, gathering herself together.

Down with it! Down! Down! Just now, at this time, when such an utterly unexpected dawn of a possible escape . . . to give way again.

She thought suddenly, 'Suppose I give up the New-Thought way, always distracting your attention to something else, always suppressing your desire, resisting the pull you want to yield to. Suppose I try the Freud way, bringing the desire up boldly, letting yourself go, unresisting.' It was worth trying.

She sat down in a chair, her elbows on the dressing-table, and let herself go, gorgeously, wholly, epically, as she had been longing to ever since she had first intercepted that magnetic interchange of looks between Marsh and Marise, the day after her arrival, the day of the picnic-supper in that stupid old woman's garden. That was when she had first known that something was up.

Why, how easy it was to let yourself go! They were right, the Freudians, it was the natural thing to do, you did yourself a violence when you refused to. It was like sailing off above the clouds on familiar wings, although it was the first time she had tried them. . . . Marise would fall wholly under Marsh's spell, would run away and be divorced. Neale would never raise a hand against her doing this. Eugenia saw from his aloof attitude that it was nothing to him one way or the other. Any man who cared for his wife would fight for her, of course.

And it was so manifestly the best thing for Marise too, to have a very wealthy man looking out for her, that there could be no disturbing reflexes of regret or remorse for anybody to disturb the perfection of this foreordained adjustment to the Infinite. Then with the children away at school for all the year, except a week or two with their father . . . fine, modern, perfect schools, the kind where the children were always out of doors, Florida in winter and New England hills in summer. Those schools were horribly expensive . . . what was all her money for? . . . but they had the best class of wealthy children, carefully selected for their social position, and the teachers were so well paid that of course they did their jobs better than parents.

Then Neale, freed from slavery to those insufferable children, released from the ignoble, grinding narrowness of this petty manufacturing business, free to roam the world as she knew he had always longed to do . . . what a life they could have . . . India with Neale . . . China . . . Paris . . . they would avoid Rome perhaps because of unwelcome memories . . . Norway in summer-time. Think of seeing Neale fishing a Norway salmon brook . . . she and Neale on a steamer together . . . together . . .

She caught sight of her face in the mirror . . . that radiant, smiling, triumphant, *young* face, hers!

Yes, the Freud way was the best.

Chapter 17: *The Soul of Nelly Powers*

July 20.

THE big pine was good for one thing, anyhow, if it did keep the house as dark as a cellar with the black shade it made. The side-porch was nice and cool even on a hot summer day, just right for making butter. If it wasn't for the horrid pitch-piney smell the tree wouldn't be so bad. The churning was getting along fine too. The dasher was beginning to go the blob-blob way that showed in a minute or two the butter would be there. It had been a real good idea to get up early and get the work out of the way so that the churning could be done before it got so hot. A thunderstorm was coming, too, probably. You could feel it in the air. There, perhaps the butter had come now. Nelly pushed the dasher down slowly and drew it back with care, turning her ear to listen expertly to the sound it made. No, not yet, there wasn't that watery splash yet that came after it had separated.

She went on with the regular rhythmic motion, her eyes fixed dreamily on the round hole in the cover of the churn, through which the dasher-handle went up and down and which was now rimmed with thick yellow cream. She loved to churn, Nelly thought. She loved to have milk to look out for, anyhow, from the time it came in from the barn, warm and foamy and sweet-smelling, till the time when she had taken off the thick, sour cream, like shammy-skin, and then poured the loppered milk spatteringly into the pigs' trough. She liked seeing how the pigs loved it, sucking it up, their eyes half shut because it tasted so good. There wasn't anything that was better than giving people or animals what they liked to eat. It made her feel good all over to throw corn to the hens and see how they scrabbled for it. She just loved to get a bag of stick candy at the store, when she went to town, and see how Addie and Ralph and little 'Gene jumped up and down when they saw it.

And then it was so nice to be forehanded and get the churning out of the way before noon. She would have time this afternoon after the dishes were done to sit right down with that sprigged calico dress for little Addie. She could get the seams all run up on the machine before supper-time, and have the hand-work, buttonholes and finishing for pick-up work for odd minutes. She just loved to sit and sew in a room all nice and picked up, and know the housework was done.

That would be a *real* pretty dress, she thought, with the pink sprigs and the pink feather-stitching in mercerized cotton she was going to put on it. Addie would look sweet in it. And if it was washed careful and dried in the shade it wouldn't fade so much. It was a good bright pink to start with. Only Addie ought to have a new hat to wear with it. A white straw with pink flowers on it. But that would cost a couple of dollars, anyhow, everything was so dear now. Oh well, 'Gene would let her buy it. 'Gene would let her do most anything.

She thought with pity of her sisters, mill-hands in West Adams still, or married to mill-hands, men who got drunk on the sly and didn't work regular, and wanted a full half of all they made for themselves. 'Gene and his mother were always scolding about the money they could have had if they'd kept that wood-land on the mountain. They'd ought to ha' been really poor the way she had been, so's you didn't know where the next meal was coming from, or how the rent was going to be paid. She had been awfully lucky to get 'Gene, who let her decide how much money ought to be spent on the children's clothes and hers, and never said a thing, or scolded or bothered. He was kind of *funny*, 'Gene was, always so sober and solemn, and it was a *sort* of bother to have him so crazy about her still. That had been all right when they were engaged, and first married. She had liked it all right then, although it always seemed sort of foolish to her. But men *were* that way! Only now, when there were three children and another one coming, and the house to be kept nice, and the work done up right, and the farmwork and everything going so good, and so much on her mind, why, it seemed as though they'd ought to have other things to think about beside kissings and huggings. Not that 'Gene didn't do his share of the work. He was a fine farmer, as good as anybody in the valley. But he never could settle down, and be comfortable and quiet with her, like it was natural for old married folks to do. If she went by him, close, so her arm touched him, why then, if nobody was there he'd grab at her and kiss her and rumple her hair, and set her all back in her work. With all she had to do and think of, and she did her work as good as anybody if she did say it who shouldn't, she had her day planned before she turned her feet out of bed in the morning. And she liked to have things go the way she planned them. She *liked* 'Gene all right, only she had her work to get done.

She churned meditatively, looking off towards the mountain where the Eagle Rocks heaved themselves up, stiff and straight and high. 'Gene's mother came to the door, asked if the butter was coming all right, looked at her, and said, 'My! Nelly, you get better looking every day you live,' and went back to her bread-baking.

Nelly went on with her reflections about 'Gene. It was more than just that he bothered her and put her back with her work. She really didn't think it was just exactly nice and refined to be so crazy about anybody as that. Well, there was a streak in the Powerses that wasn't refined. 'Gene's mother! gracious! When she got going, laughing and carrying-on, what wouldn't she say, right out before anybody! And dancing still like a young girl! And that hateful old Mrs. Hewitt, just after they'd moved back to Ashley, didn't she have to go and tell her about

'Gene's being born too soon after his father and mother were married? 'Gene took it from his mother, she supposed; he wa'n't to blame, really. But she hoped Addie and Ralph would be *like* her folks. Not but what the Powerses were good-hearted enough. 'Gene was a good man, if he was queer, and an awful good papa to Addie and Ralph and little 'Gene. None of her sisters had got a man half so good. That sprigged dress would look good with feather-stitching around the hem, too. Why hadn't she thought of that before? She hadn't got enough mercerized thread in the house, she didn't believe, to do it all; and it was such a nuisance to run out of the thread you had to have, and nobody going to the village for goodness knows when, with the farmwork behind the way it was, on account of the rains.

She shifted her position and happened to bring one of her feet into view. Without disturbing a single beat of the regular rhythm of the dasher, she tilted her head to look at it with approbation. If there was one thing she was particular about it was her shoes. She took such comfort in having them nice. They could say what they pleased, folks could, but high heels *suited* her feet. Maybe some folks, that had great broad feet like that old Indian Touclé, felt better in those awful, sloppy old gunboats they called 'Common-sense shoes,' but *she* didn't! It would make her sick to wear them! How they did look! Was there anything so pretty, anyhow, as a fine-leather shoe with a nice pointed toe, and a pretty, curved-in heel? It made you feel refined, and as good as anybody, even if you had on a calico dress with it. That was another nice thing about 'Gene, how he'd stand up for her about wearing the kind of shoes she wanted. Let anybody start to pick on her about it, if 'twas his own mother, he'd shut 'em up short, and say Nelly could wear what she liked, he guessed. Even when the doctor had said so strict that she hadn't ought to wear them in the time before the babies came, 'Gene never said a word when he saw her doing it.

There, the butter was just almost there. She could hear the buttermilk begin to swash! She turned her head to call to her mother-in-law to bring a pitcher for the buttermilk, when a sound of galloping hoofs echoed from the road. Nelly frowned, released her hold on the dasher, listened an instant, and ran into the house. She went right upstairs to her room as provoked as she could be. Well, she would make the bed and do the room-work anyhow, so's not to waste *all* that time. She'd be that much ahead, anyhow. And as soon as Frank had finished chinning with Mother Powers, and had gone, she'd go back and finish her churning. She felt mad all through at the thought of that cream left at just the wrong minute, just as it was separating. Suppose Frank hung round and *hung* around, the way he did often, and the sun got higher and the cream got too warm, and she'd have to put in ice, and go down cellar with it, and fuss over it all the rest of the day? She was furious and thumped the pillows hard with her doubled-up fist. But if she went down, Frank'd hang around worse, and talk so foolish she'd want to slap him. He wa'n't more'n half-witted, some- times, she thought. What was the *matter* with men, anyhow? They didn't seem to have as much sense as so many calves! You'd think Frank would think up something better to do than to bother the life out of busy folks, sprawling around all over creation the way he did. But she never had any luck! Before Frank it had been that old Mrs. Hewitt, nosing around to see what she could pick fault with in a person's housekeeping, looking under the sink if you left her alone in the kitchen for a minute, and opening your dresser drawers right before your face and eyes. Well, Frank was getting to be most as much of a nuisance. He didn't peek and snoop the way Mrs. Hewitt did, but he *bothered*; and he was getting so impudent, too! He had the big-head because he was the best dancer in the valley, that was what was the matter with him, and he knew she liked to dance with him. Well, she did. But she would like to dance with anybody who danced good. If 'Gene didn't clump so with his feet, she'd love to dance with him. And Frank needn't think he was so much either. That city man who was staying with the old man next to the Crittendens was just as good a dancer as Frank, just exactly as light on his feet. She didn't like him a bit. She thought he was just plain fresh, the way he told Frank to go on dancing with her. What was it to him! But she'd dance with him just the same, if she got the chance. How she just loved to dance! Something seemed to get into her when the music struck up. She hardly knew what she was doing, felt as though she was floating around on that thick, soft moss you walked on when you went blue-berrying on the Burning above the Eagle Rocks . . . all springly. . . . If you could only dance by yourself, without having to bother with partners, that was what would be nice.

She stepped to the door to listen, and heard 'Gene's mother cackling away like an old hen. How she would carry on with anybody that came along! She hadn't never settled down, not a bit really, for all she had been married and was a widow and was old. It wa'n't nice to be so lively as that at her age. But she *wasn't* nice, Mother Powers wasn't, for all she was good to Addie and Ralph and little 'Gene. Nelly liked nice people, she thought, as she went back to shake the rag rugs out of the window; refined ladies like Mrs. Bayweather, the minister's wife. That was the way *she* wanted to be, and have little Addie grow up. She lingered at the window a moment looking up at the thick dark branches of the big pine. How horrid it was to have that great tree so close to the house! It shaded the bed-room so that there was a musty smell no matter how much it was aired. And the needles dropped down so messy too, and spoiled the grass.

Frank's voice came up the stairs, bold, laughing, 'Nelly, Nelly, come down here a minute. I want to ask you some-thing!'

'I can't,' she called back. Didn't he have the nerve!

'Why can't you?' the sceptical question came from half-way up the stairs. 'I saw you on the side-porch, just as I came up.'

Nelly cast about for an excuse. Of course you had to have some *reason* for saying you couldn't see a neighbour who came in. She had an inspiration. 'I'm washing my hair,' she called back, taking out the hairpins hastily as she spoke. The great coils came tumbling down on her shoulders. She soused them in the water pitcher, and went to the door, opening it a crack, tipping her head forward so that the water streamed on the floor. 'Can't you ask Mother Powers for whatever it is?' she said impatiently. She wished as she spoke that she could ever speak right out sharp and scratchy the way other people did. She was too easy, that was the trouble.

'Well,' said Frank, astonished, 'you be, for a fact.'

He went back down the stairs, and Nelly shut the door. She was hot all over with impatience about that butter. When it wasn't one thing to keep her from her work, it was another. Her hair all wet now. And such a job to dry it!

She heard voices in the kitchen, and the screen-door open. Thank goodness, Frank was going away! Oh my! Maybe he was going to the village! He could bring some of the pink mercerized cotton on his way back. He might as well be of *some* use in the world. She thrust her head out of the window. 'Frank, Frank, wait a minute!' she called. She ran back to her

215

work-basket, cut a length from a spool of thread, wound it around a bit of paper, and went again to the window. 'Say, Frank, get me two spools of cotton to match that, will you, at Warner and Hardy's.'

He rode his horse past the big pine, under her window, and stood up in the stirrups, looking up boldly at her, her hair in thick wet curls about her face. 'I'd do anything for you!' he said jokingly, catching at the paper she threw down to him.

She slammed the window down hard. How provoking he was! But anyhow she would have enough thread to feather-stitch that hem. She'd got that much out of him. The thought made up to her for some of the annoyance of the morning. She put a towel around her shoulders under her wet hair, and waited till he was actually out of sight around the bend of the road. It seemed to her that she saw something stir in the long grass in the meadow there. Could the woodchucks be getting so close to the house as that? She'd have to tie Towser up by her lettuce, nights, if they were.

Gracious, there it was thundering, off behind the Rocks! She'd have to hustle if she got the butter done before the storm came. When Frank had really disappeared, she ran downstairs, and rushed out to her churn. She felt of it anxiously, her face clearing to note that it seemed no warmer than when she had left it. Maybe it was all right still. She began to plunge the dasher up and down. Well, it had gone back some, she could tell by the feel, but not so much, she guessed, but what she could make it come all right.

As she churned, she thought again of Frank Warner. This was the limit! He got so on her nerves, she declared to herself she didn't care if he *never* danced with her again. She wished she had more spunk, like some girls, and could just send him packing. But she never could think of any sharp things to say to folks in time. She was too easy, she knew that, always had been. Look how long she had put up with Mrs. Hewitt's snooping around. And then in the end she had got cold feet and had had to stick 'Gene on to her, to tell her they didn't want her sitting around all the time and sponging off them at meal-times.

But somehow she didn't want to ask 'Gene to speak to Frank that way. She was afraid somehow it would get 'Gene excited. Mostly he was so still, and then all of a sudden he'd flare up and she never could see a thing to make him then more than

216

any time. The best thing to do with Gene was to keep him quiet, just as much as she could, not do anything to get him started. That was why she never went close up to him or put her arms around his neck of her own accord. She'd *like* to pet him and make over him, the way she did over the children, but it always seemed to get him so stirred up and everything. Men were funny, anyhow! She often had thought how nice it would be if 'Gene could only be another woman. They could have such good times together.

Why, here was 'Gene himself come in from cultivating corn right in the middle of the morning. Maybe he wanted a drink. He came up on the porch without looking at her and went into the house. How heavy he walked. But then he always did. That was the trouble with his dancing. You had to step light to be a good dancer.

There was a crack of thunder again, nearer than the first one. She heard him ask his mother, 'Frank Warner been here?'

And Mother Powers say, 'Yes, he come in to ask if we could loan him our compass. He's going to go up to-morrow in the Eagle Rock woods to run out the line between the Warner and the Benson woodlots. The Warners have sold the popple on theirs to the Crittenden mill, and Frank says the blazes are all barked over, they're so old.'

Oh goody! thought Nelly, there the butter was, come all at once. The buttermilk was splashing like water. Yes, even there around the hole you could see the little yellow specks. Well, she needn't have got so provoked after all. That was fine. Now she could get at that sprigged dress for Addie, after all, this afternoon.

'Gene came out on the porch again. She looked at him and smiled. She felt very happy and relieved that the butter had come so that she could finish working it over before noon.

'Gene glowered at her smiling face and at her hair curling and shining all down her back. How cross he looked! Oh bother! Excited too. Well, what could the matter be, *now*? She should think any man would be satisfied to come in right in the middle of the morning like that, without any warning, and find his house as spick and span as a pin, and the butter churned and half the day's work out of the way. She'd like to know what more he wanted? Who else could do any better? Oh bother! How queer men were!

Yes, it would really be lots nicer if there were only women and children in the world. Gracious! how that lightning made her jump! The storm had got there quicker'n she'd thought. But the butter had come, so it was all right.

PART III

Chapter 18: *Before the Dawn*

July 21.

NEALE had lain so long with his eyes on the place where the window ought to be, that finally he was half-persuaded he could see it, a faintly paler square against the black of the room. Very soon dawn would come in that window, and another day would begin.

At the thought the muscles of his forearms contracted, drawing his fingers into rigidly clenched fists, and for a moment he did not breathe.

Then he conquered it again; threw off the worst of the pain that had sprung upon him when he had wakened suddenly, hours before, with the fear at last there before him, visible in the darkness.

What was this like? Where before had he endured this eternity of waiting? Yes, it was in France, the night when they waited for the attack to break, every man haggard with the tension, from dark till just before dawn.

He lay still, feeling Marise's breathing faintly stirring the bed.

There in France it had been a strain almost beyond human power to keep from rushing out of the trenches with bayonets fixed to meet the threatened danger, to beat it back, to conquer it, or to die and escape the suspense. Now there was the same strain. He had the weapons in his hands, weapons of passion and indignation and entreaty and reproach, against which Marise would not stand for a moment.

But there in France that would have meant possibly an insignificant local success and the greater victory all along the line imperilled. And here that was true again. There hadn't been anything to do then but wait. There was nothing to do now but wait.

Yes, but it was harder to wait now! There in France they had at least known that finally the suspense would end in the fury of combat. They would have the chance to resist, to conquer, to impose their will. And now there was no active part for him. He must wait on, and hold back his hand from the attack which would give him the appearance of victory, and which would mean everlasting defeat for him, for Marise, the death and ruin of what they had tried to be for each other, to build up out of their life together.

What did he mean by that? Wasn't he fooling himself with words, with priggish phrases? It was so easy to do that. And he was so mortally fatigued with this struggle in the dark. He had been thinking about it so deeply, so desperately, ever since he had faced it there, squarely, those endless black hours ago. He might have lost his way.

Now, once more, slowly, step by step, once more over the terrible road that led him here. Perhaps there was another way he had overlooked. Perhaps this time it would lead him to something less intolerable. Quiet now, steady, all that he had of courage and honesty and knowledge of Marise, and of life, and of himself, put to work.

His brain began again to plod up the treadmill it had laboured on for so many black hours. He set himself to get it clear in his own mind, forcing those fierce, burning thoughts of his into words, as if he had been speaking aloud. 'Now, now here I am. What must I do? What ought I to do? There must be some answer if I can only think clearly, feel aright. *What is it that I want?*'

The answer burst from him, as though in a cry of torture from his brain, his body, his passion, his soul, '*I want Marise!*'

And at this expression of overmastering desire, memory flooded his mind with a stream of unforgotten pictures of their life together; Marise facing him at the breakfast-table; Marise walking with him in the autumn woods; Marise with Paul a baby in her arms; Marise, almost unknown then, the flame-like divinity of her soul only guessed at, looking into his eyes as the Campagna faded into darkness below them. 'What was it she asked me then? Whether I knew the way across the dark plain? I was a confident young fool then. I was sure I could find the way *with her*. I've been thinking all these years that we were finding it, step by step . . . till now. And now, what is it I am afraid of? I'm afraid she finds herself cramped, wants a fuller existence, regrets . . . no, that's dodging. There's no use lying to myself. I'm afraid that Marise is in love with Vincent Marsh. Good God! no! It can't be that . . . not

220

Marise! This is all nonsense. This is something left over from sleep and a bad dream. I must wake up. I must wake up and find it not true.'

He lay perfectly still, his fists clenched tight, perspiration standing out on his rigid body. Then sternly he forced his mind to go forward again, step by step.

'I suppose it's possible. Other women have. There's a lot in her that must be starved here. I may not be enough for her. She was so young then. She has grown so greatly. What right have I to try to hold her if she is tired of it all, needs something else?'

He hesitated, shrinking back as from fire, from the answer he knew he must give. At last he forced it out, 'I haven't any right. I don't want her to stay if she wants to go. I want Marise. But even more I want her to be happy.'

The thought, with all its implications, terrified him like a death-sentence, but he repeated it grimly, pressing it home fiercely, 'I want her to be happy.'

He realized where this thought would lead him, and in a panic wildly fought against going on. He had tried to hold himself resolute and steady, but he was nothing now save a flame of resentment. 'Happy! She won't be happy that way! She can't love that man! She's being carried away by that damnable sensibility of hers. It would be the most hideous, insane mistake. What am I thinking of . . . all these *words*! What I must do is to keep her from ruining her life.'

On the heels of this outcry, there glided in insinuatingly a soft-spoken crowd of tempting, seductive possibilities. Marise was so sensitive, so impressionable, so easily moved, so defence-less when her emotions were aroused. Hadn't he the right, the duty, he who knew her better than anyone else, to protect her against herself? Wasn't he deceiving himself by fantastic notions? It would be so easy to act the ardent, passionate young lover again . . . but when had he ever 'acted' anything for Marise! No matter, no matter, this was life or death; what was a lie when life and death hung in the balance? He could play on her devotion to the children, throw all the weight of his personality, work on her emotions. That was what people did to gain their point. Everybody did it. And he could win if he did. He could hold her.

Like the solemn tolling of a great bell there rang, through all this hurried, despairing clutching at the endurable and lesser, a call to the great and intolerable. The immensity of his love for Marise loomed up, far greater than he; and before that sacred thing he hung his head, and felt his heart breaking.

'No, that won't do. Not when it is Marise who is in question. The best, the very best I can conceive is what I must give to Marise. A cage could not hold her, not anything but her body, and to force her decision would be to make a cage. No, I mustn't use the children either. They are hers as much as mine. If all is not right between us, what would it avail them to be with us? They must take what life brings them, like the rest of us. If the years Marise and I have passed together, if what we have been to each other, and are to each other, if that is not enough, then nothing is enough. That would be a trick to play on her . . . to use my knowledge of her vulnerable points to win. That is not what I want. What *do* I want? I want Marise to be happy.'

He had advanced a step since the last time he had told himself this, for now he said it with a dreadful calm, his heart aching but not faltering.

But he could go no farther. There were limits to what he could endure. He fell into a trance-like state of passivity, his body and mind exhausted.

As he lay thus, fallen and prostrate, there soared up out of a part of him that was neither mind nor body, but was nevertheless himself, something swift and beautiful and living, something great enough at last to measure its greatness with the immensity of his love for Marise.

What was it?

It was this . . . for a moment he had it all clear, as though he had died and it were something told him in another world . . . he did not want Marise for himself; he did not even want her to be happy; he wanted her to be herself, to be all that Marise could ever grow to be, he wanted her to attain her full stature so far as any human being could do this in this life.

And to do that she must be free.

For an instant he looked full at this, his heart flooded with glory. And then the light went out.

He was there in the blackness again, unhappy beyond any suffering he had thought he could bear.

He lay still, feeling Marise beside him, the slow, quiet rhythm of her breathing. Was she awake or sleeping? What would happen if he should allow the fear and suffering which racked him to become articulate? If he should cry out to her, she would not turn away. He knew Marise. She would never turn away from fear and suffering. 'But I can't do that. I won't work on her sympathy. I've promised to be true to what's deepest and truest in us both. I have been, by God! and I will be. If our married life has been worth anything, it's because we've both been free and honest . . . true with one another. This is her ordeal. She must act for herself. Better die than use my strength to force her against her own nature. If I decide . . . no matter how sure I am I'm right . . . it won't be her decision. Nothing would be decided. I must go on just as before . . .' he groaned, 'that will take all the strength I have.'

It was clear to him now; the only endurable future for them, such as they were to each other, would come from Marise's acting with her own strength on her own decision. By all that was sacred, he would never by word or act hamper that decision. He would be himself, honestly. Marise ought to know what that self was.

He had thought that this resolve would bring to him another of these terrible racking instants of anguish, but instead there came almost a calm upon him, as though the pain had passed and left him in peace, or as though a quiet light had shone out in the darkness. Perhaps the dawn had come. No, the square of the window was still only faintly felt in the blacker mass of the silent room.

Then he knew why the pain had left him. It had been driven away by the certainty that there was a worse fear than any he knew, or ever would know. No matter what risk or catastrophe lay before them, Marise would never look at him out her clear eyes and act a thing that was not true. Marise would always be Marise. Why then, whatever came he could bear it.

Life might be cruel and pitiless, but it was not base, when it had among its gifts such a certainty as that, rock-like under his feet, bearing him up in his pain.

He moved to her in the bed, felt for her hand and put it gently to his lips.

Then, holding it in his, on his breast, he turned his eyes towards the window, waiting for the dawn.

Chapter 19: *Mr. Welles Lights the Fuse*

THAT early-morning talk with Mr. Welles had left Marise trembling with helpless sorrow and exasperation. She sat on the bench where he had left her, and felt the nervous tears stinging her eyes. When she looked up and saw Vincent Marsh was standing there, extremely pale, as visibly shaken as she, as visibly little in control of himself, she burst out, 'So you too know. He has just told me that he is really going. The very date is set. His cousin has a room in her boarding-house engaged for him. He's going to work as a clerk to pay for the extra expenses of the life there. *Oh!*' She struck her hand on the back of the bench.

Vincent Marsh sat down beside her, his eyes on hers. He said in a curious, low voice, rough and husky, 'I wish you would do something for me. I wish you would think with all your might, deeply, just why you are so opposed to his doing what evidently seems to him a very saintly and heroic action; and then tell me why it is.'

Marise felt this as a challenge. He was always challenging everything. This time she was more than ready. 'I don't need any time to think of reasons!' she cried. 'It's obvious to anyone with any sense for the reality of human values, who isn't fooled by threadbare old words. It's one of those wasteful, futile, exasperating tricks people play on themselves in the name of "duty." He's throwing away something real and true, something that could add to the richness of human life, he's throwing away the happiness that comes of living as suits his nature, and so creating a harmony that enriches everybody who touches him. And what's he doing it for? To satisfy a morbid need for self-sacrifice. He's going to do harm, in all probability, mix up a situation already complicated beyond solution, and why is he? So that he can indulge himself in the perverse pleasure of the rasp of a hair-shirt. He doesn't really use his intelligence to think, to keep a true sense of proportions; he takes an outworn and false old ideal of self-sacrifice, and uses it not to do anybody any real good, but to put a martyr's crown on his head.'

She became conscious that her words were having a singular effect upon Vincent. A dark flush had come over all his face. His gaze on her was extraordinary in its intentness, in its eagerness, in its fierceness. She stopped suddenly, as though he had broken in on what she was saying.

He did not stir from his place, but to her he seemed to tower taller. Into his dark, intent face came an exultant look of power and authority which fell on her like a hot wind. With a loud knocking of her heart she knew. Before he spoke, she knew what he would say. And he saw that.

He opened those burning lips and said in the same low voice, rough with its intensity, 'You see what you have done. You have spoken for me. You have said at last what I have been silently and desperately calling out to you. You know what has happened. You have said it, it is obvious to anyone with any sense of human values. Make an end! Make an end! Come away from a position where only an outworn old ideal holds you to futility and waste. Come away where you will really live and know the fullness of life. Come away from that false notion of duty which makes you do for the children what you know is not best for them, only because it is the traditional thing to do, only because it gives you a martyr's crown to wear. I don't say anything now, as I would to any other woman in the world, as I would have said to you weeks ago before I knew all that you are . . . I don't say anything about the imbecility of keeping such a woman as you are here in this narrow, drab hole, this sordid prison . . . you born, if ever a human being was, to rich and warm and harmonious living! It is your birthright. Let me give it to you. All that, even that, a whole world of beauty and fullness waiting for you to create it to glorious being, all that is nothing compared to what has come to pass between us, you and me; compared to the other world of impassioned living existence that is waiting for you. Come away from the man who is nothing more to you than the house you live in . . . nothing but a habit.'

She started at this, moving out of the stony immobility in which she gazed at him, listened to him. She did not know that she had moved, was incapable of willing to do so. It had been a mere reflex start as though she had been struck. But at the sight of it, the flame in his eyes leaped up. 'No, no, no!' he cried with an insistent triumph, 'he is nothing more to you than a habit. And you are nothing more to him. You were right, on that evening when you shrank away from the sight of the place in Italy where in your ignorant youth you made the mistake of trying to join your life to his. There is not a breath you draw, not a turn of your head or body . . . I know them all . . . that does not prove that he is nothing to you now. I have seen you take a handkerchief from his pocket as you would take it from a bureau-drawer. I have seen him set you on one side, to pass through a door, as he would set a chair on one side. You don't even see him any more when you look at him, and he doesn't see you. Whatever there may have been between you, if there was ever anything real, it is dead now, dead and buried . . . and you the most living woman who ever wore flesh and blood! And I am a living man! You know, I don't need to say it, you know what happens when our looks meet. Our looks only! Life flares up like a torch in both of us. You know if I but brush against your skirt, how I cannot speak! You know how when our hands touch, every drop of blood in our two bodies burns! You are a grown woman. You know life as well as I do. You know what this means. You are no longer even a part of his life. You are all of mine. Look at me now.'

He flung out his hands, shaking uncontrollably. 'Do you see how I show this, say this anywhere, tell this to you here, now, where anyone could hear me? I am not ashamed of it. It is not a thing to hide. It is a thing to glory in. It is the only honestly living thing in all our miserable human life, the passion of a man and a woman for each other. It is the only thing that moves us out of our cowardly lethargy of dead-and-alive egotism. The thing that is really base and false is to pretend that what is dead is still alive. Your marriage is dead. Your children do not need you as you pretend. Let yourself go in this flood that is sweeping us along. I had never thought to know it. I could fall down and worship you because you have shown it to me. But I will show it to you, that and the significance of what you will be when you are no longer smothered and starved. In all this crawling ant-heap of humanity, there are only a handful of human beings who ever really live. And we will be among them. All the rest are nothing, less than nothing, to be stamped down if they impede you. They have no other destiny. But we have! Everything comes down to that in the end. That is the only truth. That . . . and you and I!'

In the distance, someone called Marise's name. He thought she made a move, and said, leaning towards her, the heat of his body burning through to her arm where he touched her, 'No, no, none of those trivial, foolish interruptions that tie you hand and foot can tie us any longer. They have no real strength. They can't stand for an instant against something alive. All that rattles in your ears, that keeps you from knowing what you really are . . .'

Someone was hurrying down the walk towards them, hidden by the hedge. Marise could not have turned her head if her life had hung on the action.

Vincent looked straight at her, straight and deep and strong into her eyes, and for an instant his burning lips were pressed on hers. The contact was terrible, momentous.

When he went on speaking, without haste, unafraid although the hurrying steps were almost there, she could scarcely hear his voice, although it was urgent and puissant as the impact of his eyes. 'You can't get away from this now. It is here. It has been said. It lives between us, and you are not strong enough, no power on earth is strong enough, to put it down.'

And then the outer world broke in on them, swept between them with an outcry. Someone was there, someone who drew short sobbing breaths, who caught at her and clung to her. It was Cousin Hetty's old Agnes . . . why in the world was she here? . . . and she was saying in a loud voice as though she had no control of it, 'Oh, oh! Come quick! Come quick!'

Marise stood up, carrying the old woman with her. She was entirely certain now that she was in a nightmare, from which she would presently awake, wet with cold sweat.

'Come! Come!' cried the old woman, beating her hands on Marise's arm. 'Perhaps it ain't too late. Perhaps you can do something.'

'What has happened?' asked Marise, making her voice sharp and imperative to pierce the other's agitation.

'I don't know. I don't know,' sobbed Agnes. 'She didn't come down for breakfast. I went up to see . . . oh, go quick! Go quick!'

She went down, half on the bench, half on the ground.

Marise and Marsh stood for an instant, petrified.

There was only the smallest part of Marise's consciousness which was alive to this. Most of it lay numbed and bewildered, still hearing, like a roll of thunder, the voice of Vincent Marsh.

Then she turned. 'Look out for her, will you,' she said briefly. 'No, don't come with me. I'll go by the back road. It's the quickest, but it's too narrow for a car. You drive to Ashley and bring the doctor in your car.'

She ran down the path and around the house to the road, not feeling the blinding heat of the sun. She ran along the dusty road, a few steps from the house before the turn into the narrow lane. She felt nothing at all but a great need for haste.

As she ran, putting all her strength into her running, there were moments when she forgot why she was hurrying, where she was going, what had happened; but she did not slacken her pace. She was on the narrow back road now, in the dense shade of the pines below the Eagle Rocks. In five minutes she would be at Cousin Hetty's. That was where she was going.

She was running more slowly now over the rough, uneven, stony road, and she was aware, more than of anything else, of a pain in her chest where she could not draw a long breath. It seemed to her that she must be now wholly in the bad dream, for she had the nightmare sensation of running with all her strength and not advancing at all. The sombre, thick-set pines seemed to be implacably in the same place, no matter how she tried to pass them, to leave them behind, to hurry on. Everything else in the silent, breathless, midsummer forest was rooted immovably deep in the earth. She alone was killing herself with haste, and yet futilely . . . not able to get forward, not able to . . .

And then, fit to turn her brain, the forest drew aside and showed her another nightmare figure, a man, far away to her right, running down the steep incline that sloped up to the Rocks. A man running as she had been wishing she could run, a powerful, roughly dressed man, rapt in a passion of headlong flight, that cast him down the rough slope, over the rocks, through the brambles, as though his flight were part of an endless fall.

Marise stopped stock-still, shocked out of every sensation but the age-old woman's instinct of fear and concealment.

The man plunged forward, not seeing her where she stood on the road across which he now burst, flinging himself out of the pines on one side and into the thicket of undergrowth on the other.

Far from him as she was, Marise could hear, through the forest hush, the terrible sound of his breathing as he ran, as he stumbled, as he struggled to his feet, fighting crazily with the thick undergrowth. Those loud hoarse gasps . . . it was as though he were being choked to death by a hand on his throat.

He was gone, down the slope towards the valley road. The

228

leaves closed together behind him. The forest was impenetrably silent again. Marise knew who he was, then, recognized him for 'Gene Powers beyond any doubt.

She felt a strange mixture of pity and scorn and envy. To be so primitive as that . . . to think, even for an instant's madness, that you could run away on your own two poor human feet from whatever life brought to you!

She herself was hurrying forward again. What was she going to? What had she left behind? The passage of the other runner had not taken a single moment's time. She was now at the path which led to Cousin Hetty's side-door.

She darted along this, and found herself in the yard before the door, open as Agnes had left it when she rushed out for help.

A tea-kettle on the kitchen-stove sang in a low murmur. The clock ticked loudly, wagging its pendulum back and forth. The cat, stretched at full length on the floor in a yellow square of sunlight, lifted a drowsy head and looked at her. There was a smell of freshly made coffee in the air. As she stood there for an instant till the whirling in her head should stop, a stick of wood in the fire broke and fell together.

Marise went through into the dining-room where the table laid for breakfast stood in a quiet expectancy. The old house, well-kept and well-loved, wore a tranquil expression of permanence and security.

But out in the dusky hall, the white stairs stood palely motioning up. There Marise felt a singular heavy coolness in the stagnant air. She went up the stairs, leaning on the balustrade, and found herself facing an open door.

Beyond it, in a shuttered and shaded room, stood a still white bed. And on the bed, still and white and distant, lay something dead. It was not Cousin Hetty. That austere, cold face, proud and stern, was not Cousin Hetty's. It was her grandmother's, her father's, her uncle's face, whom Cousin Hetty had never at all resembled. It was the family shell which Cousin Hetty had for a time inhabited.

Marise came forward and crossed the threshold. Immediately she was aware of a palpable change in the atmosphere. The room was densely filled with silence, which folded her about coldly. She sank down on a chair. She sat motionless, looking at what lay there so quiet, at the unimaginable emptiness and remoteness of that human countenance.

This was the end. She had come to the end of her running and her haste and her effort to help. All the paltry agitations and sorrows, the strains and defeats and poor joys, they were all hurrying forward to meet this end.

All the scruples, and sacrifices, and tearing asunder of human desires to make them fit words that were called ideals, all amounted to this same nothingness in the end.

What was Cousin Hetty's life now, with its tiny inhibitions, its little passivities? The same nothingness it would have been, had she grasped boldly at life's realities and taken whatever she wanted.

And all Cousin Hetty's mother's sacrifices for her, her mother's hopes for her, the slow transfusion of her mother's life to hers; that was all dead now, had been of no avail against this nothingness. Some day Elly would lie like that, and all that she had done for Elly, or could do for her, would be only a pinch of ashes. If she, if Cousin Hetty, if Cousin Hetty's mother, if Elly, if all of them, took hotly whatever the hours had to give, they could not more certainly be brought to nothingness and oblivion in the end. . . .

Those dreams of her . . . being one with a great current, sweeping forward . . . what pitiful delusions! . . . There was nothing that swept forward. There were only futile storms of froth and excitement that whirled you about to no end, one after another. One died down and left you becalmed and stagnant, and another rose. And that would die down in its turn. Until at the end, shipwreck, and a sinking to this darkly silent abyss.

Chapter 20: *A Primæval Heritage*

July 21. Evening.

COUSIN HETTY lay coldly dead; and Marise felt herself blown upon by an icy breath that froze her numb. The doctor had come and gone, queerly, and bustlingly alive and full of talk and explanations; Agnes had come back and, silently weeping, had walked endlessly and aimlessly around the house, with a broom in her idle hand; one after another of the neighbours had come and gone, queerly alive as usual, they too, for all their hushed and awkward manners; Neale had come, seeming to feel that cold breath as little as the others.

And now Neale was gone, after everything had been decided, all the incredibly multitudinous details that must be decided. The funeral was set for the day after to-morrow, and until then, everything in everybody's life was to stop stock-still, as a matter of course. Because Agnes was in terror of being left alone for an instant, Marise would not even leave the house until after the funeral, and one of the thousand petty unescapable details she and Neale had talked of in the hushed voice which the house imposed on all in it, was the decision as to which dress and hat were to be sent to her from the wardrobe at home.

She was to stay there with Agnes, she, who was all the family old Cousin Hetty had left, for the last watch over what lay up there on the bed in her bedroom. Neale would look out for the children (there was no one else for the moment, Touclé was gone, Eugenia quite useless), would telegraph the few old friends who would care to know the news, would see Mr. Bayweather about the funeral, would telephone the man in West Ashley who dug graves, would do what was to be done outside; and she would do what was to be done inside, as now, when she sat on the stairs waiting in case the undertaker needed something.

She was glad that the undertaker was only quiet, white-bearded old Mr. Hadley, who for so many, many years had given his silent services to the dead of Ashley that he had come to seem not quite a living figure himself, hushed and stilled by his association with everlasting stillness. Marise, cold and numbed with that icy breath upon her, knew now why the old undertaker was always silent and absent. A strange life he must have had. She had never thought of it till she had seen him come into that house, where she and Agnes waited for him, uncertain, abashed, not knowing what to do. Into how many such houses he must have gone, with that same quiet look of unsurprised acceptance of what everybody knew was coming sometime and nobody ever expected to come at all. How extraordinary that it had never occurred to her that Cousin Hetty, old as she was, would some day die. You never really believed that anybody in your own life was ever going to die, or change, any more than you really believed that you yourself were ever going to grow old, or change, or that the children were ever really going to grow up. That threadbare old phrase about the death of old people, 'it always comes as a shock,' that was true of all the inevitable things that happened in life

231

which you saw happen to everyone else, and never believed would happen to you.

This was the last tie with the past gone, the last person disappeared for whom she was still the little girl she felt herself now, the little girl who had lost her way and wanted someone to put her back in the path. She had a moment of very simple, sweet sorrow, sitting there alone in the hall, warm tears streaming down her cheeks and falling on her hands. Cousin Hetty gone, dear old Cousin Hetty, with her bright living eyes, and her love for all that was young. How much she owed her . . . those troubled years of her youth when Cousin Hetty and the old house were unfailing shelter. What shelter had she now?

The pendulum of her mind swung back . . . of course this was silly traditional repeating of superstitious old words. There was no shelter; there could be none in this life. No one could show her the path, because there *was* no path; and anyone who pretended to show it was only a charlatan who traded on moments of weakness like this.

Mr. Hadley opened the door quietly and asked in that seldom-heard voice of his for a couple of soft, clean towels. Where did Cousin Hetty keep her towels? In the chest of drawers at the end of the hall. An odour of cloves came up spicily into the air as Marise opened the drawer. How like Cousin Hetty to have that instead of the faded, sentimental lavender. She had perhaps put those towels away there last night, with her busy, shaking old hands, so still now. All dead, the quaintness, the vitality, the zest in life, the new love for little Elly, all dead now, as though it had never been, availing nothing. There was nothing that did not die.

She handed in the towels and sat down again on the stairs leaning her head against the wall. What time could it be? Was it still daylight? . . . No, there was a lamp lighted down there. What could she have been doing all day, she and Agnes and the doctor and Mr. Hadley? She wondered if the children were all right, and if Neale would remember, when he washed Mark's face, that there was a bruise on his temple where the swing-board had struck him. Was that only yesterday morning? Was it possible that it was only last night that she had lain awake in the darkness, trying to think, trying to know what she was feeling, burning with excitement, as one by one those boldly forward-thrusting movements came back to her from the time when he had cried out so angrily, '*They* can't love her. They're not capable of it!' to the time when they had

232

exchanged that long reckless gaze over Elly's head? And now there was the triumphant glory of security which had been in his kiss . . . why, that was this morning, only a few hours ago! Even through her cold numbed lassitude she shrank again before the flare-up of that excitement, and burned in it. She tried to put this behind her at once, to wait, like all the rest, till this truce should be over, and she should once more be back in that mêlée of agitation the thought of which turned her sick with confusion. She was not strong enough for life, if this was what it brought, these fierce, clawing passions that did not wait for your bidding to go or come, but left you as though you were dead and then pounced on you like tigers. She had not iron in her either to live ruthlessly, or to stamp out that upward leap of flame which meant the renewal of priceless youth and passion. Between these alternatives, she *could* make no decision, she could not, it would tear her in pieces to do it.

The pendulum swung back again, and all this went out, leaving her mortally tired. Agnes came to the foot of the stairs, a little, withered, stricken old figure, her apron at her eyes. From behind it she murmured humbly, between swallowing hard, that she had made some tea and there was bread and butter ready, and should she boil an egg?

A good and healing pity came into Marise's heart. Poor old Agnes, it was the end of the world for her, of course. And how touching, how tragic, how unjust, the fate of dependants, to turn from one source of commands to another. She ran downstairs on tiptoe and put her arm around the old woman's shoulder. 'I haven't said anything yet, Agnes,' she told her, 'because this has come on us so suddenly. But of course Mr. Crittenden and I will always look out for you. Cousin Hetty . . . you were her best friend.'

The old woman laid her head down on the other's shoulder and wept aloud. 'I miss her so. I miss her so,' she said over and over.

'The thing to do for her,' thought Marise, as she patted the thin heaving shoulders, 'is to give her something to work at.' Aloud she said, 'Agnes, we must get the front room downstairs ready. Mr. Hadley wants to have Cousin Hetty brought down there. Before we eat we might as well get the larger pieces of furniture moved out.'

Agnes stood up, docilely submitting herself to the command, stopped crying, and went with Marise into the dim old room, in which nothing had been changed since the day, twenty years ago, when the furniture had been put back in place after Cousin Hetty's old mother had lain there, for the last time.

The two women began to work, and almost at once Agnes was herself again, stepping about briskly, restored by the familiarity of being once more under the direction of another. They pulled out the long haircloth sofa, moved the spindle-legged old chairs into the dining-room, and carried out one by one the drawers from the high-boy in the corner. From one of these drawers a yellowed paper fell out. Marise picked it up and glanced at it. It was a letter dated 1851, the blank page of which had been used for a game of Consequences. The foolish incoherencies lay there in the faded ink just as they had been read out, bringing with them the laughter of those people, so long dead now, who had written them down in that pointed, old-fashioned handwriting. Marise stood looking at it while Agnes swept the other room. Cousin Hetty had been ten years old in 1851, just as old as Paul was now. Her mother had probably left something she wanted to do, to sit down and laugh with her little daughter over this trivial game. A ghostly echo of that long-silent laughter fell faintly and coldly on her ear. So soon gone. Was it worth while to do it at all? Such an effort, such a fatigue lay before those children one tried to keep laughing, and then . . .

Someone came in behind her, without knocking or ringing. People had been coming and going unannounced in that house all the day as though death had made it their own home. Agnes came to the door, Marise looked up and saw Nelly Powers standing in the doorway, the second time she had been there. 'I come over again,' she said, 'to bring you some hot biscuit and honey. I knew you wouldn't feel to do much cooking.' She added, 'I put the biscuits in the oven as I come through so they'd keep warm.'

'Oh, thank you, Nelly, that's very kind and thoughtful,' said Marise. As she spoke and looked at the splendid, enigmatic woman standing there, the richness of her vitality vibrating about her, she saw again the nightmare vision of 'Gene and heard the terrible breathing that had resounded in the Eagle Rock woods. She was overwhelmed, as so often before in her life, by an amazement at the astounding difference between the aspect of things and what they really were. She had never entirely outgrown the wildness of surprise which this always brought to her. She and Nelly, looking at each other so calmly, and speaking of hot biscuits!

She listened as though it were an ironically incongruous speech in a play to Agnes' conscientious country attempt to make conversation with the caller, 'Hot to-day, ain't it? Yesterday's storm didn't seem to do much good.' And to Nelly's answer on the same note, 'Yes, but it's good for the corn to have it hot. 'Gene's been out cultivating his, all day long.'

'Ah, not all day! Not all day!' Marise kept the thought to herself. She had a vision of the man goaded beyond endurance, leaving his horses plodding in the row, while he fled blindly, to escape the unescapable.

An old resentment, centuries and ages older than she was, a primæval heritage from the past, flamed up unexpectedly in her heart. *There* was a man, she thought, who had kept the capacity really to love his wife; passionately to suffer; whose cold intelligence had not chilled down to . . .'

'Well, I guess I must be going now,' said Nelly in the speech of the valley. She went away through the side-door, opening and shutting it with meticulous care, so that it would not make a sound. . . . As though a sound could reach Cousin Hetty now!

'I don't like her biscuits,' said Agnes. 'She always puts too much sody in.' She added, in what was evidently the expression of an old dislike, 'And don't she look a fool, a great hulking critter like her, wearing such shoes, teeterin' along on them heels.'

'Oh well,' said Marise vaguely, 'it's her idea of how to look pretty.'

'They must cost an awful sight too,' Agnes went on scoldingly, 'laced half-way up her leg that way. And the Powerses as poor as Job's turkey. The money she puts into them shoes'd do 'em enough sight more good if 'twas saved up and put into a manure spreader, I call it.'

She had taken the biscuits out of the oven and was holding them suspiciously to her nose, when someone came in at the front door and walked down the hall with the hushed, self-conscious, lugubrious tiptoe step of the day. It was Mr. Bayweather, his round old face rather pale. 'I'm shocked, unutterably shocked by this news,' he said, and indeed he looked badly shaken and scared. It came to Marise that Cousin Hetty had been of about his age. He shook her hand and looked about for a chair. 'I came to see about which hymns you would like sung,' he said. 'Do you know if Miss Hetty had any favourites?' He broke off to say, 'Mrs. Bayweather wished me to be sure to excuse her to you for not coming with me to-night to see if there was anything she could do. But she was stopped by old Mrs. Warner, just as we were leaving the house. Frank, it seems, went off early this morning to survey some lines in the woods somewhere on the mountain, and was to be back to lunch. He didn't come then and hasn't showed up at all yet. Mrs. Warner wanted my wife to telephone up to North Ashley to see if he had perhaps gone there to spend the night with his aunt. The line was busy of course, and Mrs. Bayweather was still trying to get them on the wire when I had to come away. If she had no special favourites, I think that "Lead, Kindly Light, Amid th' Encircling Gloom" is always suitable, don't you?'

Something seemed to explode inside Marise's mind, and like a resultant black cloud of smoke a huge and ominous possibility loomed up, so darkly, so unexpectedly, that she had no breath to answer the clergyman's question. Those lines Frank Warner had gone to survey ran through the Eagle Rock woods!

'Or would you think an Easter one, like "The Strife Is O'er, the Battle Won," more appropriate?' suggested Mr. Bayweather to her silence.

Agnes started. 'Who's that come bursting into the kitchen?' she cried, turning towards the door.

It seemed to Marise, afterwards, that she had known at that moment who had come and what the tidings were.

Agnes started towards the door to open it. But it was flung open abruptly from the outside. Touclé stood there, her hat gone from her head, her rusty black clothes torn and disarranged.

Marise knew what she was about to announce.

She cried out to them, 'Frank Warner has fallen off the Eagle Rocks. I found him there, at the bottom, half an hour ago, dead.'

The savage old flame, centuries and ages older than she, flared for an instant high and smoky in Marise's heart. '*There* is a man who knows how to fight for his wife and keep her!' she thought fiercely.

Chapter 21: *The Counsel of the Stars*

IT had been arranged that for the two nights before the funeral Agnes was to sleep in the front bedroom, on one side of Cousin Hetty's room, and Marise in the small hall bedroom on the other side, the same room and the same bed in which she had slept as a little girl. Nothing had been changed there, since those days. The same heavy white pitcher and basin stood in the old wash-stand with the sunken top and hinged cover; the same oval white soap-dish, the same ornamental spatter-work frame in dark walnut hung over the narrow walnut bedstead.

As she undressed in the space between the bed and the wash-stand, the past came up before her in a sudden splashing wave of recollection which for a moment engulfed her. It had all been a dream, all that had happened since then, and she was again eight years old, with nothing in the world but bad dreams to fear, and Cousin Hetty there at hand as a refuge even against bad dreams. How many times she had wakened, terrified, her heart beating hammer-strokes against her ribs, and trotted shivering, in her night-gown, into Cousin Hetty's room.

'Cousin Hetty! Cousin Hetty!'

'What? What's that? Oh, you, Marise. What's the matter? Notions again?'

'Oh, Cousin Hetty, it was an *awful* dream this time. Can't I get into bed with you?'

'Why yes, come along, you silly child.'

The fumbling approach to the bed, the sheets held open, the kind old hand outstretched, and then the haven . . . her head on the same pillow with that of the brave old woman who was afraid of nothing, who drew her up close and safe and with comforting assurance instantly fell asleep again. And then the delicious, slow fading of the terrors before the obliterating hand of sleep, the delicious slow sinking into forgetfulness of everything.

Standing there, clad in the splendour of her physical maturity, Marise shivered uncontrollably again, and quaked and feared. It was all a bad dream, all of it, and now as then Cousin Hetty lay safe and quiet, wrapped in sleep which was the only escape. Marise turned sick with longing to go again, now, to seek out

237

Cousin Hetty and to lie down by her to share that safe and cold and dreamless quiet.

She flung back over her shoulder the long shining dark braid which her fingers had been automatically twisting, and stood for a moment motionless. She was suffering acutely, but the pain came from a source so deep, so confused, so inarticulate, that she could not name it, could not bring to bear on it any of the resources of her intelligence and will. She could only bend under it as under a crushing burden, and suffer as an animal endures pain, dumbly, stupidly.

After a time a small knock sounded, and Agnes' voice asked through the door if Miss Marise thought the door to . . . to . . . if the 'other' door ought to be open or shut. It was shut now. What did people do as a general thing?

Marise opened her own door and looked down on the old figure in the straight, yellowed night-gown, the knotted, big-veined hand shielding the candle from the wandering summer breeze which blew an occasional silent, fragrant breath in from the open windows.

'I don't know what people do as a rule,' she answered, and then asked, 'How did Miss Hetty like best to have it, herself?'

'Oh, open, always.'

'We'd better open it, then.'

The old servant swayed before the closed door, the candle-stick shaking in her hand. She looked up at Marise timidly. 'You do it,' she said under her breath.

Marise felt a faint pitying scorn, stepped past Agnes, lifted the latch, and opened the door wide into the blackness of the other room.

The dense silence seemed to come out, coldly and softly. For Marise it had the sweetness of a longed-for anæsthetic, it had the very odour of the dreamless quiet into which she longed to sink. But Agnes shrank away, drew hastily closer to Marise, and whispered in a sudden panic, 'Oh, don't it scare you? Aren't you afraid to be here all alone, just you and me? We'd ought to have had a man stay too.'

Marise tried to answer simply and kindly, 'No, I'm not afraid. It is only all that is left of dear Cousin Hetty.' But the impatience and contemptuous surprise which she kept out of her words and voice were felt none the less by the old woman. She drooped submissively as under a reproach. 'I know it's foolish,' she murmured, 'I know it's foolish.'

She began again to weep, the tears filling her faded eyes and

238

running quietly down her wrinkled old cheeks. 'You don't know how gone I feel without her!' she mourned. 'I'd always had her to tell me what to do. Thirty-five years now, every day, she's been here to tell me what to do. I can't make it seem true, that it's her lying in there. Seems as though every minute she'd come in, stepping quick, the way she did. And I fairly open my mouth to ask her, "Now, Miss Hetty, what shall I do next?" and then it all comes over me.'

Marise's impatience and scorn were flooded by an immense sympathy. What a pitiable thing a dependant is! Poor old Agnes! She leaned down to the humble, docile old face, and put her cheek against it. 'I'll do my best to take Cousin Hetty's place for you,' she said gently, and then, 'Now you'd better go back to bed. There's a hard day ahead of us.'

Agnes responded with relief to the tone of authority. She said with a reassured accent, 'Well, it's all right if *you*'re not afraid,' turned and shuffled down the hall, comforted and obedient.

Marise saw her go into her room, heard the creak of the bed as she lay down on it, and then the old voice, 'Miss Marise, will it be all right if I leave my candle burning, just this once?'

'Yes, yes, Agnes, that'll be all right,' she answered. 'Go to sleep now.' As she went back into her own room, she thought passingly to herself, 'Strange that anyone can live so long and grow up so little.'

She herself opened her bed, lay down on it resolutely, and blew out her candle.

Instantly the room seemed suffocatingly full of a thousand flying, disconnected pictures. The talk with Agnes had changed her mood. The dull, leaden weight of that numbing burden of inarticulate pain was broken into innumerable fragments. For a time, before she could collect herself to self-control, her thoughts whirled and roared in her head like a machine disconnected from its work, racing furiously till it threatens to shake itself to pieces. Everything seemed to come at once.

Frank Warner was dead. What would that mean to Nelly Powers?

Had there been enough bread left in the house till someone could drive the Ford to Ashley and buy some more?

Ought she to wear mourning for Cousin Hetty?

What had happened on the Eagle Rocks? Had Frank and 'Gene quarrelled, or had 'Gene crept up behind Frank as he sighted along the compass?

How would they get Cousin Hetty's friends from the station at Ashley out to the house, such feeble old people as they were? It would be better to have the services all at the church.

Had anything been decided about hymns? Someone had said something about it, but what had she . . . oh, of course that had been the moment when Touclé had come in, and Mr. Bayweather had rushed away to tell Frank's mother. Frank's mother. His mother! Suppose that were to happen to Mark, or Paul? No, not such thoughts. They mustn't be let in at all, or you went mad.

Was it true that Elly cared nothing about her, that children didn't, for grown-ups, that she was nothing in Elly's life?

She was glad that Touclé had come back. There would be someone to help Neale with the children. . . .

Neale . . . the name brought her up abruptly. Her mind, hurrying, breathless, panting, was stopped by the name, as by a great rock in the path. There was an instant of blankness, as she faced it, as though it were a name she did not know. When she said that name, everything stopped going around in her head. She moved restlessly in her bed.

And then, as though she had gone around the rock, the rapid, pattering, painful rush of those incoherent ideas began again. Queer that nobody there, Mr. Bayweather, Agnes, Touclé, none of them seemed to realize that Frank had not fallen, that 'Gene had . . . but of course she remembered they hadn't any idea of a possible connection between Frank and the Powers, and she had been the only one to see 'Gene in that terrible flight from the Rocks. Nelly had thought he had been cultivating corn all day. Of course nobody would think of anything but an accident. Nobody would ever know.

Yes, it was true; it was true that she would touch Neale and never know it, never feel it . . . how closely that had been observed, that she could take a handkerchief from his pocket as from a piece of furniture. It was true that Neale and she knew each other now till there was no hidden corner, no mystery, no possibility of a single unexpected thing between them. She had not realized it, but it was true. How could she not have seen that his presence left her wholly unmoved, indifferent now? But how could she have known it, so gradual had been the coming of satiety, until she had to contrast with it this fierce burning response to a fierce and new emotion? . . .

Had she thought 'indifference'? and 'satiety'? Of whom had she been thinking? Not of *Neale*! Was that what had come of the great hour on Rocca di Papa? *Was that what human beings were?*

She had gone farther this time, but now she was brought up short by the same blankness at the name of Neale, the same impossibility to think at all. She could not think about Neale to-night. All that must be put off till she was more like herself, till she was more steady. She was reeling now, with shock after shock; Cousin Hetty's death, 'Gene's dreadful secret, the discovery no longer to be evaded of what Vincent Marsh meant and was. . . .

She felt a sudden hurried impatient haste to be with Vincent again, to feel again the choking throb when she first saw him, the constant scared uncertainty of what he might say, what she might feel, what they both might do, from one moment to the next . . . she could forget, in those fiery and potent draughts, everything, all this that was so hard and painful and that she could not understand and that was such a torment to try to understand. Everything would be swept away except . . .

As though she had whirled suddenly about to see what was lurking there behind her, she whirled about and found the thought, 'But I ought to tell someone, tell the police, that I saw 'Gene Powers running away after he had killed the man who wanted to take his wife from him.'

Instantly there spoke out a bitter voice, 'No, I shall tell no one. 'Gene has known how to keep Nelly. Let him have her for all his life.'

Another voice answered, 'Frank's mother . . . his mother!'

And both of these were drowned by a tide of sickness as the recollection came upon her of that dreadful haste, those horrible laboured breaths.

She sat up with a great sweeping gesture of her arms, as though she must fight for air. The little room seemed palpably crammed with those jostling, shouting, battling thoughts. She slid from the bed and went to the window, leaning far out from it, and looking up at the sky, immeasurably high and black, studded thick with stars.

They looked down disdainfully at her fever and misery. A chilling consolation fell from them upon her, like a cold dew. She felt herself shrink to imperceptible proportions. What did they matter, the struggles of the maggots who crawled about the folds of the globe, itself the most trifling and insignificant of all the countless worlds which people the aimless disorder of the universe? What difference did it make? Anything they did was so soon indistinguishable from anything else. The easiest way . . . to yield to whatever had the strongest present force . . . that was as good as any other way in the great and blind confusion of it all.

After she had gone back to bed, she could still see the silent multitude of stars above her, enormous, remote beyond imagination, and it was under their thin, cold, indifferent gaze that she finally fell asleep.

Chapter 22: *Eugenia Does What She Can*

July 22.

AGNES brought upstairs an armful of white roses. 'The lady that visits at your house, she brought them from your garden and she wants to see you if she can.'

Eugenia of course. That was unexpected. She must have made an effort to do that, she who hated sickness and death and all dark things.

'Yes, tell her I will be down in a moment. Take her in a glass of cold water, too, will you please, Agnes? The walk over here must have been terribly hot for her.'

The roses showed that. They were warm to the touch and as she looked at them intently, at their white clear faces, familiar to her as those of human beings, bent on her with a mute message from the garden, she saw they had begun to droop imperceptibly, that the close, fine texture of their petals had begun ever so slightly to wither. She sprinkled them, put their stems deep into water and went downstairs, wiping her moist hands on her handkerchief.

Eugenia in mauve organdie stood up from the deep Windsor chair where she had sunk down, and came forward silently to greet her. They kissed each other ceremoniously in token of the fact that a death lay between them and the last time they had met . . . was it only yesterday morning?

'Were you able to sleep at all, Marise? You look shockingly tired.'

'Oh yes, thanks. I slept well enough. Are the children all right?'

Eugenia nodded, 'Yes, as usual.'

'Did their father tell them the news of Cousin Hetty's death? How did they take it? Elly perhaps was . . .'

242

Eugenia did not know about this, had not happened to hear anybody say. But old Touclé was back, at least, to do the work.

'I knew she must be,' said Marise. 'She was here last night. It was she, you know, who found Frank Warner's body at the foot of . . . of course you've heard of that?'

Eugenia made a little wry face. Of course she had heard of that, she said with an accent of distaste. Everybody was talking about the melodramatic accident, as probably they would still be talking about it a hundred years from now, up here where nothing happened. People had come all the way from North Ashley to look at the place, and some of the men and boys had gone around up to the top of the Eagle Rocks to see where Frank had lost his footing. They found his surveyor's compass still set upon its staff. It was where the line ran very near the edge and Frank must have stepped over the cliff as he was sighting along it. They could see torn leaves and stripped twigs as though he had tried to save himself as he fell.

She stopped speaking. Marise found herself too sick and shaken to venture any comment. There was rather a long silence, such as was natural and suitable under the circumstances, in that house. Presently Marise broke this to ask if anyone knew how Frank's mother had taken the news, although she knew of course Eugenia was the last person of whom to ask such a question. As she expected, Eugenia had only lifted eyebrows, a faint slow shake of her head and a small graceful shrug of her shoulders, her usual formula for conveying her ignorance of common facts, and her indifference to that ignorance.

But Marise, looking at her, as they sat opposite each other in the twilight of the closely shuttered room, was struck by the fact that Eugenia did not seem wholly like herself. Her outward aspect was the same, the usual exquisite exactitude of detail, every blond hair shining, and in its place the flawless perfection of her flesh as miraculous as ever, her tiny white shoe untouched by dust through which she must have walked to reach the house. But there was something . . . in her eyes, perhaps . . . which now looked back at Marise with an expression which Marise did not understand or recognize. If it had not been impossible to think it of Eugenia, Marise would have imagined that her eyes looked troubled, excited. Was it possible that even in her safe ivory tower of aloofness from life, she had felt the jarring blow of the brutally immediate tragedy of

243

the Eagle Rocks? Or perhaps even Cousin Hetty's disappearance . . . she had always hated reminders of death.

As Marise, surprised, looked at her and wondered thus passingly if she felt any reverberation from the tragedy-laden air about them, Eugenia's face hardened back into its usual smooth calm; over the eyes that had been for an instant transparent and alive with troubled brightness slid their acquired expression of benignant indifference. She answered Marise's faintly inquiring gaze by getting up as if to go, remarking in a clear low tone (she was the only person who had come into the house who had not succumbed to that foolish, instinctive muffling of the voice), 'I forgot to give you a message from Neale. He is obliged to be away to-day, on business, something about a deed to some wood-land.'

Marise was slightly surprised. 'Where is he going?' she asked. 'In the Ford? On the train?' How little she had thought about the mill of late, that she should be so entirely blank as to this business trip.

'Oh, I didn't even try to understand,' said Eugenia, smoothing the shining silk of her parasol. 'Business finds no echo in me, you know. A man came to supper last night, unexpectedly, and they talked interminably about some deal, lumbering, lines, surveys, deeds . . . till Touclé came in with the news of the accident. The man was from New Hampshire, with that droll, flat New Hampshire accent. You know how they talk, "bahn" and "yahd" for barn and yard.'

The words 'New Hampshire' and 'deeds' stirred a disagreeable association of ideas in Marise's mind. The shyster lawyer who had done the Powers out of their inheritance had come from New Hampshire. However, she supposed there were other people in the state besides dishonest lawyers.

Eugenia went on casually. 'It seemed quite important. Neale was absorbed by it. He told me afterward, Neale did, that the man had acted as agent for him some years ago in securing a big tract of woodland around here, something that had been hard to get hold of.'

Marise was startled and showed it by a quick lift of her head. She had never known Neale to employ an agent. She looked hard at Eugenia's quiet, indifferent face. The other seemed not to notice her surprise, and returned her look with a long clear gaze, which apparently referred to her hair, for she now remarked in just the tone she had used for the news about Neale, 'That way of arranging your coiffure *is* singularly becoming to you. Mr. Marsh was speaking about it the other day, but I hadn't specially noticed it. He's right. It gives you that swathed close-coifed Leonardo da Vinci look.' She put her handkerchief into a small bag of mauve linen, embroidered with white and pale-green crewels, and took up her parasol.

Marise felt something menacing in the air. Eugenia frightened her a little with that glass-smooth look of hers. The best thing to do was to let her go without another word. And yet she heard her voice asking, urgently, peremptorily, 'What was the name of the man from New Hampshire?'

Eugenia said, 'What man from New Hampshire?' and then, under Marise's silent gaze, corrected herself and changed her tone. 'Oh yes, let me see: Neale introduced him, of course. Why, some not uncommon name, and yet not like Smith or Jones. It began with an L, I believe.'

Marise said to herself, 'I will not say another word about this,' and aloud she said roughly, brusquely, 'It wasn't Lowder, of course.'

'Yes, yes,' said Eugenia, 'you're right. It was Lowder. I *thought* it was probably something you'd know about. Neale always tells you everything.'

She looked away and remarked, 'I suppose you will inherit the furniture of this house? There are nice bits. This Windsor chair; and I thought I saw a Chippendale buffet in the dining-room.'

Marise, immobile in her chair, repeated, 'It wasn't Lowder. You didn't say it was Lowder.'

'Yes, it was Lowder,' said Eugenia clearly. 'And now you speak of it once more, I remember one more thing about their talk although I didn't try to understand much of it. It was all connected with the Powers family. It was their woodlot which this Mr. Lowder had bought for Neale. I was surprised to know that they had ever had any wood-land. They have always seemed too sordidly poverty-stricken. But it seems this was the only way Neale could get hold of it, because they refused to sell otherwise.'

She looked again at Marise, a long, steady, and entirely opaque gaze which Marise returned mutely, incapable of uttering a word. She had the feeling of leaning with all her weight against an inner door that must be kept shut.

'Did Neale *tell* you this man had secured the Powers woodlot for him, for Neale, for our mill?' she heard her voice asking, faint in the distance, far off from where she had flung herself against that door.

'Why yes, why not? Not very recently he said, some time ago. We had quite a talk about it afterwards. It must be something you've forgotten,' said Eugenia. She took up a card from the table and fanned herself as she spoke, her eyes not quitting Marise's face. 'It's going to be as hot as it was yesterday,' she said with resignation. 'Doesn't it make you long for a dusky, high-ceilinged Roman room with a cool, red-tiled floor, and somebody out in the street shouting through your closed shutters, "Ricotta! Ricotta!"' she asked lightly.

Marise looked at her blankly. She wished she could lean forward and touch Eugenia to make sure she was really standing there. What was it she had been saying? She could not have understood a word of it. It was impossible that it should be what it seemed to mean – impossible!

A door somewhere in the house opened and shut, and steps approached. The two women turned their eyes towards the hall-door. Old Mrs. Powers walked in unceremoniously, her gingham dress dusty, her lean face deeply flushed by the heat, a tin pan in her hands, covered with a blue-and-white checked cloth.

'I thought maybe you'd relish some fresh doughnuts as well as anything,' she said briskly, with no preliminary of greeting.

Something about the atmosphere of the room struck her oddly for all the composed faces and quiet postures of the two occupants. She brought out as near an apology for intruding as her phraseless upbringing would permit her. 'I didn't see Agnes in the kitchen as I come through, so I come right along, to find somebody,' she said, a little abashed.

Marise was incapable of speaking to her, but she made a silent gesture of thanks, and, moving forward, took the pan from the older woman's hand.

Mrs. Powers went on, 'If 'twouldn't bother you, could you put them in your jar now, and let me take the pan back with me? We hain't got any too many dishes, you know.'

Marise went out to the pantry with the older woman, feeling with astonishment the floor hard and firm under her feet as usual, the walls upright about her. Only something at the back of her throat contracted to a knot, relaxed, contracted, with a singular, disagreeable, involuntary regularity.

'You look down sick, Mis' Crittenden,' said Mrs. Powers with a respectful admiration for the suitability of this appearance. 'And there ain't nothing surprising that you should. Did you ever see anybody go off more sudden than Miss Hetty?

Such a good woman she was, too. It must ha' gi'n you an awful turn.' She poured the doughnuts into the jar and, folding the checked cloth, went on, 'But I look at it this way. 'Twas a quick end, and a peaceful end without no pain. And if you'd seen as many old people drag along for years, as I have, stranglin' and chokin' and half-dead, why, you'd feel to be thankful Miss Hetty was spared that. And you too!'

'Marise,' said Eugenia, coming to the pantry door, 'your neighbours wanted me, of course, to bring you all their sympathetic condolence. Mr. Welles asked me to tell you that he would send all the flowers in his garden to the church for the service to-morrow. And Mr. Marsh was very anxious to see you to-day, to arrange about the use of his car in meeting the people who may come on the train to-morrow, to attend the funeral. He said he would run over here any time to-day, if you would send Agnes to tell him when you would see him. He said he wouldn't leave the house all day, to be ready to come at any time you would let him.'

Mrs. Powers was filled with satisfaction at such conduct. 'Now that's what I call real neighbourly,' she said. 'And both on 'em new to our ways too. That Mr. Welles is a real nice old man, anyhow. . . . There! I call him "old" and I bet he's younger than I be. He acts so kind o' settled down to stay. But Mr. Marsh don't act so. That's the kind o' man I like to see, up-and-coming, so you never know what he's a-goin' to do next.'

Eugenia waited through this, for some answer, and still waited persistently, her eyes on Marise's face.

Marise aroused herself. She must make some comment, of course. 'Please thank them both very much,' she said finally, and turned away to set the jar on a shelf.

'Well, you goin'?' said Mrs. Powers, behind her, evidently to Eugenia. 'Well, good-bye, see you at the funeral to-morrow, I s'pose.'

Marise looked around and caught a silent, graceful salutation of farewell from Eugenia, who disappeared down the hall, the front door closing gently behind her.

Mrs. Powers began again abruptly, 'Folks is sayin' that Frank Warner must ha' been drinking, but I don't believe it. He wa'n't no drinker. And where'd he git it, if he was? It was heedless, that's what it was. He always was a heedless critter from a little boy up. He was the one that skated right ahead into the hole and most drowned him, and he was fooling with

247

his gran'father's shot-gun when it went off and most blew him to pieces. 'S a wonder he lived to grow up: he come so nigh breaking his neck, before this.'

Marise was surprised to hear Eugenia's voice again, 'Marise, I stepped back to ask you if there are any errands I could do for you, any messages to take. I pass by the door of Mr. Welles' house. I could perfectly easily stop there and tell Mr. Marsh he could see you now, for instance.'

Marise seemed to see her from afar. She heard what she said, but she was aware of it only as an interruption. There was a question she must ask old Mrs. Powers. How could she think of anything else till that had been answered? She said to Eugenia at random, using the first phrase that came into her mind, 'No, no. Later. Some other time.'

Eugenia hesitated, took a step away from the door, and then came back in, deliberately, close to Marise. She spoke to her in Italian, very clearly, 'He is not a man who will wait.'

To this Marise, wholly engrossed in her inner struggle, opposed a stupid blankness, an incapacity to think of what Eugenia was saying, long enough to understand it. In that dark inner room, where she kept the door shut against the horror that was trying to come in, she dared not for an instant look away. She merely shook her head and motioned impatiently with her hand. Why did not Eugenia go away?

And yet when Eugenia had gone, she could not bring the words out because of that strange contraction of her throat.

'My! but you ought to go and lie down,' said Mrs. Powers compassionately. 'You're as white as a sheet. Why don't you just give up for a while? Agnes and I'll tend to things.'

Marise was filled with terror at the idea of not getting her answer, and spoke quickly, abruptly. 'Mrs. Powers, you never heard, did you, you never thought, in that trouble about losing your wood-land . . . nobody ever thought that Mr. Lowder was only an agent for someone else, whose name wasn't to be known then.'

'Oh sure,' said Mrs. Powers readily. ''Gene found out from a man that had lived in his town in New Hampshire that Lowder didn't do no lumbering of his own. He just makes a business of dirty deals like that for pay. He always surmised it to be some lumber-company; somebody that runs a mill. Lots of men that runs mills do that sort of thing, darn 'em!'

Marise leaned against the pantry shelf. The old woman glanced at her face, gave a cry, and pushed her into a chair, running for water. At the sound, Agnes came trotting, and showed a scared rabbit-like face. 'She's just beat out with the shock of Miss Hetty's going off so sudden,' explained Mrs. Powers to Agnes.

Marise got to her feet angrily. She had entirely forgotten that Cousin Hetty was dead, or that she was in her house. She was shocked that for a moment she had relaxed her steady pressure against that opening door. She flung herself against it now. What could she do next?

Instantly, clearly, as though she had heard someone saying it to her, she thought, 'Why, of course, all I have to do is to go and ask Neale about it!'

It was so simple. Somehow, of course, Neale could give the answer she must have. Why had she not thought of that the instant Eugenia had begun to speak?

She drank the glass of water Agnes gave her and said, 'Mrs. Powers, could you do something for me? I promised I would stay here till the funeral and I know Agnes is afraid to stay alone. Would you mind waiting here for perhaps half an hour till I could get to the mill and back? There is something important I must see to.'

Mrs. Powers hesitated. 'Well now, Mis' Crittenden, there ain't nothing I wouldn't do for you. But I'm kind o' *funny* about dead folks. I don't believe I'd be much good to Agnes because I feel just the way she does. But I'll run over to the house and get Nelly and 'Gene to come. I guess the four of us together won't be nervous about staying. 'Gene ain't workin' to-day. He got a sunstroke or something yesterday, in the sun, cultivatin' his corn and he don't feel just right in his head, he says.'

She went out of the door as she spoke, calling over her shoulder, 'I wun't be gone long.'

Marise sat down again, there in the pantry, leaned her head against the door and looked steadily at the shelves before her, full of dishes and jars and bottles and empty jelly glasses. In her mind there was only one thing, a fixed resolve not to think at all, of anything, until she had been to Neale's office and had Neale explain it to her. Surely he would not have started on that trip whatever it was. It was so early still. She must not think about it at all, until she had asked Neale. Eugenia had probably made a mistake about the name. Even if Neale had gone she would be able to ask about the name and find that Eugenia had made a mistake. That would make everything all right. Of course Eugenia had made a mistake about the name.

She was still staring fixedly at the shelves, frowning and beginning again to count all the things on them, when Mrs. Powers' voice sounded from the kitchen. 'I met 'em on the way is why I'm back so soon,' she explained to Agnes. 'Nelly had some flowers to bring. And they've been down by the river and got a great lot of ferns too.'

Marise started up, for an instant distracted from her concentration on what Eugenia had said. This was the first time she had seen Nelly and 'Gene since Frank's death. How would they look? How did people go on living? How would they speak, and how could they listen to anything but their own thoughts? What had Frank's death meant to Nelly?

She turned shrinkingly towards Nelly. Nelly was bending down and flicking the dust from her shoes with her handkerchief. When she stood up, she looked straight at Marise. Under the thick-springing, smooth-brushed abundance of her shining fair hair, her eyes, blue as precious stones, looked out with the deep quiet which always seemed so inscrutable to the other woman.

She held out an armful of flowers. 'I thought you'd like the white phlox the best. I had a lot of pink too, but I remembered Mrs. Bayweather said white is best at such times.'

Marise drew a long breath. What superb self-control!

'Were the biscuits good?' asked Nelly, turning to Agnes. 'I was afraid afterward maybe they weren't baked enough.'

Marise was swept to her feet. If Nelly could master her nerves like that, she could do better herself. She took the flowers, carried them to the kitchen, and set them in a panful of water. She had not yet looked at 'Gene.

She went to find an umbrella to shield her hatless head from the sun, and on her way out only cast a swift glance at 'Gene. That was enough. All the blazing, dusty way to the mill, she saw hanging terribly before her that haggard ashy face.

At the mill, she paused in the doorway of the lower office, looking in on the three desk-workers tapping on their machines, leaning sideways to consult note-books. The young war-cripple, Neale's special protégé, seeing her, got to his feet to ask her what he could do for her.

Marise considered him for a moment before she answered. *Was* there anything he could do for her? Why had she come? All she could remember for the moment was that singular contraction of her throat, which had come back now.

Then she remembered, 'Is Mr. Crittenden here?'

'No, he was called away for the day, urgent business in New Hampshire.'

Marise looked about her helplessly. 'May I sit down for a moment?'

The young stenographer ran, limping and eager, to offer her a chair, and then, shyly, swung his swivel-chair towards her, not wishing to go back to his work, uncertain what to say to his employer's wife.

'When will Mr. Crittenden be back?' asked Marise, although she knew the answer.

'No later than to-night, he said,' answered the stenographer. 'He spoke particularly about coming back because of Miss Hetty Allen's funeral.'

'Yes, of course,' said Marise.

There was nothing more to be said, she knew that, nothing more to be done until Neale came back. But it seemed physically impossible for her to live until then, with the clutch in her throat.

She ought to get up now, at once, and go back to Cousin Hetty's. The Powers were waiting for her return. But her consternation at finding Neale really gone was a blow from which she needed a breathing time to recover. She couldn't have it so. She could never endure a whole day with this possibility like a threatening powder-mine under her feet, ready to go off and bring her inner world to ruin and despair. She put her hand out to take her umbrella and struggled up.

'Any message to leave for Mr. Crittenden?' asked the stenographer, seeing her ready to go.

She shook her head. Her eye fell on the waste-paper basket beside the desk. On one of the empty envelopes, torn in two, the words, 'Return to C. K. Lowder,' stood out clearly. She turned away and stood motionless, one hand at her temple. She was thinking to herself, 'This is simply incredible. There is some monstrous mistake. If I could only think of a way to find it out before it kills me.'

She became aware that the young cripple was looking at her anxiously, and saw in his startled, agitated face a reflection of what hers must be. She made an effort to speak quietly, and heard herself say, 'Do you happen to remember if Mr. Crittenden was alone as he drove away?'

'Oh no,' said the other. 'He had had someone with him ever since the afternoon train came in yesterday. Mr. Crittenden drove the car in himself to the Ashley station to meet him. Somebody here on business.'

'What sort of a man, do you remember?' asked Marise.

'Well, a clean-shaven man with a queer thin long mouth, like the pictures of William Jennings Bryan's. And he talked out of one corner of it, the way . . . see here, Mrs. Crittenden, you look awfully tired. Wouldn't you better sit down and rest a moment more?'

Marise shook her head with an impatient gesture. Now she needed to get away from that office as much as she had wished to go to it. The place was hateful to her. The young man's eyes were intolerable. He was one of the people, one of the many, many people who had grown up trusting in Neale.

She swung suddenly to a furious incredulity about the whole thing. It was nonsense! None of it could be true. What were all these people saying to her, Eugenia, Mrs. Powers, this boy . . .? She would never forgive them for trying to do such an infamous thing. They were trying to make her believe that Neale had been back of Lowder in the low-down swindle that had been practised on the Powers. They were trying to make her believe that for seven years Neale had been lying to her with every breath he drew. Because other men could lie, they thought they could make her believe that Neale did. Because other women's husbands had done base things in business, they thought she would be capable of believing that about Neale. They didn't know how preposterous it was, how close she and Neale had always been, how deeply a part of the whole aspect of life to her Neale's attitude towards his work had become. Those people did not realize what they were trying to make her believe, it was not only that her husband had been the instigator of a mean little cheat which had cost years of suffering to helpless neighbours, it was the total destruction of all that she had thought Neale to be . . . *thought* him? Known him to be.

'I must get back at once,' she said with a resentful accent, and moved towards the door.

Chapter 23: *Marise Looks Down on the Stars*

July 22.

SHE passed out from the office into the yellow glare of the sun, her feet moving steadily forward, with no volition of hers, along the dusty road. And as steadily, with as little volition of hers,

252

march, march, came . . . first what Eugenia had said, the advance from that to Mrs. Powers' words, from that to the stenographer's, to the name on the envelope . . . and then like the door to a white-hot blast-furnace thrown open in her face, came the searing conception of the possibility that it might be true, and all the world lost.

The extremity and horror of this aroused her to a last effort at self-preservation so that she flung the door shut by a fierce incapacity to believe any of those relentless facts which hung one from another with their horrible enchaining progression. No, she had been dreaming. It was all preposterous!

The heat wavered up from the hot earth in visible pulsations and there pulsed through her similar rhythmic waves of feeling; the beginning . . . what Eugenia had said, had said that *Neale had told her* . . . what Mrs. Powers had said, 'Lots of men that run mills do that sort of thing' . . . what the stenographer had said . . . the name on the envelope . . . *suppose it should be true.*

She was at Cousin Hetty's door now; a give-and-take of women's voices sounding within. 'Here's Mrs. Crittenden back. Come on, Nelly, we better be going. There's all the work to do.'

Marise went in and sat down, looking at them with stony indifference, at 'Gene this time as well as at the women. The drawn sickness of his ashy face did not move her in the least now. What did she care what he did, what anyone did, till she knew whether she had ever had Neale or not? The women's chatter sounded remote and foolish in her ears.

If Neale had done that . . . if that was the man he was . . . but of course it was preposterous, and she had been dreaming. What was that that Eugenia had said? The descent into hell began again step by step.

The Powers went out, the old woman still talking, chattering, as if anything mattered now.

After they were gone, Agnes ran to the door calling, 'Mis' Powers! You forgot your pan and towel after all!' And there was Mrs. Powers again, talking, talking.

She had been saying something that needed an answer apparently, for now she stood waiting, expectant.

'What was that, Mrs. Powers? I was thinking of something else.'

'I was just tellin' you that there's going to be a big change over to our house. 'Gene, he told Nelly, as he was setting here waiting for you, how he was going to cut down the big pine

253

one of these days, like she always wanted him to. You know, the one that shades the house so. 'Gene's grandfather planted it, and he's always set the greatest store by it. Used to say he'd just as soon cut his grandmother's throat as chop it down. But Nelly, she's all housekeeper and she never did like the musty way the shade makes our best room smell. I never thought to see the day 'Gene would give in to her about that. He's gi'n in to her about everything else though. Only last night he was tellin' her he was going to take something out'n the savings-bank and buy her an organ for Addie to learn to play on, that Nelly always hankered after. Seems 'sthough he can't do enough for Nelly, don't it?'

Marise looked at her coldly, incapable of paying enough attention to her to make any comment on what she said. Let them cut down all the trees in the valley, and each other's throats into the bargain, if Neale had . . . if there had never been her Neale, the Neale she thought she had been living with all these years.

Mrs. Powers had gone finally, and the house was silent at last, so silent that she could now hear quite clearly, as though Eugenia still sat there, what the sweet musical voice was saying over and over. Why had they gone away and left her alone to face this deadly peril which advanced on her step by step without mercy, time after time? Now there was nothing to do but to wait and stand it off.

She was sitting in the same chair, her umbrella still in her hand, waiting, when Agnes came in to say that she had lunch ready. She turned eyes of astonished anger and rebuke on her. 'I don't want anything to eat,' she said in so strange a voice that Agnes crept back to the kitchen, shuffling and scared.

She was still sitting there, looking fixedly before her, and frowning, when Agnes came to the door to say timidly that the gentleman had come about using his car to meet the train, and wanted to know if he could see Mrs. Crittenden.

Marise looked at her, frowning, and shook her head. But it was not until late that night that she understood the words that Agnes had spoken.

She was still sitting there, rigid, waiting, when Agnes brought in a lighted lamp, and Marise saw that evening had come. The light was extremely disagreeable to her eyes. She got up stiffly, and went outdoors to the porch, sitting down on the steps.

The stars were beginning to come out now. The sight of them suggested something painful, some impression that belonged to that other world that had existed before this day, before she had conceived the possibility that Neale might not be Neale, might never have been Neale, that there was no such thing for her as human integrity. Was it she who had leaned out from the window and felt herself despised by the height and vastness of the stars? From the height and vastness of her need, she looked down on them now, and found them nothing, mere pin-pricks in the sky, compared to this towering doubt of her, this moral need which shouted down all the mere matter on the earth and in the heavens above the earth. Something eternal was at stake now, the faith in righteousness of a human soul.

She had thought childishly, shallowly last night that she had had no faith, and could live with none. That was because she had not conceived what it would be to try to live without faith, because she had not conceived that the very ground under her feet could give way. At that very moment she had had a faith as boundless as the universe, and had forgotten it. And now it was put in doubt. She could not live without it. It was the only vital thing for her.

Was she the woman who had felt forced into acquiescing when Vincent Marsh had said so boldly and violently that she loved her husband no more, that he was nothing to her now? It seemed to her at this moment that it was a matter of the utmost unimportance whether she *loved* him or not; but she could not live without believing him. That was all. She could not live without that. Life would be too utterly base . . .

Neale nothing to her? She did not know *what* he was to her, but the mere possibility of losing her faith in him was like death. It was a thousand times worse than death, which was merely material. This mattered a great deal more than the physical death of someone's body . . . it was the murder, minute by minute, hour by hour, month by month, year by year of all her married life, of all she had found lovable and tolerable and beautiful and real in life.

Of course this could not be true . . . of course not . . . but if it were true, she would find the corrosive poison of a false double meaning in every remembered hour. She did not believe any of those hideously marshalled facts, but if they were true, she would go back over all those recollections of their life together and kill them one by one, because every hour of her life had been founded on the most unthinking, the most absolute, the most recklessly certain trust in Neale. To know that past in peril, which she had counted on as safe, more surely than on anything in life, so surely that she had almost dismissed it from her mind like a treasure laid away in a safe hiding-place . . . to know those memories in danger was a new torture that had never before been devised for any human being. No one had the safe and consecrated past taken from him. Its pricelessness shone on her with a blinding light. What if it should be taken away, if she should find she had never had it at all . . .?

The idea was so acute an anguish to her that she startled herself by a cry of suffering.

Agnes' voice behind her asked tremblingly, 'Did you call me, Miss Marise?'

Marise shifted her position, drew a breath, and answered in a hard tone, 'No.'

She knew with one corner of her mind that Agnes must be terrified. What if she were? Marise's lifelong habit of divining another's need and ministering to it vanished like a handful of dust in a storm. What did she care about Agnes? What did she care about anything in the world but that she should have back again what she had valued so little as to lose it from her mind altogether? All of her own energy was strained in the bitterness of keeping her soul alive till Neale should come. She had not the smallest atom of strength to care about the needs of anyone else.

She looked up at the stars, disdainful of them. How small they were, how unimportant in the scheme of things, so much less able to give significance to the universe, than the presence of integrity in a human soul.

If she could have Neale back again, as she had always had him without thinking of it, if she could have her faith in him again, the skies might shrivel up like a scroll, but something eternal would remain in her life.

It seemed to her that she heard a faint sound in the distance, on the road, and her strength ran out of her like water. She tried to stand up but could not.

Yes, it was the car approaching. The two glaring headlights swept the white road, stopped, and went out. For an instant the dark mass stood motionless in the starlight. Then something moved, a man's tall figure came up the path.

'Is that you, Marise?' asked Neale's voice.

She had not breath to speak, but all of her being cried out silently to him the question which had had all the day such a desperate meaning for her, 'Is that *you*, Neale?'

PART IV

Chapter 24: *Neale's Return*

July 22. Evening.

HE stooped to kiss her and sank down beside her where she sat cowering in the dark. Although she could not see his face clearly Marise knew from his manner that he was very tired, from the way he sat down, taking off his cap, and his attitude as he leaned his head back against the pillar. She knew this without thinking about it, mechanically, with the automatic certainty of a long-since acquired knowledge of him. And when he spoke, although his voice was quiet and level, she felt a great fatigue in his accent.

But he spoke with his usual natural intonation, which he evidently tried to make cheerful. 'I'm awfully glad you're still up, dear. I was afraid you'd be too tired, with the funeral coming to-morrow. But I couldn't get here any sooner. I've been clear over the mountain to-day. And I've done a pretty good stroke of business that I'm in a hurry to tell you about. You remember, don't you, how the Powers lost the title to their big woodlot? I don't know if you happen to remember all the details, how a lawyer named Lowder . . .'

'I remember,' said Marise, speaking for the first time, 'all about it.'

'Well,' went on Neale, wearily but steadily, 'up in Nova Scotia this time, talking with one of the old women in town, I ran across a local tradition that, in a town about ten miles inland, some of the families were descended from Tory Yankees who'd been exiled from New England after the Revolution. I thought it was worth looking up, and one day I ran up there to see if I could find out anything about them. It was Sunday and I had to . . .'

Marise was beside herself, her heart racing wildly. She took hold of his arm and shook it with all her might. 'Neale, quick! quick! Leave out all that. *What did you do?*'

She could see that he was surprised by her fierce impatience,

258

and for an instant taken aback by the roughness of the interruption. He stared at her. How *slow* Neale was!

He began, 'But, dear, why do you care so much about it? You can't understand about what I did, if I don't tell you this part, the beginning, how I . . .' Then, feeling her begin to tremble uncontrollably, he said hastily, 'Why, of course, Marise, if you want to know the end first. The upshot of it all is that I've got it straightened out, about the Powers woodlot. I got track of those missing leaves from the Ashley Town Records. They really were carried away by that uncle of yours. I found them up in Canada. I had a certified copy and tracing made of them. It's been a long complicated business, and the things only came in yesterday's mail, after you'd been called over here. But I'd been in correspondence with Lowder, and when I had my proofs in hand, I telephoned him and made him come over yesterday afternoon. It was one of the biggest satisfactions I ever expect to have, when I shoved those papers under his nose and watched him curl up. Then I took him back to-day, myself, to his own office, not to let him out of my sight till it was all settled. There was a great deal more to it . . . two or three hours of fight. I bluffed some, about action by the bar-association, disbarment, a possible indictment for perjury, and seemed to hit a weak spot. And finally I saw him with my own eyes burn up that fake warranty-deed. And that's all there is to that. Just as soon as we can get this certified copy admitted and entered on our Town Records, 'Gene can have possession of his own wood-land. Isn't that good news?'

He paused and added with a tired, tolerant, kindly accent, 'Now Nelly will have fourteen pairs of new shoes, each laced higher up than the others, and I won't be the one to grudge them to her.'

He waited for a comment and, when none came, went on doggedly making talk in that resolutely natural tone of his. 'Now that you know the end, and that it all came out right, you ought to listen to some details, for they are queer. The missing pages weren't in that first town I struck at all. Nothing there but a record of a family of Simmonses who had come from Ashley in 1778. They had . . .'

Marise heard nothing more of what he said, although his voice went on with words the meaning of which she could not grasp. It did not seem to her that she had really understood with the whole of her brain anything he had said, or that she had been able to take in the significance of it. She could think of nothing but a frightening sensation all over her body, as though the life were ebbing out of it. Every nerve and fibre in her seemed to have gone slack, beyond anything she had ever conceived. She could feel herself more and more unstrung and loosened, like a violin string let down and down. The throbbing ache in her throat was gone. Everything was gone. She sat helpless and felt it slip away, till somewhere in the centre of her body this ebbing of strength had run so far that it was a terrifying pain, like the approach of death. She was in a physical panic of alarm, but unable to make a sound, to turn her head.

It was when she heard a loud insistent ringing in her head and saw the stars waver and grow dim that she knew she was fainting away.

Then she was lying on the sofa in Cousin Hetty's sitting-room, Neale bending over her, holding a handkerchief which smelled of ammonia, and Agnes, very white, saying in an agitated voice, 'It's because she hasn't eaten a thing all day. She wouldn't touch her lunch or supper. It's been turrible to see her.'

Marise's head felt quite clear and lucid now; her consciousness as if washed clean by its temporary absence from life. She tried to sit up and smile at Neale and Agnes. She had never fainted away in all her life before. She felt very apologetic and weak. And she felt herself in a queer, literal way another person.

Neale sat down by her now and put his arm around her. His face was grave and solicitous, but not frightened, as Agnes was. It was like Neale not to lose his head. He said to Agnes, 'Give me that cup of cocoa,' and when it came, he held it to Marise's lips. 'Take a good swallow of that,' he said quietly.

Marise was amazed to find that the hot sweet smell of the cocoa aroused in her a keen sensation of hunger. She drank eagerly, and taking in her hand the piece of bread and butter which Neale offered to her, she began to eat it with a child's appetite. She was not ashamed or self-conscious in showing this before Neale. One never needed to live up to any pose before Neale. His mere presence in the room brought you back, she thought, to a sense of reality. Sometimes if you had been particularly up in the air, it made you feel a little flat as she certainly did now. But how profoundly alive it made you feel, Neale's sense of things as they were.

The food was delicious. She ate and drank unabashedly,

finding it an exquisite sensation to feel her body once more normal, her usual home, and not a scaring, almost hostile entity, apart from her. When she finished, she leaned against Neale's shoulder with a long breath. For an instant, she had no emotion but relieved, homely, bodily comfort.

'Well, for Heaven's sake!' said Neale, looking down at her.

'I know it,' she said. 'I'm an awful fool.'

'No, you're not,' he contradicted. 'That's what makes me so provoked with you now, going without eating since morning.'

Agnes put in, 'It's the suddenness of it that was such a shock. It takes me just so, too, comes over me as I start to put a mouthful of food into my mouth. I can't get it down. And you don't know how *lost* I feel not to have Miss Hetty here to tell me what to eat. I feel so gone!'

'You must go to bed this minute,' said Neale. 'I'll go right back to the children.'

He remembered suddenly. 'By George, I haven't had anything to eat since noon myself.' He gave Marise an apologetic glance. 'I guess I haven't any stones to throw at your foolishness.'

Agnes ran to get him another cup of cocoa and some more bread and butter. Marise leaned back on the sofa and watched him eat.

She was aware of a physical release from tension that was like a new birth. She looked at her husband as she had not looked at him for years. And yet she knew every line and hollow of that rugged face. What she seemed not to have seen before, was what had grown up little by little, the expression of his face, the expression which gave his presence its significance, the expression which he had not inherited like his features, but which his life had wrought out there.

Before her very eyes there seemed still present the strange, alien look of the dead face upstairs, from which the expression had gone, and with it everything. That vision hung, a cold and solemn warning in her mind, and through it she looked at the living face before her and saw it as she had never done before.

In the clean, new, sweet lucidity of her just-returned consciousness she saw what she was not to forget, something like a steady, visible light, which was Neale's life. That was Neale himself. And as she looked at him silently, she thought it no wonder that she had been literally almost frightened to death by the mere possibility that it had not existed. She had been right in thinking that there was something there which would outlast the mere stars.

He looked up, found her eyes on him, and smiled at her. She found the gentleness of his eyes so touching that she felt the tears mounting to her own. . . . But she winked them back. There had been enough foolishness from her for one day.

Neale leaned back in his chair now, looked around for his cap, took it up, and looked back at her, quietly, still smiling a little. Marise thought, 'Neale is as *natural* in his life as a very great actor is in his art. Whatever he does, even to the most trifling gesture, is done with so great a simplicity that it makes people like me feel fussy and paltry.'

There was a moment's silence, Neale frankly very tired, looking rather haggard and grim, giving himself a moment's respite in his chair before standing up to go; Marise passive, drawing long quiet breaths, her hands folded on her knees; Agnes, her back to the other two, hanging about the sideboard, opening and shutting the drawers, and shifting their contents aimlessly from one to the other.

Then Agnes turned, and showed a shamed, nervous old face. 'I don't know what's got into me, Miss Marise, that I ain't no good to myself nor anybody else. I'm afraid to go back into the kitchen alone.' She explained to Neale, 'I never was in the house with a dead body before, Mr. Crittenden, and I act like a baby about it, scared to let Mrs. Crittenden out of my sight. If I'm alone for a minute, seems 'sthough . . .' She glanced over her shoulder fearfully and ended lamely, 'Seems 'sthough I don't know what might happen.'

'I won't leave you alone, Agnes, till it is all over,' said Marise, and this time she kept contempt not only out of her voice, but out of her heart. She was truly only very sorry for the old woman with her foolish fears.

Agnes blinked and pressed her lips together, the water in her eyes. 'I'm awful glad to hear you say that!' she said fervently.

Marise closed her eyes for a moment. It had suddenly come to her that this promise to Agnes meant that she could not see Neale alone till after the funeral, to-morrow, when she went back into life again. And she found that she immensely wanted to see him alone this very hour, now! And Agnes would be there . . .!

She opened her eyes and saw Neale standing up, his cap in his hand, looking at her, rough and brown and tall and tired and strong; so familiar, every line and pose and colour of him;

as familiar and unexciting, as much a part of her, as her own hand.

As their eyes met in the profound look of intimate interpenetration which can pass only between a man and a woman who have been part of each other, she felt herself putting to him clearly, piercingly, the question which till then she had not known how to form, '*Neale, what do you want me to do?*'

She must have said it aloud, and said it with an accent which carried its prodigious import, for she saw him turn very white, saw his eyes deepen, his chest lift in a great heave. He came towards her, evidently not able to speak for a moment. Then he took her hands . . . the memory of a thousand other times was in his touch . . .

He looked at her as though he could never turn his eyes away. The corners of his mouth twitched and drew down.

He said in a deep, trembling, solemn voice, 'Marise, my darling, I want you always to do what is best for *you* to do.'

He drew a deep, deep breath as though it had taken all his strength to say that; and went on, 'What is deepest and most living in you . . . that is what must go on living.'

He released one hand and held it out towards her as though he were taking an oath.

Chapter 25: *Marise's Coming-of-Age*

July 23. Dawn.

EVEN after the old child, Agnes, had been soothed and reassured, over and over, till she had fallen asleep, and the house lay profoundly quiet, Marise felt not the slightest approach of drowsiness or even of fatigue. She lay down on her bed, but could not close her eyes. They remained wide open, looking not at a wild confusion of incoherent images as they had the night before, but straight into blackness and vacancy.

It was strange how from the brawling turmoil of impressions which had shouted and cried out to her the night before, and had wrought her to frenzy by their insane insistence, not an echo reached her now. Her mind was as silent and intent as the old house, keeping its last mute watch over its mistress. Intent on what? She did not know. On something that was waiting for her, on something for which she was waiting.

In an immense hush, like the dusky silence in a cathedral

aisle or in the dark heart of the woods, there was something there waiting for her to go and find it.

That hush had fallen on her at the sight of Neale's face, at the sound of his voice, as he had looked at her and spoken to her at the last, just before he went away back to the children. Those furiously racing pulses of hers had been stilled by it into this steady rhythm which now beat quietly through her. The clashing thoughts which had risen with malevolent swiftness, like high, battling shadowy genii, and had torn her in pieces as they fought back and forth, were stilled as though a master word had been spoken which they must all obey.

The old house, silent under the stars, lay quiet in its vigil about her, but slept no more than she; the old house which had been a part of her childhood and her youth now watched over her entry into another part of her journey.

For as she lay there, wideawake, watching the light of the candle, she felt that she knew what was waiting for her, what she must go to find. It was her maturity.

And as she lay quiet, her ears ringing in the solemn hush which Neale's look and voice had laid about her, she felt slowly coming into her, like a tide from a great ocean, the strength to go forward. She lay still, watching the candle flame hovering above the wick which tied it to the candle, reaching up, reaching up, never for a moment flagging in that transmutation of the dead matter below it, into something shining and alive.

She felt the quiet strength come into her like a tide. And presently, as naturally as a child wakes in the morning, refreshed, and feels the impulse to rise to active effort again, she sat up in bed, folded her arms around her knees, and began to think.

Really to think this time, not merely to be the helpless battle-field over which hurtling projectiles of fierce emotions passed back and forth! She set her life fairly there before her, and began to try to understand it.

As she took this first step and saw the long journey stretching out before her, she knew on what staff she leaned. It was Neale's belief that she was strong and not weak, that she could find out, if she tried, what was deepest and most living in her heart. With this in her hand, with that great protecting hush about her, she set forth. She was afraid of what she might find, but she set forth.

She must begin at the beginning this time, and go steadily forward from one step to the next, not her usual involuntary plunge, not the usual closing over her head of those yelling waters of too vivid impression.

The beginning had been . . . yes, the first conscious beginning had been the going away of little Mark, out of his babyhood into his own child-life. He had gone out and left an empty place behind him, which till then had been filled with the insistent ever-present need for care for the physical weakness of babyhood. And she had known that never again would Mark fill that place.

Emptiness, silence, solitude in the place of constant activity; it had frightened her, had set before her a vision that her life had reached its peak, and henceforth would go down the decline. Into that empty place had come a ringing, peremptory call back to personal and physical youth and excitement and burning sensations. And with that blinding rebirth of physical youth had come a doubt of all that had seemed the recompense for the loss of it, had come the conception that she might be letting herself be fooled and tricked out of the only real things.

There had been many parts to this: her revolt from the mere physical drudgery of her life, from giving so much of her strength to the dull, unsavoury, material things. This summer, a thousand times in a thousand ways, there had been brought home to her by Vincent, by Eugenia, the fact that there were lives so arranged that other people did all the drudgery, and left one free to perceive nothing but the beauty and delicacy of existence. Now, straight at it! With all the knowledge of herself and of life which she had gathered – straight at it, to see what this meant! Did their entire freedom from drudgery give them a keener sense of the beauty and delicacy of existence? Were they more deeply alive because of the ease of their lives?

She cast about her for evidence, in a firm, orderly search among the materials which life had brought to her. Had she seen anything which could give evidence on that? There was Eugenia; Eugenia and her friends had always lived that life of rich possessions and well-served ease. What had it made of them? Was their sense of beauty deeper and more living because of it? No, not in the least.

She turned her inward eye on Eugenia's life, on the lives of the people in that circle, in a long searching gaze. Was it deep in eternal values? Was it made up of a constant recurrence of sensitive aliveness to what is most worth responding to? Odd, that it did not seem to be! They were petulant and bored, and troubled about minute flaws in their ease, far more than they were deep in communion with beauty.

Another piece of evidence came knocking at the door now, a picture of quaint and humble homeliness . . . herself standing before the stove with the roast on a plate, and little Mark saying fastidiously, 'Oh, how nasty raw meat looks!' She recalled her passing impatience with the childishness of that comment, her passing sense of the puerile ignorance of the inherent unity of things, in such an attitude of eagerness to feed on results and unwillingness to take one's share of what leads up to results. Yes, it was more there, than in looking at Eugenia, that she could find evidence. Did she want to be of those who sat afar off and were served with the fine and delicate food of life, and knew nothing of the unsavoury process of preparing it? It had seemed to her this summer, a thousand times with Vincent's eyes on her, scornful of her present life, that she did want it, that she wanted that more than anything else. Now let her look full at it. She was a grown woman now who could foresee what it would mean.

She looked full at it, set herself there in her imagination, in the remote ivory tower and looked out from its carven windows at the rough world where she had lived and worked, and from which she would henceforth be protected . . . and shut out. She looked long, and in the profound silence, both within and without her, she listened to the deepest of the voices in her heart.

And she knew that it was too late for that. She had lived, and she could not blot out what life had brought to her. She could never now, with a tranquil heart, go into the ivory tower. It would do her no good to shut and bar the golden door a hundred times behind her, because she would have with her, everywhere she went, wrought into the very fibre of her being, a guilty sense of all the effort and daily strain and struggle in which she did not share.

She saw no material good accomplished by taking her share. The existence in the world of so much drudgery and unlovely slavery to material processes was an insoluble mystery; but a life in which her part of it would be taken by other people and added to their own burdens . . . no, she had grown into something which could not endure that!

Perhaps this was one of the hard, unwelcome lessons that the war had brought to her. She remembered how she had hated the simple comforts of home, the safety, the roof over her head, because they were being paid for by such hideous sufferings on the part of others; how she had been ashamed to lie down in her warm bed when she thought of Neale and his comrades in the trench mud, in the cold horror of the long drenching nights, awaiting the attack; and she had turned sick to see the long trains of soldiers going out while she stayed safely behind and bore no part in the wretchedness which war is. There had been no way for her to take her part in that heavy payment for her safety and comfort; but the bitterness of those days had shocked her imagination alive to the shame of sharing and enjoying what she had not helped to pay for, to the disharmony of having more than your share while other people have less than theirs.

This was nothing she had consciously sought for. She felt no dutiful welcome that it had come; she bent under it as under a burden. But it was there. Life had made her into one of the human beings capable of feeling that responsibility, each for all, and the war had driven it home, deep into her heart, whence she could not pluck it out.

She might never have known it, never have thought of it, if she had been safely protected by ignorance of what life is like. But now she knew, living had taught her; and that knowledge was irrevocably part of the woman she had become.

Wait now! Was this only habit, routine, dulled lack of divining imagination of what another life could be? That was the challenge Vincent would throw down. She gazed steadily at the wall before her, and called up, detail by detail, the life which Vincent Marsh thought the only one that meant richness and abundance for the human spirit. It hung there, a shimmering mass of lovely colours and exquisite textures and fineness and delicacy and beauty. And as she looked at it, it took on the shape of a glorious, uprooted plant, cut off from the very source of life, its glossy surfaces already beginning to wither and dull in the sure approach of corruption and decay. But what beauties were there to pluck, lovely fading beauties, poignant and exquisite sensations, which she was capable of savouring, which she sadly knew she would live and die without having known, a heritage into which she would never enter; because she had known the unforgettable taste of the other heritage, alive and rooted deep!

This faded out and left her staring at the blank wall again, feeling old and stern.

Nothing more came for a moment, and restless, feeling no

bodily fatigue at all, she got out of her bed, took up the candle, and stepped aimlessly out into the hall. The old clock at the end struck a muffled stroke, as if to greet her. She held up her candle to look at it. Half-past two in the morning. A long time till dawn would come.

She hesitated a moment and turned towards the door of a garret room which stood open. She had not been in there for so long – years perhaps; but as a child she had often played there among the old things, come down from the dead, who were kept in such friendly recollection in this house. Near the door there had been an old, flat-topped, hair-covered trunk . . . yes, here it was, just as it had been. Nothing ever changed here. She sat down on it, the candle on the floor beside her, and saw herself as a little girl playing among the old things.

A little girl! And now she was the mother of a little girl. So short a time had passed! She understood so very little more than when she had been the little girl herself. Yet now there was Elly who came and stood by her, and looked at her, and asked with all her eyes and lips and being, 'Mother, what is the meaning of life?'

What answer had she to give? Was she at all more fit than anyone else to try to give Elly the unknowable answer to that dark question? Was there any deep spiritual reality which counted at all, which one human being could give to another? Did we really live on desert islands, cut off so wholly from each other by the unplumbed, salt, estranging sea? And if we did, why break one's heart in the vain effort to do the impossible, to get from human beings what they could not give?

Her heart ached in an old bitterness at the doubt. Did her children . . . could they . . . give her the love she wanted from them, in answer to her gift of her life to them? They were already beginning to go away from her, to be estranged from her, to shut her out of their lives, to live their lives with no place for her in them.

She sat there on the old trunk and saw the endless procession of parents and children passing before her, the children so soon parents, all driven forward by what they could not understand, yearning and starving for what was not given them, all wrapped and dimmed in the twilight of their doubt and ignorance. Where were they going? And why? So many of them, so many!

Her humbled spirit was prostrate before their mystery, before the vastness of the whole, of which she and her children were only a part, a tiny, lowly part.

With this humbling sense of the greatness of the whole, something swollen and sore in her heart gave over its aching, as though a quieting hand had been laid on it. She drew a long breath. Oh, from what did it come, this rest from that sore bitterness?

It came from this, that she had somehow been shown that what she wanted was not love from her children for herself. That was trying to drive a bargain to make them pay for something they had never asked to have. What she wanted was not to get love, to get a place in their lives for herself, to get anything from them, but to give them all that lay in her to give. If that was what she wanted, why, nothing, nothing could take it away. And it was truly . . . in this hour of silence and searching . . . she saw that it was truly what she wanted. It was something in her which had grown insensibly to life and strength, during all those uncounted hours of humble service to the children. And it was something golden and immortal in her poor, flawed, human heart.

A warm bright wave of feeling swept over her . . . there, distinct and rounded against the shadowy confused procession of abstract ideas about parents and children, there stood looking at her out of their clear loving eyes, Paul and Elly and little Mark, alive, there, a part of her; not only themselves but her children; not only her children but themselves; human life which she and Neale had created out of the stuff of the universe. They looked at her and in their regard was the clear distillation of the innumerable past hours when they had looked at her with love and trust.

At the sight of them, her own children, her heart swelled and opened wide to a conception of something greater and deeper in motherhood than she had had; but which she could have if she could deserve it; something so wide and sun-flooded that the old selfish, possessive, never-satisfied ache which had called itself love withered away, its power to hurt and poison her gone.

She had no words for this . . . she could not even try to understand it. It was as solemn a birth-hour to her, as the hour when she had first heard the cry of her new-born babies . . . she was one mother then, she had become another mother now. She turned to bless the torment of bitter, doubting questioning of what she had called mother-love, which had forced her forward blindly struggling, till she found this divination of a greater possibility.

She had been trying to span the unfathomable with a mean and grasping desire. Now she knew what she must try to do; to give up the lesser and receive the greater.

This passed and left her, looking straight before her at the flickering shadows, leaping among the dusky corners of the dark slant-ceilinged room. The old clock struck three in the hall behind her.

She felt tired now, as she had after the other travail which had given her her children, and leaned her head on her hand. Where did she herself, her own personal self come in, with all this? It was always a call to more effort which came. To get the great good things of life how much you had to give! How much of what seemed dearly yourself you had to leave behind as you went forward! Her childhood was startlingly called up by this old garret where nothing had changed: she could still see herself running about there, happily absorbed in the vital trivialities of her ten years. She had not forgotten them, she knew exactly the thrill felt by that shadowy little girl as she leaned over the old chest yonder, and pulled out the deep-fringed shawl and quilted petticoat.

It had been sweet to be a little girl, she thought wistfully, to have had no past, to know only the shining present of every day with no ominous, difficult future beyond it. Ineffably sweet too was the aroma of perfect trust in the strength and wisdom of grown-up people, which tinctured deep with certainty every profoundest layer of her consciousness. Ineffably sweet . . . and lost for ever. There was no human being in the world as wise and strong as poor old Cousin Hetty had seemed to her then. A kingdom of security from which she was now shut out.

And the games, the fantastic plays – how whole and rounded and entire the pleasure in them! She remembered the rainy day she had played paper-dolls here once, with little Margaret Congdon . . . dead, years ago, that much-loved playmate of past summer days . . . and how they had taken the chest for the house for Margaret's dolls, and the hair-trunk where she sat for hers; how they had arranged them with the smallest of playthings, with pasteboard furniture, and bits of coloured tissue-paper for rugs, and pieces of silk and linen from the rag-bag for bedclothes; how they had hummed and whistled to themselves as they worked (she could hear them now!); and how the aromatic woodsy smell of the unfinished old room and the drone of the rain on the roof had been a part of their deep content.

Nothing had changed in that room, except the woman who sat there.

She got up with a sudden impulse, and threw back the lid of the trunk. A faint musty odour rose from it, as though it had been shut up for very long. And . . . why, there it was, the doll's room, just as they had left it, how long ago! How like this house! How like Cousin Hetty never to have touched it!

She sat down on the floor and, lifting the candle, looked in at the yellowed old playthings, the flimsy, spineless paper-dolls, the faded silk rags, the discoloured bits of papers, the misshapen staggering pasteboard chairs and bed, which had seemed so delightful and enchanting to her then, far better than any actual room she knew. A homesickness for the past came over her. It was not only Margaret who was dead. The other little girl who had played there, who had hung so lovingly over this creation of her fancy, was dead too, Marise thought with a backward look of longing.

And then the honest, unsparing habit of her life with Neale shook her roughly. This was sentimentalizing. If she could, would she give up what she had now and go back to being the little girl, deeply satisfied with makeshift toys, which were only the foreshadowings of what was to come? If she could, would she exchange her actual room at home for this, even to have again all the unquestioning trust in everyone and everything of the child who had died in her heart? Would she choose to give up the home where her living children had been born, at no matter what cost of horrid pain to herself, and were growing up to no matter what dark uncertainties in life, for this toy inhabited by paper-dolls? No, no, she had gone on, gone on, and left this behind. Nor would she, if she could, exchange the darker, heavier, richer gifts for the bright small trinkets of the past.

All this ran fluently from her mind, with a swiftness and clarity which seemed as shallow as it was rapid; but now there sounded in her ears a warning roar of deeper waters to which this was carrying her.

Before she knew what was coming, she braced herself to meet it; and holding hard and ineffectually, felt herself helplessly swept out and flung to the fury of the waves . . . and she met them with an answering tumult of welcome. That was what Vincent Marsh could do for her, wanted to do for her – that wonderful, miraculous thing – give back to her something she had thought she had left behind for ever; he could take her, in the strength of her maturity with all the richness of growth, and carry her back to live over again the fierce, concentrated intensity of newly born passion which had come into her life, and gone before she had had the capacity to understand or wholly feel it. He could lift her from the dulled routine of life beginning to fade and lose its colours, and carry her back to the glorious forgetfulness of every created thing, save one man and one woman.

She had had a glimpse of that in the first year of her married life, had had it, and little by little had lost it. It had crumbled away insensibly, between her fingers, with use, with familiarity, with the hateful blunting of sensitiveness which life's battering always brings. But she could have it again; with a grown woman's strength and depth of feeling, she could have the inheritance of youth. She had spent it, but now she could have it again. That was what Vincent meant.

He seemed to lean over her now, his burning, quivering hand on hers. She felt a deep hot flush rise to her face, all over her body. She was like a crimson rose, offering the splendour of its maturity to be plucked. Let her have the courage to know that its end and aim and fulfilment lay in being plucked and gloriously worn before the coming of the inevitable end! Thus and thus only could one find certainty, before death came, of having lived as deeply as lay in one to live.

Through the glowing pride and defiance with which she felt herself rise to the challenge, felt herself strong to break and surmount all obstacles within and without, which stood in the way of that fulfilment of her complete self, she had heard . . . the slightest of trivialities . . . a thought gone as soon as it was conceived . . . nothing of the slightest consequence . . . harmless . . . insignificant . . . yet why should it give off the betraying clink of something flawed and cracked? . . . She had heard . . . it must have come from some corner of her own mind . . . something like this, 'Set such an alternative between routine, traditional, narrow domestic life, and the mightiness and richness of mature passion, before a modern, free European woman, and see how quickly she would grasp with all her soul for passion.'

What was there about this, the veriest flying mote among a thousand others in the air, so to awaken in Marise's heart a deep vibration of alarm? Why should she not have said that? she asked herself, angry and scared. Why was it not a natural thought to have had? She felt herself menaced by an unexpected enemy, and flew to arms.

Into the rich, hot, perfumed shrine which Vincent's remembered words and look had built there about her, there blew a thin cool breath from the outside, through some crack opened by that casual thought. Before she even knew from whence it came, Marise cried out on it, in a fury of resentment . . . and shivered in it.

With no apparent volition of her own, she felt something very strong within her raise a mighty head and look about, stirred to watchfulness and suspicion by that luckless phrase.

She recognized it . . . the habit of honesty of thought, not native to Marise's heart, but planted there by her relation with Neale's stark, plain integrity. Feeding unchecked on its own food, during the long years of her marriage it had grown insensibly stronger and stronger, till now, tyrant and master, with the irresistible strength of conscious power, it could quell with a look all the rest of her nature, rich in coloured possibilities of seductive self-deceit, sweet illusions, lovely falsities.

She could no more stop its advance now, straight though it made its way over treasures she fain would keep, than she could stop the beating of her heart.

A ruthless question or two . . . 'Why did you say that about what a modern, free European woman would do in your place? Are you trying to play up to some trumpery notion of a rôle to fill? And more than this, did you really mean in your heart an actual, living woman of another race, such as you knew in Europe; or did you mean somebody in an Italian, or a French, or a Scandinavian book?' Marise writhed against the indignity of this, protested fiercely, angrily against the incriminating imputation in it . . . and with the same breath admitted it true.

It was true. She was horrified and lost in grief and humiliation at the cheapened aspect of what had looked so rich before. Had there been in truth an element of such trashy copying of the conventional pose of revolt in what had seemed so rushingly spontaneous? Oh no, no . . . not that!

She turned away and away from the possibility that she had been partially living up to other people's ideas, finding it intolerable; and was met again and again by the relentless thrust

273

of that acquired honesty of thought which had worn such deep grooves in her mind in all these years of unbroken practice of it. 'You are not somebody in a book, you are not a symbol of modern woman who must make the gestures appropriate for your part . . .' One by one, that relentless power seated in her many-coloured tumultuous heart put out the flaring torches.

It had grown too strong for her, that habit of honesty of thought and action. If this struggle with it had come years before she could have mastered it, flinging against it the irresistible suppleness and lightness of her ignorant youth. But now, freighted heavily with experience of reality, she could not turn and bend quickly enough to escape it.

It had profited too well by all those honest years with Neale . . . never to have been weakened by a falsehood between them, by a shade of pretence of something more, or different from what really was there. That habit held her mercilessly to see what was there now. She could no more look at what was there and think it something else, than she could look with her physical eyes at a tree and call it a dragon.

If it had only been traditional morality, reproaching her with traditional complaints about the overstepping of traditional bounds, how she could have overwhelmed it, drowned out its feeble old voice, with eloquent appeals for the right to growth, to freedom, to the generous expansion of the soul, of the personality, which Vincent Marsh could give. But honesty only asked her neutrally, 'Is it really growth and freedom, and generous expansion of the soul?' Poor Marise felt her arms fall to her side, piteous and defenceless. No, it was not.

It was with the flatness of accent which she hated, which was so hard for her, that she made the admission. It was physical excitement – that was what it was. Physical excitement, that was what Vincent Marsh could give her which Neale no longer could. . . . That and great ease of life, which Neale never would. There was a pause in which she shivered, humiliated. She added lamely to this, a guessed-at possibility for æsthetic sympathy and understanding, perhaps more than Neale could . . . and broke off with a qualm of sickness. How horrid this was! How it offended a deep sense of personal dignity and decency! How infinitely more beautiful and gracious those rolling clouds of vagueness and impulsive illusion!

But at least, when it had extracted the plain, bare statement which it had hunted down through the many-recessed corners of her heart, that stern sense of reality let her alone. She no longer felt like a beetle impaled on a pin. She was free now to move as she liked and look unmolested at what she pleased. Honesty had no more power over her than to make sure she saw what she was pretending to look at.

But at what a diminished pile she had now to look, tarnished and faded like the once-loved bits of bright-coloured silk and paper. She felt robbed and cried out in a pain which seemed to her to come from her very heart, that something living and vital and precious to her had been killed by that rough handling. But one warning look from the clear eyes of honesty forced her, lamenting, to give up even this. If it had been living and precious and vital to her, it would have survived anything that honesty could have done to it.

But something had survived, something to be reckoned with, something which no tyrant, overbearing honesty could put out of her life . . . the possibility for being carried away in the deep full current of passion, fed by all the multitudinous streams of ripened personality. If that was all that was left, was not that enough? It had been for thousands of other women. . . .

No, not that; honesty woke to menace again. What thousands of other women had done had no bearing here. She was not thousands of other women. She was herself, herself. Would it be enough for her?

Honesty issued a decree of impartial justice. Let her look at it with a mature woman's experienced divination of reality, let her look at it as it would be and see for herself if it would be enough. She was no girl whose ignorance rendered her incapable of judging until she had literally experienced. She was no bound-woman, bullied by the tyranny of an outgrown past, forced to revolt in order to attain the freedom without which no human decision can be taken. Neale's strong hand had opened the door to freedom and she could see what the bound-women could not . . . that freedom is not the end, but only the beginning.

It was as though something were holding her gripped and upright there, staring before her, motionless, till she had put herself to the last supreme test. She closed her eyes, and sat so immobile, rapt in the prodigious effort of her imagination and will, that she barely breathed. How would it be? Would it be enough? She plunged the plummet down, past the fury and rage of the storm on the surface, past the teeming life of the senses, down to the depths of consciousness. . . .

And what she brought up from those depths was a warning

distaste, a something offending to her, to all of her, now she was aware of it.

She was amazed. Why should she taste an acrid muddy flavour of dregs in that offered cup of heavy aromatic wine, she who had all her life thanked Heaven for her freedom from the ignominy of feeling it debasing to be a woman who loved? It was glorious to be a woman who loved. There had been no dregs left from those sweet, light, heady draughts she and Neale had drunk together in their youth, nor in the quieter satisfying draughts they knew now. What was the meaning of that odour of decay about what seemed so living, so hotly more living than what she had? Why should she have this unmistakable pre-science of something stale and tainting which she had never felt? Was she too old for passion? But she was in the height of her physical flowering, and physically she cried out for it. Could it be that, having spent the heritage of youth, she could not have it again? Could it be that one could not go back there, any more than . . .

Oh, what did that bring to mind? What was that fleeting cobweb of thought that seemed a recurrence of a sensation only recently passed? When she had tried to tell herself that full-fruited passion was worth all else in life, was the one great and real thing worth all the many small shams . . . what was it she had felt?

She groped among the loose-hanging filaments of impression and brought it out to see. It seemed to be . . . could it have been the same startled recoil as at the notion of getting back the peace of childhood by giving up her home for the toy-house, her living children for the dolls?

Now for the great trial of strength. Back! Push back all those thick-clustering, intruding, distracting traditional ideas of other people on both sides; the revolt on one hand, the feeble resignation on the other; what other women did; what people had said. . . . Let her wipe all that off from the too-receptive tablets of her mind. Out of sight with all that. This was *her* life, *her* question, hers alone. Let her stand alone with her own self and her own life, and, with honesty as witness, ask herself the question . . . would she, if she could, give up what she was now, with her myriads of roots, deep-set in the soil of human life, in order to bear the one red rose, splendid though it might be?

That was the question.

With no conscious volition of hers, the answer was there, plain and irrefutable as a fact in the physical world. No, she would not choose to do that. She had gone on, gone on beyond that. She was almost bewildered by the peremptory certainty with which that answer came, as though it had lain inherent in the very question.

And now another question crowded forward, darkly confused, charged with a thousand complex associations and emotions. There had been something displeasing and preposterous in the idea of trying to stoop her grown stature and simplify her complex tastes and adult interests back into the narrow limits of a child's toy-house. Could it be that she felt something of the same displeasure when she set herself fully to conceive what it would be to cramp herself and her complex interests and adult affections back to . . .

But at this there came a wild protesting clamour, bursting out to prevent her from completing this thought; loud, urgent voices, men's, women's, with that desperate certainty of their ground which always struck down any guard Marise had been able to put up. They cried her down as a traitor to the fullness of life, those voices, shouting her down with all the unquestioned authority she had encountered so many times on that terribly vital thing, the printed page; they clashed in their fury and all but drowned each other out. Only disconnected words reached her, but she recognized the well-known sentences from which they came . . . 'puritanism . . . abundance of personality . . . freedom of development . . . nothing else vital in human existence . . . prudishness . . . conventionality . . . our only possible contact with the life-purpose . . . with the end of passion life declines and dies.'

The first onslaught took Marise's breath, as though a literal storm had burst around her. She was shaken as she had been shaken so many times before. She lost her hold on her staff . . . *what had that staff been?*

At the thought, the master words came to her mind again; and all fell quiet and in a great hush waited on her advance. Neale had said, 'What is deepest and most living in *you*.' Well, what *was* deepest and most living in her? That was what she was trying to find out. That was what those voices were trying to cry her down from finding.

For the first time in all her life, she drew an inspiration from Neale's resistance to opposition, knew something of the joy of battle. What right had those people to cry her down? She would not submit to it.

She would go back to the place where she had been set upon by other people's voices, other people's thoughts, and she would go on steadily, thinking her own.

She had been thinking that there *was* the same displeasure and distaste as when she had thought of returning to her literal childhood, when she set herself fully to conceive what it would be to cramp herself and simplify her complex interests and affections back to the narrow limits of passion, which like her play with dolls had been only a foreshadowing of something greater to come.

She spoke it out boldly now, and was amazed that not one of the clamorous voices dared resist the authenticity of her statement. But after all, how would they dare? This was what she had found in her own heart, what they had not been able, for all their clamour, to prevent her from seeing. She had been strong enough to beat them, to stand out against them, to say that she saw what she really did see, and felt what she really did feel. She did not feel what traditionally she should feel, that is what a primitive Italian woman might feel, all of whose emotional life had found no other outlet than sex. . . .

Well, if it was so, it was so. For better or for worse, that was the kind of woman she had become, with the simple, forthright physical life subordinate, humble; like a pleasant, lovable child playing among the strong, full-grown, thought-freighted interests and richly varied sympathies and half-impersonal joys and sorrows which had taken possession of her days. And she could not think that the child could ever again be master of her destiny, any more than (save in a moment of false sentimentality) she could think that she would like to have her horizon again limited by a doll-house. To be herself was to go on, not to go back, now that she knew what she had become. It seemed to her that never before had she stood straight up.

And in plain fact she found that somehow she had risen to her feet and was now standing, her head up, almost touching the rafters of the slant ceiling. She could have laughed out, to find herself so free. She knew now why she had never known the joy of battle. It was because she had been afraid. And she had been afraid because she had never dared to enter the battle, had always sent others in to do her fighting for her. Now she had been forced into it and had won. And there was nothing to be afraid of there!

She spread out her arms in a great gesture of liberation. How had she ever lived before, under the shadow of that coward fear? This . . . this . . . she had a moment of vision . . . this was what Neale had been trying to do for her, all these years, unconsciously, not able to tell her what it was, driving at the mark only with the inarticulate wisdom of his love for her, his divination of her need. He had seen her, shivering and shrinking in the shallow waters, and had longed for her sake to have her strike out boldly into the deep. But even if he had been ever so able to tell her, she would not have understood till she had fought her way through those ravening breakers, beyond them, out into the sustaining ocean.

How long it took, how *long* for men and women to make the smallest advance! And how the free were the only ones who could help to liberate the bound. How she had fought against Neale's effort to set her free, had cried to him that she dared not risk herself on the depths, that he must have the strength to swim for her . . . and how Neale, doggedly sure of the simple truth, too simple for her to see, had held to the certainty that his effort would not make her strong, and that she would only be free if she were strong.

Neale being his own master, a free citizen of life, knew what a kingdom he owned, and with a magnanimity unparalleled could not rest till she had entered hers. She, not divining what she had not known, had only wished to make the use of his strength which would have weakened her. Had there ever before been any man who refused to let the woman he loved weaken herself by the use of his strength? Had a man ever before held out his strong hand to a woman to help her forward, not to hold her fast?

Her life was her own. She stood in it, knowing it to be an impregnable fortress, knowing that from it she could now look abroad fearlessly and understandingly, knowing that from it she could look at things and men and the world and see what was there. From it she could, as if for the first time, look at Vincent Marsh when next she saw him; she would look to see what was really there. That was all. She would look at him and see what he was, and then she would know the meaning of what had happened, and what she was to do. And no power on earth could prevent her from doing it. The inner bar that had shut her in was broken. She was a free woman, free from that something in her heart that was afraid. For the moment she could think of nothing else beyond the richness of that freedom. Why, here was the total fulfilment she had longed for. Here was the life more abundant, within, within her own heart, waiting for her!

The old clock in the hall behind her sounded four muffled strokes and, as if it had wakened her, Agnes stirred in her bed and cried out in a loud voice of terror, 'Oh, come quick, Miss Marise! Come!'

Marise went through the hall and to her door, and saw the frightened old eyes glaring over the pulled-up sheet. 'Oh . . . oh . . . it's you . . . I thought . . . Oh, Miss Marise, don't you see anything standing in that corner? Didn't you hear . . . Oh, Miss Marise, I must have had a bad dream. I thought . . .' Her teeth were chattering. She did not know what she was saying.

'It's all right, Agnes,' said Marise soothingly, stepping into the room. 'The big clock just struck four. That probably wakened you.'

She sat down on the bed and laid her hand firmly on Agnes' shoulder, looking into the startled old eyes, which grew a little quieter now that someone else was there. What a pitiable creature Agnes' dependence on Cousin Hetty had made of her. . . .

Like the boom from a great bell came the thought, 'That is what I wanted Neale to make of me, when the crucial moment came, a dependant . . . but he would not.'

'What time did you say it is?' Agnes asked, still breathing quickly but with a beginning of a return to her normal voice.

'Four o'clock,' answered Marise gently, as to a child. 'It must be almost light outside. The last night when you have anything to fear is over now.'

She went to the window and opened the shutter. The ineffable sacred pureness of another dawn came in, grey, tranquil, penetrating.

At the sight of it, the dear light of every day, Marise felt the thankful tears come to her eyes.

'See, Agnes,' she said in an unsteady voice, 'daylight has come. You can look around for yourself, and see that there is nothing to be afraid of.'

Chapter 26: *Marise Looks and Sees What is There*

A Torch in a Living Tree

July 24.

NOT since his fiery, ungovernable youth had Vincent felt anything like the splendid surge of rich desire and exultant certainty which sent him forward at a bound along the wood-road into which he had seen Marise turn. The moment he had been watching for had come at last, after these three hideous days of sudden arrest and pause. The forced inaction had been a sensation physically intolerable to him, as though he had been frozen immobile with every nerve and muscle strained for a great leap.

He felt himself taking the leap now, with such a furious, triumphant sense of power released, that he came up beside her like a wind in the forest, calling her name loudly, his hands outflung, his face glowing, on fire with joy and his need for her.

For an instant he was dumbfounded by the quiet face she turned on him, by his instant perception of a profound change in her, by an expression in her long dark eyes which was new to him, which he felt to be ominous to him. But he was no untried boy to be cast down or disconcerted by sudden alterations of mood in a woman. He was a man, with a man's trained tenacity of purpose and experienced quickness of resource.

He wasted no time. 'What has happened to you?' he demanded, peremptorily as by right to know, and with the inner certainty of over-riding it, whatever it was.

She did not seem tacitly or otherwise to deny his right to know, but she seemed to have no words for it, continuing to look at him silently, intently, with no hostility, with a sort of steady, wondering attention in her face, usually so sensitively changing. He felt a resentment at its quiet, at its lack of that instant responsiveness to his look which had given him such moments of exquisite pleasure, which had been her own, her wonderful gift to him. She was looking at him now as she might have looked at anyone else, merely in order to see what was there.

Well, he would show her what was there! The will to conquer rose high and strong in him, with an element of fierceness it had not had before because no resistance had called it out.

He did not show this, indeed only allowed it the smallest corner of his consciousness, keeping all the rest tautly on the alert for the first indication of an opening, for the first hint of where to throw his strength.

But standing in suspense on the alert was the last rôle he could long endure, and in a moment, when she did not answer, he took a step towards her, towering above her, his hands on her shoulders, pouring out with a hot sense of release all his longing into the cry, 'Marise, Marise my own, what has happened to you?'

How he hated the quiet of her face! With what hungry impatience he watched to see it break. How surely he counted on its disappearance at his touch. For he had the certainty of his power to kindle her left intact from the last time he had seen her, tinder to his spark, helplessly played upon by his voice.

But now it was as though he had held a torch aloft into the green branches of a living tree. A twitch of surface agitation on her face and that was all.

And when she spoke, as she did at once, the sound of her voice was strange and alien to him. With an extreme directness, and with a deep sincerity of accent which, even to his ears, made his own impassioned outcry to her sound inflated and false, she said earnestly, 'I don't believe I can tell you what has happened. I don't believe you could understand it.'

He did not believe a word of this, but with his brilliant suppleness of mind he perceived that he was in the wrong key. She was not, for the moment, to be kindled to flame, she who miraculously was never the same. Perhaps it was the moment for a thrust of sheer power, straight at the obstacle, for of course he knew the obstacle.

'I know what has happened,' he said, 'without your telling me. Your husband has made a scene, and overborne you, and is trying to force you back into the hen-yard of domestic virtue. . . .' He changed his manner. He said in a low, beautiful, persuasive voice, his eyes deeply on her, sure of himself with that sureness that no one had ever resisted, 'But you can never do that now, you bird-of-paradise! You would only . . .'

He was brought up short by a change in her. This time his words had had the power to move her face from the quiet he hated. It was suddenly alive with a strong emotion. But what emotion? He could not guess at its meaning, nor why she should step quickly away, shaking his hands from her shoulders, and looking at him sadly, her eyebrows drawn up as if in pain. He hung uncertain, daunted by his inability to read her face, feeling for the first time an instantly dismissed doubt of his mastery over her.

She said very quickly, with the accent and manner of one who, shocked and pitying, tries to save another from going on with an involuntary disclosure in him of something shaming and unworthy.

'No, oh no! Not that. Neale has done nothing . . . said nothing . . . except as he always has, to leave me quite free, all free.'

As he was silent for a moment, watchful, not especially moved by her words, which seemed to him unimportant, but alarmed by some special significance which they seemed to have for her, she went on with the single, only note of blame or reproach which was to come into her voice. 'Oh, how *could* you think that?' she said to him, with a deep quavering disappointment, as though she were ashamed of him.

He knew that he was the cause of the disappointment, although he could not imagine why, and he regretted having made a false move; but he was not deeply concerned by this passage. He did not see how it could have any importance, or touch what lay at issue between them. These were all woman-ish, up-in-the-air passes and parries. He had only not yet found his opening.

He flung his head back impatiently. 'If it is not that, what is it?' he demanded. 'A return of hide-bound scruples about the children? You know that they must live their own lives, not yours, and that anything that gives you greater richness and power makes you a better mother.'

'Oh yes, I know that,' she answered. 'I have thought of that myself.'

But he had a baffled feeling that this was not at all the ad-mission the words would make it seem.

His impatience began to burn high, and a dawning alarm to translate itself into anger. He would not be played with by any woman who ever lived! 'Marise,' he said roughly, 'what under the sun is it?' In his tone was all his contemptuous dis-missal of it, whatever it might be . . . outworn moral qualms, fear of the world's opinion, inertia, cowardice, hair-splitting scruples, or some morbid physical revulsion . . . there was not one of them which he knew he could not instantly pounce on and shake to rags.

Marise stood very still, her eyes bent downward. 'Aren't you going to answer me?' he said, furious.

She nodded. 'Yes, I'm going to answer you,' she said, without raising her eyes. He understood that he must wait, and stood opposite to her, close to her, looking at her, all the strength of his passion in that avid gaze.

She was stamped on his mind in every detail as she looked at that instant, infinitely desirable, infinitely alluring, in her thin white dress, her full supple woman's body erect and firm with a strong life of its own, her long sensitive hands clasped before her . . . how many times in his dreams had he held them in his . . . her shining dark hair bound smoothly about her head and down low on each side of her rounded forehead. Her thick white eyelids, down-dropped, were lowered over her eyes, and her mouth with its full lips and deep corners . . . at the sight of her mouth on which he had laid that burning kiss, Vincent felt a barrier within him give way . . . here he was at last with the woman he loved, the woman who was going to give herself to him . . . Good God! all these words . . . what did they mean? Nothing. He swept her into his arms and drew her face to his, his eyes closed, lost in the wonder and ecstasy of having reached his goal at last.

She did not make the startled virginal resistance of a girl. She drew away from him quietly . . . the hatred for that quiet was murderous in him . . . and shook her head. Why, it was almost gently that she shook her head.

How dared she act gently to him, as though he were a boy who had made a mistake! How dared she not be stirred and mastered! He felt his head burning hot with anger, and knew that his face must be suffused with red.

And hers was not, it was quiet. He could have stamped with rage, and shaken her. He wanted to hurt her at once, deeply, to pierce her and sting her back to life. 'Do you mean,' he said brutally, 'that you find, after all, that you are a cold, narrow, cowardly, provincial woman, stunted by your life, so that you are incapable of feeling a generous heat?'

As she remained silent, he was stung by the expression on her face which he did not understand. He went on vindictively, snatching up to drive home his thrust the sharpest and cruelest weapon he could conceive, '*Perhaps you find you are too old?*'

At this she looked away from him for an instant, up to the lower branches of the oak under which they stood. She seemed to reflect, and when she brought her eyes back to his, she answered, 'Yes, I think that is it. I find I am too old.'

He was for years to ponder on the strangeness of the accent with which she said this, without regret, with that damnable gentleness as though to hide from him a truth he might find hard to bear, or be incapable of understanding.

How could any woman say 'I find I am too old' with that unregretting accent? Was it not the worst of calamities for all women to grow old? What was there left for a woman when she grew old?

But how preposterous, her saying that, she who stood there in the absolute perfection of her bloom!

He found that he did not know what to say next. That tolerant acquiescence of hers in what he had meant to sting intolerably . . . it was as though he had put all his force into a blow that would stun, and somehow missing his aim, encountering no resistance, was toppling forward with the impetus of his own effort. He recovered himself and looked at her, choking, 'You don't mean . . .' he began, challenging her incredulously, and could go no further.

For she nodded, her eyes on his with that singular expression in them which he did not understand, and which he intensely resented.

He was so angry that for a moment he could not speak. He was aware of nothing but anger. 'It's impotence and weakness on your part, that's all it is!' he cast out at her, hating her savagely as he spoke, 'no matter what fine words you've decided to call it to cloak your own feebleness. It's the littleness of the vital spark in you. Or it's cowardly inertia, turning from the real fulfilment that calls for you, back to chips and straw because you are used to them. It's being a small, poor, weak, cowed creature, traditional-minded, instead of the splendid, brave, living woman I thought I loved. I am *glad* to leave you behind, to have no more of you in my life. I have no use for thin-blooded cowards.'

She made no answer at all, not a word. His flaming eyes fell away from her face. He turned from her abruptly and walked rapidly away, not looking back.

Then he found he had ceased to advance rapidly, had stopped and was standing still, wrung in so dreadful a pain that his hand was at his side as though he had been stabbed. With no thought, with no awareness of what he was doing, he ran back to her, his hands outstretched, suffering so that he must have help. He did not mean to speak, did not know what he was to say . . . he cried out to her, 'Marise, Marise . . . I love you! *What can I do?*'

The cry was desperate, involuntary, forcing its way out from unfathomed depths of feeling below all his anger and resentment, and tearing him to pieces as it came. It was as though he had taken his heart out and flung it at her feet.

Her face changed instantly and was quiveringly alight with a pale and guilty agitation. 'No . . . oh *no*, Vincent! I thought you only . . . I had thought you could not really . . . Vincent, forgive me! Forgive me!' She took one of his hands in both hers . . . the last unforgotten touch he was ever to have of her. . . .

It came to him through those words which he did not understand that she was pitying him; and stung to the quick, he drew back from her, frowning, with an angry toss of his head.

Instantly she drew back also, as though she had misinterpreted something.

He stood for an instant looking full at her as though he did not see her; and then with a wide gesture of utter bewilderment, strange from him, he passed her without a look.

This time he did not turn back, but continued steadily and resolutely on his way.

Chapter 27: *The Fall of the Big Pine*

§ 1

August 2.

WHEN Marise reached the place on the wood-road where she had had that last talk with Vincent Marsh, she stopped, postponing for a moment the errand to the Powers which she had so eagerly undertaken. She stood there, looking up into the far green tops of the pines, seeing again that strange, angry, bewildered gesture with which he had renounced trying to make anything out of her, and had turned away.

It remained with her, constantly, as the symbol of what had happened, and she looked at it gravely and understandingly. Then, very swiftly, she saw again that passing aspect of his which had so terribly frightened her, felt again the fear that

286

he might be really suffering, that she might really have done a hurt to another human being.

This brought her a momentary return of the agitation it had caused in her that day, and she sat down abruptly on a tree-trunk, her knees trembling, her hands cold.

That fear had come as so totally unexpected a possibility, something which his every aspect and tone and word up to then had seemed to contradict. Strange, how unmoved he had left her till that moment! Strange the impression of him, that first time after she had known herself strong enough to stand up and be herself, not the responsive instrument played on by every passing impression. Strange, how instantly he had felt that, and how passionate had been his resentment of her standing up to be herself, her being a grown woman, a human being, and not a flower to be plucked. How he had hated it, and alas! how lamentable his hatred of it had made him appear. What a blow he had dealt to her conception of him by his instant assumption that a change in her could only mean that Neale had been bullying her. It had been *hard* to see him so far away and diminished as that had made him seem, so entirely outside her world. It had dealt a back-hand blow to her own self-esteem to have him seem vulgar.

How strange an experience for her altogether to be able to stand firm against noise and urgent clamour and confusion, and to see, in spite of it, what she was looking at; to see, back of the powerful magnetic personality, the undeveloped and tyrannical soul, the cramped mind without experience or conception of breadth and freedom in the relations between human beings; to be able to hear Vincent cry out on her with that fierce, masterful certainty of himself that she was acting from cowed and traditional-minded motives and not to believe a word of it, because it was not true; not even to feel the scared throb of alarm at the very idea that it might be true; to have it make no impression on her save pity that Vincent should be imprisoned in a feeling of which possession was so great a part that failure to possess turned all the rest to poison and sickness.

What had happened to her, in truth, that she had this new steadfastness? She had told Vincent he could not understand it. Did she understand it herself? She leaned her chin on her two hands, looking deep into the green recesses of the forest. High above her head, a wind swayed the tops of the pines and sang loudly; but down between the great brown columns of their trunks, not a breath stirred. The thick-set, myriad-leaved young maples held all their complicated delicately edged foliage motionless in perfect calm.

It was very still in the depths of Marise's complicated mind also, although the wind stirred the surface. Yes, she knew what had happened to her. She had seen it completely happen to three other human beings, miraculously, unbelievably, certainly; had seen the babies who could not tell light from dark, heat from cold, emerge by the mere process of healthful living, into keenly sensitive beings accurately alive to every minutest variation of the visible world. It must be that like them she had simply learned to tell moral light from dark, heat from cold, by the mere process of healthful living. What happened to the child who at one time could not grasp the multiplication table, and a few years later, if only he were properly fed and cared for, had somehow so wholly changed, although still the same, that he found his way lightly among geometric conceptions, and only a few years after that was probing with expert fingers at some unsolved problem of astronomy? He had grown up, that was all. By calling the miracle a familiar name we veiled the marvel of it. Insensibly to him, with no visible change from one day to the next, he had acquired a totally different conception of the universe, a totally different valuation of everything in life.

That was what had happened to her. She had grown up ... why should not a woman grow up to other valuations of things as well as her comrade in life?

And it had happened to her as it did to the child, because someone stronger than she had protected her while she was growing ... not protected from effort, as though one should try to protect the child from learning his lessons. ... Back there, such ages ago in Italy, in her ignorant ... how ignorant! ... and frightened girlhood, she had begged Neale, without knowing what she did, to help her grow up, to help her save what was worth saving in her, to help her untangle from the many-coloured confusion of her nature what was best worth keeping. And Neale had done it, had clung steadily to his divination of what was strong in her, in spite of her clamour to him to let it go.

But Vincent had not grown up, was back there still in confusion, holding desperately with all that terrific strength of his to what could not be held, to what was impermanent and passing in its nature. Why should he do that? Neale knew better than that. Then she saw why: it was because Vincent conceived of nothing but emptiness if he let it go, and horribly feared that imaginary emptiness. Out of the incalculable richness of her kingdom she wondered again at his blindness. . . . And made a pitying guess at the reason for it . . . perhaps for him it was *not* imaginary. Perhaps one of the terms of the bargain he had made with life was that there *should* be nothing later but emptiness for him. Yes, she saw that. She would have made that bargain, too, if it had not been for Neale. She would have been holding terrified to what was not to be held; with nothing but that between her and the abyss. Who was she to blame Vincent for his blindness?

That, perhaps, had been the meaning of that singular last moment of their talk together, which had frightened her so, with its sudden plunge below the surface, into the real depths, when, changed wholly into someone else, he had run back to her, his hands outstretched, his eyes frightened, his lips trembling . . . perhaps he had felt the abyss there just before him. For an instant there, he had made her think of Paul, made her remember that Vincent himself had, so short a time ago, been a little boy too. She had been so shocked and racked by pity and remorse, that she would have been capable of any folly to comfort him. Perhaps she had seen there for an instant the man Vincent might have been, and had seen that she could have loved that man.

But how instantly it had passed! He had not suffered that instant of true feeling to have space to live, but had burned it up with the return of his pride, his resentment that anyone save himself should try to stand upright, with the return of the devouring desire-for-possession of the man who had always possessed everything he had coveted. There was something sad in being able to see the littleness of life which underlay the power and might of personality in a man like Vincent. He could have been something else.

She wondered why there should slide into her mood just now a faint tinge of regret. . . . Why should there be anything there but the bright gladness of thanksgiving for the liberation from the chains which her own nature might have forged about her? She had at last stepped outside the narrow circle of personal desire, and found all the world open to her. And yet there was room in her heart for a shade of wistful wonder if perhaps all this did not mean that she might be sliding from the ranks of those who feel and do, into the ranks of those who only understand.

But one glance at the life that lay before her scattered this hanging mist-cloud . . . good heavens! what feeling and doing lay there before her!

Had she thought that Neale was nothing to her because he had become all in all to her so that he penetrated all her life, so that she did not live an instant alone? Had she thought the loss of the amusing trinket of physical newness could stand against the gain of an affection all massy gold? Would she, to buy moments of excitement, lose an instant of the precious certainty of sympathy and trust and understanding which she and Neale had bought and paid for, hour by hour, year by year of honest life-in-common? Where was real life for her? Had she not known? Where were the real depths, where the real food for the whole woman she had grown to be? Neale had opened the door so that she could go away from him if that was what she needed, or go back to stand by his side; and through the open door had come the flood of daylight which had shown her that she could not go back to stand by his side because she had been there all the time, had never left it, never could leave it, any more than she could leave half of her body in one place, and go on to another.

§ 2

There was other feeling and doing now, too, before her, this instant, which she had forgotten, idling here in her much-loved forest, as much a part of her home as her piano or her own roof-tree. She had been trying to understand what had been happening that summer. Let her try first of all to understand what she must do in that perfectly definite and concrete dilemma in which she had been placed by that strange sight of 'Gene Powers fleeing back from the Eagle Rocks. She must look squarely at what she supposed was the legal obligation . . . she instantly felt a woman's impatience of the word legal as against human, and could not entertain the thought of the obligations of the situation. She must see, and think and try to understand, with Neale to help her. She had not yet had time to tell Neale.

But not to-day. To-day she was only the bearer of the good tidings to Nelly and 'Gene, tidings which would wipe out for her the recollection of a day which was shameful to her, the day when she had conceived the possibility of believing something base against Neale. It was not that she had believed it — no, she had stood it off till Neale came back. But there was shame for her in those recurrent spasms of horror when she had conceived the possibility that she might believe it. There had been proof of it, of course, Eugenia's positive statement . . . strange how Eugenia could have so entirely misunderstood the affair! . . . But what was mere proof against human certainty? No, she had been attacked suddenly and for an instant had failed to rise to defend what was hers to defend. It was a failure to live down.

She stood up and moved forward along the path, changing the thick envelope in one hand to the other. She had already lost time. She ought to have been by this time through the forest and out in the edge of the Powers' pasture.

She became aware that for some time she had heard a distant sound, a faint toc-toc-toc, like the sound of chopping. This being associated in her mind with snow and winter woods, she had not thought it could be the sound of the axe which it seemed to be. Nobody could be felling trees in the height of the farming season, and on this day of swooning heat. But as she came to the edge of the woods and turned into the path along the brook, she heard it more plainly, unmistakable this time, not far now, the ringing blows delivered with the power and rhythmic stroke of the trained chopper. It came not from the woods at all, she now perceived, but from the open farming land, from the other side of the pasture, beyond the Powers' house.

But there were no woods there, only the Powers' big pine which towered up, darkly glorious, into the shimmering summer haze.

As she looked at it wondering, it came into her mind . . . had somebody told her, or had she overheard it somewhere? . . . that 'Gene had promised Nelly at last to cut down the big pine he and his fathers had so cherished.

Could it be that? What a sacrifice! And to a foolish whim of Nelly's. There had been no musty smell in the house till Nelly came there to keep the shutters closed so that the sun would not fade the carpets. The old pine was one of the most splendid things of beauty in the valley. And it was something vital in 'Gene's strange, choked, inarticulate life. She stopped to listen a moment, feeling a chill of apprehension and foreboding. It was dreadful to have 'Gene do that. It was as though he were cutting at his own strength, cutting off one of his own members to please his wife. Poor 'Gene! He would do that too, now, if Nelly asked him.

The resonant winter note rang out loud, strange in that sultry summer air. She looked from afar at the tree, holding its mighty crest high above the tiny house, high above the tiny human beings who had doomed it. So many winters, so many summers, so many suns and moons and rains and snows had gone to make it what it was. Like the men who had planted it and lived beneath its shade, it had drawn silently from the depths of the earth and the airy treasures of the sky food to grow strong and live its life. And now to be killed in an hour, in attempted expiation of a deed for which it bore no guilt!

Marise was coming closer now. The axe-strokes stopped for a moment as though the chopper drew breath. The silence was heavy over the breathless summer field.

But by the time she had arrived at the back door of the house, the axe-blows were renewed, loud, immediate, shocking palpably on her ear. She knocked, but knew that the ringing clamour of the axe drowned out the sound. Through the screen-door she saw old Mrs. Powers standing by the table, ironing, and stepped in. The three children were in the pantry beyond, Ralph spreading some bread and butter for his little brother and sister. Ralph was always good to the younger children, although he was so queer and un-childlike! Nelly was not there. Mrs. Powers looked up at Marise and nodded. She looked disturbed and absent. 'We're at it, you see,' she said, jerking her head back towards the front of the house. 'I told you 'bout 'Gene's sayin' he'd gi'n in to Nelly about the big pine.'

Marise made a gesture of dismay at this confirmation. The old woman went on, 'Funny thing . . . I ain't a Powers by birth, Lord knows, and I never thought I set no store by their old pine tree. It always sort o' riled me, how much 'Gene's father thought of it, and 'Gene after him . . . sort of silly, seems like. But just now when we was all out there, and 'Gene heaved up his axe and hit the first whack at it . . . well, I can't tell you . . . it give me a turn most as if he'd chopped right into *me* somewhere. I got up and come into the house, and I set to ironin' as fast as I could clip it, to keep my mind off'n it. I made the children come in too, because it ain't no place for kids around, when a tree that size comes down.'

Marise demurred, ''Gene is such a fine chopper, he knows to a hair where he'll lay it, of course.'

'Well, even so, who knows what notion a kid will take into his head? They was playin' right there on a pile of pole-wood
292

'Gene's brought in from the woods and ain't got sawed up into stove-lengths yet. I didn't want to take no chances; maybe they wouldn't ha' moved quick enough when their papa yelled to them. No, ma'am, I make 'em come in, and here they'll stay. Nelly, she's out there, walkin' round and round watchin' 'Gene. She's awfully set up havin' it come down. 'Gene he's told her he'll give her the money from the lumber in it. There'll be a sight of boards, too. It's the biggest pine in the valley.'

Marise went to the window and looked at the scene, penetrated by the strangeness of the difference between its outer and inner aspect: 'Gene, his faded blue overalls tucked into his ploughman's heavy cow-hide boots, his shirt open over his great throat and chest, his long corded arms rising and falling with the steady effortless rhythm of the master woodsman. Nelly, in one of her immaculate blue ginghams, a white apron over it, a white frilled shade-hat on her head, her smartly shod small feet treading the ground with that inimitable light step of hers, circling slowly about, looking at 'Gene as he worked, looking up at the crown of the tree, high, so insolently high above her head, soon to be brought low by a wish from her heart, soon to be turned into money for her to spend.

'I came over to talk to 'Gene and Nelly about some business,' Marise said, over her shoulder, to Mrs. Powers, not able to take her eyes from the trio in the drama out there, 'but I'd better wait till the tree is down before I speak to them.'

''Twon't be long now. 'Gene's been at it quite a while, and he's stavin' away like all possessed. Seems as if, now he's started in, he couldn't get it over with quick enough to suit him. He acted awful queer about it, I thought.'

She left her ironing and, looking over her shoulder at the children, came closer to where Marise stood. Then she stepped back and shut the door to the pantry. 'Mis' Crittenden,' she said in an anxious troubled voice, ''Gene ain't right these days. He acts to me like he's comin' down with a sick spell, or something. He ain't *right*. To-day Nelly told me she woke up in the night last night and 'Gene wasn't there. She hollered to him, and he didn't answer. It scared her like everything, and she scrambled out of bed and lighted the lamp, and she said she 'most fainted away when she see 'Gene, rolled up in a blanket, lying on the floor, over against the wall, his eyes wide open looking at her. She said she let out a yell . . . it scairt the life out of her . . . and 'Gene he got right up. She says to him, "For the Lord's sake, 'Gene, what *ails* you?" And what

293

do you suppose he says to her, he says, "I didn't know whether you wanted me there or not, Nelly." What do you think of that? She says back, "For goodness' sake, 'Gene Powers, where *would* you be nights, except in your own bed!" He got back and for all Nelly knows slept all right the rest of the night. She says she guesses he must have had some sort of funny dream, and not been really all waked up yet. But it must ha' gi'n her a turn, for all she ain't one of the nervous kind.'

Marise turned sick with shocked pity. The two women looked at each other, silently, with shadowed eyes of foreboding. Mrs. Powers shook her head, and turned back into the pantry, shutting the door behind her. Marise heard her speaking to the children in the cheerful, bantering, affectionate, grandmother tone she had always had for them. She was brave, old Mrs. Powers, she always said she could 'stand up to things.' She was the sort of woman who can always be depended on to keep life going, no matter what happens; who never gives up, who can always go on taking care of the children.

Marise herself did not feel at all brave. She sat down heavily in a chair by the window looking out at the man who for his wife's sake was killing something vital and alive. He had done that before, 'Gene had. He went at it now with a furious haste which had something dreadful in it.

Nelly, who had sat down to rest on the pile of brush and poles, seemed a carved and painted statuette of ivory and gold.

She took off her ruffled pretty hat, and laid it down on the white-birch poles, so that she could tip her head far back and see the very top of the tree. Her braids shone molten in the sunshine. Her beautiful face was impassive, secreting behind a screen all that Marise was sure she must have been feeling.

'Gene, catching sight of her now, in a side-glance, stopped abruptly in the middle of a swing, and shouted to her to 'get off that brush-pile. That's jus' where I'm lottin' on layin' the tree.'

Somewhat startled, Nelly sprang up and moved around to the other side, back of him, although she called protestingly, 'Gracious, you're not *near* through yet!'

'Gene made no answer, returning to the fury of his assault on what he so much loved. The great trunk now had a gaping raw gash in its side. Nelly idled back of him, looking up at the tree, down at him. What was she thinking about?

Marise wondered if someone with second-sight could have seen Frank Warner there between the husband and wife?

'Gene's face was still grey in spite of the heat and his fierce exertion. Glistening streams of perspiration ran down his cheeks.

What did the future hold for 'Gene? What possible escape was there from the tragic net he had wrapped stranglingly around himself?

Very distantly, like something dreamed, it came to Marise that once for an instant the simple, violent solution had seemed the right one to her. *Could she have thought that?*

What a haunted house was the human heart, with phantoms from the long-dead past intruding their uninvited ghastly death's-heads among the living.

The axe-strokes stopped; so suddenly that the ear went on hearing them, ghost-like, in the intense silence. 'Gene stood upright, lifting his wet, grey face. 'She's coming now,' he said.

Marise looked out, astonished. To her eyes the tree stood as massively firm as she had ever seen it. But 'Gene's attitude was of strained, expectant certainty: he stood near Nelly and as she looked up at the tree, he looked at her. At that look Marise felt the cold perspiration on her own temples.

Nelly stepped sideways a little, tipping her head to see, and cried out, 'Yes, I see it beginning to slant. How *slow* it goes!'

'It'll go fast enough in a minute,' said 'Gene.

Of what followed, not an instant ever had for Marise the quality of reality. It always remained for her a superb and hideous dream, something symbolical, glorious and horrible which had taken place in her brain, not in the lives of human beings.

Nelly . . . looking down suddenly to see where the tree would fall, crying out, 'Oh, I left my hat where it'll . . .' and darting, light as a feather, towards it.

'Gene, making a great futile gesture to stop her as she passed him, shouting at her, with a horrified glance up at the slowly leaning tree, 'Come back! Come back!'

Nelly, on the brush-pile, her hat in her hand, whirling to return, supple and swift, suddenly caught by the heel and flung headlong . . . up again in an instant, and falling again, to her knees this time. Up once more with a desperate haste, writhing and pulling at her shoe, held by its high heel, deep between the knotty poles. . . .

'Gene, bounding from his place of safety, there at her feet, tearing in a frenzy at the poles, at her shoe. . . .

Above them the great tree bearing down on them the solemn vengeful shadow of its fall.

Someone was screaming. It was Nelly. She was screaming, "Gene! 'Gene! 'Gene!' her face shrunken in terror, her white lips open.

And then, that last gesture of 'Gene's when he took Nelly into his great arms, closely, hiding her face on his shoulder, as the huge tree, roaring downward, bore them both to the earth, for ever.

Chapter 28: *Two Good-Byes*

August 10.

MARISE welcomed the bother about the details of Eugenia's departure and Mr. Welles', and flung herself into them with a frightened desire for something that would drown out the roaring wind of tragedy which filled her ears in every pause of the day's activities, and woke her up at night out of the soundest sleep. Night after night, she found herself sitting up in bed, her nightgown and hair damp with perspiration, Nelly's scream ringing knife-like in her ears. Then, rigid and wide-eyed, she saw it all again, what had happened in those thirty seconds which had summed up and ended the lives of 'Gene and Nelly.

But one night as she sat thus in her bed, hammered upon beyond endurance, she saw as though she had not seen it before what 'Gene had finally done, his disregard of possible safety for himself, his abandon of his futile, desperate effort to free Nelly from the tangle where her childish vanity had cast her, the grandeur and completeness of his gesture when he had taken Nelly into his strong arms, to die with her. Marise found herself crying as she had not cried for years. The picture, burned into her memory, stood there endlessly in the black night till she understood it. The tears came raining down her face, and with them went the strained, wild horror of the memory.

But the shadow and darkness hung about her like a cloud, through which she only dimly saw the neat, unhurried grace of Eugenia's preparations for departure and far travels, and felt only a dimmed, vague echo of the emotion she had thought to feel at the disappearance of Mr. Welles, poor, weary, futile old crusader on his Rosinante.

On that last morning of their stay she drove with them to the station, still giving only a half-attention to the small episodes of their departure. She did see and smile at the characteristic quality of an instinctive gesture of Eugenia's as they stepped up on the platform of the station. Two oddly shaped pieces of metal stood there, obviously parts of a large machine. Paul stumbled over them as he climbed out of the car, and held tight to Mr. Welles' hand to save himself from a fall. Eugenia saw them instantly from afar as an element in life which threatened the spotlessness of her grey travelling cloak, and as she passed them she drew the thick folds of velvet-like wool about her closely. Marise thought to herself, 'That's Eugenia's gesture as she goes through the world.'

Neale turned off his switch, listened a moment to see if the Ford were boiling from the long climb up the hill to the station, and now made one long-legged step to the platform. He started towards Eugenia with the evident intention of making some casual pleasant remarks, such as are demanded by decency for a departing guest, but in his turn his eyes caught the curiously shaped pieces of metal. He stopped short, his face lighted up with pleasure and surprise. All consciousness of anyone else on the platform disappeared from his expression. 'Hello!' he said to himself, 'those mandrels here.' He picked up one in his strong hands on which the metal left a grey dust, and inspected it. He might have been entirely alone in his shop at the mill.

Marise noted with envy how he gave all of himself to that momentary examination, entirely escaped from any awareness of that tyrannical self which in her own heart always clamoured like a spoiled child for attention. The impersonal concentration of his look as he turned the metal about between those strong dusty hands gave to his face the calm, freed expression not to be bought for any less price than a greater interest in one's work than in one's self. 'They'll do,' pronounced Neale. This was evidently a thought spoken aloud, for it did not occur to him to make any pretence of including the two women in his interest. He set down the casting he held, and went off into the freight-house, calling loudly, 'Charlie! Charlie! Those mandrels have come. I wish you'd . . .' his voice died away as he walked farther into the dusky freight-shed.

Marise happening to glance at Eugenia now, caught on her face an expression which she took to be annoyance at a breach of manners. She reflected, 'Eugenia must find Neale's abrupt American ways perfectly barbaric.' And she was surprised to feel for the first time a rather scornful indifference to all that was involved in Eugenia's finding them barbaric. Heavens! What did it matter? In a world so filled with awful and portentous and glorious human possibilities, how could you bother about such things?

There was a silence. Mr. Welles and Paul had been standing near, aimlessly, but now, evidently taking the silence for the inevitable flatness of the flat period of waiting for a train, Mr. Welles drew the little boy away. They walked down the cinder-covered side-tracks, towards where the single baggage truck stood, loaded with elegant, leather-covered boxes and wicker basket-trunks, marked 'E. Mills. S.S. Savoie. Compagnie Générale Transatlantique.' Among them, out of place and drab, stood one banal department-store trunk labelled, 'Welles. 320 Maple Avenue. Macon, Georgia.'

The departure of the old man and the little boy left the two women alone. Eugenia stepped closer to Marise and took her hand in her own gloved fingers. She looked at it intently, with the expression of one who is trying to find words for a complicated feeling. Marise made an effort to put herself in the receptive mood which would make the saying of it easier, but failed. The fall of the big pine roared too loudly in her ears. She looked without sympathy or admiration at Eugenia's perfection of aspect. 'To look like that, she must care for looks more than anything else. What can she know about any real human feeling?' Marise asked herself, with an intolerance she could not mitigate.

And yet as she continued to peer at Eugenia through that dark cloud of tragedy, it seemed to her that Eugenia showed signs of some real human emotion. As she gazed at her in the crude brilliance of the gaudy morning sun, she saw for the first time signs of years in Eugenia's exquisite small face. There was not a line visible, nor a faltering of the firmness of the well-cared-for flesh, but over it all was a faint, hardly discernible flaccid fatigue of texture.

But perhaps she imagined it, for even as she looked, and felt her heart soften to think what this would mean to Eugenia, an inner wave of resolution reached the surface of the other woman's face, and there was Eugenia as she always had been, something of loveliness immutable.

She said impulsively, 'Eugenia, it's a stupidly conventional thing to say, but it's a pity you never married.'

As Eugenia only looked at her, quietly, she ventured further,

'You might really be happier, you know. There is a great deal of happiness in the right marriage.' She had never said so much to Eugenia.

Eugenia let Marise's hand drop and with it, evidently, whatever intention she might have had of saying something difficult to express. Instead, she advanced with her fastidious, delicate note of irony, 'I don't deny the happiness, if that sort of happiness is what one is after. But I think my appetite for it . . . that sort . . . is perhaps not quite robust enough to relish it.'

Marise roused herself to try to put a light note of cheerfulness into this last conversation. 'You mean that it seems to you like the coarsely heaped-up goodies set before a farmhand in a country kitchen . . . chicken and butter and honey and fruit and coffee, all good but so profuse and jumbled that they make you turn away?'

'I didn't give that definition of domestic life,' corrected Eugenia, with a faint smile, 'that's one of *your* fantasies.'

'Well, it's true that you get life served up to you rather pell-mell, lots of it, take-it-as-it-comes,' admitted Marise, 'but for a gross nature like mine, once you've had that, you're lost. You know you'd starve to death on the delicate slice of toasted bread served on old china. You give up and fairly enjoy wallowing in the trough.'

She had been struck by that unwonted look of fatigue on Eugenia's face, had tried to make her laugh, and now, with an effort, laughed with her. She had forgotten her passing notion that Eugenia had something special to say. What could she have? They had gone over that astonishing misconception of hers about the Powers' woodlot, and she had quite made Marise understand how hopelessly incapable she was of distinguishing one business detail from another. There could be nothing else that Eugenia could wish to say.

'How in the world shall I get through the winter?' Eugenia now wondered aloud. 'Biskra and the Sahara perhaps . . . if I could only get away from the hideous band of tourists. They say there are swarms of war-profiteers from Italy now everywhere, low-class people with money for the first time.' She added with a greater accent of wonder, 'How in the world are *you* going to get through the winter?'

Marise was struck into momentary silence by the oddness of the idea. There were phrases in Eugenia's language which were literally non-translatable into hers, representing as they

299

did ideas that did not exist there. 'Oh, we never have to consider that,' she answered, not finding a more accurate phrase. 'There won't be time enough to do all we'll try to do, all we'll have to do. There's living. That takes a lot of time and energy. And I'll have the chorus as usual. I'm going to try some Mendelssohn this year. The young people who have been singing for five or six years are quite capable of the "Elijah." And then any of the valley children who really want to come to me for lessons, you know. The people in North Ashley have asked me to start a chorus there this year, too. And in the mill, Neale has a plan to try to get the men to work out for themselves some standards of what concerns them especially, what a day's work really is, at any given job, don't you know.'

What an imbecile she was, she thought, to try to talk about such things to Eugenia, who could not, in the nature of things, understand what she was driving at. But apparently Eugenia had found something understandable there, for she now said sharply, startled, 'Won't that mean less income for you?'

She did not say, '*Even* less,' but it was implied in the energy of her accent.

Marise hesitated, brought up short by the solidity of the intangible barrier between their two languages. There were phrases in her own tongue which could not be translated into Eugenia's, because they represented ideas not existing there. She finally said vaguely, 'Oh perhaps not.'

Her pause had been enough for Eugenia to drop back into her own world. She said thoughtfully, 'I've half a notion to try going straight on beyond Biskra, to the south, if I could find a caravan that would take me. That would be something new. Biskra is so commonplace now that it has been discovered and exploited.' She went on, with a deep, wistful note of plaintiveness in her voice, 'But *every*thing's so commonplace now!' and added, 'There's Java. I've never been to Java.'

It came over Marise with a shock of strangeness that this was the end of Eugenia in her life. Somehow she knew, as though Eugenia had told her, that she was never coming back again. As they stood there, so close together, in the attitude of friends, they were so far apart that each could scarcely recognize who the other was. Their paths which in youth had lain so close to each other as to seem identical, how widely they had been separated by a slight divergence of aim! Marise was struck by her sudden perception of this. It had been going on for years, she could understand that now. Why should she only see it in this quiet, silent, neutral moment?

An impalpable emanation of feeling reached her from the other woman. She had a divination that it was pain. Perhaps Eugenia was also suddenly realizing that she had grown irrevocably apart from an old friend.

The old tenderness felt for the girl Eugenia had been, by the girl Marise had been, looked wistfully down the years at the end.

Marise opened her arms wide and took Eugenia into them for a close, deeply moved embrace.

'Good-bye, Eugenia,' she said, with sadness.

'Good-bye, Marise,' said Eugenia, looking at her strangely.

Neale came back now, frankly consulting his watch with Neale's bluntness in such matters. 'Train's due in a minute or two,' he said. 'Where's Mr. Welles?'

Marise said, 'Over there with Paul. I'll go tell them.'

She found them both, hand in hand, sitting on the edge of the truck which carried the leather-covered boxes and wicker basket-trunks, bound for Biskra or beyond, or Java; and the square department-store trunk bound for Maple Avenue, Macon, Georgia.

'Mother,' said Paul, 'Mr. Welles has promised me that he'll come up and visit us summers.'

'There's no house in the world where you'll be more welcome,' said Marise with all her heart, holding out her hand.

Mr. Welles shook it hard, and held it in both his. As the train whistled screamingly at the crossing, he looked earnestly into her face and tried to tell her something, but the words would not come.

As she read in his pale old face and steady eyes what he would have said, Marise cried out to herself that there do not exist in the world any things more halting and futile than words. She put her arms around his neck and kissed him. 'Good-bye, dear Mr. Welles,' was all she said, but in the clinging of his old arms about her, and in the quivering, shining face he showed as they moved down the platform together, she knew that he too had not needed words.

Paul clung to his hand till the last moment, gazing up at him constantly, silently. Marise looked down on the little boy's tanned, freckled, sober face and strained, rapidly winking eyes, and had the intuition, 'This is one of the moments Paul will never forget. He will always be able to shut his eyes and see this old Don Quixote setting forth.' With a rush of her old, jealous, possessive mother-love, she longed to share this with him and to have him know that she shared it; to put her arms around him and *make him let her in.* But she knew better now. She yearned over him silently, and did not touch him.

'Well, good-bye, Paul,' said Mr. Welles, shaking hands with him.

'Well, good-bye,' said Paul dryly, setting his jaw hard.

'Oh, this is the day-coach!' cried Eugenia. 'Where is the drawing-room car?'

'At the far end,' said the conductor with the sweeping gesture of a man used to talking with his arms.

'Good-bye, Mr. Welles,' said Eugenia, giving him for an instant a small, pearl-grey hand. 'Bon voyage! Good luck!'

'Same to you,' said the old gentleman, scrambling up the unswept, cinder-covered steps into the day-coach.

At the front end of the train, the baggage man was tumbling into the express car the fine, leather-covered boxes and the one square trunk.

Neale carried Eugenia's two small bags down to the drawing-room car and now handed them to the porter.

The two women kissed each other on both cheeks, hurriedly, as someone cried, 'All aboard!'

Eugenia took Neale's outstretched hand. 'Good-bye, Neale,' she said.

With the porter's aid, she mounted the rubber-covered steps into the mahogany and upholstery of the drawing-room car.

'Good luck, Eugenia! Bon voyage!' called Neale after her. She did not turn around or look back.

Marise noted that characteristically Eugenia had forgotten Paul. But Paul had forgotten her, too, and was now back near the day-coach searching one window after another.

The conductor signalled widely, the whistle shrieked, the wheels groaned. Neale drew Marise a little back out of the whirl of dust and stood holding her arm for an instant.

It seemed to Marise as they stood thus, Neale holding her arm, that she caught a last glimpse of Eugenia behind plate-glass, looking at them gravely, steadily.

Paul suddenly caught sight of Mr. Welles' face at a window, snatched off his cap, and waved it frantically, over and over, long after the train was only an echoing roar from down the tracks.

Then the mountain silence settled down about them calmly, and they could hear their own hearts beat, and knew the thoughts in their minds.

As they went back to their battered Ford, Marise said thoughtfully, 'Somehow I believe that it will be a long time before we see Eugenia again.'

Neale permitted himself no comment on this, nor showed the alteration of a line in his face as he stepped into the car and turned on the switch, but Marise cried out to him accusingly, 'You might as well say it right out, that you can support life if it is.'

Neale laughed a little and put his foot on the starter. 'Get in the back seat, Paul,' was all he said, as the little boy came up silently from the other side of the station.

He added as they started up the hill road, 'First time in my life I was ever sort of sorry for Eugenia. It seemed to me this morning that she was beginning to show her age.'

Marise hid the fact that she had had the same idea and opposed, 'Eugenia would laugh at that from you, the husband of such a frankly middle-aged thing as I.'

Neale was silent for a moment, and then, 'You'll always look younger than she. No, not younger, that's not it at all. It's *living*, you look. I tell you what, she's a cut flower in a vase that's beginning to wilt, and you're a living plant.'

'Why, *Neale!*' said Marise, astonished and touched.

'Yes, quite a flight of fancy for me, wasn't it?' commented Neale casually, leaning forward to change the carburettor adjustment.

Marise felt Paul lean over her shoulder from the back of the car. 'Say, Mother,' he said in her ear, 'would you just as soon get in back with me for a while?'

Neale stopped the car. Marise stepped out and in, and seated herself beside Paul. He had apparently nothing to say after all, looking fixedly down at his bare brown feet.

But presently he moved nearer to his mother and leaned his head against her breast. This time she put her arm around him and held him close to her, the tears in her eyes.

Chapter 29: *Vignettes from Home-Life*

August 20.

PAUL had been sent for blue-berries through the Eagle Rock woods to the high upland pasture where the Powers' cows fed during the day. On the upper edge of that, skirting a tract of slash left from an old cutting, was a berry-patch, familiar to all the children of Crittenden's valley.

When at four o'clock there was no sign of him, and then at five still none, Marise began to feel uneasy, although she told herself that nothing in the world could happen to Paul on that well-known mountain-side. He had taken Médor with him, who would certainly have come for help if Paul had fallen and hurt himself. She excused herself to the tall, awkward lad from North Ashley come to try over his part in a quartet, asked Touclé to help Elly set the supper things on the table if she should be late, and set off at a rapid pace by the short-cut over the ledges.

As she hurried over the rough trail, frankly hastening, now frankly alarmed, she thought that probably for all the life-time of the people in the valley the death of Frank Warner would set a sinister element of lurking danger in those familiar wooded slopes. Nothing *could* have happened to Paul, but still she hurried faster and faster, and as she came near the upper edge of the pasture she began to shout loudly, 'Paul! Paul!' and to send out the high yodel-cry that was the family assembly call. That act of shouting brought her a step nearer to panic.

But almost at once she heard the little boy's answer, not far from her saw his dog bounding through the bushes, and as she emerged from the woods into the open pasture she saw Paul running towards her, pail in hand, evidently astonished to know her there. But there was about him something more than astonishment, something which Marise's mother-eye catalogued as furtive, that consciousness of something to hide which always looks to grown-ups like guilt. She gave no sign of seeing this, however, stopping short to catch her breath, smiling at him, and wondering with great intensity what in the world it could be. He looked a little frightened.

He came up to her, answering her smile uneasily, and she saw that he had only a few berries in his pail. At this she was relieved, thinking that possibly all that had happened was that he had lingered to play. But when she glanced back at his face, she had the impression that there was something more, very much more. He had received some indelible impression and it was his instinct to hide it from his mother. Her heart sank forebodingly.

'What is the best thing to do?' she asked herself. 'To speak about it first, or to wait till he does?'

She sat down on a stone, fanning herself with her hat, watching him, trying to make out the meaning of every shift of expression, turn of eye, position of his hands, carriage of his head, bringing to this all her accumulated knowledge of Paul, afire with the sudden passion to protect him which had flamed up with her intuition that something had happened to him.

(Come and gone with the dry rapidity of fingers snapped, she had thought, 'The point is, that other people may be more clever than mothers, but nobody else *cares* enough, always, always to try to understand!')

'I thought I'd come up and walk back with you,' she offered.

'I haven't got very many,' said Paul, abashed, looking down at the few, blue, bloom-covered balls in the bottom of his shining tin pail. 'I was trying to hurry up and get enough for supper, anyhow.'

Marise, in spite of herself, moved by pity for his confusion, offered him a way out. It always seemed to her too dreadful for anyone not to have a way out, even if it implied a fib. 'Weren't there very many on the bushes?' she asked.

But he refused it with a characteristic integrity. 'Oh yes, there were lots there,' he said.

A silence fell. The little dog, sensitively aware of something wrong, whined uneasily, and pawed at Paul's hand. But Paul did not look down at him. He stood, his bare feet wide apart, the empty pail in his hand, looking down the beautiful green slope of the pasture, golden now in the long rays from the sun poised low on the line of the mountains opposite.

Marise looked at him, seeing nothing in all the world but that tanned, freckled, anxious little face. With what an utter unexpectedness did these moments of crisis spring on you? something vital there, and no warning, no chance to think.

'Anything the matter, Paul?' she said gently.

He nodded, silent.

'Anything you can tell Mother?' she asked, still more gently.

Paul said gruffly, 'I don't know: it's about Ralph Powers.

305

He was up here this afternoon.' He looked down at his brown, bramble-scratched legs.

Marise's imagination gave an unbridled leap of fear. She had always felt something strange and abnormal about Ralph. But she thought, 'I mustn't tyrannize over Paul, even by a too-waiting expectant silence,' and stooped over with the pretext of tying her shoe. A lump came to her throat. How terribly, helplessly, you *cared* about what came to your children!

When she lifted her head, Paul had come nearer her and was looking down at her with troubled eyes. 'Say, Mother, he didn't *say* not to tell you. Do you suppose it would be fair?'

She made a great effort at loyalty and said, 'I can't tell, Paul. You saw him. You know better than I, if you think he meant you not to tell. Try to remember if he said anything about it.'

Paul thought hard. 'You wouldn't tell anybody?' he asked.

'Not if you don't want me to,' she answered.

Paul sat down by her and drew a long breath. 'I don't believe he would care, *your* knowing it, if you never told anybody else, nor said anything to him. Mother, I was going along up there by the big rock where the white birches grow, and I saw Ralph. . . . He was in front of a sort of table he'd fixed up with a long piece of slate-stone, and he had some queer-shaped stones on it . . . oh, *Mother* . . . he was crying so, and talking to himself! And when he saw me he got as mad! And he told me about it, just as mad all the time, as though he was mad at me. Mother, it's an altar!'

'An altar!' said Marise, stupidly, utterly disconcerted by the word, so totally other than what her fears had been foreboding.

'Yes, an altar, and he says the stones on it are idols, and he bows down and worships them, the way the Bible says it's wicked to.'

Marise was too much astonished to open her lips.

Paul said, 'Mother, Ralph says he hates God, and isn't going to say his prayers to him any more. He says God let his father and mother both get killed, and he don't know what the devil could do any worse than that. He said he started in having an altar to idols because he thought from what the Bible said that if you did you'd be so wicked lightning would strike you dead. But it didn't, and now he doesn't believe *anything*. So he's going on having idols because the Bible says not to.'

Marise's first rounded and exclusive emotion was of immense

relief. Nothing had happened to her own son, and beside this relief, nothing for the moment seemed of any consequence. She drew Paul to her with a long breath of what was, she recognized it the moment afterward, her old, clear, undiluted, ferocious, hateful mother-egotism. For that instant she had not cared an atom what happened to another woman's child, so long as hers was safe.

But the next instant, the awareness of her hard heart cut across her like the lash of a whip. She shrank under it, horrified. She hung her head guilty and ashamed, divining the extremity of the other child's misery.

As she sat there, with her living arms around her own little son, the boy whose mother was dead came and stood before her in imagination, showing those festering, uncared-for wounds of sorrow and bitterness and loneliness, and furious, unavailing revolt from suffering too great to be borne.

She felt the guilt driven out from her narrow heart as it swelled larger to take him in. Any child who needed a mother so much was *her own child*. He had no longer any mother who would care enough to try to understand, but *she* would care enough.

'He bowed down and worshipped,' said Paul, in a shocked, frightened voice. 'He knocked his head on the stones and cried like anything. He said he hated God.'

'Oh!' cried Marise, intolerably stung by sympathy and pity. She started up to her feet, her heart burning, the tears on her cheeks. Her arms ached with emptiness till she should have drawn that suffering into them.

Paul said shyly, 'Say, Mother, it's *awful* hard on those Powers' kids, isn't it, not having anybody but their grandmother. Say, Mother, don't you think maybe we could . . . we could . . .' He turned his freckled, tanned, serious little face up to hers.

His mother stooped to kiss him, furiously, burningly, passionately, as she did not often kiss Paul, and he clung to her with all the strength of his strong little arms. 'Yes, yes, you darling, you darling,' she told him brokenly. 'Yes, yes, yes.'

§ 2

September 10.

Marise was slowly going through a passage of Scriabine, which had just come in the mail. She was absorbed in the difficulties and novelties of it, her ear alert to catch a clue to the meaning of those new rhythms and progressions, her mind opened wide to understand them when she heard them.

It was with an effort that she brought her attention back to Elly, who had come in behind her and was saying something urgently. Marise turned around on the piano-stool, her head humming with the unfamiliar, tantalizing beauties and intricacies of the page she had left half unread, and considered the little girl for an instant before she heard what she said. How Elly did grow! That dress was already much too small for her.

Well, Elly was not the only one who had grown out of her old clothes this summer . . . the old garments that had been large enough and now must be laid aside! . . . Elly was saying, 'Mother, one of my chickens looks sick, and I don't know what to do. I *wish* you'd come!'

Marise began a process of mentally weighing which was more important, Scriabine or Elly's chicken. Elly looked at her mother with imploring eyes. 'Mother, he looked *awfully* sick. And he is my nicest little Downy-head, the one I've always loved the best. I've tried to take *such* good care of him. Mother, I'm *worried* about him.'

Marise decided that Scriabine had at least the capacity to wait, while the chicken might not. She got up, saying, 'All right, Elly, we'll see what we can do.'

Elly pulled her along rapidly to the chicken-yard where grossly self-satisfied hens scratched in trash and filth undiscriminatingly, and complacently called their families to share what they had found there, or indeed at times apparently to admire them for having found nothing. Marise stood regarding them with a composed, ironic eye. It was good, she reflected, to be able to know that that was the way you looked from the outside, and not to care a bit because you knew firmly that there was something else there that made all the difference. All the same, it was a very good thing to have had the scaring thought that you were like that . . . 'there but for the grace of God. . . .' Was it complacent to say that? Oh, what did it matter what you called it – complacent or not, if you *knew*! It all came back to not caring so much about what things could be called, if you knew what they were.

Elly had disappeared into the chicken-house and now came back with a perplexed face. 'Downy-head *was* there, by the nests, and now he's gone.' Marise caught in the child's eyes the realness of her anxiety and thrilled to it, as she always did

308

to any real emotion. 'I'll help you look,' she said, turning her eyes about the chicken-yard, crowded with voluble, intently self-centred, feather personalities. 'Which hen is his mother, Elly?'

'This one, Old Speckle. Oh, Mother, there he is, lying down. He must be feeling worse!' She ran forward and stooped over a little panting yellow ball.

Across the intervening space and beyond all those carelessly alive bodies, Marise's eyes caught the unmistakable aspect of death in the tiny creature lying there.

'Mother!' cried Elly, 'his eyes look so! He can't get his breath. *Mother!*' Marise felt the child's agitation and alarm knock at her heart. She looked down helplessly at the dying creature. That tiny, tiny scrap of down-covered flesh to be alive, to contain the miracle and mystery of life, and now to be struggling, all alone, with the miracle and mystery of death!

The little thing opened its glazing eyes once more, drew a long breath, and lay still. An age-old inherited knowledge and experience told Elly what had happened. She gave a scream, picked it up and held it in her cupped hands, her little face drawn in horrified incredulity. She looked up at her mother and said in a whisper, 'Mother, he's *dead*.'

Marise nodded silently. Poor Elly! She wished she could think of something comforting to say. But what is there to say? For her there had never been anything but stoic silence.

The mother hen clucked unconcernedly at their feet, and with coaxing guttural sounds called the rest of the chickens to eat a grain. The strong ammonia smell of the chicken-yard rose in the sunshine. Elly stood perfectly still, the little ball of yellow down in her hand, her face pale.

Marise looked down on her with infinite sympathy. Her child, flesh of her flesh, meeting in this uncouth place the revelation of the black gulf! But she remained silent, not knowing what to say.

Elly spoke in a low voice, 'But, Mother, how *can* he be dead, just so quick while we were looking at him? Mother, he was alive a minute ago. He was breathing. He looked at me. He knew me. And in just a minute like that . . . nothing!'

She looked around her wildly. '*Mother, where has his life gone to?*'

Marise put her arm around the little girl's shoulders tenderly, but she still only shook her head without a word. She did not know any more than Elly where his life had gone.

And surely loving silence was better than tinkling words of falseness.

Elly looked up at her, glistening drops of sweat standing on her temples. 'Mother,' she asked, urgently, in a loud, frightened whisper, 'Mother, do we die like that? Mother, will *you* die like that? All in a moment . . . and then . . . nothing?'

It came like thunder, then, what Marise had never thought to feel. With a clap, she found that this time she had something to answer, something to say to Elly. Looking deep, deep into Elly's eyes, she said firmly with a certainty as profound as it was new to her, 'No, Elly, I don't believe we do die like that . . . all in a moment . . . nothing.'

She was astonished by what she said, astonished by the sudden overflowing of something she had not known was there, but which was so great that her heart could not contain it, 'comme une onde qui bout dans une urne trop pleine.' And she was as moved as she was astonished. Elly came into her arms with a comforted gasp. They clung to each other closely, Marise's ears humming with the unfamiliar beauty and intricacy of that new page at which she had had that instant's glimpse. Here was a new harmony, a new progression, a new rhythm to which her ear had just opened . . . heard here in this uncouth place!

That evening, after the children were in bed, she stopped her reading of the new music for a moment to say to Neale, 'You know those ideas that other people are better for children than their parents are?'

'Yes,' said Neale, laying down the baseball page of his newspaper, instantly all there, looking at her intently.

'Well, I don't believe a word of it,' said Marise.

'I should say it depended on which parents and on which children were meant,' advanced Neale guardedly.

Marise had at first an affectionate smile for this, and then a laugh. She got up from the piano-stool and went to kiss him. He said with a whimsical suspicion of this, 'Why so?'

'Because you are so entirely you,' she told him, and went back to Scriabine.

§ 3

September 22.

It was the half-hour of pause after lunch. The children played idly with the fox-terrier and lounged on the steps of the

310

side-porch, strong and brown, living cups filled to the brim with life. Neale had pushed his chair back from the table, lighted his pipe, and sat meditating. Presently he put out his hand and laid it on Marise's, who had turned to look down the sun-flooded valley.

It was high-noon, dreamy, entranced, all the world golden with the magnificent weather as a hollyhock is golden with pollen. From the brook came the living voice of the water, with the special note of brave clarity it always had for brilliant noons.

It seemed to Marise that she too was all gold-powdered with the magnificence of life, that in her heart there sang a clear living voice that did not fear high-noons.

§ 4

October.

Would Vincent come back at all? Marise had wondered so often. Not Vincent in the flesh; that last angry bewildered gesture had finality in it. He had given her up then, totally. But would he come back to haunt her in those inevitable moments of flat ebb-tide in life, when what should be moist and living, withered and crisped in the merciless drought of drudgery and routine? She feared it, frankly dreaded it at first, and tried to think how to brace herself against it.

But it was not then that he came, not when she was toiling with dishes to wash, or vegetables to pare, or the endless care of the children's never-in-order clothes. Instead she found in those moments, which had been arid before, a curious new savour, a salt without which life would seem insipid, something which gave her appetite for the rest. 'This is all Tolstoyan nonsense and sentimentality,' she told herself mockingly, 'there is nothing sacred about scrubbing the floor.' Or on another day, 'I wonder if it's a twist of the absurd mediæval ascetic perversity left over?' Or again, 'All it does for me is to take off the curse of belonging to the bourgeoisie.' But no matter what sceptical name she called it, nor how much she minimized the reality of it, she felt some odd value in it which she would not have gone without. Once she said to herself, 'It's ballast, to a person like me,' although she did not know exactly what this meant. And another time she said, 'Perhaps it's that I'm making an honest effort to do my share.'

But it was true and real, the fact that after such work the

311

reading of the day's news of the world brought her a less oppressive sense of guilt. And stranger than this, music had greater vitality for her. She felt it a deeper, richer soil than even she had dreamed of, and struck her roots profoundly into depths which kept her whole complicated organism poised, steady, and upright.

And here it was that Vincent came back. Not the Vincent of the hawk-like imperious face, or burning eyes of desire, which had seemed to him his realest self. But the Vincent who had come in from the porch that day in March when she had first played to him, who had smiled at her, the good, grateful, peaceful smile, and had said to her music, 'Go on, go on.' It was the same Vincent of the afternoon in Cousin Hetty's garden when the vulture of the desire to possess had left him for a moment in peace. Often and often he came thus as she played and leaned his head back and said, 'Go on.' And thus Marise knew he would always come. And thus she welcomed him.

This was what was left of him in the house he had so filled with his smoky, flaming brilliance.

§ 5

December.

They had been talking around the fire of the stars and their names and stories, she and Neale and the children. Presently interest overcoming inertia they decided to go out and see if the clouds had blown away so that the stars could be seen. They huddled on hastily found wraps, thrust their feet into flapping, unbuckled overshoes, and leaving the still, warm, lamp-lit room, they shuffled out, laughing and talking, into the snow which lay thick and still before the house.

At first they carried out between them so much of the house atmosphere that it hung about them like warm fog, shielding them from the fiercely pure, still cold of the air, and from the brilliant glitter of the myriad-eyed black sky. They went on talking and laughing, pointing out the constellations they knew, and trying to find others in the spangled vault over their heads.

'A bear!' cried Mark. 'I could draw a better bear than that any day!' And from Paul, 'They can call it Orion's belt all they want to, but there's no belt to it!' And from Elly, 'Aldebaran! Aldebaran! Red-eyed Aldebaran!'

But little by little the house-air began to be thinned about them, to blow away from between them in wisps and wreaths, off into the blackness. The warmed, lighted house dwindled to nothing. There were only the great cold black sky and the small cold white earth. Their voices were lowered; they stood very still, close together, their heads tipped back, their faces and hearts upraised silently to receive the immensity above and about them.

Elly murmured under her breath, 'Doesn't it seem funny, our world being just one of all those, and such a little one, and here we are, just these few of us, standing on the world and looking at it all.'

Marise thought, 'We seem to be the only living things in all creation.' In that huge, black, cold glittering universe how tiny was the little glow of life they made!

Tiny but unquenchable! Those myriads of hard staring eyes could not look down the immortal handful of human life and love which she and Neale had created between them.

There was a silence, filled with still, breathless cold; with enormous space, with infinity.

Marise felt a rigorous shudder run over her, as though something vital were coming to her, like the rending pang of pain which heralds child-birth. After this, did she close her eyes for a moment, or did it come to her while she continued to gaze wide-eyed at the stern greatness of the universe? What was this old, familiar, unknown sensation?

. . . as though, on a long journey in the dark it had grown light, so that she had suddenly recognized which way she was going.

Then she knew what it was. Conscious and awake, she was feeling herself one with the great current, advancing with an irresistible might, majesty and power, in which she shared, to which she gave her part.

§ 6

January.

She was putting away the clean sheets from the washing on the shelves at the end of the hall, upstairs, her mind entirely on the prosaic task, wondering when she would have to replace some of the older ones, and wishing she could put off buying till the outrageous post-war prices went down. Someone stirred behind her and she turned her head quickly to see who was there. It was Neale, come in early. He was standing, looking at her back; and in the instant before he saw that she had turned, she caught the expression on his face, the tender fathomless affection that was there.

A warm gush of happiness surged up all over her. She felt a sudden intense physical well-being, as though her breath came more smoothly, her blood ran more sweetly in her veins.

'Oh, *Neale*!' she said, under her breath, flushing and turning to him. He looked at her, his strong, resolute face and clear eyes smiled, and opening his arms he drew her into them.

The ineffable memory of all the priceless past, the ineffable certainty of the priceless future was in their kiss.

That evening, after a long golden hour at the piano, she chanced to take down the Largo in the Chopin sonata. As she began it, something stirred in her mind, some memory that instantly lived with the first notes of the music. How thick-clustered with associations music became, waking a hundred echoes and overtones!

This was the memory of the time when she had played it, almost a year ago, and had thought how intimacy and familiarity with music but deepened and enriched and strengthened its hold on you. It was only the lower pleasures of which one grew tired, – had enough. The others grew with your growing capacity to hold them. She remembered how that day she had recalled the Wordsworth sonnet, 'A beauteous evening, calm and free,' and had thought that music took you in to worship quite simply and naturally at the Temple's inner shrine, that you adored none the less although you were at home there and not breathless with adoration like the nun: because it was a whole world given to you, not a mere pang of joy, because you could live and move and be blessedly and securely at home there.

She finished the last note of the Largo and sat silent. She was thinking that her marriage was like that, too.

Presently she got up, took out the old portfolio of photographs, and pinned upon the wall over the piano the view taken from Rocca di Papa.

§ 7

February 24.

Marise had been drilling the chorus in the Town Hall of Ashley after the men's working-hours, and now in the dimming light of the early evening was going home on snow-shoes, over the hill-path. She liked to use snow-shoes and occasionally said

314

that she could walk more easily and more lightly on them than on bare ground. She trod over the tops of the deep drifts with an accentuation of her usual strong free step.

The snow fell thickly and steadily, a cold, finely spun, straight-hung curtain, veiling all the muffled sleeping valley. There was an inconceivable silence about her as she drew her snow-shoes over the velvet-like masses of the snow. But within her were ringing echoes of the rhythms and cadences of the afternoon's struggle, imperfectly sung most of them, haltingly, or dully, or feebly, or with a loud misunderstanding of the phrase. At the recollection of these failures, she clenched her hands hard inside her fur gloves with an indomitable resolution to draw something better from her singers the next time.

But mingled with them was a moment of splendour. It was when the men had tried over the passage she had explained to them the week before. She had not known then, she did not know now, how clearly or definitely she had reached them with her summary of the situation of the drama: the desperate straits of the Israelites after the three-year drought, the trial by fire and water before the scorning aristocracy, Elijah stark and alone against all the priesthood of Baal, the extremity of despair of the people . . . and then the coming of the longed-for rain that loosened the terrible tension and released their hearts in the great groaning cry of thanksgiving. She had wondered how clearly or definitely she had reached their understanding, but she knew that she had reached their hearts, when suddenly she had heard all those men's voices pealing out, pure and strong and solemn and free, as she had dreamed that phrase could be sung.

Thanks be to God! He lav-eth the thirs-ty land.

The piercing sweetness of the pleasure this had brought to her came over her again in a wave. She halted on the crest of the hill, and for a moment in place of the purples and blues of the late snowy afternoon there hung before her eyes the powerful, roughly clad bodies of those vigorous men, their weather-beaten faces, their granite impassivity, under which her eye had caught the triumph of the moment, warming them as it did her, with the purest of joys this side of heaven, the consciousness of

315

having made music worthily. The whole valley seemed to be filled to its brim with that shout of exultation. It had taken all of her patience, and will-power, and knowledge of her art and of these people to achieve that moment. But it had lifted her high, high above the smallness of life, up to a rich realm of security in joy.

The snow fell more and more thickly, covering her as she stood with a fine, soft mantle of white. She had heard the men that afternoon saying they had seen signs of the winter break-up, and she wondered at it now, looking about the frozen, buried, beautiful valley and up to the frozen towering mountains, breathing in the cold air, as pure as the ether itself. It seemed to her that spring was as remote and unreal and impossible an imagination of the heart as a child's fairy-tale.

Then suddenly, bursting out of the dimming distance, close in front of her, flying low, silently, strongly, a pair of wild geese went winging off towards the north, their grey shapes the only moving thing in all the frost-held world.

Marise drew a great breath of delight in their strong and purposeful vitality. She looked after them, her heart rising and singing with comradely pride in them. She would have liked to shout an exultant greeting after them, 'Hurrah!'

They went beating off, fast and straight, for their unseen destination, while, treading the velvet-like snow-drifts with her strong free tread, Marise went home.

§ 8

March 2.

It was the first warm day of the year. The hard-frozen ruts of the road thawed on top and glistened. The snow-banks shrank visibly from one hour to the next under a warm wind and a hazy sun. The mountains were unbelievably beautiful and seductive in a shimmer of blue and silver. The children had brought home a branch of pussy-willows, and as Marise and Neale stood for a moment at the open door breathing in the new softness, they saw Touclé, old and stooped and shabby, her reticule bag bulging, her flat feet in enormous overshoes plodding up the road towards the mountain.

They smiled at one another. It was in truth the first day of

316

spring. Marise said, after a pause, 'Do you know what she goes off for?'

Neale shook his head with a wide indifference as to the reason. 'Because she's an Injun,' he conjectured casually.

'She told me once,' said Marise, with a sudden wonder what Neale would think of that glimpse into the old mystic's mind, how he would (for she knew beforehand he would) escape the wistfulness which struck at her even now, at the thought of that door to peace. She repeated to him word for word what Touclé had told her on that hot August day.

Neale gave her his usual careful attention. Marise thought to herself, 'Neale is the only person I ever knew who *could* listen to other people's ideas.' But when she finished he made no comment. She asked him, 'Did you ever think that old carven-image had that in her? How profound a disdain for us busy-about-nothing white people she must have!'

Neale nodded. 'Most likely. Everybody has a good deal of disdain for other people's ideals.'

'Well, you haven't for hers, have you?' challenged Marise.

Neale looked thoughtful. 'I'm no mystic. Their way of managing life often looks to me like sort of lying down on the job. I'm no mystic and I'm no fish. Looks to me as though the thing to do isn't to go off in a far corner to get your momentary glimpse of daylight, but to batter a hole in the roof of your cave and let daylight in where you live all the time. I can't help being suspicious of a daylight that's so uncertain you have to go away from life and hold your breath before you can see it for a minute. I want it where I do my work.'

Marise looked at him, thinking deeply. That was just what Neale did. But when she looked back at the old Indian woman, just now turning into the wood-road, she sighed wistfully, and did not know why.

There was so very much growing always to be done in life.

§ 9

March 10.

(*A letter from Eugenia:*)

'. . . I'm planning perhaps to make the trip to the temples in the Malay jungle. Biskra was deadly, and Italy worse . . . vulgarity and commonness everywhere. What an absolutely dreary outlook wherever one turns one's eyes! There is no corner of the modern world that is not vulgar and common.

317

Democracy has done its horrible levelling down with a vengeance . . .'

(*A letter from Mr. Welles:*)
'. . . The life here is full of interest and change, and it's like dew on my dusty old heart to see the vitality of the joy-in-life of these half-disinherited people. I'm ashamed to tell you how they seem to love me and how good they are to me. Their warmness of heart and their zest in life . . . I'm just swept back into youth again. It makes me very much mortified when I think what a corking good time I am having and what sanctimonious martyr's airs I put on about coming down here. Of course a certain amount of my feeling younger and brisker comes from the fact that, working as I am, nobody feels about me the laid-on-the-shelf compassion which everybody (and me too) was feeling before. I *am* somebody here and every time I say "Dr. Martin" to a well-educated Negro physician whom another white man has just hailed as "Andy" I feel not only a real sense of righteous satisfaction but the joyful mischievous fun that a small boy has. Give my love to Paul (speaking of small boys) and tell him I'm saving up for the fishing-pole I am going to use when I go fishing with him next summer. He said in his last letter he wanted to come down here and make me a visit; but you tell him I think he'd better get his growth before he does that.'

§ 10

March 15, 1921.
From a profound sleep, serene warm infinity of rest, Marise was wakened by a little outcry near the bed, a sobbing voice saying through chattering teeth, 'Mother! Father!'
Still drowned in sleep, Marise cried out, 'What? What's that?' and then, 'Oh, you, Elly. What's the matter, dear? Notions again?'
'Oh, Mother, it was an awful dream this time. Can't I get into bed with you?'
'Why yes, come along, you dear little silly.'
The fumbling approach to the bed, Marise holding the sheets open and stretching out her hand through the cold darkness towards the little fingers groping for her; the clutch at her hand with a quick anguish of relief and joy. 'Oh, *Mother*!'
Then the shivering body rolling into bed, the little cold arms

318

tight around her neck, the cold smooth petal-like cheek against hers.

Marise reached over beyond Elly and tucked the covers in with one arm, drew the child closer to her, and herself drew closer to Neale. She wondered if he had been awakened by Elly's voice, and the little stir in the room, and hoped he had not. He had been off on a very long hard tramp over mountain trails the day before, and had been tired at night. Perhaps if he had been wakened by Elly he would drowse off again at once as she felt herself doing now, conscious sleepily and happily of Elly's dear tender limbs on one side of her and of Neale's dear strong body on the other.

The strong March wind chanted loudly outside in the leafless maple-boughs. As Marise felt her eyelids falling shut again it seemed to her, half-awake, half-asleep, that the wind was shouting out the refrain of an old song she had heard in her childhood, 'There's room for all! There's room for all!' What had it meant, that refrain? She tried drowsily to remember, but instead felt herself richly falling asleep again, her hands, her arms, her body . . .

'There's room for all! There's room for all!'

She was almost asleep . . .

Someone was speaking again. Elly's voice, calmer now, wistful and wondering, as though she were lying awake and trying to think.

'Mother.'

'Yes, dear, what is it?'

'Mother, aren't you and father afraid of *any*thing?'

Marise was wide-awake now, thinking hard. She felt Neale stir, grope for her hand and hold it firmly . . . Neale's strong hand!

She knew what she was saying. Yes, she knew all that it meant when she answered, 'No, Elly, I don't believe we are.'

The first Virago Modern Classic was published in London in 1978, launching a list dedicated to the celebration of women writers and to the rediscovery and reprinting of their works. While the series is called "Modern Classics," it is not true that these works of fiction are universally and equally considered "great," although that is often the case. Published with new critical and biographical introductions, books appear in the series for different reasons: sometimes for their importance in literary history; sometimes because they illuminate particular aspects of women's lives, both personal and public. They may be classics of comedy or storytelling; their interest can be historical, feminist, political, or literary. In any case, in their variety and richness they promise to confuse forever the question of what women's fiction is about, while at the same time affirming a true female tradition in literature.

Initially, the Virago Modern Classics concentrated on English novels and short stories published in the early decades of the century. As the series has grown, it has broadened to include works of fiction from different centuries and from different countries, cultures, and literary traditions; there are books written by black women, by Catholic and Jewish women, by women of almost every English-speaking country, and there are several relevant novels by men.

Nearly 200 Virago Modern Classics will have been published in England by the end of 1985. During that same year, Penguin Books began to publish Virago Modern Classics in the United States, with the expectation of having some forty titles from the series available by the end of 1986. Some of the earlier books in the series were published in the United States by The Dial Press.

PENGUIN/VIRAGO MODERN CLASSICS